The Perfectionist

The Perfectionist

H M Beaumont

authorHOUSE®

AuthorHouse™
1663 Liberty Drive
Bloomington, IN 47403
www.authorhouse.com
Phone: 1-800-839-8640

First published by AuthorHouse   09/14/2011

ISBN: 978-1-4567-9614-3 (sc)
ISBN: 978-1-4567-9616-7 (ebk)

Printed in the United States of America

Dedication

"This book is dedicated to Maggie Kenny, my dear friend, inspiration and motivation for writing anything at all, and is in memory of her beloved husband, Mike. Maggie gave me the confidence to write the first words and the encouragement to finish what I had to say. Thank you Little Blossom."

Chapter 1

Finally, I'd managed to cut through the mesh that was the second line of defence into the secret comms cabin. The dark side of my life was pushing me forwards despite the anxiety of being in places as clandestine as this. The cabin's alarms went directly back to the Guardroom, their Special Forces on hand to deal with foreign predators. Like me. My nerves were prancing inside me but I needed to pause for breath to stop my hands from shaking as the mesh came down.

I reached for the little tool bag, dragging it along behind me as I slid through the hatch and into the full void that was now exposed. I tried to stop the fear from owning me in the semi-darkness. The data racks were laid out in neat rows overhead, humming and chattering as millions of bytes of data flowed through the copper and fibre optics back to the main server room in Paris. I should not be here. Why did I always take the jobs that Turtle gave me? My stomach churned at my life's many regrets. I was on my own, there was no-one else. It had to be me. The adrenalin swelled inside me, still bounding to be let out. It had to me because I *wanted* it to be me, needed it in fact. This was my life's purpose but I could have bitten off too much this time. This one was difficult. After all these years was I actually scared? The churning stopped. I would not be afraid. The power of the decision came to me in a surge, taking over my everyday persona and linking arms with the dark animal within me. Blossom was gone for tonight, my skin merely riding my animal's strength until it had served it purpose.

Hands not shaking now, I brought the little compact mirror in the pink jewelled case out of the tool bag. How pretty it looked, sparkling in the half light. Pushing the jewels in the 3 and 9 o'clock positions I felt a clunk inside the case. The magnet was on. I reached through the next gap to position the mirror carefully over the top of the detector beam position. The laser wasn't visible but I had been memorising the plans for months and knew almost by instinct where it was. The drawings had been delivered to Turtle as soon as the British built cabin was finished and he had saved them for a special occasion. Like this one. He needed information and I needed to get it for him. A perfect partnership.

Once attached to the wall, the scanner sprung out of the top of the mirror, its arm winding out for it to take a look around the room. The detector beam below it would glow handsomely for the scanner to see, all I could do was sit and wait. My body pulsed with trepidation. I watched the scanner finding its target. The mirror was to snap into place, reflecting the beam seemlessly to its partner, hiding my presence in the void underneath the darkened cabin, or . . . well, I wasn't going to think about 'or'. The French didn't take kindly to intruders in their secret data communications. Without thinking, I reached into my holster and checked the little pistol sitting patiently there. Although I knew, I felt compelled to make sure I was ready just in case 'Or' scenarios came about. The few seconds it took was enough to tell me that the mirror had done its job, fooling the laser into a false sense of security. Security I was now ready to pull apart.

Boom boom boom my heart whacked against my rib cage. Rising from my easy seat I lifted myself into position next to the detector beam. In tricking the laser I had opened up enough of a gap in the last line of defence that I could just squeeze myself through. It would be tight. I held in my chest, hoping that the booming heart inside wouldn't leap around enough for the other detector beams to see. Slithering through the tiny space I was glad I didn't suffer from the usual weight paranoia that most women I knew succumbed to. Every conversation with the few associates I allowed myself were based on the same problem – how to be skinnier, loose their flabby bits, be more attractive. If they could see me in this black catsuit they would have a field day, going on about bingo wings and big bottoms. None of this was any concern to me right now. If I was seen in the suit I was in a lot more trouble than being accused of a fat arse.

My chest held, my heart didn't manage to warp my ribcage with its fight to escape while I made my way through the gap. My ego throbbed with pleasure as it realised I was inside and as yet unscathed. The data rack I needed was the third one from the front, between us was a nest of wires and traywork that came in and out through holes in the cabin's floor above my head. Without seeing the detector beams there was a strong chance I would stumble into one as I passed by, which could lead to a little inconvenience. I took out the can of deodorant I had stowed in the spare holster in the back of the catsuit and pushed the top down until it clicked. A steady satisfying stream of vapour leaked out of the top of the can, sinking to the floor. The eerie stillness of the cabin was made more intense as the fog filled the void slowly as I watched. The dust particles floated and sparkled as they hit the cold glow of the lasers, the light reflected for an instant as it passed through the arrow straight beams. I was mesmerised by the beautiful sight, showing me the path to continue into the danger zone. Picking my way through was still difficult, the area was tight and full of barriers to my easy passage. My uncooperative limbs were squeezed through the smallest of spaces until they became quite sullen in their operation. I found a convenient place to rest them as close to the target data rack as I could fit into.

I needed a breath but was too animated, sensing I was close. I breathed out deeply, emptying my lungs completely while I concentrated on what I had come to steal. The data would be running from the rack directly above my head. I looked on the traywork where all the cables were clipped together in neat bundles. The fat yellow one was bulkier than the others. It looked so innocuous, hardly the focus of a potential international incident. Turtle's briefing had been extensive and exhausting, "Blossom, the method of extraction for this type of data is still unknown to the French. We have only just perfected it and they are not aware yet. Its only a matter of time before they find out but in the meantime they haven't strengthened the communications network because they think its unfathomable even if we get inside." Turtle wasn't one for overtalking a situation, "the same defences are in place, which we need to exploit now before they tighten them up. This is of paramount importance, Blossom, you must find that yellow cable and capture what you can," he had been most insistent. I had to go in. As he said the words, all those months before, my excitement had started to pant at the prospect. Turtle knew how to bait me into making me do these foolish things to make him happy. The yellow cable had haunted my existence for several weeks, now here in front of me was my prize.

The space was impossible to get anything like comfortable, I had to jam my legs into a small section with little in it as I took off my watch and flipped open the side. The stubby pin stuck out of the back of the watch. I pushed my USB stick into the slot that was now exposed and fastened the strap around the chunky cable, pushing the pin into the yellow flesh. The connection was tight, just as Turtle had said it should be, the ruby in the 12 o'clock position started to flash on the watch face. The data was being copied as it passed through.

"This data centre is one of the hubs of communication that keep the French military and covert operatives in touch with their political handlers," Turtle had told me when the subject had first been introduced.

"Each contact and report is made, recorded and backed up in a single night's transactions."

"What about instructions going back out to the field?" I asked him, "Yes, that too. All the information to conduct, instruct and condone military policy around the world is dealt with as cleanly and crisply as if it were a bank statement," he answered. It sounded cold, but I knew the British methods weren't any more huggable. This was the modern method of data exchange whether the outcome was an overdraft or a deadly order.

The wait for the data to change hands was almost complete. Pins and needles were piercing my legs, I couldn't remain still a second longer. Another of the racks above beeped to tell its long gone technician that it had finished its night's data run. My night's work was complete too. My nerves had settled docilely as I waited for the watch to capture its trophy, but now it was time to move again they startled me with their presence, breathing down my neck to have me dash away. The vapour was only just visible in the air, the sparkles becoming duller as the last specks of dust fell slowly to the floor. It was enough to guide me back to the open passage, tantalisingly close in the small cabin but insisting on making me work hard to return. My legs were leaden as the blood flowed into them after lying stiff in the void while the watch did its dirty work for so long.

I could almost feel the fresh air outside. I squeezed through the gap and reached back to press the button on the mirror to allow the beam to resume its rightful track. It happened in an instant, the arm snapped back and I clicked the buttons to release it from the wall. I would sink or swim in the details of the trail I left, or didn't leave, as I escaped from the cabin. Eventually the French would find out I had been in there but I could do with it not being tonight.

"This time it's important that you are completely invisible, Blossom," Turtle had tried to instil the importance in me all the way through the briefings, "the normal methods of creating diversions and taking out the guards to get in and out of a target can't be used this time I'm afraid."

"What if I'm in trouble?" I'd enquired, "Then you need an arsenal of plausible natural distractions with you to plant on your way out, but you can't use too many or they in themselves would attract some attention." I had to admit that he was making no sense at the time but in subsequent months of training for this one and only night's assignment I had finally understood.

"So what you're saying is that I have to get in and out without anything happening within the army base at all," I'd summed it up.

"That's basically it, yes," if I could have seen him at that moment I would have bet any money that he would have been smiling. Nothing of any interest could happen while I was inside the base, nothing of note was to be worthy of reporting. I had to be completely invisible, never seen nor heard, while I was there. Sounded easy and obvious. This night could not be marked out as the possible one when the data was taken, or it could lead to who was staying on the base at the time. My name was on the guest list.

Remembering Turtle's 'non impact' instructions, I replaced the cut mesh with the one I brought with me to hide my foray into the secret labyrinth. Good as new. I stuffed the tool bag into the front of the catsuit and crept to my makeshift entrance in the side of the cabin, emerging into the night like a nervous rabbit, waiting for the fox to pounce.

The sky still looked suitably black, no sign of the rising sun coming to greet me. I needed the darkness to make my way back to Claire's barrack room. I had managed to get away alright but if I wasn't there by morning my night's enterprises in being invisible would prove rather a waste. Looking up, I was suitably impressed by the moonless skyscape. The black clouds that enveloped the scene with darkness were a welcome friend. I shuddered as I drew from the cabin's front corner to a side with more cover from anyone else who may be venturing out.

I watched and waited, almost tasting the air to sense another presence. CCTV cameras were trained on the perimeter fence twenty metres from the other end of the cabin but the infra red detectors were focussed on the front. If I had emerged a metre to my right I would have been caught by the sensors and the cameras would have shifted to look in my direction, showing my red outline to the entire Guardroom. I looked at the cameras, dutifully recording the view of the fence, not budging in their strict regime. Fifty metres in the other direction was the building I needed to reach to be out of range of the prying electronic eyes.

I was still laid on the ground when something wild inside me roared with excitement. For a second I forgot to breathe, transfixed by what my senses were trying to tell me. My hearing strained. Footsteps. Were they coming for me? The temptation to run was strong but the cameras would have been on me the second

I showed myself at the front of the cabin. I clung to the floor as if it would throw me up in the air. There it was, a steady rhythmic plodding, far to my left. My body pulsed as my heart hit out, these steps were too slow to be racing to stop an intruder. The steady feet scuffed along, grazing the tarmac. Not one but two sets of footsteps, lazily making their way towards me. The pair of guards were getting closer. A stone skittered along the floor as a bored patrol foot knocked it onwards. They came slowly into view. Wait. Don't move. Don't breathe too loud.

My heart thumped, my instinct was fighting to be away. I kept watching the cameras and listening to the footsteps as they grew ever louder. The patrol's path would cross exactly where I needed to be. One step closer . . . two . . . three . . . the soldiers should be visible to the infra red detectors. The cameras began to move, following the highly detectable outlines of the guards as they passed by. It was working, the Guardroom would be filled with the images of their own men, black and white pictures of the two guards on their rounds. They would have no need to switch to the infra red view because the cameras were picking up a real heat signature, not a ghost. The ghost was me, stalking out from my hiding place, low in the background as they passed by. Black against the night, no visible trace for them to catch.

The cameras did their work well, taking the biggest signal and trailing it. They saw nothing of me as I matched the footsteps of the soldiers, growing softer as they went round the other side of the cabin and further away. The ever decreasing noise was enough to disguise my movements in the darkness as I sped out of one shadow into the welcome arms of another. Looking back, the patrol had disappeared on its way, the cameras returned to their daily grind of surveying the fenceline. I felt safe now that I was out of their reach. The pressure eased, I calmed a little in the soft black velvet hug the building was offering me. With one more check that I had everything with me I needed, I made my way back through the maze of scattered block buildings until I reached an isolated long wooden hut. Behind it stood the entrance to the Residential area where the barracks were. Where I needed to be. Right now, please.

My earpiece crackled for the first time, I was back in range of the tiny transmitter in my bag in Claire's room, hopefully too small to be detected. On the receiving end was Turtle. It was all in his big plan of invisibility. If I only had a small reception range, it would be harder to pick up. I was only allowed to use it if there was an emergency. If I was blown I was on my own. I knew that. My arsenic cap was implanted under the loose skin between my left thumb and index finger. All I had to do was bite into it and I would be dead within a minute. I knew that, too. It made DIY quite interesting, you'll never see anyone more cautious when hammering in a nail. Funny really, the scrapes I had already been through and the thought to use it never occurred to me once. I didn't seem to be able to detect defeat. It was all that had kept me alive at times and now I needed that same sense again, to see if there was a guard in the sentry box at the other side of this wooden hut.

Sentry duty at this position was used as a punishment. There was not normally a guard, but if there had been a misdemeanour in the ranks, this is where he would serve his time. Caution would have to prevail until I could see if he was there or not.

Like a stick insect I squashed myself flat against the hut's shingled wall and shimmied along, trying to blend in. The wood felt warm after the cold bricks. It smelled of old creosote, reminding me, somehow, of school. Laid on the cold floor I took the compact mirror back out and turned it to show me the next possible target.

Shifting the angle, I ran the view through the mirror, all along the fence to the gate. It was open, as usual. This perimeter was not one of the rings of security and the gate was just a doorway from one area to another. Next to it was the tiny sentry box, the fibreglass cabin was big enough for a door on the left and a window on the right and no more. A light was on, showing the little plastic buffet for the guard to perch on while the hours passed idly by. No wonder this was a punishment shift. I checked the full length of the fence that could be seen from the mirror's viewpoint, reflected clearly back to my hiding place. No guard was visible. I got to my knees, ready to run for the gate but something was holding me back. I searched my senses to feel what they were telling me, why I had to wait. They were telling me to be sure before presuming the area was clear. I forced the urge to run back down, a little annoyed at myself for preferring to check before making a dash for home.

I scanned as far and wide as I could, straining to see the feared image of an errant soldier on duty. Instead I saw a plume of smoke rise up from the other side of the hut. The cloud dissipated and carried towards me on the night's breeze. Tobacco. So I had found him at last. Our friend was having a crafting one in the shelter of the opposite side of the wooden hut. He must be in a blind spot for the cameras not to see him. Looking further, I could see his footsteps from the sentry box to the hut in the dewy morning grass. I was torn, my aggression had built throughout the night. The more I conquered, the more I wanted to succeed. The dark animal inside sang to be let out. My teeth were bared, ready to go straight over and lay him out with a growl, but I had to think of Turtle's instructions, "Invisible, Blossom, don't forget. Nothing remarkable must happen while you're there or they'll be on to you in a muzzleflash."

A noise of scuffling feet made me look back towards the other end of the hut. A couple of steps and I could see him clearly, pacing as he smoked. He attempted to whistle a little tune while the nicotine infused his lungs. I had never been a smoker but sometimes the smell of someone else's cigarettes seemed very appealing. I breathed in deeply at the smoke blowing gently closer but these were a cheap French brand and couldn't be less attractive. He turned, following the wafting cloud as it rose and disappeared into the air just beyond me. I inverted the mirror so he couldn't see the sparkling surface staring back at him. The military boots crunched on the stony floor but it sounded different to the pacing. I had to dare myself to look back in the mirror to see what he was doing. I quickly wished I hadn't dared to look, the answer was shockingly revealed, he was walking towards me.

A pulse soared through me and exploded in my chest. I clambered up from the floor, trying to crush myself further into the wall. My brain was scrambling, trying to find a scenario in my adventurous past that would suit the current circumstances and show me a plausible solution. Fight or flight were the main themes. Not many options there, I'm afraid. That was it, my brain shut down, it could think of nothing else. Fight or flight. Fight or flight, Blossom? The guard's steps were getting a little, not hurried but definitely moving this way. Fight or flight – was that all I could muster? Somewhat disappointing after ten years working in the field.

"Invisible, Blossom, don't forget," Turtle's words chastised at me for my dark thoughts of what I would do the guard when he discovered me, but tonight he would escape a violent surprise and a trip to the hospital. I had no option but to flee.

He was half way along the end wall and I was still on the corner. Without a second thought I carried myself noiselessly down the length of the hut. I rounded the opposite end just as he reached the point where I had sat inhaling his nasty cigarettes. I had moved so fast, I paused to catch my breath. The mirror once more revealed the guard's plans, he had turned and was heading down the path I had just skimmed across. This was my opportunity. He was blind to the expanse of grass between the hut and the gate. His cigarette was nearly finished. I needed to take the chance while it was offered. I thought about it no more. Putting the mirror away so there was no chance of dropping it while I ran, a last look gave me all the information I needed. The guard was nearly at the hut's door. My nerves swelled, the sickness welled. It was time to let It out, the chance would soon pass. I pulled my black cap further over my face, took a deep breath and was gone.

I can cover a hundred metres in just under twelve seconds. I was calculating our relative speeds while running flat out. I would be well inside the gate by the time he appeared around the last corner. The remnants of the fear I was trying not to acknowledge pushed me all the way, leaping and screaming as It exploded with the force to get me to the gate without looking back. I ran in the line that the guard had taken, the one he had shown me was not visible to the cameras. Thanks friend. The blurred image I would portray as I whisked through the gate would be a strange one if they bothered to pick it up. A lumpy black misshapen blur would pass in a flash. A blip on the camera screen, no more.

The barrack block doorway was the only shaft of light. It was quiet and secluded. I realised I was panting and covered in sweat. The strains of the night take their toll in one way or another. Three long clicks on my transmitter told Turtle I was home and the job was done. I waited for a second in the entrance while I put my excitement back in its place, deep in my stomach. It had done well. My pulse returned to a normal rate as the growl of the dark animal inside me grew softer, shrinking back to a murmur.

Inside Claire's barrack room I could hear her cascading her insides into the toilet bowl upstairs. I had to be a normal person now. She had been suitably plastered when I had put her to bed late last night. Mainly because I had filled her enormous glass every two minutes while drinking very little myself. We were old friends. She had copied my deliberate body language without realising. I swigged at my glass often, actually putting little of the acid dry local wine in my mouth but she wasn't to know. As we laughed and chatted away about parties and old boyfriends I slowly made sure she would be unconscious for my need to explore the surroundings.

In normal person mode I had to go and see if she was alright. I took off my catsuit and stashed the tool bag. Just in my bra and panties I noisily clumped up the stairs to where the poor inflicted girl was bent over the white porcelain. I held her long blonde hair from her face and wiped her brow with a cold clean flannel.

"Aww, thanks Blossom. You're such a good friend," she slurred at me, her bloodshot eyes exuding mascara and inviting sympathy. This unwitting pawn had outgrown her usefulness.

"Never you mind that," I handed her a glass of water, "drink this and get yourself back to bed."

"Thanks Blossom, its been lovely to see you after all this time," she had mentioned it about a thousand times since I had bumped into her while shopping a few months before.

"I still can't believe it. All the people in Paris in the summer and I manage to bump into my oldest friend in the whooole world," she threw her arms out to demonstrate the point, almost overbalancing into the bath. A few million people in Paris, indeed there were. It had taken me three days to be in just the right place for her to pick me out.

That was Turtle's idea too. When Claire had applied for the civilian position as PA to one of our Generals liaising with the French on weapons development it had flagged up on the security check that we knew one another. I thought it was too big a risk having her there, my old University room-mate was one of the few links to my past. A link I preferred to avoid, just like all the others, but Turtle disagreed. He was now, of course, right. I had been able to get into the base and use her as a perfect alibi. It was over now, though, the source exhausted. I would not be coming back—for her protection as well as mine.

I poured poor Claire back into her bed and made sure her door was closed. It was too risky for a verbal report but the data on the USB drive would be safer sent straight away. Then if anything happened to me . . . well, at least the work would not go to waste. Turtle pinged back that the message had been received. At last I could fully relax. A feeling of extreme tiredness came swooping down on me, sapping the last of the energy I had saved for the assignment. Claire was still a good alibi, she would find me still ensconced in the duvet when she finally arose.

It was quite late when Claire did get me up, I made the pretence of being very disorganised, "Oh my God, is that the time already, I need to go, Honey, or I'll miss my flight. I can't be too late I've got work in the morning" making normal-person-like disgruntled noises about the dreaded 'work'. I jumped up and threw my clothes on, the black catsuit and its special accessories were already packed into the hidden compartment in the bottom of my little overnight bag.

"Oh, it's a shame you have to rush straight off, Blossom, we hardly seem to have talked at all. Hang on, I'll make you some breakfast before you go," Claire gulped, still looking green from her intimate night-time discussions with the toilet.

"It's OK," I tried to resist a guilty chuckle, "I'll grab a coffee at the airport." But I had to allow myself a small smile when the look of relief crossed Claire's face as she was released from cooking until her stomach felt less like cold tripe.

Claire was still thinking about the previous night, all I wanted to do was to get out without leaving any trail. She still had questions about the past that I had turned away from years before.

"Hey, do you still keep in touch with Tommy?" she asked. This discussion was getting uncomfortable. My relationship with Tommy had come to an end amicably so she naturally presumed we had stayed friends.

"Erm, no," I had to reply, as well as "No's" regarding all the other people Claire had asked about last night. I jammed the last of my possessions into my bag, hurrying to get away.

"So how's the new job going?" I deflected Claire into a conversation she could not resist. Claire's work made her excited. My exciting work made me an island. What acquaintances I had were kept at a necessary distance. Girls confide in each other too much, none of them knew the story of my past. The association with Claire was a danger, being one of the handful of people who knew my real history before the covert life began. It was a risk worth taking. Once.

A rare emotion hit me. A pang of jealousy seemed to be gnawing at me for Claire's carefree life. I was a different person now to that young, ambitious girl starting out at Uni. My innocence forever gone, I had willingly said goodbye to it long ago, now I was feeling strangely jealous of this estranged old friend, far from a saint, but not the sinner that I was.

Quickly dressed and fully packed, it was time to take leave from this old acquaintance.

"Sorry I have to dash, I'll call you soon," I falsely insisted.

"When are you likely to be back over here?" Claire innocently enquired.

"Oh, well, I never really know with this job. I can't really say, it changes all the time," I had to remain vague, "But I'll be in touch as soon as I can, OK?" I extracted Claire from my reassuring hug, turned and walked away, waving happily and smiling to the hungover pawn. I shouted back towards the doorstep with every motion for Claire to look after herself, promising to call soon and arrange another visit, all the while knowing I never would.

The plane touched down two minutes early. I felt worse for having fallen asleep on the flight and only catching an hour. Sometimes a little sleep is worse than none at all. Coupled with the too hot cabin, it made me feel sick as I reached for the luggage in the overhead locker. The air felt stale and hot. It was clammy and I couldn't wait to get off the plane. The other passengers were mostly business men and women with the occasional couple having been to Paris to renew some faded romance.

"Total bollocks," I thought. A weekend in Paris sounded like a beautiful thing but the roads were busy, the bars crowded and it all cost more than a trolley dash through Harrods. I took down my hand luggage and reminded myself I was growing too old and cynical.

Once off the plane the bags were deposited safely and I headed for one of the public phones, all laid out in a neat row. In the privacy of the hooded booth I unscrewed the little electronics pack from my case and pulled out the mini scrambler. Looking as though I was finding a number in the phone book, one end went over the mouthpiece, the other in my ear. There was no other way to call him from here.

"Hi, its me I'm down" I fired at him, not attempting to hide my bad mood.

"Ah, bonjour, mon amie!"

"Yeah, whatever. Did we get the goods?" was the dry response to Turtle's greeting. Sometimes he forgets about being up all night, his humour was not always what I wanted to hear.

"Yes, we did," he was seemingly unaffected by my rude bad humour, "the recording comes up one and a half times while you were connected, so you've done really well. They are listening to some kind of a deal, so we know they have broken their promise. We can now manoeuvre to put some measures in place to see what's going on a bit closer to the source. Well done, Dear Girl." Turtle stopped talking as he seemed to hesitate on his side of the conversation. I thought that maybe I knew what he had to say next and that it would not be received very well. I felt light-headed at the prospect of what was coming but had to pursue it anyway.

"So, my Lovely, I need you to listen very carefully now" he tried to carry on cheerfully but I knew him too well. My heart sunk. I felt my bottom lip extending, my greatest fear manifesting in the tiny earpiece, "I need you to listen, so that you are fully aware that this mission is now at an end. I repeat for your attention, Blossom May, that this mission is now complete and at an end. Can you confirm?"

A sigh escaped from my body. I understood alright. A year's work was done and I would now be stood down until another suitable opportunity presented itself. My particular specialities in surveillance and infiltration were not always in demand. They tended to save me for the most difficult jobs while they trained up the younger officers with the easier tasks. Now I was faced with the prospect of just being a gadget salesman for the next few months until they found an opening worthy of my carefully honed talents. One rest period had lasted almost a year with only the elite forces training to keep me amused. The gloom spread and increased the sickness in the pit of my stomach.

"Yes, I understand. Confirmed," I said finally, somehow resisting the urge to throw down the receiver. I know it was childish but I was always the same at the end of an assignment. I had been through it more than once, Turtle knew exactly what was going on at this end of the line and would have been pouring over the words to make it easier.

"Tell you what, why don't you go to a safe house and have a look at the data you collected. You can use it as a partial debrief to see how it came out. Number Four is free and there's a secure laptop there you can use. I'll e-mail it over and call you later to talk it through, eh?" It was his best sales pitch to let me down gently so we could talk later when the ending of the job had settled in a bit.

So, I would have to make do with the day job for a while. I had an excellent cover job as a salesman for a techno company selling gizmos and electronic gadgets. The title said it all, 'International Sales Executive' meant I came and went as I pleased without attracting suspicion. My handy sales case was a cover in itself, a haven for all the techno bits I needed in both jobs and papers to get it through customs as quickly and easily as a movie star. If I was off assignment then I would need the day job for a while but I didn't have to be back until the morning. Monday morning blues would be very real for me tomorrow. Until then, I could go to House Four, make a full report, check the data then head home for some proper sleep.

"OK, speak to you there later," I put the phone down on Turtle and waved to the airport security cameras looking down on me which he was guaranteed to be remotely monitoring, my ID and location now confirmed.

In many ways he was the love of my life. Not sexual but a deep, reverend love. Unconditional, like a parent. With no siblings I couldn't compare him to anyone else. I had thought many times what I would say and do if we ever met, but while the need was in me and the ability to satisfy it, I knew Turtle would be a distant love. It was far too dangerous for me to know who he really was. Apart from my Father, he was the person that knew and understood me without question. Our unconscious link, our bond, formed through so many years of adversity, was complete. I would try to be nicer to him when he called later on.

Chapter 2

Once I was close to Number Four, I took all the usual precautions for entering a Safe House. These places were the last haven for covert operatives. They were places nobody else knew, somewhere to hide, a place to stay where nobody could find you. They were hidden in plain sight, using old council properties, like this one, as well as remote private houses or one of many flats in a large block. Safe was supposed to be for everyone who used them.

Changing route several times to make sure I wasn't being followed, the slow approach from the back of the property allowed time to make sure I was unobserved. The implications of the data captured the night before was in the forefront of my mind as I sat in the lay up position to observe the area before being sure it was safe to enter. If I had been detected during the stay in France, they would still be on my trail here. I had to be doubly careful. The house as well as the officer needed to be protected and I could not afford to compromise.

The smooth brass master Yale key felt soft as I turned it over in my fingers. I took a last look around. Quickly, I stepped through the back garden and into the house. Once inside the house I drew my weapon and waited. Standing behind the door, the staleness of the air and the empty hollowness of the house that was not a home hit me. Nobody had lived here for a long time. I imagined a family running around, little girls clomping up and down the stairs in their mother's shoes, young boys firing imaginary guns with their fingers. Here I stood, real gun drawn, waiting to see if an attack might come.

The house was deserted on a small uninteresting street. No neighbours enquired about the health of the occupants, no washing hung out on the line. All was still. I cleared each room to make sure there were no hidden guests, my heart not really in the tedious work but following the standard Safe House orders anyway.

Coming straight from an eventful night's work I could not afford to miss anything that would leave me vulnerable. I quickly secured the doors and checked the windows, leaving an adequate escape route and making sure my little gun was easily to hand. The holster under my arm which contained the tiny Glock 27 .40 Subcompact Thunderbolt pistol was always present. My other best friend in many times of need, the light, compact gun was designed as a backup weapon, but its small size and close range stopping power meant it was ideal for easy concealment under a jacket or a jumper – it had even slipped into my bra a couple of times when necessary. I placed the gun back in its holster but removed my jacket so I could extract it quickly if necessary.

The laptop was fired up, closely followed by the kettle, making a green tea to cleanse and overcome the sick feeling I still carried with me. Sitting at the little dining table I logged on to the secure system to check the plethora of e-mails sitting unread in my inbox. As always the necessary plough through the rubbish that I had collected was the first task. Thank you, Turtle, here it is. Everything else went Ctrl/A Delete.

On opening the mail there were two documents attached. I downloaded them both while sipping the green tea, starting to recover. The first file was the complete transmission of what had been captured, the other was a condensed version, just outlining the relevant points we were interested in. The raw data sent to Turtle had been downloaded and transferred to files that could be read in a standard PC format. It wasn't the tea that gave me a warm feeling of satisfaction that we had been able to see it, the translation technology was so new the French thought their communications were safer than they actually were. When they find out the Brits have cracked the method of extracting the data they will be furious.

I had to retrace the work of the previous night as I composed what would be my verbal report for Turtle. The sights and sounds replayed as I remembered where I had been. The French were as good as the Brits at espionage but were somewhat less inclined towards sharing. Occasionally, I would find myself in a foreign part of the world to dip a slender hand into the French intelligence cookie jar, taking only what Turtle needed. I had to resist the temptation to be greedy. This assignment had been time limited, the release of the technology to understand the data would come eventually, we had to grab what we needed right now.

Time to kill and nothing else to occupy me, I might as well read the whole file captured and see what was there. I had to wait for Turtle to call before I could do much else and he would be busy reporting on the information for a while. The full transmission would allow me to properly admire my handiwork. The file loaded up quickly, it started a quarter of the way through the part I had been looking for. Lines of text scrolled up the screen, the occasional missing letter showing how the glitches in the software capture were still being ironed out. I read each line with interest, filling in the gaps to understand what was being said. E-mail conversations discussing weapons deals, terrorists and – ironically – how top secret the whole thing was came to me line by line. It was pure poetry. I laughed. The noise surprised me in the empty house. I looked around for someone to share the joke with, until remembered I had only my dim shadow for company. I sighed again, a reminder of the ending of the mission came back to me glumly while the rest of the transmission unfolded.

After going through the series of e-mail traffic, I allowed it to keep streaming on to the screen as I sipped more tea and stared, glassy eyed, through the dusty net curtains of the window. The street was empty. The rows of suburban semi-detached ex-council houses just like this one were untroubled by traffic in or out. The emptiness stretched out in a yawn inside me. This was the end of the mission. How many times more would I be of use to Turtle and his masters? This was a game for the youngest and fittest. At 32 I already felt a good deal older than most of my peers. There were no guarantees with this work, if someone younger and stronger could be of more use they would go with them, not me. The potential of a droll housewife's existence did nothing to inspire my imagination. Every so often I flashed a glance at the screen to see what it was revealing to me. Wrestling with the paranoia and insecurities that came over me more and more these days when an assignment closed was not a sport to indulge in too often. My stomach started to growl. I wished I had eaten the sandwich on the plane, or at least brought it with me.

An instinct roused me from my glassy eyed review of the state of my world. My self obsession shaken away, I saw a word in the transmissions that alerted me. Rewind that back a bit. The electronic traffic rolling across the screen was showing details of an interrogation. Rewind it a bit further. It was a girl. She was being asked about a place in England. The mention of the place in a transmission like this sent a lightning bolt through me, I knew the place they were asking about but even with my experience I had never managed to get inside. Alarmed now, I put down the tea to look through the data in earnest. Something was badly wrong, I tried to hold on to my nerve at the thought. The place they were asking about was the most secret of them all.

The French e-mails said that a girl had been captured and was being held in North Africa. The French were keeping observations on the people asking the questions. Questions I didn't like the sound of, they were about a research facility in Malvern, Worcestershire. The officers spying on the questioning were asking their handers if the information was still useful and whether to carry on listening to the interrogations or take other measures. Suddenly the previous night's work was a distant memory and I was wide awake, my tired eyes forgotten. I didn't like the sound of the other measures Who was this girl that had been so cruelly taken? I mused over the bottom of my drained tea cup. Was the Malvern site missing one of its junior scientists? As if to shake me from my ponderings, the phone rang, making me jump.

"How do you like your handiwork then?" said the too cheerful voice of Turtle, trying to keep my chin up, thinking I didn't know.

"Fine," I replied, still distracted as he conducted the semi debrief.

When he didn't mention it I was impatient and took the first opportunity to ask about the girl, "Have you looked at the rest of the information we caught?"

"What? No, I just had time to snatch a glimpse of the relevant bits before sending it all off to you." I couldn't help but be a little disappointed that he had not been more thorough with the data that could have killed me to extract for him.

"What have you found?" he asked, his voice suspicious that I was meddling beyond my remit. Not for the first time, if I was forced to admit.

"A girl has been kidnapped and is being held in Tunisia," I told him, wondering if he already knew what I was about to say, "she is being questioned about a British facility."

He was quiet, waiting for me to enlighten him. I couldn't deny I was pleased that, for once, I had all the information. I paused only slightly longer to enjoy this unique position, "Its Malvern."

The simplicity of the statement was designed to accentuate its impact. I waited for his response. It didn't come. He was silent. All my thunder at amazing him rolled away. I was about to check that he was still there when I heard.

"I'll call you back" and the humming of the line as the phone went dead. I sat for a second to try and figure out what I had unwittingly uncovered. Going back over the text on the laptop, I scoured it for further information that I could have missed first time. I couldn't see anything else about the girl and where she was being held. Tunisia, that wasn't good for me.

My mobile was a cute device that looked just like an ordinary phone but was a satellite enabled encrypted transmitter/receiver that didn't go through the normal networks for 'business' calls. The built in scrambler kicked in automatically when the caller recognition detected Turtle's number. It was a lot easier than the manual switch over on the previous models. Ten minutes of pain later, it flashed into life as 'ICE' displayed on the screen. It was Turtle.

"Thanks for that, Blossom, we are checking the information now and will get on to it straight away. You've done a great job, my Lovely, and your end of assignment bonus will be in your usual account by the morning. You make sure you get some rest tonight, you must be shattered. Thanks again, Dear Girl, if we get anything for you we'll let you know . . ."

"No . . . Turtle . . . wait, I need to ask you . . . no, hang on . . . wait, no, Turtle!" I tried to halt the onslaught of thanks and dismissals from my mentor but it was no use. I was left in the emptiness wondering what had just happened. It was no use ringing him back, he would say that he knew nothing and they were still investigating, then he would remind me that the mission was complete and when he needed my assistance again he would call.

The coldness of the room drew away my energy, I realised the evening was darkening. Safety first, better leave the house before any observers had complete cover. I logged off the laptop and wiped its memory as well as the keyboard and screen for fingerprints. Everything I had touched in the house received the same care and attention to leave it in a clinical state. I looked out of the window into the semi darkness of the street to see if the house was being watched. Nothing moved, as if the whole area was frozen. Nobody walked by, no cars cluttered the road. Still alone, my constant state. My presence had done nothing to change the hollowness of the house. Even with me inside, it seemed chilly and uninviting. A reflection of myself, perhaps. Gun at the ready, I unlocked the door, bracing for action. No resistance came, I sped out through the back garden and quickly into the woods at the back of the houses.

Hungry now, I needed some dinner and an early night. Work in the morning, don't forget. The thought of the humdrum existence was gradually sinking in. A normal person job, why did it fill me with such dread? On the way to my warm and comfortable home I thought about the sly dog of a controller I worked for and what he was up to. I pondered how far away the next mission could be while trying to put out of my head the timid thoughts I was entertaining of a possible return to North Africa. The words on the screen came back to me, 'kidnapped' was such a fearful state to be in. I looked down to see my right hand rubbing the position of the invisible capsule in my left palm. At least I had a choice. I became perturbed at the plight of this unknown girl. Maybe Turtle would ring back. Maybe I could do some work of my own tomorrow. The thought was comforting as a plan began to form. I reached my home, ordered a Chinese and slumped into the big leather armchair by the window to wait for the delivery.

Chapter 3

The following evening, after an expectedly dull day at the office, I decided it was time to call my parents. They were the only people in my life I could truly rely on, for totally different reasons. One was strong and practical, the other active and adventurous. I liked to think I had inherited qualities from both. I loved them dearly for all they gave me, but I was closer to my inspirational Father than my common sense Mother. If she ever found out what I did in my day job – especially that Dad put me up to it after his own Special Forces experiences – you would be able to see the fireworks from Mars. We kept it between us as our little secret, as much to spare our hides as protect my Mother's heart.

Although we shared a lot of things, Mother was an alien to me at times, seeming never to have understood or wanted the same things as I did. Dad, on the other hand, was precisely my type, an ex Royal Marine whose long career abroad had more affect on me than anything else. He would be eager to know what progress I had made over the weekend. He maintained a keen interest in everything I did. For me it was like having another specialist as a personal reference. Since he retired, it was all the excitement his sedentary life would allow. To get to him I would have to speak to Mother, there was nothing else for it, I prepared myself by sighing and shaking my head as I dialled the number, wondering what minor misdemeanour I would be discredited for tonight.

"Oh, there you are, Blossom, thank goodness. I have been ringing you all weekend, where on earth have you been?" she started as soon as I said "Hello."

"Do you have any idea that I might want to actually talk to you and know that you're OK? Not a word I've had back from you . . . what have I said about keeping in touch . . ." she went on. And on.

I dutifully apologised (several times), which seemed eventually to halt the onslaught, at least for now. After some benign chat about the dog's sore paw and the state of the porch roof, I felt the impatient need to ask if Dad was in. He would take the call in his study. I loved his study, the dark oak panels with a large leather topped desk in the middle of the room, the smell of a thousand cigars as well as the leather of the red Chesterfield suite conjured images of being sent there as a child for some aggravation I had inflicted on my poor Mother while he was away. Out of desperation I was told to go to my Father to see if there were any fit punishment for whatever I had done. Things had not changed much. Mother transferred me through. I pictured him in the wing-back chair, his favourite seat, closing his eyes to listen as I regaled him with the story of my adventures. Our relationship was such that all I did I fed back to him. The mini scrambler I had installed in his study phone would keep our conversations safe from any interference while allowing me to brag and strut in front of the one who already admired me the most. His paternal pride shone down the phone whenever I had been successful. I could always retell my adventure to a willing audience.

Dad knew exactly what the plan had been in France. I described in detail the unfolding of events, I usually deliberately kept him in some suspense to amuse us both more but my telling this time fell far short of entertaining, "You seem less than pleased with the results, Blossom, what has happened?" He was very perceptive. I had clammed up with the debrief details, not knowing whether to mention it or not.

"Well, Turtle was fine and happy with the data capture" I continued, "until I told him about the girl" there, I had said it.

I explained the transcript of the interrogation. Dad knew all about the area I was talking of, the gravity of the situation and the delicacy of the Malvern site. Even through my little scrambler, he wouldn't mention the top secret laboratory on this line.

"How did Turtle react when you told him?" he asked.

"Well, that's the strange thing, he dismissed me completely. He said they would investigate further and let me know if they needed anything, then signed off and left me hanging there on the end of the phone," I did my best to sound outraged at the terrible treatment, playing on my Father's protective nature.

He paused long enough for me to realise I sounded like I was asking him to sort out a bully in the playground, I could almost feel my foot stamping having had my doll taken away. He was always patient, sometimes too much so, I admit. I just wanted him to be on my side and tell me how to make Turtle give the doll back. The silence continued. I suspected, with good reason, he would tell me to listen to Turtle and let him play with it for a while. I waited for his answer, bottom lip drooping down as if he could see me and not be able to resist. My stubborn response was already formulating, my big armchair silently enveloping me as my only comfort if my Father was against me. He was not going to discourage me, I was determined to find out what was going on, no matter what he said.

Once more I had underestimated my loving Father, who knew me too well to try and put me off by telling me to drop it. He was shrewder political operator than I was, opting for a cautious middle ground where Turtle's displeasure would not be raised, but maybe I could get the answers that had struck a need in me to gain.

"Blossom, I think you should contact Turtle tonight to talk it through with him. He would probably have more information by now anyway," he reasoned. The nerves in my tummy at a possible negative response from Dad immediately dispelled into relief. I thought some more, like a responsible adult rather than a petulant child, and decided to wait until tomorrow.

"I'll sleep on it, Dad, and see if he contacts me tomorrow," I would offer him another chance to give the doll back. If he didn't, I had an excuse to ring him and force his hand. I felt satisfied that a plan had been made and I had followed Dad's advice, well, more or less.

"Thanks Dad, I'll call him tomorrow. Love you loads, hugs to Mum, take care," I put the phone down feeling better with a plan in the bag.

Another plain work day, how many more would Turtle force me to endure? I was sorting through the mail before calling him. Thinking constantly about the girl and what she was going through, I had been rehearsing the words for Turtle in my head all day. Even being told at work that there was a rival for the sales targets from one of the up and coming young men in another branch failed to raise a response. Usually, this was the point where I raised my game to flatten the rival and quash any rumours that they would be taking over my coveted position and the largest of the corner offices. Last time someone muted that there was a challenger, I doubled my figures in two months, leaving my rival beaten and my name still very much top of the sales charts. This time the comment passed by without raising a hair as I was engrossed in the other side of my complicated life, unusually distracted by the pain of being dismissed.

I hoped that my attempts at taking things into my own hands had been subtle enough to escape Turtle's notice. The words were running through my mind a final time as I picked up the phone, bracing myself, but it sprang into life before I had a chance to dial. The screen read "ICE." I answered a little sheepishly, "Hi, I was just about to ring you" I said, trying not to sound rattled by the previous conversation. Turtle gave no time to continue, "I'm calling about the girl" he forced in, I thought I had better stay silent, he didn't sound amused.

"We need to know exactly where she is. We can't tell from the e-mails. I see you are already booked on a flight to Tunisia for tomorrow night so carry on with that. Usual place is booked. Contact me when you arrive. Got it?"

"OK" was all I could manage before Turtle snapped shut the mobile and I was left wondering how annoyed with me he was for booking the flight without asking him. However, at least I was back on the assignment. Less than 12 hours until the flight, I would need to prepare.

My survival kit was always on my body in a neoprene skin body belt that was only removed on aeroplanes. The only other luggage would be my gadget sales case, where a myriad of covert equipment could be hidden in the open, and an overnight bag with a few items thrown together to complete the right image for checking into the hotel.

Part of me was glad of the easy stay in the hotels but there was that dark inner animal which excelled outdoors on survival. The intensive assault on the senses I had received the previous month hammered home the excitement of hunting outdoors. August is always a busy time for catching up with training. This year's was equivalent to the SAS Selection regime that tested the many hopefuls and weeded out the weakest. All Special Forces had to undergo some part of the Selection each year in order to stay operationally active. I was counted as one of these special chosen few.

The life I had chosen was all about the trying times. Why settle for a dull existence when you could strive for a fuller life, taking all the energy you could extract from its thorny grip while it had hold. Out on survival—checking my limits, striving for the basics of life—I had to push through every minute. There was nobody else to help, I lived or died by my own hand. The liberation of that control was what drove me always on. Further, fitter, better. Superior. Living a challenged life and coming through unscathed was the source of my confidence. I punished myself when being chased or interrogated but once I made it through, the animal spirit soared within, I felt unstoppable. This was what allowed me to carry on the insanely dangerous work that gave me so much energy and drive.

"Train hard, fight easy" was the phrase, the hardships of training were very real for me. I didn't operate in a patrol, when I went out, I went alone so I was singled out in training to suffer more than most. I had to be harder, tougher, more resilient than the others. After ten years on various courses, though, there was little that could surprise me. I loved the discipline and camaraderie that came with the work at these times. A rare opportunity to interact within the community was a welcome break from my usual isolation. I had even built up what could be described as friendships on these trips, but come the end, I had no option to keep in touch. The various elite forces I worked with on these occasions were always surprised to see a woman there. No special quarters or treatment were given, I slept and ate with the men and I wouldn't have it any other way. Often they found it more awkward than I did, amusingly.

Like men everywhere they didn't want to be beaten by a girl. The standard was always high so I had to prove myself, pushing on to over achieve. The proud young men would quickly go from the cock-fight of trying to chat up the only female in camp to mocking banter, then respect at my performance. I knew it looked like arrogance to the ones who don't know me, but being the best was what I needed to be, allowing me to continue in my deadly pastimes. Even the ones who know me don't take kindly to a beating. It was always amusing, the basic nature of male pride. I was glad to have the choice.

Right now a different challenge was on the horizon. The various bits of equipment came out of the secure storage area built into the inside of my divan and were carefully stowed away for the journey. My overnight case was basic, travelling as light as possible, I would buy what I needed on the way. As I laid out my clothes and decided what would be left behind I caught myself half smiling in the dressing table mirror. I also found I had picked out all the smallest, prettiest of underwear, ensuring it all matched. When I realised what I had done I snatched the flimsy garments off the bed and went looking for more sturdy apparel. What was I thinking, had I really come to this? I should be concentrating on the mission.

But the thoughts remained whether I recognised them or not, how would I track down the French spies tailing the girl. Unfortunately I knew exactly where to go for the right information. One piece of kit I would need for certain, gym gear. My heart gave away an extra couple of beats for the memory of the last time I met my Tunisian source. Goose pimples appeared on my arms and the backs of my thighs. I looked down at the hairs standing on end as I traded back the cotton bikini pants for lace, you aren't fooling anyone Blossom May.

Whenever I saw him I turned into a clumsy simpleton, my girly crush ignited and made me more ridiculous every time we met. I felt the heat welling up in my face at the thought of our last encounter. The feeling was painful, I had been walking towards him in the middle of the Club when my foot caught the thick carpet, my ankle buckled underneath me and I flailed around hopelessly trying to save myself from toppling. He reached out, grabbing me firmly but gently, saving me from falling on my very red face. I remembered his face close to mine, his smell, the stubble just brushing across my bare shoulder as he easily took my weight to save me. His concern and charm about it afterwards only made it more intolerable and embarrassing. He was always so cool and unruffled, my chaos never affected him and he was always bloody smiling. What was he so damn happy about – or was he just laughing at me? I had spent way too much time considering the question but I found it infuriatingly impossible to move on.

Danny's cover in a hotel health spa in Tunis meant working as a fitness instructor to a lot of ex-pat Europeans who wanted a western style gym with spinning classes, boxercise and yoga, just like back home. Martial arts were also popular and Danny had black belts in three of them. All the times I had visited the Club de Lac and how splendid Danny always looked there swam around my head as I thrust the soft little panties into my overnight bag. The luxurious Club overlooked the Lac du Tunis in the heart of the vibrant capital. The uniform was white, with navy blue piping round the vest and a short navy blue jacket with the Club logo on the left breast. He usually wore shorts because of the heat, teamed with cute little Daz white socks. With Danny's short mousy blond hair he reminded me of an army PT instructor. He looked fresh out of the box, newly unwrapped, always perfect just for me. These visions had to stop, I had him on a pedestal and he needed to be taken down.

Somewhere deep inside where my inner animal slept I could feel my confidence was already ebbing away as more clothes were carefully folded into the bag. That wasn't a good sign. He confused me and clouded my judgement. If that wasn't enough, he's a good five years younger than me and already accomplished and competent in his profession. My profession. Another bloody rival to contend with and one I couldn't focus on long enough to beat. I would rather not see him at all, but knew what Turtle would say if I tried to wriggle out of it.

Forget him, the association would be fleeting, concentrate on the girl. I repeated every line of the interrogation details over to myself to break his spell and shut him out. The packing done, I ate some noodles and flicked through the TV channels, not really watching anything. There were only chick flicks and soaps on offer, neither of which were welcome distractions. I picked up one of the books Mum had drawn out of her Library for me and went to bed. Gently resting on my pillows, I could feel my eyes beginning to close, revealing my memory's picture of Danny's image. A picture I tried to suppress, but the giddy excitement of knowing I was setting off to see him tomorrow made me shuffle around the bed fretfully. Turning and shifting, I was unable to push away how he looked, the softness of his eyes, the slight roundness of his face contrasting with the short sharp haircut making him look even younger. The clock turned over as often as I did, the numbers running round on the dial far too quickly. I couldn't get past thinking of Danny's taught torso and subtly bulging shoulders, it was never ending. Finally I slept, my dreams haunted by the image that was all too soon going to be a reality. This time it would be different.

Chapter 4

Another airport but this one was hot and dry. The transfer from the plane up the tunnel to Tunis-Carthage terminal made my body lather from the first flush of sweat. The air conditioning inside denied the heat entry into the building, but the short walk had betrayed the fierce temperatures outside. It would take a few hours to acclimatise from the dank dewy air of England to the dry crispness of North Africa. The shock of the cool air inside after the heat made my eyes water a little. I had slept well and was eager and alert to carry on with the vital task I had been given.

Whisking our way through customs, my case and I headed as usual for the airport phones. With the mini scrambler carefully in place, I called in, "I'm down, where to?" I asked, knowing I would get nowhere in wriggling but trying anyway. Turtle didn't sound entirely surprised by the question, he knew I had something against working with Danny but I hoped had no idea what it was. I had tried to avoid as much contact with him as possible due to sheer embarrassment, but I could hardly explain a silly crush to a world leading spy handler.

Danny was one of the best informants we had, Turtle told me every time I tried to object to his presence.

"Why are you even asking, you know exactly where to go. Suck it up and get on with your job. I have left the usual package for you at the hotel, make sure you check in with me as soon as you have made contact. I'll call you back with the next step. OK?" he commanded.

"Yes, but what if ... ?" I stuttered, but Turtle wasn't interested today, "You have your orders. Stop messing about, this is serious."

I felt suitably reprimanded, but my mentor had already hung up. Again. He was quite annoyed with me, then.

My face and neck flushed at the thought of seeing Danny that evening. Previous visits here returned to my memory, fresh and clear. He opened the door for me as he always did, wishing me luck on the last mission he had helped with. He was wearing a small t-shirt and tennis shorts, his arm passed faintly over my back as he stretched to hold open the door. I looked back and thanked him, his eyes soft blue under the Club's low fluorescent lights, the smile planted on his pink lips and the little dimple on his left cheek making its usual appearance. I had all that to come again. Better get on and get it out of the way. I jumped into a taxi outside.

The highly decorated white exterior with the giant ornately detailed front portico and square balconies protruding from the side of the gleaming edifice rolled up to greet me as we arrived at the Tunisia Palace Hotel. It was a favourite haunt and I was glad to be back. Inside, the high plasterwork ceilings enticed me towards the walnut Reception desk with the heavy brass rail running along its length. The cool tactile surface was smooth from many years of hands rubbing against it; I touched it again, just for the pleasure of feeling its under my hands. A feeling of homely warmth and safety met me. Turtle's package was handed over with the key-card for a quietly placed room on the second floor.

After appreciating the simple but luxuriously furnished room it was straight to work for me, I changed into my gym kit. Before I left, four little sensors came out of my sales case, one into each section of the room, including the bathroom. Walking round the room to make sure each electronic Telltale picked me up, I checked the signal on my mobile. I watched a picture of myself on the phone's screen. As soon as the sensors picked up that someone was nearby, the image flashed on to my phone. I would be able to see inside my room all the time I was away. Telltales in place, I could now leave my room, but a more old school approach was preferred for outside. I checked the corridor, making some pretence at checking the key-card's operation. I was alone on the short space. One of my long dark hairs was easy to pull out, I ran it through my mouth to moisten the strand. I closed the door and stuck the hair across the seal at an angle between door and frame, just above the natural eye-line. It stuck well, but would fall off if it were opened, a reliable early warning system.

The couple of miles jog to the Club de Lac was an easy and welcome stretch of the legs after the stiffness of the flight. On arrival I was careful to straighten my hair and wipe off the sweat, trying to look radiant rather than exhausted, determined to stride in confidently and show Danny I was no silly schoolgirl. I stretched out my calves to cool down, preparing to go in. I wasn't sure if my heart was racing because of the run or in nervous expectation of seeing a vision I was greedy to obtain. The jitters in my stomach confirmed it wasn't the run.

I needed to summon as much confidence as I could muster, I drew myself up to my full 5'10" height and pushed open the big glass double doors that enclosed the Club foyer. The area was full of the usual crowd, fat but important old men who had come here as their own cover as they fornicated with their secretaries in the steam room and massage tables. They would tell their ageing wives of the great workout they had and their wives wouldn't care less as long as they left them alone at night and paid off their credit cards each month.

I immediately needed to take stock and survey the scene to pinpoint anything that could be taken as suspicious. My method was to work it like a snapshot, my eyes scanned the foyer in an instant, my brain assessed everything as it passed. There were lots of people milling about aimlessly. One man sat in one of the chairs next to Reception. A woman looked at me when she came through from the changing area, I would remember to keep an eye on her and see where she went. I could see no direct threat or other signs of being observed.

A dreadful looking woman in a bright green velour leisure suit loomed in front of me, her prune of a face plastered with make-up to cover the injection marks from the Botox she had just been given. She walked towards me as I came in through the entrance. In one hand was a designer handbag with a large gym bag in the other that I concluded was more likely full of foundation than water bottles. The ghastly woman's mobile phone was ringing, I watched as she juggled the bags around to get to it as we passed each other. The stuffed holdall swung across me, swiping my leg with the corner. Searing pain went though my left leg. My hand shot down instinctively to cover the wound, I looked down to see a flap of skin peel back from the shin. It wasn't as bad as the shock of the impact had made it feel, I pushed it back together to try and stop the blood from dripping. Botox woman pushed out into the street to summon a taxi for her ride home without a backward glance. I took a mental note of the taxi details for Turtle to trace her later on.

A few people in the busy foyer that had nothing better to do saw the incident and gathered, fussing over the minor injury on my leg. I had to be on my guard, I looked around to see if there was another threat heading this way while I was supposed to be distracted. I was aware of attracting far too much attention, trying to mop up the blood with a tissue someone had given me while insisting it was nothing and I could manage. I was not feeling very invisible. That's why a plain girl was better for this work than a pretty one. Everyone would look at and be able to describe a stunning looking girl, even the women. A plain girl could change her appearance and still remain undetectable. I was trying to stop the fuss without being rude—people remembered that as well.

I held the tissue over the tear in my shin to stem the bleeding. A large tanned hand with neatly clipped white nails helped to apply some pressure then its owner knelt down on the floor bringing his face in a little too close, "We do seem to be in the wars, don't we, Miss." I didn't need to look up, the vision of the short hair, soft blue eyes and firmly engaged dimple attached to the perma-grin was already gushing into my mind. I felt light-headed, my breath quickened again. The fluttering through my insides made me feel uneasy, although I still tried to shrug off the supporting arm under my elbow to help me down the corridor to the First Aid room. We crossed the foyer and walked down past the staff room and male changing room. My excitement rose further as he walked across to open the door with that slight slow swagger, the only outward remnant of his days in the French Foreign Legion. He had joined at only seventeen and was now a covert campaign veteran. The French citizenship he was entitled to for being part of the Legion was used to great effect for the British secret services whenever they needed him.

I sat down on the treatment couch in the small First Aid room, Danny turned to open the cupboard. That was the first time I allowed myself a proper look. Here I was again, the wounded little bird he was going to save and coax back to flight. That awful bloody woman with the big bloody bag – I will trace her myself for robbing me of my grace in front of such a man.

"I need to talk to you, can we meet tonight?" I asked quickly, trying to ignore everything else and stick to the business in hand. Rather frustratingly, he ignored the work reference.

"Are you feeling OK?" he asked while he filled a small dish with water and disinfectant. My embarrassment was anxious to conclude things, "I'm fine" I snapped, "I can look after it myself with just a sticking plaster, if you would just give me one." The Freudian slip was unfortunate, I would normally laugh at something like that, but it was too close to the truth and I was aware of making things worse. My insides fluttered once more, I suddenly felt hot. I needed to be away from here, my plan to take back control, be confident and demure had failed on its arse.

Danny's grin never abated, he seemed to be enjoying my discomfort. A female member of staff whose name badge read 'Shahnia' came through the door and positioned herself where she could see what was going on. For a second I wondered what the petite young black girl was doing there, then realised she would be our chaperone. Western rules here, no unaccompanied male staff with female Club members allowed. Heaven forbid there could be an accusation of him molesting me. More likely to be the other way around, I thought, as I caught site of his muscular bottom through the little tennis shorts and even through my embarrassment I found myself wondering if he wore anything underneath when he bent over the cabinet to get another wet wipe for my leg. When he turned round, I tried to make out I had been looking at something else over there and Shahnia did the same. The little trollop. I looked daggers at her but she wasn't interested in me. I flushed a little more, feeling caught out as I realised I was just as bad.

He had taken off the short navy blue jacket as we entered the room, his toned physique exuded from the vest top as he worked away mopping up the blood that had trickled down to my sock. His slim, well defined arms and chest and the beautiful velvet skin dotted with the pretty little freckles at the shoulders made my mouth water, I swallowed hard to try and suppress the dark thoughts that needed to remain within. I tried to focus on what I had come for before he caught this pair of hungry women swarming over him with their eyes.

He knew I wanted a meet so we would have to arrange when and where. Shahnia the interloper would need to be unaware of anything that could be reported at a later date.

"What time does the Club close?" I asked, trying to sound like I was going to come back later.

"The Club closes at 8 then I shower and change and lock up about 8.30" he answered. Great, now I was thinking about him in the shower. Come on, please, could this get any more distracting. I looked at Shahnia and she smiled. We were clearly on the same channel.

"Are you in the area for long?" he asked, the grin still fixed, "Just a business appointment" I replied, "is there anywhere local you can recommend for dinner?" I hoped he didn't miss the invitation to name the venue, "There's a lovely quiet restaurant a couple of blocks away" he grinned, "it's perfect for couples, very romantic." I looked him straight in the eye for the first time. He was teasing me, the terrible flirt. I couldn't encourage that, the level of embarrassment involved for me would be terminal, I was sure, "This is strictly business" I spat the words out, spitefully, "Is there anywhere else that would suit my guest, he's a very fat old man with terrible breath, not romantic at all" see how he likes that description.

"OW!" I jumped at the stinging shot searing through my leg.

"Sorry" he said, "iodine, I needed to clean your cut. Don't want your leg falling off, do we?" Bastard. He was still grinning, he really did like to see me in pain.

He suggested a more formal restaurant and I agreed it sounded rather better. The rendez-vous set, I apologised for all the trouble and filled in the western style Health & Safety forms with the false name I was using at the hotel. I left a standard coded telephone number that Danny would be able to work out later if he needed to contact me.

On the way back to the hotel I checked out La Tavolata and booked a table at the quietest booth. The large tips for the manager and head waiter, just as I always did when I was in town, was enough to secure the best spot whenever I wanted. At the hotel I tried not to admire myself too much in the mirror once I changed into the dress I'd bought on the way back. It wasn't for his benefit, it was just for me. A longer dress would be excellent camouflage for my bandaged leg. Anyway, he wouldn't get close enough to feel the satin and halter necks were very fashionable so it was not a special outfit as far as he would be concerned.

It was all part of the plan to take back control. My beautiful new dress 's deep aubergine colour complemented my fair skin and dark hair. I felt special wearing it and padded round the hotel room deliberately, ages before I really needed to get changed. I needed the confidence of looking as good as I could. Tonight there would be no mistakes. The focus was the mission rather than the deep pools of Danny's eyes or that damn dimple. The disaster element of this encounter was now over and I was ready to move on. My green eyes seemed to sparkle as I finished my make up in the mirror. My jittery tummy returned but it was a nervous kind of looking forward to something exciting rather than the fear and dread of this afternoon.

With my subtle Telltales intact, I clicked my kitten heels out of the hotel and down the main route the few blocks to the restaurant. It was cooler now, a strong breeze blew the long dress around my knees, I had to pull my pashmina close around my shoulders, although the temperature was still in the low twenties. The street was busy and bustling, my brain took its snap shots to dissect unusual movements, taking in its surroundings, looking for anything out of place – like someone following.

I had to move carefully. Dry cleaning was all important on an assignment like this, the art of getting somewhere without being followed. I stopped at a few shops and crossed the road a couple of times, looking in windows and nonchalantly tossing my long hair over my shoulders. My plum coloured lipstick was checked in any mirrored surface as I progressed. My craft was to be stealthy and I practised it often. After a last check I entered the restaurant under cover of a few passers by, disappearing behind them as they jostled by.

At the restaurant I was met graciously by the manager himself. Earlier in the day I had checked the exits and left a weapon hidden in the service alley just in case a quick getaway was required in the next couple of hours. Even though we were both professionals I had survived this long only by being cautious, making sure I had a way out of a building before I went in.

The manager welcomed me in, his arms stretched wide like I was an old friend, "Yes, thank you, I will have a glass of champagne" I smiled at him as he offered the greeting The Head Waiter settled me into the semi-circular booth, leaving the bottle in the cooler on the table after pouring the first glass. I wouldn't be helping myself to the pleasurable slip, it was 8:45pm already, I didn't know exactly what time Danny would show up but wasn't going to be tight by the time he arrived. I took a tiny sip and finished scanning the area. The booth was selected not just because it was quiet, but it commanded a view of the whole restaurant.

Various couples were dotted around the large room. A man in a white shirt sat at the bar near the entrance with his back to me, he had been there when I walked in. The waiters busied themselves moving between customers and the kitchen, none of them were looking over at me. A woman walked in wearing a long gold dress; her platinum blonde hair was scraped back and piled up on top of her head. She wore garish make up and her long diamond chandelier earrings swung back and forth as she trotted along behind the man clearly paying for her services that night. I watched their display from my vantage point with intrigue and disgust. They sat at their table and ordered the most expensive items from the menu in the most voluminous tones. I watched them with all abhorrence in the same way you can't take your eyes from the scene of a car crash. I managed to avert my eyes from the vulgar scene when another figure entered my view.

The man in the white shirt was sitting opposite, he was also watching the loud couple while pouring himself a glass of champagne from the bottle on the table. My hand was on the leg holster containing the Magnum Research semi-automatic ME380 .38 for when my normal holster was too obtuse. I opened my mouth to challenge him when he smiled. The dimple popped up on his left cheek, the realisation struck. Danny sat there as calm as usual. I needed to look at him again, though, just to be sure. His hair looked dark in the candle lit restaurant and the white shirt betrayed nothing of the toned physique hiding underneath. Even the pretty blue eyes looked darker and deeper, more serious. No wonder I hadn't recognised him, I'd never seen him with his clothes on. The joke fell flat within me and he must have sensed it as well.

I had never seen him away from the Club, our business had always been conducted in there, a message or short note the only thing passing between us apart from hungry glances from me in his direction. He was a vivacious flirt, always light and bubbly. Here, with the light as his back, he looked darker and harder than I had thought was possible from him. Less boyish, more handsome but equally confident. I'm sure the swagger would have been evident if I'd have seen him walk through the door. The smile quickly disappeared and he leant forward on the table as a stern look overcame his features. I hadn't been prepared for this. Here was a different person, a Dark Danny I had never met before. Worst thing was, I liked this one even more.

"Did I startle you?" his voice was stern and low. Here he was, looking for the wounded bird again, he presumed he had the upper hand. Well, not tonight.

"Do help yourself to champagne," I offered, not giving him the satisfaction of thinking he had done something to surprise me.

The food was exquisite, I decided to order something light and simple that I could probably eat without spilling or wearing, a Caesar salad with dressing on the side. He ordered a steak, rare, with oysters, I gulped down a mouthful of champagne. After ordering, we settled into the booth to talk about the business in hand.

"So what can I do for Britain's finest?" he asked, casually sipping from his glass as he slid round the booth to my side so we could talk intimately while waiting to be enthralled by the meal to come. There was no smile now and no boyish naivety, this was business. I urged myself to concentrate, the revelation that he was even more attractive as a serious grown up would have to go right to the back of my mind. I thought about the kidnapped girl and the lines of the e-mails I had memorised so I could save her, I didn't think she would be too happy if she knew I was sat here daydreaming.

I gave Danny an outline of the e-mails without revealing how they were captured. I told him of the girl's interrogation but not of the other traffic or the involvement of his friends the French.

"Do you know of a girl being questioned at the moment?" I asked.

"There is one, but she's very young. Believed to be Irish, though, not English. We were just keeping an occasional eye on that one because it wasn't supposed to be anything to do with us," he answered.

"Who has her?"

"Some Tunisians have her in one of the old French safe houses. The men picked her up in Ireland but she's only about 18 or 19. I was confused because she was so young, I didn't see what use she could be to them," he looked serious.

It made sense to me. The French were able to monitor the interrogation because they had left recording equipment at the safe house maintained in their old territory. The age of the girl was a shock, so young to be going through such a terrifying experience. It made me even more determined to get her out of there.

"Where is she?" I demanded, "On the outskirts of a small town, north west of here, about 20 miles out of Tunis. An old French colonial house called San Michel near Mateur. I have it bugged but haven't had it switched on all the time to reduce the chances of detection," he looked a bit guilty at not having tracked the girl more thoroughly. It wasn't his fault, we all did the work our handlers instructed and stayed out of the business that wasn't ours. If we were wise, that was.

We drew apart as the waiter arrived with our delicious looking meals. The aroma of his succulent steak, the slight hint of garlic from his oysters made my mouth water. I had wanted to follow my instinct and order something fulfilling, but I had taken the 'girl on a first date' option and the sophisticated salad on the oversized plate was gently handled on to my place setting. It looked light and fresh, the huge shavings of flaked parmesan layered the top of the chicken and crisp leaves. I would normally enjoy the tasty treat but the first forkful of steak that passed Danny's lips made me wish I had chosen a different option. Too late now, we carried on talking while we ate.

"I can produce daily transcripts of what they are saying, if that's any use to you?" he offered, letting his lips curl up just at the corners. I felt my stare linger on the sweet smile. My heart pumped up inside my chest. I was inclined to accept anything he chose to give me. The transcripts would be welcome for the work. I knew he had pinpointed every safe house in the area himself after long and painful hours following known agents for sometimes weeks on end. His surveillance skills were excellent, perfected in the two years of this posting.

"Thank you, that would be very useful," I accepted, my eyelids fluttering slightly.

Danny picked up his mobile phone and keyed in a code for the programme he was using, "Done" he said, "it will start recording in the next few minutes. The automatic voice recognition will notate the conversations and e-mail them to me and Turtle every hour. Is that good enough for you?" I cleared my throat to disguise the admiration in my voice, "Yes, that will be fine, thank you," I coughed, "where are the devices fitted?"

"There is a main living area on the first floor which they use most often. They take their meals in there as well." He punctuated his sentence with the chewing of the delicious smelling morsels.

"We have one listening device in the cushions of the sofa and one up the chimney. There was a third in the kitchen but we don't know what happened, it stopped working some time ago," he leaned closer, confiding a sense of intimacy that mad me feel a quickening inside, "the rest of my equipment, however, is in perfect working order."

The scarlet rash burst through my skin and rushed from my chest to my cheeks in an instant. I was aware of my mouth remaining open when it should really have been closed if I was to appear at all seemly. I had to remember to breathe as I tried to disguise the joyous squirming that squeezed at my insides.

The waiter cleared our plates, the moment of his arrival opportune for me to recover. I had to take back the control, the last comment was a blip, I wasn't going to fall for any more. The silence while our table was set for the next course allowed us both time to reflect on the night's events. I had the information I needed. The house would be the next target for me but first I had to get to the end of this dinner; cool, in control, superior. Simple.

The desserts came chilled and perfectly presented. My mound of profiteroles were draped in a delicious cape of dark molten chocolate, making them so indulgent I was already proportioning up how many I would allow myself to eat in front of my equally delicious companion. I looked over to him hacking off great manly chunks of the rich, sticky cream doused cheesecake that I would have savoured every spoonful of, given the opportunity. The conversation had come to a natural end with the imparting of the girl's whereabouts. We sat quietly, licking spoons and scraping cream from plates to cover the awkwardness at the lack of any further connection.

"How's your leg?" he asked at last. He might as well have pounced at my heart with the spoon he was still holding. I squirmed at him mentioning it, I was determined my weakness in front of him that afternoon was not how he was going to remember me tonight.

"Fine, thank you. Are you busy at the Club at this time of year?" I swigged my champagne to clear my glass, getting ready to leave.

"Fairly," he answered, falling for the deflection in subject matter, "it depends on how many classes I have." He finished the champagne by refilling my glass almost to the top then toppled the empty bottle head first back into the cooler. I got the feeling there was something more being planned than a simple information exchange, but I had neither the time nor the inclination to act on a ridiculous crush.

"One of the guys has been on holiday this week so I covered his classes as well. It's been quite hectic, really, one lesson after another as well as the private clients," he continued.

"It must get very tiring, with so many people to satisfy," I sipped my way down the last glassful. He looked at me, his eyes shining, "I don't get tired, no matter how many," he said, his eyebrows rose slightly and a broad grin spread across his face. The bubbles in the last sip of champagne seemed to hit me in the back of my throat, I coughed.

"In that case you're not doing it right," I retorted, regaining my composure. The dimple in his left cheek peeked out, he laughed out loud, the first time I had heard it. It made a nice noise, round and soft. Maybe he did have a sense of humour after all. Maybe he wasn't always laughing at me?

It didn't matter, my work was done here. Time, at last, to move to the next task. I got up, the room seemed to shift under my feet just enough to make me knock into the table as I rose. I shouldn't have let Danny coerce me into that last glassful. He opened the door as I settled the bill. Cash only, no trace. I checked the room again with a snapshot on leaving to see who else was making the same move. The restaurant was unchanged as we left. Another handsome tip for the waiter and I glided out into the cool night. Danny seemed to be waiting for me to give him his next instruction, blatantly hanging back, seeming reluctant to move. I, on the other hand, had things to do and it didn't involve him, "Well, thanks again for all your help," I dismissed him, "I'll go make my report. I'm sure I'll see you again before too long."

"I know where the house is, I can take you there if you like," he offered, a little too keen. I thought about the disaster of me trying to look pretty while creeping through the shrubbery outside the marked house. If he was with me I would end up falling in to the duck pond or crashing into pots on the terrace. No. I don't need any more distractions or anyone else muscling in on my assignment, this would be a solo project from now on.

"That's very good of you," I was trying to be polite but firm, "I'll just report back to Turtle and he can take it from there. I'm sure he'll let you know if there's anything else we need." The silence was slightly awkward as he still seemed reluctant to move.

"Well, if there's nothing else I can do . . . please let me know if you need anything . . . it would have been nice to . . . erm, well. Good luck . . ." it was as if he wanted to ask something but couldn't find the right words. He took a step forward and leaned in towards me. I saw the beautiful face looming, he flicked his tongue over his lips to moisten them, my insides curdled. I withdrew, taken aback by him being able to read my mind and act out my greatest wish. I thrust my hand out to grasp his in a firm and businesslike handshake, it was either that or loose my grip on the authority I had managed to salvage.

I turned quickly and walked away, not looking back after seeing the dejected figure watch me click my tiny heels back towards the hotel. My head cleared steadily as I made my way. I had kept my composure and my command, at least for most of the night, even resisting the flirting and the certainty of a small clinch at the end. I would kick myself later, but my legs would have sunk underneath me, their power lost, if he had managed to get close enough to kiss me in the moonlight.

The Telltales showed no sign of an intruder so I went straight into my room. The sales case contained all my special gadgets, two of which were swiftly clipped together and twisted so the little red light poked out from the top. I checked the room twice for transmitting devices. The light never flashed, the room appeared clean. I thought about the devices that had remained in San Michel for over two years, maybe a little extra security was required. The signal jamming device looked just like a mobile phone charger, I plugged it in after turning off the TV. Every signal for a ten metre radius would be interrupted by the jammer, including the television remote control. I had found this out to my cost after being stuck with a Spanish soap opera for far too long one eventful afternoon in South America. Not just mine but my immediate neighbours would suffer if they were currently tired of their choice of entertainment. The lack of response from the TV remote would prompt either a slamming against the table or the usual removal of the cover and a hand rolling slowly over the batteries in the back, depending on the temperament of the occupant I was disturbing. They would all just have to manage while I made my report.

Turtle answered the first ring, he must have been waiting up, "Had a nice evening have we?" he asked, almost accusing, designing to tease me. At least he was talking to me again, but I wasn't up for the game tonight, it was almost 11:00 already and I needed to be on my way.

"Very pleasant" I replied dryly, "we have the location, it's a safe house that used to belong to the French on the outskirts of Mateur.

She would appear to be Irish rather than English, if that means anything to you?"

"Why do you think she's Irish?" Turtle asked.

"Well, Danny said that they had picked her up in Ireland, so he had kept a distance because he thought it was nothing to do with us." Turtle was very quiet on the other end of the phone. I knew his moods, he was thinking. I waited patiently to see what he wanted me to do next. I was going to the house anyway, I just needed him to say it for me.

"OK," he said at last, "Get over there and check it out. See if she's still there and make a plan just in case, usual plan. Oh, and don't get caught or I will have to send your friend in to rescue you and you don't want that, do you."

"Goodnight!" I was still not playing, and hung up.

Chapter 5

Changed and ready for the night's work, I checked myself in the long mirror on the wardrobe. The holster built in under the left arm of the black catsuit was empty for now, but the second one in the back of the waistband was full, along with the survival kit underneath. Black combat boots made of leather and canvas that sealed around the bottom of the suit completed a look even Gok Wan couldn't have created. Urban secret soldier chic.

A secret patch on the breast of the suit was built in to the fabric. Although it looked black to the naked eye, different conducting materials were woven in, embroidering a Union flag. With thermal imaging lenses the materials looked different colours, warmed by my body, showing the flag for easy identification. I could hardly walk around the streets in the strange uniform, I threw on a shirt and jogging bottoms to complete the outbreak of uncontrollable sweat that had flushed through me at the heat of being so completely encased in material. I imagined the flag at my chest glowing at the rise in temperature.

Turtle's welcome package contained everything I needed to motor out of town. The car park was on the outskirts, I had the keys along with a registration number and a code to disarm the security functions. I had another stop first, to refill my little holster with the old friend I had left behind the restaurant earlier. My escape plan had not been necessary, now I needed to retrieve the Glock from under the crate in the service alley. It was all quiet now, I jogged lazily over to the crates and slipped the gun back into its rightful place. Already I felt better, the lack of the bulk under my arm had been marked, I was naked without it. I had changed my gait to accommodate the weapon and without it I had to remember to walk normally. A steady walk to the car park on the end of the main road where the blue Suzuki Swift was waiting patiently for me.

The dinky little car was certainly deceptive. Walking past it looked like a small housewife's run-around with sweet wrappers in the footwell and a toddler's car seat in the back. A shopping bag in the passenger side gave the impression its owner had just dropped in to the shops on the way to pick up the children. These cars were not all they appeared, under the bonnet was a high capacity engine. The suspension, tyres and brakes rally spec for getting out of trouble quickly. I loved these little super-specials, a smile overtook my face as the key turned to start it up. A specially attenuated exhaust muffled the noise, making it sound more like it needed fixing than it was disguising a monster.

A command on the voice controlled system made the SatNav and tracker flip up behind the usual dials as I turned right heading slowly out of the car park. My speed, route and nearby Police car positions were all illuminated on the screen behind the dashboard. The last thing I needed was to draw the attention of the local bribe hungry lawmen. The SatNav talked through my movements with a calm reassuring female voice as I set off at a sedate pace out of town. I needed to go through a few standard checks before I reached the city limits to make sure this adventure was a solo one. For that, it was better to be going slower than the traffic's natural flow. Anyone behind would stand out, being overtaken as I now was.

A few miles along the straight road heading west I noticed a large silver Mercedes behind me. The reflection in my mirrors didn't reveal much, but it was enough to make me a little cautious. He kept a safe distance, but his presence was enough for me to want to break away.

"SatNav command" I spoke to the voice controls, "Ready" the computer responded, "Route change, display map" I told it. The map view filled the screen, I could see all roads in the area. I tapped the road I wanted to take and the lady in the dashboard obliged.

"Recalculating" the computer blinked then settled back to the SatNav view, the new route highlighted on the screen. I kept an interested eye on the friend in my mirrors.

"In one hundred yards, turn left," was the instruction I had been waiting for, the sharp turn I had programmed in loomed on the map. I maintained my position on the road, watching the Mercedes. The traffic was close, I would have to do this quickly.

"In ten yards, turn left," I waited another couple of seconds to judge the gap in the cars, without indicating I yanked the wheel over and pulled the little car round the tight bend, narrowly missing a large bus travelling the other way. I accelerated quickly along the straight road that led ultimately back into town to get some distance between me and the corner I had just rampaged through. I checked my mirrors to see whether my suspicions were justified. Almost a mile on, the traffic parted and changed lanes behind me to reveal, a little further behind than he had been, the large silver Mercedes.

My senses were bright, I loved a chase, but the work tonight was essential. I could not afford for it to be stopped no matter how intrigued I felt about who was behind me and why. The joy of being chased would have to submit to the value of the job. Another command to the voice controls and a new route was formed.

"Command, Head Up Display" I told the computer and the scene in front of me was morphed into a 3D image of my new route. Markers projected on to the windscreen showed me the distance to the next corner, my speed and a countdown in seconds of how long before I reached the turn. The image on the screen showed the hairpin right hander coming into view on the road ahead. I had to lose him here. Three seconds to the turn I accelerated. The little turbo ramped up, thrusting the vehicle forward with a kick in the back that made me want to grip more tightly on the steering wheel. The corner was approaching fast, I waited until the last moment, weaving across the lanes of traffic. As the display read only one second left I turned off the headlights and took the turn without slowing down. The tyres on the little car never even screeched, the suspension taking the brunt of the G-force trying to pull me into the surrounding buildings. I straightened the wheels as the car got the better of the narrow bend, pushed on the gas pedal and felt the little car squirt out from the turn like a harshly held bar of wet soap.

The car dashed out of harm's way. I looked behind to see if he was still there. No sign. I switched the lights back on and reset the map to SatNav only. Heading in the right direction again it took a few more discreet turns to get out of anyone's way before slipping into the traffic heading the right way on the P7 out of town. The road then headed north west and met up with the P11. After twenty minutes steady drive with no further interest, I took a bypass to encircle the house so I didn't drive straight past it on the main road.

A couple of miles north of my destination, a large wooded area at the side of a lake with a series of dirt tracks that criss-crossed through to the farm land at the other end made ideal cover to leave the car. Lac Ichkeul was a popular local spot in summer for its clear blue water and beautiful woodland border, but the locals soon retreated to their homes in autumn and the dark wood was abandoned. Pulling in and turning off the headlights, I cautiously drove down the track that led to the farthest point from the road and parked as far as I could under a large prickly shrub that overhung the track. Taking off the jogging pants and T-shirt, I got little respite from the heat now they were on the back seat of the car. The pink hat turned inside out to reveal a black lining so I could push my long hair off my face and scrape it inside to make sure it didn't get in the way.

With the direction and bearing from the SatNav as the only guide, I set off into the darkness, taking as much cover as I could from the woods and the land. Instinctively, I checked my weapon by touch as I pushed through the vegetation. The stream that fed the lake meandered through the farmland, being used for an irrigation system that had been dug out using ditches to water the crops, now these were dry I could slide into them and traverse the land without being seen. The stream's path mimicked my own as I followed its general direction upstream, creeping through the fields. I made my way silently towards the house, counting the footsteps so I could judge how far I had travelled, all the time checking my direction. Trying to distinguish landmarks, of which there were few, was proving difficult. This was a flat, featureless horizon leading only to the hills on one side where the big house would be. I would have to be careful I was on the right bearing, heading for the almost invisible line where the land met the sky.

As I steadily made my way through the ditches and crops that surrounded me I was wary of the wild perils that lay beneath my feet. Africa had snakes and venomous insects in abundance. I was being careful to avoid them, but in the darkness it was easier said than done. I flinched at one point when something moved under my foot as I trod into the bottom of one of the ditches, but whatever it was had not thought to exact revenge and I made it past unscathed.

A sudden flurry of wings made me dive into the crops as a flock of nervous birds flapped and panicked overhead. My heart pumped hard, the sound whooshing through my ears and mixing with the beating air as it washed past my face, the birds all taking off at once, squawking and circling into the sky. I settled down for a second and composed myself, looking across the fields desperately to see that there was no-one else around to hear the uproar. The birds landed further away and I set back to my task, more urgently than before. I saw a light in the distance, on top of the hill at the horizon. There it was, the single house stood out on its own.

About half a mile away I stopped and set up a recce position. Lights in the windows showed me clearly the position of the house, shedding out on to the garden and the driveway leading up from the main road. In a snapshot I noted the size of the house, its position from the road, if there were any cars parked outside and what cover was available from the large garden surrounding it on the three sides visible from my position. From this distance I could also shine the infra red torch over the entrance and see the light reflective dust through the glass filter built in to the top of the torch. Seeing the tiny glistening reflections of the dust that

Danny had put down to mark the house when he had discovered it confirmed I was in the right place. It also confirmed that Danny was a very good agent to have got that far undetected, but that thought would be blotted out for now to allow me to concentrate. It looked safe enough for me to move further in.

Up close, the large tree I had seen from the recce position was perfect, the lower limbs spread out and spanned across the grass, giving plenty of cover from the house as well as the road. My breath quickened, my senses alert as I laid in waiting, listening for any movement. A feeling of overpowering aggression built as the animal inside me growled at the hunt, approaching my prey silently. The prospect of breaking into the house almost made me salivate. I crept forward, keeping my concentration on the house for signs of movement. I sunk down to get under the low hanging branches of the giant tree without disturbing them; underneath was black, it smelt of damp pine needles and the musty old aroma of raking up wet leaves in winter. I headed for where the bottom of the trunk and the roots must be, although I could see almost nothing as my eyes adjusted to being denied even more light under the shadow of the big tree. I could feel the roots under my feet and turned round to sit on one of them to start setting up my lay up position. As I crouched close the trunk, the tree came to life behind me. I felt like a bolt of lightning hit me in a flash in the darkness. One strong hand went over my mouth and the other, just as fast, clamped around my torso.

My arms were gripped by my side, I couldn't move. My instincts took over, as fast as I was grabbed, I powered my legs to lift me up and roll forward. The man holding on to me was forced to come too as I wheeled on to my back, landing hard with him underneath. His grip loosened with the impact, I swiftly whipped round so we were face to face. I could feel his hard, sinewy muscles under his clothes, he was broad and wiry, his body strong and well developed. The hood covering his face made his figure more intense, head to toe in black, I could feel the holster under his arm, just like mine. We struggled together, each wrestling and wrenching to outmanoeuvre the other. The sparkles in his eyes were all I could distinguish as the light from the house caught the liquid pools. The look was dark and threatening, I had stumbled into a professional killer. My blood rushed through me, the hairs on the back of my neck pulled at the skin as they raised up in alarm, but my own predator was still present. I felt the growl inside me growing as I started to attack.

I turned to face my adversary as we rolled over each other, striking the tree trunk. He was still trying to grip me hard, wanting to turn me on my back and control me, yet we had not exchanged blows. This encounter was unusual; although my fear was real, I wondered why he hadn't hit me yet. We scrabbled together, I was over him, trapping him between my body and the tree. He locked his arms tightly round my torso, squeezing the air from my lungs. He could have the body, my arms were free, my hands clawing and grasping for purchase on his clothing and skin. He let go of my ribcage to grab my wrists to stop me, a brisk strike on the nose with the back of my knuckles exacted a satisfying crunch from beneath my hand, accompanied by a muffled "Oof" from under the hood.

I used the split second it took him to recover from the sudden blow to free one of my hands. Gripping the side of his black collar, I leaned across him, thrusting my forearm into his neck to stop his breathing. I pushed down with all my weight, bringing my face close to his. I heard a snarl, I wasn't sure if it was him or, in fact, me. Even while crushing his neck he still never struck me, this curious assassin not wanting to sully me with his blows.

Pulling the arm he still had hold of, he levered me over to the side to release the pressure from his throat. He kept turning, adding momentum with his legs to push me all the way over. I was thrown on to my back, a tree root slamming into my spine as I landed. My breath fell short, I couldn't fill my lungs, the pain shot through my ribs for precious moments. The agony in my shoulder blades sent my head spinning but there was no time to recover.

He was on me, regaining his mount. With his full weight upon me, he knelt on my chest, my hands hoisted above my head, pinned to the dirt. I could hardly move. My legs thrashed against the ground as I tried to knee and kick the murderous assailant. The crunch of my boots as they made contact with the back of his head gave a morbid sense of pleasure, more so as he let go of one of my hands.

He ripped off his hood and leaned over my face, his silhouette black against the light from the windows of the house. My heart pumped harder, my pulse resounding in my ears. I couldn't reach him with my boots now so I lifted my legs to wrap around his waist or chest to try and wrench myself free. His breath felt hot on my face and neck, I turned to avoid it. Hardly able to breathe now as he held up my arms, his knees pressed down on my chest. I was steadily being crushed, my lungs unable to fill, my brain going mad with fear, screaming at me urgently to breathe, breathe, breathe.

My legs caught hold of him, trying to prise him away with my knees up and under his ribs. I freed one hand to apply a skilful left hook to his jaw, resulting in a sound that turned me to ice, freezing as I was still contemplating my next strike, "Bloody 'ell" he said quietly under his breath, spitting out the blood from the inside of his cheek. How had a northern English accent make its way here to attack me in the darkness? In amazement, I turned to face my aggressive opponent as he leaned right over me.

He swooped down and kissed me, hard, on the lips, gripping my head with his one free hand. My shock turned to anger until it dawned on me that I might be in more trouble than I thought with this violent killer who had hold of me. A shot of panic tensed my weary body, the fear tearing at my insides to get away. He twisted loose of my grip on his torso and sank down, his bent knee drilling painfully into my thigh to force a way in between my legs. His chest was level with mine now, I had his weight upon me still but at least I could begin to breathe again. He continued to kiss me as I thrashed underneath him, forming my plan to finish him off.

My elbow was poised for the strike, aimed at the pressure point in the neck that would leave him unconscious at best, as I felt the situation change. The panic faded, I could see and feel clearly. I battled with my senses to try and take in what my brain was telling me. I had to follow my training and see through the red mist of the contact. Why hadn't he just shot me as I approached? Why hadn't he hit me? Why did this feel so familiar? I was confused and in pain, the adrenalin pumping making me dizzy. My elbow held aloft while I pondered the strange scene. The crippling blow would be the final act, I raised my arm. Yet my mind was telling me to wait. Now there it was, the kiss, the northern accent, the feeling. I was remembering.

My arm lowered across the back of what had been my attacker, my legs twisted together around his waist as I realised why I felt this way. He was still kissing me hard as I threw in my lot and gripped him tightly, kissing him back. He let my other wrist go so we could slide into a tight embrace. His stubble slashed my face but I couldn't care less, the fatiguing memories of our last encounter on a Welsh hillside in the middle of winter making me want more of the rugged attentions. With some embarrassment I remembered I had not shaved my legs for some time during the exercise when we met and he made a sweet comment that he liked his women wild. The blood in his cheek let him know how wild I really was. Back in Wales we were supposed to be bivvying together for warmth but things had got a bit too hot and we were almost caught by the course instructor as he approached unnoticed as we shared more than body heat.

I didn't usually succumb to the advances of my training partners but Macca was not like the others. His confidence and maturity made me trust he wouldn't be blurting his conquest all over the training camp. We had circled each other for days in our quiet attraction. I was glad now that I had previously made his acquaintance, as one of the best boxers in the Regiment I would have stood little chance against him had he decided to strike first. His hard, lean body was welcome comfort to me now, our enjoyable reunion lasting until we both relaxed to catch our breath, smiling and suppressing a mischievous giggle.

"What are you doing here?" I whispered in muted tones that would not carry, using a slight lisp to soften the words and make them less perceptible.

"I could say the same to you, my sweet wild Blossom. You get even harder to tangle with, my lovely, you caught me with a good couple of left handers there – I thought you were going to knock 'ell out of me, Lass." He nursed his swollen cheek and laughed, spitting more blood, exhausted at the battle he had only just managed to win.

"We just came in tonight. We're shadowing a couple of terror suspects and the day shift tailed them here" he said, looking up at the big house.

Aghast, I realised he said "we", that meant there were at least three others lurking around the grounds that could have witnessed our happy reunion. I coloured up instantly, looking around for signs of flashing eyes and teeth as they fell about their hiding places laughing. Mac must have sensed my discomfort and added, "The others are on the different sides of the building so we can monitor each side. I'm keeping an eye on cars as well to see what the activity is like. Don't worry," he said, "we're as good as alone," a more subtle kiss landed upon me as reassurance that our mischief would go unreported. Any successful woman was accused of sleeping her way to the top; in my male dominated world it was an accusation I could not afford. Macca understood, he had more respect for me than that. My trust was well placed.

My face beamed up at him as I put my hat back on and tucked in my hair. The darkness masked most of his looks but I could make out the square jaw and prominent cheek bones. He isn't typically handsome but rugged and confident, his body not carefully crafted from hours in the gym, but honed tirelessly out of the necessity of combat. Even the broken nose from boxing was hardly perceptible, only adding to the tough physique and manly air. In the winter his jet black hair had been quite long but it was neatly close now, matched by the permanent growth of stubble that covered his chin. He looked like a convict, and behaved like one most of the time. I didn't have to wonder why I found him so attractive, he was rough and ready, dangerous and surly; all the things Danny wasn't – he was blonde and pretty, Macca was dark and dirty. And I liked it.

"Who's in the house?" I asked, forcing a return to the task in hand.

"As far as we can tell, there's the two Tunisian terrorists that we had tailed here, plus two other geezers we don't know. They seem to be having a meeting in the living room on the first floor – second window along from the left" he pointed up to the area of the house just in front of us.

"There's been a recent increase in activity with this group, we're trying to see what they're planning. These are the men responsible for the attacks on the American Embassy, you remember, when Frank was killed? Anyway, they're planning something and the other men seem to be part of it but we're not sure of their involvement yet."

"Is that all?" I asked him, fishing to see if he could save me some time in finding the room the girl was being held in.

"Well, one of the guys around the back thought he saw someone else earlier. A ghostly figure with long hair walked past one of the windows in a bedroom on the other side, but he hasn't seen it since and he wasn't sure whether it was male or female." He seemed sceptical whether his friend had seen anyone at all, apparently not impressed by is observational skills, but it was just what I was hoping for, "That's my mark."

Mac looked surprised, "Who is it?" he asked.

I thought that was a very good question, "Don't know yet, I'm just here to confirm the girl's presence and report back" I answered.

"How long are you here for?" I was fishing again but now for an entirely different purpose.

"Just until the terrorists leave" he was almost apologetic, sensing my dusky motives, "as soon as they go, we'll go with them. Those are our current orders."

It must be big if the SAS were involved. Wait 'til I tell Dad, he'll want to know every detail if his old professional sparring partners were in the game somewhere.

Mac radioed through to the rest of the patrol that I was coming around and they were to allow free passage around the house while I made my reconnaissance. I crept across the garden, noting every detail of the property. It was a large, square building in the classic French colonial style. The lower floor was where the French dignitaries would have their parties and receptions. I made my way around the sides, receiving the occasional nod from underneath a shrub or behind a fence as my fellow interlopers showed themselves to me as I passed.

An impressive drive ran from the main road to the large entrance portico with a facade of Italian marble relief work. Beautiful long columns made the double entrance doors look even taller and more grand. My estimate at the height, however, would actually make it more than accessible for the purpose that I had in mind. Around the back of the building was the main kitchen, along with the staff accommodation in small cells with tiny windows. There were no staff here now, the windows dirty and bare. The landing window was clearly lit even at this time of night, I wondered if there was an unseen guard somewhere, keeping an eye out for British officers and SAS men trying to break in to his secret sanctum. No sign of life came from within, the light reflected on the glazed doors that led to the terrace at the top of the garden. The house's position on top of the small hill made the garden dip gently at the edges and the terrace allowed a flat surface for water features and furniture for further entertaining.

I noted the position of the chimneys relative to the bedrooms I could make out on the second floor The room Macca had indicated with the girl in it was nothing spectacular. No curtains covered the windows, no light shone from inside, the room looked empty. I completed my circuit of the property, assessing the surfaces on the way round and the cover on all sides. A detailed mental picture built for the immediate action plan that Turtle would want from me as soon as I returned. My basic plan was set, I refined it steadily, examining equipment and personnel until I had all I needed.

Macca was still under the tree, I returned to bid him a good night with another passionate clinch that lasted more blissful minutes. I gave him my hotel details and the name I was using just in case either of us were in the area for a while. I knew neither of us were likely to be, but it would keep a spark of interest alive in me for a day or two – and the thoughts of Danny out of my way.

Slight tampering with my hotel's rear fire door before I went out allowed me to slip in unannounced just before dawn. A peg in the mortice that held the door shut was enough to make it look closed but give access from outside. The staff were just starting to prepare breakfast in the kitchen as I stole through to take the service elevator to one floor below where I wanted to be. Remembering the Mercedes from the previous night, I wound my way carefully up the stairs and waited a little away from my room for any signs that things were not as they should be. On the landing of the stairwell I checked my phone, the little images of my room displayed a quiet, empty space just as I had left it. I quickly let myself in and drew my gun. The room was still. I checked the electronic Telltales had not been tampered with, cleared all the rooms, put the bolt on the door and pushed the case table behind it so I would not be disturbed. Time to relax at last.

My security electronics scanned the area for listening devices, I set up the signal jammer and called Turtle.

"She seems to be there" I reported, then told the story of my night's adventures, leaving out the bit about rolling round in the dirt with an SAS patrol sergeant like a dog on heat. Turtle agreed that it must be the girl we were looking for, "We need to extract her before its too late. How long are the Regiment on site?" he asked, "Just as long as the guys they are tailing," I gave the answer I had been given when asked in an entirely different context.

"OK, I'll find out what the situation is and see who we can use. We'll put another team in and keep tabs on the girl, let the SAS guys follow their suspects. I'll call you later. Don't forget to get some rest."

"Yes, *Mother*," I retorted in a sarcastic tone. That reminded me, I hadn't had chance to call my parents. Better do that now then get to bed. I still had the normal-person job cover appointment at lunchtime and needed to justify the sales VP title with some actual sales.

With the scramblers still in place I called my Mother at home. Margaret May was a part time librarian in the village. She was the one I inherited my love of reading from. Mum's disappointment at me not becoming a country school English teacher after studying at University she had never expressed, but she didn't have to actually say it for me to know. There were no arguments or insistences, it was just a feeling I wasn't following the path as it had been lovingly laid out for me.

Mother should have known, the life of a school teacher was not on the cards for her tearaway child. I always took after my Father, he treated me more like a son. When I was little, he would take me camping, fishing, trapping animals and shooting bows and arrows we made ourselves. He was away a lot of the time, so these trips were special, just for us. He taught me things. He told me things. We shared everything when we were away. His stories of the battles he'd been in and the men he led had me hanging on his every word. My hero in every way, I wanted to be just like him. I had always loved being away and would bring back various skinned animals for Mother to cook.

"What a gorgeous little girl I have", she used to sigh and say. Attempts get me into a pretty dress or brush my long dark hair would end in a massive fight and several slammed doors. Not just by me. I never knew why it was so important for me to wear those stupid clothes that you couldn't even run in, never mind climb trees. Now I realised what a disappointment I must be to poor Margaret, the promise of a daughter to dress up and make pretty, to bake with and go shopping had never materialised. Dolls? No. Well, maybe if you count Action Man.

For as long as I could remember, my Mother had been a special volunteer for the local Samaritans, taking phone calls on their mobile at all hours of the day and night to help people who had nowhere else to turn. I would see her after the calls, sometimes very satisfied, other times distressed, but she was always there and never failed to help somebody who needed her. As an only child, having to share my Mother when I was younger had made me jealous of the Samaritans for a while. It had been difficult coming second to whoever needed her at the time. Once I realised I got to keep what they could only borrow, I held no further grudge, appreciating that some people needed her more than me at times. Looking back, I think it made me stronger, more independent to know that at times I had to fend for myself. Every child must learn they aren't the centre of the universe, especially an only child. As an adult, I had come to terms with her unpaid work, knowing that as long as there was someone as caring and sensible as her around, she should be shared with as many people as possible.

It was the same common sense approach that convinced her husband it was time for him to retire from the service he loved so much when she finally said he was too old to be running round with the young kids in his regiment. She was fed up of worrying about him and wanted a quiet life for them both, at last. I had spoken to Dad about it at the time, being so much closer to him, but he had to admit she had a point – her logic and reasoning winning out again, so he retired. Just like that.

Margaret was always an early riser, needing very little sleep for her alert mind to stay in scintillating form. The time difference between Tunisia and England was only an hour, she would be up and getting ready to go to the library for her morning's work.

"Hello?" Mum answered, enquiring with her voice who could be calling at such an hour.

"Hi Mum," I answered the question.

"Aah, hello Darling, how are you?" the delight in her response soon giving way to a mother's tongue lashing, "My goodness, child, I thought you must have fallen off the planet. Don't they have phones in Tanzania or wherever the goodness you are this week? Honestly, Blossom, I have all on keeping up with you, why on earth haven't you phoned?" but it was too late to reply by the time the next barrage of questions came flooding towards me, "What is it like there? Is the Hotel OK? Are they looking after you?" I tried to get a word in to answer the onslaught of enquiries, wishing I'd called later and got hold of Dad instead.

"Make sure you watch out for the water, its not like back home, you know," was the usual warning. I tried to assure her I was eating properly and only drinking bottled water. With my safety confirmed it was time for Mum to start to remind me of family business.

"And don't forget your cousin Edward's wedding next Friday – its second time around for him so its very important that we all show our support, even though he's only just met this girl and it all seems a bit of a rush. Makes you wonder why it all has to happen so fast, but never mind, he would love you to be there, Blossom, its important you try to make it."

"Yeah, we'll see, Mum, I'll try; depends on what I've got on at work, you know. I can't just book days off willy nilly." Truth was I hated family weddings. I was always told it would be "your turn next" and I hated it. If I showed up with a date, they all nudged him and begged him to marry me as soon as possible. If I came alone they frowned and looked at me pitifully as if I had something wrong with me. It was all so very painful, but family was family and I knew I would definitely try. Mother had no idea what I was doing while I was away, so I humoured her efforts to look after me until it was time for her to leave for work. At last I was put through to my Father.

He was all ears. I loved to hear him so animated. The involvement of the Regiment made him even more excited and he wanted to know every detail. What was the terrain like, were there any other houses nearby, how often did a car pass by. Then it was the building itself, what were the entry points, had I seen the position of the stairs and the landing, how far to the girl's bedroom, how many floors and how high was the roof. It all had to be recounted and reported before the ex-Marine was happy with his brief. I already had a method of entry in mind, but throwing it past the old man gave a fresh scope to the plans. William was an infiltration specialist and always loved a challenge. More than once he had come up with a superior plan to mine just by using his own experience and a little extra cunning. I was ready for all the questions and enjoyed the time he spent mulling things over while I listened to him reasoning each option through out loud over the phone. William enjoyed this process as much as I did. He seemed to feel his worth again when a new challenge was proposed. The energy in his voice resounded when I needed him. My own personal reference library of infiltration was as much a joy to him to recount as it was for me to hear it. He had taught me to pick a lock when I was only 14, something I had put to good use on more than one occasion.

It wasn't until after I'd broken into his desk study to check his diary for a camping trip that I found out about tell-tales and marking objects to tell if they've been moved. I was home from school one holiday, waiting frustratedly for some commitment from William to go off somewhere. I thought that while he was away, I would just go and check his personal diary so I could see what time he had booked. I used the skills he showed me to break into his desk to get to his papers. I was lucky not to scratch the shiny brass lock and had left everything just as I had found it – a very skilful job, I had to say. He never said if he'd found out about my little foray into his private papers, if any little finger marks betrayed me, but it was after this he used to take me away to teach me more skills.

He seemed to understand I just wanted to use what I had been taught and began to think of amusing ways in which he could make me feel useful. He had honed my covert talents so I didn't feel the need to look for other ways of getting adventure and experience. He always insisted that what he showed me was put to good use and not abused. My one lapse in school, breaking into the headteacher's apartment and removing her entire glut of securely locked confiscated contraband, including the chocolate from the midnight snack I had planned until it was forcibly removed from my hand the previous night, he had never seen fit to reprimand me for, although his concerns for my honest future ran deep.

Fourteen is a dangerous age for a girl and a cause of constant worry for parents. Girls grow up fast and want their freedom, but the worry makes the parents try to keep them indoors. William took me away to learn his trade when I was in my teens. A wise move. I got the little bouts of adventure I desired without feeling hemmed in by my protective parents. He thought this worked out well, as far as I sensed and he thought I was still a virgin when I went away to University. The naivety of parents.

William was coming to his conclusions as I listened silently on, adding the odd detail when questioned.

"A downstairs entry would be difficult to transition to the girl's room, so it would be better if you went straight in at the first floor," he mused.

"The small porch over the back door would be a decent climb and you could break in at the landing window if necessary. The quickest way would be to go in to the girl's room directly, but you would need to do it very gently so that you didn't wake her or scare her if she was already awake." He was lost in the puzzle now, with no concept that I would need help from anyone, no matter what size of plan he came up with. As far as he was concerned, I was the only one he needed to consider.

"If you come over the roof you could abseil down and cause less fuss and attention at the window. That," he concluded, "was probably the best option."

We went into the finest details about equipment and numbers required, keeping it all to a minimum. Every detail was worked out until we were happy with the plan. A beautiful joint venture between two motivated professionals. A wonderful thing we had created. My Mother had left for work ages ago and it was time to sign off and get some sleep.

"Don't forget your cousin's wedding, Blossom, your Mother is going on and on about it. I know it's a pain for you, but do try your best, Darling, OK?" He knew how I felt about family do's but he knew I would make it if I could, he was just adding some extra encouragement.

"I will try, Dad, honest, we need to see where this leads first. Love you, thanks for your help. Bye."

"Good luck, Cheeky Face. See you soon."

I had gone to bed to mull over the next move but was asleep within minutes. I woke up in plenty of time to dress up as a sales executive, take my case of gizmos and gadgets and meet my contact in the same restaurant as I had dined the previous evening.

This time I was on a sales budget where I had to keep receipts and make claims for expenses, so the Champagne was swapped for Chardonnay as I pitched my sales patter at the buyer for a new mail order catalogue just setting up on the continent.

I needed to sell 50000 units at a decent margin in order to pay for the trip, so it had better be a good lunch. I gave him my best sale and showed him the case of goodies. I was dressed for the part, in a smart dark grey suit and white silk cowl neck blouse. The strappy sandals neither too sexy nor too sensible but the silk neck scarf I had set off wearing proved to be too much for the Tunis heat and it was soon tied around my handbag. I hadn't needed to be careful on the way to the restaurant this time, I was just a sales exec carrying a case full of demo items to a meeting with a client. Nobody was interested in me or my gadgets, although the Glock Thunderbolt was in its usual trusted position under my jacket.

The lunch concluded cordially, the man was impressed by the mini biometrics but thought that the solar battery chargers and wind up gadgets would be the things for an African market. We discussed prices and I gave him a satisfactory discount. There was some left in the pot if he pushed harder, but I wanted the sales at the best margin I could manage, and that meant playing the age old game of chicken with the client.

We had settled for now, but he was non-committal and left saying he would call tomorrow and may want to see me again. That was excellent. The sales door was still open and I had the perfect excuse to stay around to see out the rest of the assignment. I would talk to him again tomorrow. Good. Boring job over, now it was time to see what Turtle was thinking for the night's work ahead. I thought about the plan again as I walked back to the hotel, wishing for nightfall to arrive.

Chapter 6

I was safe and comfortable in my room. Turtle, on the scrambled and jammed line, was giving his side of the bargain of information while I laid on the bed lazily munching on an apple, admittedly a little distracted.

"The SAS tailed their targets away from the French safe house at about midday," Turtle explained, "but the other men, whom we have yet to identify, were still in the building when they left." The apple scrunched in my teeth as I listened to the latest news, thinking about the contact with Macca. I couldn't help feeling a little tinge of sadness as Turtle told me how he had now left the area, the little dream of hope I'd maintained since seeing him had gone in a mere sentence. He would not be calling on me that evening.

Turtle carried on with his briefing, "Danny is keeping up with the transcripts of activity inside the house but there has been little or no further interrogations held. Danny said that they expressed disappointment at their progress with the girl and they might have to act without all of the information as they would be able to get the rest elsewhere. Do you know what that could mean?" he interrupted my train of thought as daydreams of naughty Macca were replaced with the lovely Danny.

The question made me blink to think what he was asking. What was he saying?

"Erm, no, I have no idea," I managed to splutter, the bits of apple skin catching in my teeth.

"Well, they said she had until the weekend and if she didn't give them what they wanted by then they would dispense with her services and go to plan B," Turtle continued. Today was Friday. "We have to move tonight."

It was as if the words set off an explosion inside me, suddenly I was paying attention. I threw what was left of the soggy apple in the bin, still trying to separate the skin from my smile. Turtle gave me the RV point to meet the team we would be using and asked if I had any further questions. I went through the plan again, running back over the equipment I was going to need the team to bring and what I would take myself. All basic infiltration kit, but I wanted things specifically, it all had to be perfect. My usual quest.

The weight of inaction had been lifted, I had the go-ahead at last. We were going to extract the girl. A raft of emotions ran over me, nerves, excitement, professional angst, all tinged with just enough fear to make it really fun. I was happy and looking forward to the evening when Turtle added, "There are just a couple more things you need to consider before you go." I raised an eyebrow. He had held something back, the lousy bastard. My suspicions were aroused, just what exactly was he up to?

"This is a foreign property we are about to infiltrate," he continued. I felt a scowl form on my face as I looked down the phone. "We?" it won't be you getting the firing squad if "we" get caught, I thought, but I remained silent, listening.

"Politically we can't afford for them to know we have broken in. You will have to take the girl and make it look like she has escaped.

You will also have to leave the area clean when you are finished." Oh well, that's not so bad I would have done most of that anyway. I would just have to look after things very precisely when we left, that's all. I sensed there was something else, I waited for the rest of the 'challenges' he thought I would need to overcome.

"And the other thing is, this girl is a serious drug addict. She may be in a very poor condition. The reports from the transcripts say that this is why they are having to give her extra time to co-operate, as she can barely string two words together. She has been missing for over two weeks so she should be coming through that now. She may, however, think you are trying to hurt her if you try and take her out by force, so you need to deal with that before you start. Got it?"

Yes, I had it. I had to remove a victim there would be no reasoning with. In effect it was a double kidnap. Two weeks without a fix for a severe addict would make her mind not her own. The risk of her shouting for help from her captors was high in her state of confusion. She would have to be neutralised and removed clinically. All this without leaving a trace and making it look like she had escaped on her own. Easy.

"Got it," I acknowledged. I had everything I needed except one. I packed an extra rucksack. The plan was still solid. It was do-able with a decent team.

With preparations complete, I headed off as the night before. The little Suzuki chirped away across the countryside. Making sure I was not the object of anyone's unwelcome attention, I found to my relief I was alone on my journey this time. Focussing on the night ahead, I played the plan through several times in my mind until it was all perfect. Once happy I could execute every detail,

I ran it through again, substituting the perfect execution for what could go wrong at each stage. What if we were discovered on the roof? What if the floorboards creaked in the bedroom once we got inside? Where would we meet if we got split up? Who takes charge of getting the girl away? Risks for each manoeuvre were analysed, counter actions devised, plans revised. Take after take, the plan was gone through again.

If we were compromised at any stage we should all know how to react. With the confidence of prior planning, no team member should descend into panic or do something rash. These preparations were important in every assignment, but more so when there was a team involved. I would brief them on each aspect of what was expected. Every new team offered the same inconvenience. I always had the impression the men thought they knew best. I had been told more than once I should be at home doing the dishes, usually to much sniggering and coughed laughter in the ranks. With age came experience, I had learned to be the Alpha dominant up front. I could never be accepted as a man, I knew that, but I could still take command and execute my function. With jobs like these they had to trust me immediately without much time to get to know me, so I had to have a plan for everything.

At the RV point, I drove deep into the woods and unloaded the car. Further into the woods I stalked to the end of the dirt track. After laying up for a few minutes I stepped forward at the designated time and flashed the red LED light three times. I crouched down, waiting for the signal to continue. From the other side of the track, a little further down, a red light flashed back four times, the silhouette of the three team members stepped forward on to the road.

"Hello, are we all English speakers?" I greeted the team, "Yes, we're all field officers. What are the orders?" came a voice from the centre of the three outlines opposite.

"How much do you already know?" I asked, to establish we were all here for the right reasons.

"We know it's a snatch job and it has to be done tonight. We've had the house under surveillance since we got the nod about dusk then got into position in the grounds as night fell. We came over to RV with you here but our No1 is still on site," said the dark centre shape.

"Do we have confirmation of who is currently in the house and whether there appears to be any guard inside or out?" I asked. Any changes in how they were operating inside the house might have a severe effect on our plans.

"The house looked quiet. There was some movement from the target bedroom but not much. Three marks in the house were witnessed moving around the first floor room then went to bed around midnight. They retired to bedrooms on the same floor as the living area. One was in a room on the east elevation, the others on the north, the same as the girl's. No kind of stag was maintained that we could see," the silhouette continued.

"OK, well done. Do you have radio headsets?" I asked.

"Yes, we have one for you here," one of the other men handed me a headset to put on and test the reception.

"Right then, I'll brief you and your No 1 then we'll make our way into position," I led on, giving them all a run-down of each man's task and how to do it. I explained what the backup plans were and how to react under gunfire. The main of the brief over, I asked for any questions. A few enquiries were no trouble to answer, they accepted their instructions happily. This was unusual. I wished they could all have so much faith on first contact. Now I knew what it was like to be received like a man. I quite liked it. They silently got on with the allotted tasks, unloading the equipment out of their vehicle at the far end of the track and distributing it amongst us.

We set off back towards the house, I was thrilled with the reception I had received. My confidence shone as we followed the path of the stream where I had come in the night before. A surge of aggression built with every step, my inner animal tingling with excitement. I felt it wanting to growl with power inside me. My strength was my confidence and it was sky high after a successful briefing. We moved stealthily through the irrigation ditches, gaining on our target in the darkness. I used the two miles or so over the rough ground to get to know the team a little better and decide what roles each of them would take when they got into position. We didn't need to share real names, Curly, Larry and Moe would suffice for tonight.

The distance seemed to speed away under us, we covered it in little time. We approached the garden in silence, keeping low to the ground. My heart thumped as we came up the last section of the hill to the familiar garden. The team pointed out the large tree on the eastern side where their No 1 was laid, I knew it well. They left me to go ahead and greet him as they spread out to get into their own lay up positions on each side of the building.

Ducking under the low boughs of the tree, I flashed the red LED light three times. A faint four flashes came back, I made my way gingerly towards the light. I could barely suppress a smile thinking about the pleasant surprise I had been given by Macca the night before. Goose pimples ran up the backs of my thighs as I recalled the exciting scuffle that had taken place and its satisfying climax.

"At last we get to do some proper work together" said a muted voice from the darkness of the low roots of the trunk. He had turned off the radio, I heard Danny's voice just in front of me. The hair stood up on the back of my neck, a tingling ran up my spine, making me judder involuntarily. The shock of meeting Macca the previous night was equalled by having to deal with Danny on the operation right now. I tensed. Lousy bastard Turtle never said it was his team doing the extraction with me. Could I manage to do this with him watching, my hand ran over my hair to flatten it down and I pulled at my tight suit in the hope it would look better around my inglorious bits. I felt self conscious already. The doubts and feelings overtook me and I realised, annoyed, that I was distracted by him already.

"Are you good to go?" he asked, with some obvious concern after my strange behaviour.

"Yes, yes, absolutely," I stuttered out, gathering myself and trying to concentrate on what we were supposed to be doing. It was 12:30, we had an hour and a half to wait before starting the operation. Danny checked his watch, we were all synchronised.

"Why don't you sit here in front of me, its quite comfortable once you hunker down a bit," he whispered, "I'm afraid its not as warm a welcome as you received last night." I looked at him with a quizzical face as the lightning bolt seemed to strike me square in the chest for the second night running.

"What?" was all I could mumble, dreading the reply as my heart sank and I gulped hard, trying not to let him get the better of me again.

"I was over there, by the gate that you can just see," he continued, ignoring my discomfort.

"I saw you come in and was about to signal when your SAS man rolled over you. I was on my way to help out when I realised you were more than competent in your task, so I left you to it," he spoke the dreaded words with a light giggle in his voice.

I was glad it was so dark, my face contorted as if in pain. I felt faint with embarrassment. I thought back to the scene and how it must have looked through his eyes, the dirty slapper wrapping herself round some bloke in the undergrowth. Just as I thought I could be cool working with him, Danny had caught me out again. I felt low and incompetent. How had Mac let another operative get so close without knowing? Come to think of it, how had I? I was fuming with myself. The club sandwich from dinner repeated on me, I could feel the mustard in my throat. I looked at Danny, imagining the dimple popping out as he laughed at me under his hood. The awkwardness now was as bad as it had ever been. How could I look at him after he had seen me like that?

My superiority was paramount, I had to take back control. This wasn't a briefing, it was a full assignment. I put the radio back on and ordered absolute silence unless it was urgent. The prospect of an hour and a half's small talk with a man who distracted me at best was not a good way of getting into fight mode. The ranting in my head would keep me busy until then. I tried hard to think of Danny as a lousy upstart, a pretender to my seniority, but my mind always came back to the curve of his shoulders and his pretty blue eyes. I sat and remonstrated with myself for feeling so helpless near him.

Fuming passed the time quickly, before I was really ready it was only 20 minutes to go. It was important I had no more distractions now. I shook it all back into order after he'd jumbled it all up when I came into the garden. My countdown drill was mechanical, checking radios, calling each position, signing in at each instruction so we all knew we were ready to go. T minus 10 minutes, then I counted down from T minus 5.

Curly, Larry and Moe would be getting themselves ready too. Danny sat silently next to me. I hoped he had spent the time regretting his decision to mention my indiscretion and mentally kicking himself. I regained my composure by going through the routine of checking equipment, I was pleased to hear the echo of the same coming from the man at my side. Weapon, spare ammo, flash-bangs (just in case), radio and survival kit were all gone over one by one. I kept the order strict so nothing was missed. The preparations were robotic. One mistake could be fatal. I wondered if Danny's heart was beating as hard as mine. My breath came quickly but I fought to keep it under control. My legs went numb, the pain of sitting still in the tree roots for so long now a distant memory as the adrenalin took over and I felt new life in the stiff limbs.

T minus 3 minutes, the blood rushed through me. I thought about the girl we were about to take back, the e-mails I had read leading to this point, the importance of making sure she was safe. She was my prime concern. "That's what you're here for, Blossom," I told myself, "Don't balls it up now".

T minus 2 minutes, I was in the mission now, nothing was going to distract me. I felt the excitement rising within, invigorated by the sensations it released. The intensity of my senses almost deafened me, the predator inside began to smile.

T minus 1 minute, my body was tense, my mouth dry. The feeling of needing to pee I always got just before a fight popped up out of nowhere, quite unnecessarily. Sweat ran down my back under the black catsuit. I had already picked my steps through the shrubbery towards the house, thought about the noise they would make and how I would walk to avoid it. I ached to be on my way.

At last it was time, "Go go go," I spoke calmly into the radio even though I was screaming inside with excitement. I had to sit still and wait until the others made their ways to their positions. It wasn't my turn to move, my patience was wearing thin. The other side of the house was where Curly would be creeping forwards to start the assault, free climbing up the front portico that led to the first floor, then skilfully shinning up on to the roof. I heard nothing. The dark air around me gave no clue as to whether he was climbing or falling. I crouched under the tree, waiting. The temptation to move was too great, my senses shrieked at me to get closer so I could see what was happening. I felt my feet move underneath me, the decision made to get to the other side of the house. I arrived behind the next big shrub to see Curly's shadowy figure making his way over to the corner of the roof above the girl's bedroom window. Larry and Moe rushed out to hold taught the rope that Curly had dropped to the ground from where he stood, high above. He had made it. My heart buzzed with the thrill that we had begun.

Moe's telescopic climbing pole looked like an eight foot Christmas tree, the sturdy central rod with its sprung loaded pegs that stuck out like branches at the sides would propel us quickly towards the first floor window. Once the rungs snapped into place the mechanism was locked, Larry used the pole as a ladder to climb up the outside of the building.

Curly passed the other half of the rope around the chimney at the apex of the large roof and began his descent by feeding the rope round his body bit by bit, pulling one end while pushing the other past himself; no harness or clips to rattle and clang in the darkness, just a man's body around the taught line, lowering himself gently down until he was level with the bottom of the girl's window. My eyes were wide watching the grapples with the rope. I crept out from my hiding place towards the bottom of the pole. My feet landed silently on the soft ground, making their way to where Moe was standing, holding the rope and the pole steady for both men.

Curly took his weight in the loop of the rope and swung across the wall to the large window. The house was still very old fashioned, there was no need for sealed units and double glazing here, the opening rested on a latch that sat on a hook inside the window. He slid the long knife from his vest pocket and looked for signs of movement from inside the room. All was quiet, the house was asleep. He looked down at me for approval, Danny came over the radio, "All clear."

I nodded for Curly to continue. He nervously wiped the sweat from his top lip then slipped the knife in silently through the gap in the windows and lifted the latch. It swung away easily and the glazed panes moved towards him. He opened one leaf as Larry made it to the bottom ledge and poked his head over the top to see if the room had been disturbed. Nothing moved.

We had broken in and could not go back. The surge in power made me feel like a rubber bouncy ball, the latent energy waiting to be released. Larry heaved himself over the windowsill and was the first to set foot in the room, drawing his weapon as he landed on the tufted rug covering the old floorboards. I whisked myself quickly up the pole and into the room, Curly followed from the rope. Larry checked the door, it was locked from the outside. Good, if we were discovered it would take an extra second or so to unlock the door, giving us time to draw weapons or get out.

I crossed over to the bed to see what our prize entailed. A thin, waif of a figure laid on top of the covers. The girl looked wasted, lying in her clothes in a pile of sweat, she was soaked through. The heady smell of vomit and piss added to the disgusting mix of general nastiness within the room. This was no time to be squeamish, I reached at the uninviting figure to take her pulse. It was barely there, very faint and weak. I wondered if we were too late and they had drugged her already.

I covered the girl's mouth and pinched her ear to see if there was any reaction. She didn't make a noise but made an attempt to try and get away from the fierce nipping on her earlobe. Good, she was conscious. I felt her skinny arm, it was like running my hand over a dry stone wall. The constant injections into the already damaged skin had left her with abscesses wherever she could reach and the skin felt more dead than alive. I had to try and find a place to insert my own needle, pick a spot that didn't feel blistered with the abuse the girl had shown herself. I lifted up the arm to push the syringe into the softest part of the tricep, near the armpit. I carefully slipped the spent needle back into my pocket while its shed contents took their debilitating effect.

Curly and Larry kept guard as I checked the girl again, she was unconscious.

"She'll need immediate medical care as soon as we get her safe," I whispered into the radio mic.

"Already standing by" Danny answered. He sounded solemn in his response. Now to try and remove her from the room without breaking her. I opened the extra rucksack I had packed at the last minute and removed the spare bedsheets from the hotel room, all ripped up and tied into knots to make a long rope. The two men looked at me, disbelieving, I saw them look at each other to see if they should be questioning me more than they had done so far. It was a cliché, I know, but always plausible, I had used it before to good effect, but right now I needed to reassert my command on the fellows standing doubting with loose jaws in front of me.

I pointed at Larry and gestured towards the girl. He lifted her so Curly and I could strip the sodden, stinking bed. This last sheet was joined to the ones already being thrown out of the window to make the rope look more authentic. Curly secured the end within the room, employing a granny knot no professional would use. I wrapped the rope in coils around the girl's body then teased her gently out of the window to avoid banging her head. The men weren't sure, I could tell, looking at me and each other for reassurance. I remained quiet but gave strong eye contact whenever I felt their unrest, they did well to dangle the girl precariously without question. My confidence was growing, I knew this was going to work.

Larry and I suspended the catatonic waif over the windowsill and out into the cool air. Curly's rope, placed in a single loop around the girl, was the brake to control her speed. Moe looked up from the ground, hardly believing what he was seeing as I let go of the blankets and the girl started to fall, turning over and over gently like a doll in the hand of a child as the rope unfolded loop by loop from her waist. Tension on the brake line meant it didn't run away, Danny stood underneath with baited breath, waiting for the delicate parcel to float down to him. He caught her easily and unravelled the rest of the loops to release her and move into cover behind the large tree. I turned to the two men and smiled triumphantly, they nodded and smiled back. Maybe I wasn't crazy after all. Maybe.

There was no need to wait, as the girl had been twirling her way down to earth, Larry rushed down the pole and Curly was already half way over the windowsill. Last one out, I turned to check the room before leaving to ensure no evidence of our intrusion could be gleaned. Any personal effects needed to be found, but there was nothing. I took out the extra bedding from the empty wardrobe and used it to brush the carpet to hide our invisible footmarks, then stuffed them into the rucksack to complete the deception. One final check, I climbed over the windowsill, wiping the top. Clear and clean.

My inner predator swelled, almost satisfied with the success. Danny had hidden the girl away from the house, Curly and Larry were to take the first shift in moving her to safety. I almost ran down the climbing pole while Moe held on to guide me down. The two escorts radioed through to say they had the hidden prize, all seemed too easy until a light on the first floor came on suddenly. We dived into the nearest shrub A cracking sound came up from the deck of Moe hitting his knee on a rock as he landed. The fluid sped into the joint, I clamped his mouth shut to prevent his crying out as he winced and shook, trying to maintain his balance on the dark side of the bush.

The pool of light flooded into the garden, shining across the area we had that second vacated. There was movement in the room, I could see clearly from my position holding on to Moe in his agony. I watched to see where the night wanderer was going, my heart pounding my chest. The animal instinct was almost at a roar within me, it growled and panted for a hearty fight. We had to be away from here. Tonight was not the night for this particular satisfaction. I squeezed Moe tighter as my body tensed when I saw a black something leaning against the wall. A glance back in the direction of the house revealed, with horror, that the climbing pole was still in position. My hands turned in the loose clothing at Moe's shoulders, wrapping my fingers deeper into the fabric as I thought of what to do. This was not one of my pre-prepared disasters.

My mind spun as it flooded with things to be done. Our tiny hiding place was bathed in the light from the window, I wouldn't dare venture out. If the pole was left there, we might as well have knocked on the front door. I would wait until it was clear enough to pick up the damning evidence. I whispered into the radio, "Curly, Larry, pick up the package and get back to the ERV. Moe and I will stay here until clear to move. No 1, you go as backup for the package."

The orders were out there, but it was too late, out of the corner of my eye I saw a dark figure approaching next to the wall of the house. My gun was drawn, my eyes unblinking with concentration, trying to recognise the threat softly approaching. The figure came nearer, slinking against the wall. I released the safety catch on my little pistol and turned to take aim. I lifted the barrel skyward as I recognised the spider creeping slowly along the side of the wall, it was Danny.

As long as nobody looked out of the lit room, he could not be seen underneath, I signalled him to carry on as he slithered to the pole, unlocked the mechanism and silently collapsed it back down to the size of a retractable umbrella. He slid it into the leg pocket of his combats. I watched in anticipation, waiting for the figure in the lit bedroom to take a look out of the window. My gun was still drawn, Moe had his back to the action and squirmed to see what was going on. My free hand buffed him across the back of the head to keep still. I looked around the house, there was no movement anywhere else inside. I signalled 'OK', Danny began to pick his way back to his hideout when the light snapped off inside the house. Plunged into darkness once again, Danny leaped for the shrubbery. I didn't need to wait for another potential tragedy, after a last look around, we each made our way out of the garden. Moe limped along with his badly swollen knee, trickles of blood spreading down his trouser leg.

Curly and Larry were waiting further out. I took the girl's shoes from her feet and put them in my pockets. Danny volunteered to carry her on his back. I agreed, putting her on in a piggy back to spread the load, then using the bedsheets I had taken to tie the girl in position so he didn't have to use his energy holding on to her. I ripped a strip of bedding off and tied it round Moe's leg to help stem the blood and give his knee some support.

"Go back to the RV position and wait for me there" I instructed.

"Hey, wait . . ." Danny interjected, trying to stop me from wandering off on my own.

"Enough." I held up my hand, "Back to the RV. I'll join you when I'm done. If I'm not there within half an hour, carry on to the safe house. Now do as you are ordered." They walked off into the darkness. The final part of my plan was ready to be completed.

Back in the garden, I covered the faint tracks we'd made by brushing the area with twigs and branches, then covering up with leaves to disguise our presence. I liked to tidy up after a job if I could, this one was more important than most, they might look for her if she disappeared, they still needed her. I needed to make her vanish as convincingly as possible. I worked my way towards the house, brushing and cleaning every area the men had been positioned. Under the bedroom window I took the girl's shoes out of my pocket and put them over my own feet. She was smaller than me, I had to squeeze my toes into the ends so they could stay on. With stumbling movements I walked towards the front gate of the house then out to the main road at the end of the drive. I took my time, making sure the tracker marks I left pointed in the right direction, away from where we had actually been. In the little shoes, I made it to the main road. I'd headed across the grass away from the door to leave plenty of tracks for the kidnappers to spot.

With the last piece of subterfuge in place, I was content with my night's work. I ran down the road then tracked inside to pick up the team where they would be making their way back to the woods. As I approached at the edge of the woods, I could hear them swishing through the undergrowth. When I was close enough to see them, they were in a ready position with their weapons drawn, waiting to see who the visitor was. A flush of pride swept through me from working with such a professional team. I flashed the light three times, they flashed back four. Curly put his arm around my shoulders as a welcome without speaking, I smiled at him silently in the darkness to express the pleasure of a plan well executed. Danny arrived at the vehicle first, laid up at the edge of the woods, waiting for us to arrive.

It was 03:15, we were all still alive, we had the girl and were back to the RV without a shot being fired. It wasn't time to celebrate yet. We took a patrol's exit, covering all the firing angles while Danny and I bundled the girl gently into the back of the estate car at the end of the track. Danny reached up and threw the boot lid down, it was a large Mercedes in a pale colour that could have been silver. I looked at him but he averted his eyes, not willing to surrender to the questions my stare was asking. So, in fact, I had my answer.

I thanked them all quietly for a job well done but still couldn't bear to look at Danny. I had been impressed by his bravery in retrieving the climbing pole and how well trained and professional his men were, he must be the reason why they had been so attentive to my briefing all those hours ago, but I was still embarrassed by his presence and wasn't sure why he'd had me followed the previous night. He held out his hand to congratulate me on a successful operation but I couldn't stand the feelings he brought out in me. I pushed the radio set into his outstretched palm, "Yours, I believe," I walked past him. He didn't have time to speak, let alone apologise. I looked up only once to see the deep disappointment on his boyish face then continued on my way.

I turned my back to the team after waving to all but one. Danny got into the driver's seat and wound cautiously down the trail leading out of the woods. I waited slightly longer to make sure there was enough of a gap between us, then started the little car and drove back into town. As I drove, I dissected each part of the night's adventure as it came back into my mind. I replayed each stage over again. I decided I was content with the execution, the plan had worked well. William would be pleased. But the long, lingering thought that remained, the thing that cursed my whole night was how Danny had seen me making out in the shrubbery – worse than that, I'd had no idea.

I wasn't sure which bothered me most, the fact that I hadn't detected him or that he'd seen me so unreserved with Macca – not once but twice. Rolling around on the floor with stray soldiers as I come across them in the undergrowth wasn't the usual image I liked to project, especially to those I would quite like to roll around with myself. I winced as I thought of wrapping my legs round Macca's waist as I had enjoyed his passion. The thought that it bothered me so much bothered me even more.

Still slightly annoyed, I arrived back at the hotel and slipped in through the doctored fire escape. I decided not to disturb Turtle with a separate report, Danny would call in on the way then again once he arrived at our own safe house. A hot bath was calling me, the need to relax and cleanse myself. I shaved my legs and thought about going to bed but knew I wouldn't be able to sleep. I felt guilty about writhing around with Mac. I didn't like guilt. I'd had to wrestle with my conscience more than once during my long career. Some things I did were good, others only my maker could judge me for. I decided I had done worse and drifted off to sleep after emptying the mini-bar.

Chapter 7

Five hours deep sleep later I needed to sort my mind into order about the night's work and mentally compile the report for Turtle. It all flooded back to me, the success, the regrets, a little guilt with a double vodka and tonic. I dragged myself out of bed, set up the necessary devices and called in for my next instructions.

"What now?" I asked, the brief of the operation completed without a mention of Danny's indiscretion. Turtle had been non-committal all the way through, as though he was thinking about something else. He normally drove me mad with a thousand questions about everything that happened. I felt myself waiting for some bad news but I wasn't sure quite why. I started to think about my parents and wonder if they were OK.

"OK, yes, well, good job, well done, dear girl. That's all for now, thank you, Blossom" said Turtle after considering the question.

"What do you mean? That's all?" my feeling of uneasiness was growing.

"Well, you've done very well. We have nothing on the radar to say they suspect us. You might as well come home now," he answered, I had the feeling of being kept out of something. Come home? Why would I be coming home?

"Now hang on," I tried to stay calm, "I found this girl, I extracted her, we still need to know who she is and what the connection is to the facility in England as well as how she got here and what they wanted with her." My mind was racing, thinking through all the conversations we'd had about this girl over the last week. Then it hit me, jolting me back to the reality of the work that I do. The one question I had never asked Turtle was who this girl was. Until now I had presumed that everyone was as much in the dark as I was and I would be asking the questions to find out. Instead I was being sent home.

It dawned on me like a shower of light flowing down to make the path in front of me appear for the first time. They already knew who she was. They had probably known all along. Not for the first time I had the feeling of being used and slightly abandoned. My usual bubble of knowing I was at the top of the information tree had burst. I had been used as a blunt instrument, not as the trusted officer that I normally enjoyed.

"You knew all along," I said, quietly smouldering but needing to communicate effectively.

"Yes" was the only response. A blunt tool. Not the first time and probably not the last. It wasn't Turtle's fault, he had a job to do too. Whenever he had to use me, unable to tell the full story, he was always honest enough to admit it when I eventually figured it out. I still wanted the closure that had taken me so far into the job but I was also curious, as any woman talking to friends who has a snippet of gossip and wants to know more. I wanted to know who was important enough that a major international incident was risked to bring her home.

"Are you going to tell me?" I asked.

"I can't talk about it, even on this line, dear girl," Turtle remained an impenetrable wall.

"Please, just come home and I will arrange a Data Meet for when you get back. I'll brief you on what I know. It was a preventative extraction so we could hold some information. We're not even sure she has it, but we had to stop her from talking."

"At any cost?" my bitterness showing, knowing what it would have meant for the girl if we had failed to take her.

"Yes" came the simple response. There were times when I didn't like this job very much. I tried to make sure it was always for the greater good, but wondered which one of the team members had the kill order last night if it had all gone wrong. I thought back to the scene of last night's adventure, imagined the light from the house going on and a shout going up inside as we bundled the girl through the garden. Minutes later the terrorists reaching her lifeless body, left for them to deal with, our task complete and the girl silenced. The thought made me feel sad at the prospect. I regretted calling the team after the three stooges now, this could have been anything but a laughing matter.

It didn't matter now. The work was complete and we hadn't needed to resort to orders.

"OK, I'll come home" I acquiesced. The futility of resistance made me unnecessarily tired.

"Have a good flight," said Turtle, probably feeling it best to leave me alone for a while.

The feeling of foreboding about my parents coupled with an uncontrollable urge to sulk made me want to call home. I braced myself for the annoyance and dialled the number.

"Hi Mum, how are you?" it felt better to hear her voice, nagging and disapproving as it was.

"I'm fine, Blossom, how has your work gone? Did you sell all the erm, unit thingies or whatever it is you have to do?" sometimes she befuddled herself did my loving Mother. The following dull ramblings about her forthcoming weekend in London with Auntie Dot surprised me with how much better I felt afterwards. Maybe I should only ring her when I'm in a bad mood. Dad was out so I cut the conversation as short as I dared by saying I was on my way home.

I tried to cast aside my disappointment at the end of the mission. My careful execution of a well crafted plan had saved a girl's life. Anything else didn't matter, especially not my feelings, I got ready to pack them up in my sales case with my secret life. Anything else didn't matter, I should remember that, whoever the girl was, I would find out when I got home.

Before I could leave there was the little matter of the catalogue contact I needed some business from to cover my time in Tunisia. With no gadgets to protect my privacy I made the call to the prospective buyer. He wanted to haggle some more but in my surly state, I was in no mood to negotiate further, wanting to stand my ground and let my confidence grow back. My feet were planted, the game of chicken was won. He placed an order for 250,000 units, mostly the solar chargers and wind up electrical equipment that we had talked about the day before. The success was complete, I had doubled my sales target for the month and paid easily for the trip. Maybe we could have had Champagne instead of Chardonnay. Another job well done, but the feelings of emptiness and disappointment strangely not leaving me alone. I was ready to go home.

*   *   *

Getting off the flight back in England from Tunisia was like landing in a muddy puddle. The autumn weather had deteriorated in the few days I had been away and the air was damp and grey. My hair frizzed and I felt uneasy about the whole episode I had just been through. Once home, I sorted my hair first, then called Turtle to arrange the Data Meet for the following Monday.

Usually somewhere in London in a government location, the building would be de-bugged, scanned and cleaned thoroughly by another branch of the service before we arrived for the meeting. The site would then be continuously guarded while audio visual equipment was brought in to allow me to get as close as I was ever allowed to my mentor. Turtle would not be there in front of me, it was too much of a security risk for me to know what he looked like. We would communicate through a web-cam and screen, with Turtle posting up any pictures he needed as part of his briefing.

No image was available for Turtle, he appeared as a synthesised voice on the screen, a graphical line which jumped and vibrated as he spoke. He would be in another room, looking at a similar screen with the web-cam's portrait of me in front of him. The synthesis of his voice gave him a slight tinny resonance that I had always associated with his identity, whether here or on the phone, the sound was the same, the false manifestation of my superior.

He was friend and mentor, guide and inspiration all rolled into one. I carried round in my head the image of a tall, thin gentleman with short white hair and a goatee beard. He had a long, thin face, like Christopher Lee, and was well spoken, gentle and handsome. This was my impression of my guardian angel that was conjured up whenever we spoke. Manned satellite stations all over the world conducted our phone calls. If he ever didn't answer, help could be summoned if that's what I needed, but Turtle had never not answered. One day I would get to hold his hand and say thank you.

I had always felt we complimented each other well, the girl of action and the mature steadying hand. Turtle brought me up, along with Dad's gentle encouragement, to be the best field officer in the past ten years. They hadn't known how they were going to use me when I joined, although I already had several years of amateur experience which made me rise to the top with the cream of my classes. In his old fashioned way, Turtle had tried to put me off, selling me an alternative life where I settled down and forgot the idea of dangerous, heartbreaking assignments.

Once I had done so well in field-craft training, thanks to my Father's unique education, the bosses of our organisation insisted I went into active fields. To get someone with my talent for breaking and entering so young was unique, especially of my gender. Normally the ranks were filled by experienced soldiers and ex Special Forces who have taken on some extra activities, so Turtle struck a deal to allow me to be left alone to study through university. When I finished, they trained me properly, starting to give me more critical work. Summer holidays were used to hone and update skills, teaching new ones plus latest techniques. They got me the job as the sales rep for the gadget company as the perfect cover and the company had been rewarded by me outselling all the other reps. Purely incidental, I just don't like to be beaten.

This Data Meet had been set up at a secure holding area in what had been an old warehouse. The Government kept areas like this in London in case of major incidents when they needed to get troops and equipment in close without being noticed. It would act as a base for special forces to eat, sleep and prepare for any incident or exercise that demanded their unique brand of justice.

I parked some distance away and walked through the normal looking entrance to sign in at the innocent Reception. The receptionist was taking calls for the imaginary business whose property this was, an occupied building in the middle of London was less likely to attract any undue attention. I signed in, without a word the receptionist gestured for me to go through the nearby frosted glass door that led to a long corridor. The corporate blue of the company that was supposed to be based there adorned the walls, with art deco pictures and a company mission statement in a frame. I was already on camera, Turtle would be watching as I approached. I hated the feeling of walking into these places, one door after the other would force me in to tighter and tighter spaces. I went through the first open door and continued to walk. A buzz and a snap meant the magnetic lock on the top of the door at the far end of the corridor was released. I pushed my way through.

The next area was in stark contrast to the one I had just passed through. The corporate blue tones had been replaced with a stony white, the door opening fully to reveal a small waiting area with a couple of comfortable chairs and a little oak table with a rose carved into the top. My nerves began to rise, swelling up as I took each steady step closer to the inner sanctum waiting for me. This was perfect ambush territory, my instincts were on edge. I wondered who would be waiting here for me to come out, the next meeting queuing up behind to use the facilities for the fleeting time they would be available.

The next door had an electronic keypad, I entered my code. The tones on the keypad playing 'Edelweiss' as I pushed the digits, which always amused me. The code accepted, a small part of the wall slid upwards and a horizontal wedge popped out like the bird in a cuckoo clock. I rested my chin on the wedge and tried not to tense up as a flash in my eyes made me jump, even though I'd been expecting it. This did not amuse me quite so much.

The lock snapped open, I was in the next chamber. A very small compartment. The door in front could not open until the door behind had fully closed and locked. I hated this bit the most, standing there waiting like a rat caught in a trap. The slight pause for the door to unlock after the other one had shut behind me was the moment they had taken the X-ray to check for concealed weapons and listening devices so Turtle knew that the inner space was clean. That was the last check, I was inside.

The door opened to welcome me into the space of a huge open warehouse of grey concrete. I wasn't sure whether it was my spy's brain that could not shut down or the nerves in my stomach that pushed me to be on my guard, but even though this was one of the most protected places in Britain right at this moment, I still scanned the dim area around me, half waiting for an attack to spring out of the shadows. I walked almost a hundred steps in a straight line to get to the only part of the room that was lit. The AV equipment set out was bathed in a slim pool of light showing the large plasma screen on its frame with a laptop in front of it and a stool for me to sit on. With a last glance around the eerie space I felt satisfied enough to push my right index finger on to the laptop pad for a scan of my fingerprint to bring the large screen to life.

"Hello dear girl," Turtle's voice danced and jumped on the screen as his graphic came to life. We were in the same building, the closeness comforted me, my nerves relaxing at the proximity. I felt like the duvet had been lovingly warmed before I'd got in to bed.

"Hello Boss," I replied, happy to 'see' him. This was as much as I knew about what he looked like.

"OK," he started, "you are aware that you are in a secure location, you understand that any information given to you in this location is strictly 'need to know', it is not to be told to any third party and is of the highest classification. Can you confirm that you understand?" Turtle was serious for a moment. He had to reiterate what he was about to tell me. There would be no file to download, no record of this meeting, this encounter did not happen and I could not repeat what I was about to hear. Even my Father wouldn't get the full extent, only if we were somewhere we could not possibly be overheard. Last time I briefed him on a Meet it was a particularly windy November morning half way up Scafel Pike when there was no chance of any device being able to detect what we were discussing.

"I understand" I said solemnly, this was equivalent to signing the Official Secrets Act again, I was bound by my verbal agreement.

"OK then," said Turtle, the formality of the interview over with, we could both relax a little in each other's company, "as you are aware, we have in our safe custody a young girl of nineteen. Her name is Susie Fairfield," he paused, evidently waiting for a reaction. The name meant nothing to me, I remained silent, waiting to be enlightened.

"No?" he tried to prompt me, "you don't know the name Brian Fairfield? *Dr* Brian Fairfield?" the name came back to me, for a second I wondered what context I knew it under, a little bell was ringing in my head. A scientist, I had seen the name in print many times and was going through the images racked up in my memory.

"Well, I'll put you out of your misery, your face looks a picture when you're confused," Turtle tormented, making me giggle slightly, "His work is top classification secret, he works in the Defence Research Agency site in Malvern. He is in charge of all new weapons as well as looking at foreign developments. All of our new weapons come from one of his teams and he unravels all our competition's state of the art technologies, writing about them for the secret community. That's where you will have seen his name. Any publications with weapons analysis in will be by him. Susie is his daughter." Now I understood. This girl was taken to get information on her father's work in weapon's development, but why now? They thought she had some information and either didn't know about the drug problem, or thought it would help them get what they needed.

As Turtle talked about the girl, he put on the screen for me to see some photos of Susie with her father when she was little and he was a leading young scientist just climbing the ladder. The pictures were typical family photos, ID cards, passport photos. Susie and her father looked so happy and bright together on the pictures. They reminded me of my relationship with my own father and I felt sad that this girl had been made to suffer for hers like this.

Turtle continued, "Susie is Brian's only daughter but they have grown a little apart after some family rows at home. All typical teenage girl stuff about freedom and being allowed to grow up, but he still dotes on her despite the arguments, you know the kind of thing. She now lives in Ireland, having chosen to leave the family home to go to Dublin City University there. She had taken up with a bad crowd and started to use hard drugs." I loved Turtle's old fashioned phrases, they were always so inappropriate – 'taken up with a bad crowd' was an understatement.

"While they were in the safe house in Africa, we could gather transcripts of what was going on due to the efficient bugging that Danny had in place." It seemed he couldn't resist the tease of mentioning his name in front of me and seeing the reaction; my toes twitched slightly but otherwise I kept my cool and my face never changed, he would be looking for signs of discomfort.

"We could hear the interrogation as well as the meeting with the terror suspects that your SAS patrol were tailing." I tensed, why had he said "Your" SAS team? Had Danny blabbed about the liaison? It was none of his damn business. I managed to stay calm and keep listening, although my foot twitched involuntarily once more.

"We also had one of our best agents debriefing her afterwards and we think we have a clearer picture of what was going on, but the information I've had so far is not complete so I arranged for the agent to come and get us both up to speed while we're here and we have the facility." Turtle pushed a button, the door at the end of the corridors snapped off its lock and opened, throwing a shaft of bright light into the dim warehouse. It made me screw up my eyes in defence against the assault on my dimmed pupils.

All I could make out was the dark silhouette of a man in what looked like a smart dark suit and white shirt, left open at the neck. He stepped into the dimness and walked towards me. The door closed behind him with a clunk, blotting out the harsh light. My heart bumped an extra couple of beats. The slight swagger as he made his way the one hundred steps to where I was sitting was now perceptible as my eyes readjusted once again. I still couldn't clearly see the face of the new visitor to the scene but I knew who it was by five steps in. The swaggering walk, the tight frame, the short hair and boyish curve to the face. I wanted to run but the urge to stay and look at his face rooted me to the spot, I was frozen, unable to move. He had taken the transcripts and translated them from his bugs in the safe house, his team had made the extraction with me, he had removed the girl and taken her for debriefing and now he was here to tell us what he had found.

He walked up to me and flashed a small, sheepish smile of greeting, showing a few nerves of his own, then turned to the big screen to address Turtle, "May I?" his deep voice was quiet but confident. I found myself watching him as he moved towards the screen to be in full view of the web-cam, my eyes ran down the length of his back to take in the whole delicious view. Even from behind he looked good, the suit sitting perfectly on his carefully measured shoulders. His exposed neck at the front made me think of the soft skin against my lips. I pursed mine together to let the blood flow in, making them full and red.

"Please, proceed" said Turtle, graciously accepting the help of someone whom he obviously had a great respect for, no matter what I thought or felt.

Danny inserted a data stick into the laptop to bring up the pictures he had taken of Susie recovering in the safe house, including the ones he had taken that morning before setting off for our meeting. I remembered her abscessed arms and the vomit stained hair and clothes. The pictures showed a freshly washed and groomed young woman with new clothes and a meal in front of her. She looked as though she hadn't eaten in weeks, so gaunt and wasted by her addictions. I knew she was only nineteen but her face was aged and haggered like a woman of more than twice that.

"Susie is still in a bit of cold turkey, we have her over the worst of it with some help from the doctor," said Danny, "I thought you might be concerned, Blossom, so I brought these pictures to show you she was in a lot better state now," he said, turning to address me personally with a hopeful look on his face. I was still mad with him for the other night so gave him no reaction to the expression of concern and his attempt at reassurance. He had to carry on without the acknowledgement he seemed to turn to me for.

"She is in the best medical care and progressing well, but she's not out of danger yet and we will have to keep an eye on her for a while. The medicine she has been given is a fairly new treatment that has been proven to be very successful. Buprenorphine is used just to stop the cravings, and it can't be abused as it contains blockers in it so it doesn't work if injected, therefore there is no transfer of addition. We will need to monitor her behaviour to make sure she doesn't try to escape from us as well. She can't remember much about the French safe house or what they were questioning her about. She knows they were asking about her father's work, but as she doesn't know anything about it, she could tell them nothing."

Danny looked sad as he gave an account of her terrible story and how she came to be where we found her. He had delicately undertaken the debriefing, being careful and considerate to her needs.

"We can only question her for about an hour at a time, so it's a slow business, but we don't want to scare her and its more productive to look at the transcripts and question her specifically about anything we don't know than to ask random questions that she doesn't seem to understand." A twinge of jealousy ran over me as I saw the empathy Danny showed to his dainty charge and wondered why he cared so much for that dirty young addict when he treated me so cruelly.

He went on, "Susie had been using just about full time when the men had snatched her in Ireland. She hadn't been home for days, maybe weeks. She wasn't sure how long and only knew she had been in a squat on the outskirts of Dublin," he continued.

"She had been put up with a dealer by an Albanian working at the Uni who gave her free fixes from time to time. With the drugs available all the time at the squat, her abuse and addiction spiralled downhill until one day a car arrived outside and this dealer pushed her into it," Danny paused, reflecting sorrowfully about what the poor girl had told him of her ordeal. I listened intently. Turtle's line laid flatly across the screen, showing nothing of the man or the emotion he might be feeling at the telling of the harrowing tale.

"Susie thought the man the Albanian spoke to all the time had been living in the house for a while before she arrived," Danny went on.

"They put something wet over her face when she got into the car and she only remembered waking up being too hot and feeling sick. During the interrogations they were asking about a launch of a large project that her father was in charge of. The transcripts show that they were asking about some sort of ants."

Danny paused to allow Turtle to enlighten us about what this meant, but his silence forced Danny into carrying on.

"Susie knew nothing about any sort of ants and was coming down from a massive high, all the time begging for more, so they could get no sense at all and decided to leave her to sweat it out for a bit longer."

Danny was talking fluently about the poor girl he felt so much pain for. He paced the area in front of the screen slightly as he explained what had been happening, each time he turned, he looked at me for my interest and approval. Every time, I averted my eyes to avoid his gaze. I was listening closely but chose to make him think I couldn't care less, not impressed by his work. He seemed to be trying to engage me and this made me more determined to appear to ignore him.

He had clearly had enough. He stood in front, his body turned to face me, legs slightly apart, stance challenging me not to look at him. He was still talking, I was trying to look at the screen but the vision of Danny stood between us. Slowly, I raised my eyes to his as he spoke. I decided to maintain the steady blank stare if that's what he wanted. His eyes smiled in recognition as he talked.

"We have had further reports from the SAS team that were on site," he said, his look never wavering from mine, as if to punish me. I felt hot, trying not to shuffle in my seat, I wondered what he was going to say next. A flash of glee lit up his face. My insides all squashed together in the internal agony that he was mentioning it again – here. Danny turned away as if he'd had his fun.

"They reported that the men they were tailing were suspects from the same group that did the Embassy attacks. From their conversations in the house and what the SAS heard, the men inside the house at Mateur were arms dealers looking to broker a supply agreement."

I understood the information better than most. To me, as it would be to Turtle, this made sense. Why were the French so interested in monitoring the interrogation? They were keeping tabs on the arms deal, wanting to see what was being sold. It all added up, a throw back to my previous assignment, that particular jigsaw wasn't finished yet.

Danny was progressing with his briefing, his back turned to me, looking at the screen.

"When the Tunisian terrorists arrived, they had been shown into the room where Susie was being kept. We don't have any transcripts because there were no bugs in there, but when they went back into the main room to talk about the meeting, the terrorists were not amused and didn't think they were going to get the results from her that they wanted. The arms dealers gave them some sales talk about getting assured results and that they had it all under control, but the Tunisians were not happy and the dealers had to promise to have the information from her by the weekend or they would have to get it through the alternative route," I felt he was addressing Turtle more than me, he had obviously finished having his fun at my expense.

"That's where the deadline had come from and why we had to take her immediately," his audience were still, he was the only animated object in the huge dim space.

"Now," he continued "the transcripts show that they were asking about the launch of these 'ants'. They also teased her about her drug habit and promised her drugs if she would co-operate, but she was in too much of a state to be able to help," he paused, looking wistful about the poor delicate frame of a girl he had left that morning. He seemed to be waiting to see if there were any questions, he had been pacing up and down as he gave his report but now he turned to the screen to try and judge his next move.

"In short, these unknown men have struck a deal with the Tunisian terrorists in which they find out the launch date of these ants in return for a supply agreement for weapons on a very large scale." He was looking at the screen, the voice pattern showed no movement while Turtle listened to his report, he looked to the figure behind the voice, to understand that we had uncovered something really big and action was required immediately.

His stance was no longer challenging, he looked as if he was appealing to Turtle, his hands dropped beside him, his head cocked to one side. He was about to ask a question and was already begging for the answer.

He'd decided to make his pitch, "We must act now, Turtle, to get to the agents and find out what it is they are trying to do for the terrorists. I propose that we go to Ireland, see if we can find the squat and track down the Albanian and the dealer that pushed Susie into the car. There is a plane at 15:00 that will have us there in time to make a good start." He took a step back and dropped his head to look at his feet for a second. I wondered if he'd laid it on a bit thick there with suggesting the plane time.

As I listened to the veiled plea, I was immediately stunned by its bluntness. He was making a play for my mission. Did he really want to kick me out of the way and carry it through himself? Surely Turtle wouldn't do that. Would he? This was what I had always feared but never thought it would play out right in front of me. In my imagination it was always going to materialise in an uncomfortable phone call saying there were no suitable current assignments. A "Don't call us . . ." scenario. My heart surged with panic, I stared at the man in front of me, transfixed, wanting to rush up and kick him between the shoulder blades. The trouble was, he was right, we did need to act now, but any support I voiced might make Turtle side with this interloper and I would be going home while he took off with the next phase of the mission. I sat silently, hoping that if I was still enough Turtle would forget to dismiss me.

For a painful few seconds Danny stood, looking imploringly into the screen for any signs that he had been successful in convincing the big man that he could handle the job. As we both waited for what seemed an eternity I could almost hear his heart pounding, there was sweat on his brow and his mouth smacked, trying to summon up some saliva for his dry throat. I sat on the stool, looking as demure as I could manage, I had to remain calm and appear in control. If anyone was going onwards, it ought to be me but I wasn't going to argue my case. My power here was in my silence.

"OK," Turtle's voice broke the silence, the screen suddenly animated, "Take Susie with you to locate the squat. You are already booked on the flight to Dublin." Danny looked at me, I tried to rearrange my face as a picture of innocence and hurt. There was no reference to me in Turtle's instructions. The lustful animal inside me bounced with anger, wanting to shriek and scream and thrash about. I sat quietly and seethed, plotting my revenge instead.

"Turtle," Danny interrupted, "we will need personal protection and a chaperone for Susie if we are going back to Dublin, we need

Blossom to come too," he looked at me. My eyes screwed up with suspicion as I looked at him to try and fathom what he was up to.

"Like I said, you are already booked on the flight," the luminous green lines lit up on the screen as Turtle gave our instructions, "You'd both better get going as soon as we've finished. Blossom will meet you at the airport, Danny, you go get Susie ready to travel," he ordered.

"Blossom, this girl is delicate, you will have to support her and make sure she isn't put at risk." my heart leaped. Danny had asked for me to come too, maybe he wasn't trying to get rid of me. He turned to me, we exchanged a strange knowing glance that seemed to bring us together, just enough for my hurt to subside.

"You both go, but you need to know what you are looking for," Turtle's words danced across the monitor. "The reason this is a Data Meet is the involvement of Dr Fairfield and the work he has been doing for us."

"The ants?" I asked, "Yes," Turtle's voice came down a notch, he was deadly serious. The purpose for the Data Meet was not the girl, it's what we took her to protect.

"This is the most important technological advancement in modern weapons research. It is not a typical delivery system and the ants are seen as the key to the future of warfare. We have been working on them for ten years, with miniaturisation in the forefront of the technology. We have had some other spin off successes that have helped to fund the programme, but the development of the ants has been the culmination of many different fields of electronics. Dr Fairfield, as head of the various teams, is one of the only people that know the system's many capabilities. Each team has only had the brief for their little part. A separate team of just Fairfield and a couple of others have the overall picture. You have both done very well in your tasks to get us to this point, but we are aware now that there is an intention to give these terrorists information about the ants and when they are to be launched. As you can imagine, we cannot afford for anyone to know what the full capability of these systems are."

I knew that the Malvern site was the heart of modern technologies. What on earth had they come up with this time?

Turtle barely drew breath, he had a lot to brief us about and we were on a deadline now.

"We have developed a tiny electronic system that can be dropped in peacetime and lie in wait until they are activated by a remote satellite signal. The All Terrain Tracked System, or AnTTS, can be used for many different functions including detonating explosives and jamming electrical circuits. This is the ultimate weapon and we can't afford for it to be kidnapped. We knew the girl had gone off the radar, as she was watched periodically while in Ireland. When she took off with the dealers we were trying to track her down locally when you found the transmission – well done Blossom. We didn't know for sure she had been taken until then. We also knew the potential risk she posed, due to her position in the Fairfield family and that she could not be allowed to divulge any information she may have picked up from her Father's work."

The slight shift in Danny's feet at these words was subtle but discernible. I was glad I had listened to my Father and made the right preparations for a successful outcome. This officer would not have failed in his part if we had been compromised.

"A demonstration has been organised for the launch of the AnTTS sometime next week. I don't know any more than that, but it involves the heads of government attending a meeting and a showcase of the project. This demonstration will decide if they will put the AnTTS into full production, so it is key to the Malvern men that it goes successfully."

That was all the information Turtle could explain at the moment. Now it was time to go.

"Your new passports are waiting for you at Susie's safe house. Go there immediately and a car will be along shortly to take you to the airport for your flight. Call in when you land, as usual," said Turtle, "Good luck my dears, take care" and the screen went blank.

We were left in the warehouse, looking at each other. Everything we had done up to now was mere preparation, this was the actual mission, find the agents and make them betray the Tunisian plot. The full details of the meeting had not fully sunk in, I was absorbed now in the next task in hand. All I knew was that I was excited, looking forward to whatever Ireland brought me.

We made our separate ways out of the building without a word passing between us, taking different routes to the next rendez-vous. I had genuinely believed he was going to push me out and it was surprise mixed with relief when he did the opposite. This plus the rush of the new discovery made me feel giddy, my engine roared as I dashed to the house to start this next adventure.

Chapter 8

Ireland was as cold and wet as it always was. The emerald isle never failed to instil me with the feeling that it was magical and beautiful, but it was always, always wet. No wonder it was so green and lush. A steady drizzle covered the passengers of the budget flight from the cattle truck with wings as we made our way out of the airport and on to our final destinations.

A stag party passed by outside the airport as we climbed into a waiting taxi with a shout of "Bitch!" following me as we drove away. Danny turned and raised an eyebrow, "Just an admirer," I said, an enigmatic smile passing over my lips. We pulled out of the Terminal car park as I thought how the minor incident could have had a major impact on our mission, almost drawing far too much unwanted attention on the short crossing. While I had been waiting outside the solitary toilet on my own, the lewd inhabitant had opened the door, "Hellooo there, Baby, hows about you come in here and we have a little fun on the way over, eh?" His hair was matted and his shirt covered with the debris of the two day stag party they had just decided they were going to finish in Dublin. He stunk of stale beer and looked like he had missed the toilet completely at some point, if not right now. He fell about the cubicle, stumbling on the threshold as he tried to reach out and drag me inside. The invitation to join the mile high club was so loud that the people nearby looked round to see what was occurring. I smiled and declined his kind offer, dodging his attempts to grab my wrists.

"Thank you," I said, quietly, trying not to attract more attention than he had already, "but no thank you", I smiled demurely, taking a step back to avoid the clawing hands.

"Aahh, come on, you know you want it, Baby," he protested, pushing his trousers down around his knees. The more I tried to convince him I didn't want to come in for any 'fun', the louder he became.

"What's wrong with you?" He started shouting and swearing at the back of the plane, causing more passengers nearby to turn and look at the drunken commotion. One of the hostesses was coming back to investigate the noise.

I could ill afford the attention and decided that it would be easier just to go into the cramped space with him.

"OK," I said, stepping into the tiny cubicle. The two of us could barely fit inside, let alone enjoy any frivolities. He thought his luck had changed and could barely contain his amazement. Part of me wanted to wait there and see if he could make a show of things but all he could manage was to try and fumble his way into my blouse while falling onto the toilet. How attractive, if only he could see himself.

"Well, thank you, this was lovely," I said, using the little space I had to twist my arms and hit him so hard with the heel of my hand on his left temple that he fell immediately on to the seat, knocked out by the blow. I sat him upright, leaning against the sink with his head resting on the cold bowl. I retired to my seat, maybe I would freshen up when we landed instead. The blow would not leave a mark and he would be lucky if he could explain to his friends what had happened when they picked him out of the facilities.

We settled into the journey with the wipers dragging across the windscreen the only sound. Our driver dropped us at the hotel and reported back to Turtle that we had successfully been delivered. There was no chance to relax just yet, we were short of time and had to keep moving. Quickly, we booked into our rooms. Adjoining rooms meant we would have a little freedom of movement, beds for all three and, most importantly, an alternative means of escape if we needed one. Our hotel had been chosen due to its proximity to where Susie thought the squat was, it certainly wasn't chosen for its charm. The old Victorian terrace house had been converted into a hotel in the 1930s, apparently that was the the last time it had been decorated. The carpets were shiny with decades of grime, the wallpaper peeled in the damp patches where the roof had leaked down the stairs. The comparison with the beautiful Tunisia Palace Hotel was non existent, this run down parlour nothing like the luxury I had been treated to last week. The staff seemed friendly enough, being no exception to the standard multi-cultural mix working in hotels all over Europe. The Receptionist sounded Polish, the porter was muttering in Hungarian as he pointed from the end of the Reception desk to the rickety lift to our room, stuck out at the back of the hotel, overlooking a car park. Most delightfully appointed. It was too dark to see anything else just yet but I could hardly contain my excitement for the stimulating vista which would await us in the morning, I was sure.

We dumped our bags with no time to unpack. Susie sat mournfully on the bed while Danny and I scanned the area, getting ready for our next instruction from Turtle, "All phones set to constant streaming, we'll keep an eye on you from the satellite positioning, the driver will be a couple of streets away if you need an evac' or to bring you back when you're done. Codeword is 'Fallen'. Blossom and Susie up front, Danny, you follow behind. Everybody ready?

Good, let's go," the three of us in the little room looked at one another after Turtle gave the command to start the operation.

"Susie, are you ready to go?" I knelt down in front of her so I could look into her face. She looked up nervously at me, then at Danny, "You don't have to, Susie, its up to you," he offered. He spoke the words but his body language wasn't as forgiving, he was pressing her to shepherd us on in the gentlest way possible. We were entirely sunk without her.

Because we weren't far away we set out on foot, careful to leave the TellTales in the room for Turtle to monitor in our absence. Danny and I were both armed, thanks to the friendly taxi driver. We made our way across the quiet road and down the hill towards the end of town that, unbelievably, was the rougher end. Susie and I looked like any other pair of girlfriends, walking arm in arm and chatting as we went. Susie began to pick out where she was supposed to be going, more by following landmarks than a full knowledge of the layout of the streets. I could feel her arm stiff under mine, her hands cold, the fingers clinging to the folds of my coat. The doctor had given her some medicine to stop the cravings, but in her old environment, the feeling of being a predator, looking for drugs, seemed to come back to her as she got closer to the den. The fear of being snatched hadn't fully soaked through her yet, she had been out of it at the moment she was taken, not realising the danger she was in until she woke up in a foreign land. At least we wouldn't have to battle against that fear as well. Not yet, anyway.

Now it was different. I was trying to keep the pace and the chatter nice and light so Susie didn't spook and run, we needed this location as quickly as possible and she was the only real lead, "You're doing really well, Susie. Do you recognise this place?

That's great, keep going, there's nothing to be scared of, Danny and I are here," I talked gently to keep her calm and focussed while she looked around her to see where we should go to next. I kept up the commentary into my phone, Turtle answering in single words to tell me to keep moving. We made our way through the terrible estate, warily passing by street after lonely street.

Danny walked behind us, tailing nonchalantly from about 50 metres away. From there he could observe and cover us from another angle if trouble came our way. The streets were fairly empty with just a few people rushing home to get in from the rain. Nobody was out for a walk or hanging around, which made his job easier.

The surroundings got more derelict with every street we passed through. Some windows were boarded up and rusting machinery laid rotting in gardens with supermarket trolleys and old sofas. I amused myself thinking of the old Ikea advert to 'chuck out your chintz', these people appeared to have taken it literally.

We were both soaked in the heavy rainfall that was pouring down upon us. Our beige overcoats dripped and our hair curled at the ends below our hats. The whole atmosphere was grey and dank. At the end of the last street, I started when Susie suddenly grabbed my arm so tightly, I was amazed at the strength of the frail girl.

"That one, third on the left," she indicated the house about a quarter of the way up the street. I spoke the accurate address into the phone as we walked past as casually as we could muster. Susie was as stiff as a board under my arm, every fibre of her appeared to be terrified. I looked closely at her. She was drenched now, the rain smacked into her cheeks, giving them a rosy glow but I could see the fear etched into her face. I thought about turning back, now that we had the house, but we still needed the right occupant. I had to jolt her out of the nightmare, "Its OK," I said gently, holding her hands in mine, "Danny is right behind us, it'll be fine. OK?"

The front of the house was boarded up, just like its immediate neighbours. Susie mumbled that there was an opening round the back that everyone used. It was darker now, the street felt no more attractive with the orange glow of the dirty old lampposts. No lights showed through the boarding of the house. We split up, Susie and I went to the far end of the street and came back down via the narrow path that led from the back gardens of each house. Danny doubled back to the other end of the path and was the first to get to the back entrance of the squat, checking the garden for movement. I slowed down.

"OK, all clear on the back garden, I see no movement in the house or the street. Clear to enter," was my cue from Danny to head in. He was under the kitchen window, the entry point for all the users of the sordid house. His dark manner reminded me of my own lust for the aggression that lived inside me, I had suppressed the animal while I looked after Susie but now it was time to enter the house, I felt my power rise as I checked my weapon. I looked at Danny properly for the first time in what seemed like a very long time. The brief second that passed between us gave away the bonding moment of a pair in conflict. Our own differences would need to be forgotten here, we didn't know what was behind the loose board I was about to displace. Danny held the wood to one side and I slipped past into the kitchen with Susie close behind, Danny would provide cover from outside.

"I'm inside," I kept up the commentary, as much to remind myself I was not alone.

The kitchen was dark and smelled of stale beer and pot. A nasty mouldy, foisty smell made me want to retch. I paused for a second to collect two very deep breaths to get the smell into my system and get over it. I could taste the disgustingness of the squalor. The house was silent. Susie seemed frozen to the spot, I grabbed her arm, "Which way?" I asked her, "where will they be if they're here?" Susie's glazed eyes were fixed on the doorway as if I wasn't there. She had withdrawn in to her own world of pain, the rancid smells prompting the memory of her stay in this hellish place.

"Susie. Susie! Where will they be?" I repeated the question twice, shaking her arm to bring her back to here and now. Susie was unable to speak but pointed a shaking finger in the direction of the front door and to the right.

I moved stealthily across the tacky floor and headed for the door in the corner of the room, pushing Susie in front of me so I could keep her in view. I wondered what I might be walking in but tried not to think about it too hard. Susie opened the door. Slumped in the hallway was the figure of a man, unshaven and barely clothed, his torso covered in the track marks of his habit. Susie instinctively clutched her leathery limbs, hardly healed since she stopped her own abuse. I reached down and checked his neck, he had a very faint pulse, just as Susie's on the night we took her back. He was alive but wouldn't be causing us any trouble. I left him in his self induced stupor.

"Man in the hallway, looks like he might need an ambulance once we're done here," I whispered in Turtle's ear to try and give the strewn man a chance of surviving the week.

We crossed the hall, stepping over the man's legs. At the next door, I could hear voices in low tones. My heart boomed in my chest, the growl rising up to be satisfied. My teeth were bared, Susie had to push hard to make the next door open as it caught the loose carpet on the living room floor. She shoved it far enough to allow us both to enter then in a shielding motion I pulled her back to get between her and the contents of the room.

I felt alive. The throng of my heart's pounding ran through me as I readied at the prospect of a conflict. I was eager for them to be the ones, just the men we were looking for. My eyes felt wide as saucers, fully adjusted to the poor light. I could see to the opposite end of the room to survey the whole scene inside. In a flash, I had the image in my mind. Two men were sat on a moth eaten old sofa on the right hand side of the room. Another man was laid unconscious on the floor in the place where the family dog would have laid in front of the fire, had there been anything but an empty hole in the wall.

The two men on the sofa looked up, these were no ordinary punters waiting for their dealer. The men stopped their conversation as we entered the room. They looked at each other, smiling, evidently pleased at the fresh meat that had stumbled into their lair.

I strode confidently into the room and smiled at the two of them. I had already weighed them up and could see where the threat would come from if they were who we expected. The closest was a large man with dark, close cut hair receding at the front. His build was heavy and he wore a loose fitting cotton shirt hung out of his shiny, over-pressed suit trousers with oil spots on the sides. The fingers of his right hand were yellow with nicotine. As he looked up I could see his teeth were a disgusting shade as well. He was the muscle man and would fight with his fists.

The other man was smaller, his flat brown hair matted to his head, his clothes looked fresh from the charity emporiums of Dublin. Despite wearing a brown suit, he looked more untidy and bedraggled than his companion. The growth of hair on his face was neither designer nor appealing. I thought a hot bath should be the order of the day for this dirty specimen, then reprimanded myself for turning into my Mother. This slimy piece would shrink from physical conflict, letting his friend do the hard stuff.

I took my position on the other side of the door as Susie peered in. I watched them carefully, their smiles faded and faces changed as they realised that we were not the usual strawberries. I saw the moment pass over their faces when they recognised the girl in the doorway as the one they had sold a couple of weeks before. Their reaction to her presence confirmed these were the men we had come for. The adrenalin rushed through me, making my heart pump harder. Time appeared to slow down as I waited to see how events would unfurl.

My inner animal boomed to be set free. My body tensed, ready for the fight my senses knew was coming. The big man moved to stand up while the other pushed his hand into his jacket. I was faster than both of them. I pushed the door back on to Susie, knocking her out of the room to protect her from the scene. Her senses were not wired the same way as mine, she let out a squeal as she was bustled through the door, not knowing what was about to happen in the darkened room.

I stepped back towards the door, more to keep Susie from entering than to plot my own escape. I turned and pointed to the small man, telling him not to move, I didn't want to wait the split second to see what came out of his jacket.

"Don't draw it, Mister, put your hands where I can see them," I shouted for him to stop and drop it, but he wasn't as fast as he thought he was. Blood was still racing through me, but the booming pulses of my heartbeat seemed to be minutes apart.

My hand was still empty but he had to have heard me, he had to let go of the gun before he drew it, he had to or I wouldn't be able to stop, "Don't do it! Drop it NOW" I screamed at him. He appeared not to know when he was beaten. The seconds between my heartbeats sounded boom . . . . boom . . . . boom. As his hand withdrew from the jacket I saw the glint of gunmetal on a long barrel. Foolishly, he levelled the gun to fire. I thrust my hand forward, pointing a finger at the man just taking aim to fire. The gun in my sleeve shot forward with the thrust, directly into my palm. My finger was aiming, all I had to do was squeeze the handle to fire. I let out two rounds. Double tap, pop pop, one in the chest the other in the head. I tried to stop him, he should have listened. My consciousness returned to normal time as the gun fell from his hand. The weapon banged on the floor as he slumped into the dirty upholstery, his head reeling back, eyes wide open, staring blankly at the ceiling.

All this had passed in an instant. The big man had only just stood up, he was two steps away but lunged forward to swing a clumsy punch in the direction of my face. I felt my aggression roar, the power surging, screaming up from my core to rejoice that the fight was finally on. Simply, I stepped back, letting the fist fly past. His weight was all on his front foot, the effort he had put into the misused punch had left him off balance. My arms drew slightly back, ready to strike. I had time as he tried to regain his footing, I could pick my spot. He straightened up, his face rising to mine. My eyes locked on to his for the first time, he looked angry and upset. His clenched fist pulled back to take another shot but I was waiting.

My hips twisted as my own missile launched, the two first knuckles made contact, straight into his fleshy side, near the kidneys, rising up into the ribcage towards the centre of his body, twisting and grinding at the soft tissue they ripped past. The big man buckled under the blow, his ribs broken, I had felt the crack against my knuckles. His face contorted. Sharp pain would be cutting through his back, feeling like every breath he took was tearing through another part of his fleshy core. My second jab was to the back of his ear with the butt of my handgun, a light tap just to make sure he didn't get up too quickly.

I checked the rest of the room to make sure I hadn't disturbed the other residents, but the comatosed man was still laid out in the hearth and had not even moved as the all too quick surge of aggression had subsided, satisfied, and peace took over me once more. I trained the gun back on to the wounded figure as he lay, winded, on the tarred carpet. My adrenalin, still beating, made me spin round, gun at the ready, to check the voices behind me. I could hear Danny making sure Susie was OK before the door pushed back open for him to enter the morbid scene. I had my foot on the big man's back as he lay, my gun still smoking from making the dead agent on the sofa look permanently skyward.

I nodded acknowledgement to Danny as he entered to indicate that everything was under control. He picked up the bleeding man and threw him on to the sofa with his dead friend.

"Who are you?" I asked, kicking him in the shins to focus his attention as he writhed with pain and confusion.

"Susie!" my urgent tone summoning the girl back into the room, "do you recognise either of them?" Susie looked at the injured man but looked confused and shook her head. When she saw the body in the crumpled suit her brain didn't comprehend at first that she was looking at a corpse. The blood looked like a single black spot in the dim light. Her shocked mind innocently made her look at the ceiling in wonder at what was so interesting there that he couldn't stop staring. Then she started to shake, her senses frozen as she realised he was dead. The shock was too much for her.

"Susie is fallen. Repeat "Susie is Fallen." Pick up, immediately, we'll see you at the end of the street. Wait for us round the corner til my next instruction." A beep over the line confirmed my message had been received.

"Susie, do you know either of these men, you must answer me quickly, we need to leave here now. Do you understand me, Susie?"

"Yes," said Susie, "he's the one that pushed me into the car. He used to talk to the Albanian man and give me free stuff when I needed it." At the thought of it, the memory returned to her of being taken from this house and shoved into the car outside. The images swam around in her head and she was sick with the fright.

We had what we needed. I bustled Susie out of the room once more while Danny took care of the incapacitated agent. He retrieved the wallet and weapon of the dead man and we dragged ourselves out of there before any more of their friends turned up to see what the noise had been. Susie was beside herself by now, shaking and sobbing. I put my coat around her shoulders and tried to keep her moving.

"Pick up, ready," I ordered as we came out of the cursed house. The car pulled up at the end of the path and we all bundled in.

The taxi drove off quickly in the opposite direction to the hotel. Danny blindfolded the captured agent and we travelled through the Dublin streets to lose any unwanted followers that might have tagged along. When the driver thought we were safe, he returned us to the hotel, entering through the back to go up the stairs and into our room.

The blood had stopped flowing from the injured man's head and he was now sniffing and nursing his damaged ribs. The bruising was so deep that it would take several days to come out but for now even breathing would be agony. I took Susie to the adjoining room and gave her something to help her sleep then put her to bed after drying her hair. It had been a traumatic day for her and she needed to rest now.

I searched the injured man's pockets then dropped him into the bath with a gun trained at his head as the blindfold was removed. I wanted to know quickly who he was and who he was working for. The questions came slowly and steadily, taking into account his injuries and the mist that must have been encompassing his mind, but the more he resisted I knew he was being obtrusive rather than befuddled and gave him another sharp tap with the butt of the gun, bang on the same spot I'd hit him already.

I hit more gently this time, simply enlivening the original pain, causing him to curl up in the bottom of the bath to reject any further attention. His memory returned, however, with this persuasive argument.

"My name is L'Arnout," he murmured for me to stop the pain, but I wanted more from the dazed man.

"Alright, alright. I only work when they need me, I get paid per job I'm not with them all the time. I was told to meet Casson," So that was his name, the man whose body had just been found by his formerly unconscious friend from the hearth of the squat. As I was questioning our captive, the alarm was going up in the drug den and the occupants were abandoning the nest into the arms of the local police, who had been forewarned and were waiting outside.

"You have been here for two months" I stated after inspecting the contents of his pockets. L'Arnout looked up, "Yes," he confirmed.

"So you were here to help him look for the girl, the one you saw tonight," again, I was telling, not asking. He nodded, looking at me suspiciously.

"What did they want with her?" I wanted to know.

"I don't know. They didn't say."

I twiddled with the gun, spinning it until the butt was exposed. L'Arnout hid his head under his arms.

"I don't know, I don't know I tell you," his anxiety growing as his body shifted underneath him but there was no escape.

"What *do* you know?" my deliberate, calm manner made him even more nervous.

"I came here to meet Casson. He was looking for that girl and I helped him find her. I don't know why they wanted her, but a couple of weeks ago he told me he put her into a car and sent her to his handler."

"Handler?"

"Yes, he met him every Tuesday in Dublin. He was the one who called me here."

Casson had apparently enjoyed his stay in the squat so much he decided to move in after Susie had been shipped off. It was good for his cover and virtually indetectable by the normal means. He could also seek the comforts of the frequent strawberries that visited the den looking for their fix, he always had money and they always needed it.

L'Arnout told us Casson met his contact at lunch in the Long Stone pub on Townsend Street. That was all we required from him. We heaved him out of the bath and sat him down on the bed in the room.

"Can you see me?" I asked.

"Yes, of course," he replied.

"Can you hear me, L'Arnout?"

"Why, yes," he said, puzzled. I stood up in front of him, raising his face to mine with the ends of my fingers, a quick flick of my fingertips caught him uncomfortably in the throat.

"Look at me" I said, "and understand what I am about to tell you. I am letting you go L'Arnout. I don't need you any more, I have all your details. I know where you live now and where your family are." At the mention of his family, his attention was complete.

"You have a mobile phone, call your wife right now."

The tone of my voice made him nervous, wondering what I had done to his girl back home. He flipped up the screen and quick-dialled his wife. He tried not to sound nervous but asked if she was OK. Apparently she was fine. I watched and listened to the responses between the two, I could see he was relieved but not convinced that I was finished.

"Ask her if there is anyone sat outside in the street," I told him and he obeyed. His wife answered there were two men outside the shop down the road who had not yet moved away. He looked at me, I could see the rage welling up inside him, the feeling of wanting to strike at me almost bursting through until he remembered his snapped bones and ripped muscles.

"Tell her its fine and you'll be home soon. Put the phone down. Good. So now you know, I know where you get your coffee on a morning, I know where you ride your bicycle. I am going to let you go, but please don't think that you are getting away. If you go back to the agent with our details, I will know. If you come back to any British or Irish land, I will know. I am letting you go, but you will never escape from me. Do you understand?" I stared intently into his eyes so he didn't misconstrue what I was telling him.

"You will never work here again, got it?" He understood. He knew I had tagged him, his picture would be everywhere by now. He nodded in recognition.

"OK" was his only response; I could see that he had taken in the gravity of his situation. He was, at least, a professional and knew when he was beaten. This time it was literally, as the driver sped him away I told him to stop by the hospital before flying him back home. If there was any internal bleeding he would need to be checked out.

The tale of being mugged by a gang of youths in the depths of the Dublin backstreets where he could hardly describe his environment got him treated with care at the hospital. The injuries were bad but there was no permanent internal damage, my skill and accuracy implied that he had been very fortunate not to have had his spleen ruptured by the blows from the gang. He could seldom admit that the single punch was administered by a girl half his size and the gang story was embellished until the point when the police arrived to take his statement, by which time our driver had made him mysteriously disappear.

"Bicycle?" Danny asked, as L'Arnout was taken away.

"He has a bicycle and rides it regularly, probably to the same places he visits each day," I told him, but he still looked slightly baffled.

"The oil spots on the trousers," I explained, "from his bicycle chain. I have no idea where he lives or who his wife is, and if you're about to ask where he gets his coffee on a morning, I don't know that either, but you don't get teeth that brown and such nasty breath from drinking anything else," my confidence already high, Danny's look of surprise and admiration filled me with pride as I continued, "I didn't know his wife before, but I sure as hell can trace her now he's called her on his mobile that I tagged earlier." At the end of my sentence Danny laughed out loud, he said nothing, just shaking his head.

Together, we sat and talked through the day's events while Susie slept in the next room. Our tones were hushed, like parents who had just got the baby off to sleep, stealing a moment together to plan the night feeds. Sat on the bedroom floor with our shoes off, resting our backs against the beds, it was the first opportunity we'd had to examine what had happened since Tunisia, our heads still spinning from the developments we had made. This was as relaxed as we had ever been with each other. We were more like a team now, having come through some genuine trauma. I felt I'd performed particularly well and sat back now in a smug mood, waiting for Danny's acknowledgement and congratulations. Good job I wasn't holding my breath.

All Danny could talk about was Susie and how vulnerable she still was. He was asking me if I thought Susie needed more medical support but I was wrapped up with why he wasn't telling me how great I was after a gruelling day. My jealousy sparked up again and the green eyed monster was particularly obnoxious in my form, I knew. I kept it under wraps for the most part, but my crush on Danny was drawing it ever more annoyingly to the surface.

"So, what do you think?" he asked me again, "Shall I get another doctor to look at her?" I wondered why he was so attracted to women who needed saving, why so interested in the poor mouse when I was here, strong and independent? I regretted the thought the moment I realised what I was thinking. Have a word with yourself, Blossom. The young girl had been through quite a week. I put the hurt with the jealousy and shut the closet door back on their feelings, Susie was in our care and I needed to be a bit more forgiving.

"Let's leave it until the morning," I advised, "she's sedated right now and we're taking her home tomorrow. She will be back with her family by teatime. We'll arrange for the work's doctor to come and have another look at her there".

"Yes, of course, Blossom, you're right as usual," he smiled at me for the first time in what felt like ages, turning to look at me face on. Satisfied, I glanced at him then looked deeply into my hot chocolate. The dimple was encouraging me to look some more and I desperately wanted to in the soft hazy light in the hotel room. I swirled the cocoa powder round in the bottom of the cup and looked into it as if it would show his handsome face gazing back. I amazed myself at how relaxed I was feeling, our awkwardness was gradually fading.

Everything in the room was still and quiet. I was tired now but we still had to guard Susie overnight.

"If I take a shower now then have a sleep, can you take the first stag?" I asked.

"No problem," he agreed, still seeming excited from his day's work, maybe wanting to impress me with his staying power? I had a better method of testing but we wouldn't be exploring that, I had to remind myself. He appeared to be more than happy to let me sleep first.

I checked my gun and left it wrapped in a towel in the bathroom sink, leaving the door unlocked in case there was trouble outside. Having come straight from the data meet, I had no clean clothes with me, so I washed out my underwear and hung it on the heated towel rail to dry while I stepped into the too hot shower and allowed it to cascade over my head and into my ears and mouth.

I washed my hair to soak out the day's blood and toil as events came back to me. Better him than me; he wasn't hesitating and gave no warning. I was just faster – today. The soap bubbles meandered down my body as I rinsed out my hair and let the scalding water turn my skin pink. I scrubbed and rubbed and washed away the bad thoughts. It was done now, I had to put it in the closet with the rest of my skeletons, popping out occasionally for further examination but largely remaining hidden. I was ready to sleep now. My skin was so hot that it didn't need drying, the steam evaporated as I got out of the shower, leaving me with a smooth, radiant feel. I put on the barely dried underwear and got dressed.

Exhaustion overtook me as I climbed into the bed next to Susie's. It was the one closest to the room door and to the connecting one through to where Danny was still sitting. My weapon went under the pillow where I could feel it and retrieve it if required.

Danny had left the interconnecting door open so that I could see him. Turtle had reminded us after our evening's report that we needed to be extra vigilant to make sure there were no surprises in the time until we got the girl back home the following day. Susie would need to be delivered back to her father in a fair state, this was one of our own we were looking after, one that had never been given the choice of whether she wanted to be involved, she just was.

I was used to grabbing my sleep when it was offered and could manage on stag for long periods. I would need to be up again in three hours feeling as refreshed as I could. Danny was still alive with the day, let him stay up and wear himself out slowly. I knew I could trust him to keep a decent watch so I could sleep soundly, I shifted myself into the bed to get comfortable then instantly fell in to a delta sleep.

What seemed like moments later it was time for me to be up. A warning something raised me from the depth of my sleep. I didn't move. My hand was already on my gun under the pillow. There was a presence close to me, I could feel it, sensing silent breath drawing in and out. Someone was next to the bed. I could hear Susie's sleepy mumbling and snoring, same as before. It wasn't her. The someone took another step towards me. It was stealthy and gentle. I wasn't sure how I knew it was there as I heard nothing tangible, but I knew it was closer. My senses were alert but my body still, my muscles slowly tensing, ready to strike wherever I would need them in the next five seconds. There was a predator in the room. Before it had time to do what it had come to do I clicked the gun's safety off and opened a wary eye. Danny was crouched down at the side of the bed, his hand raised above my shoulder, frozen as he heard the familiar 'click'. The smile on his face never abated, he seemed almost gleeful in discovering I could not be shaken awake.

On finding him so close I opened the other eye to welcome in the view. He looked like a dream, his hair slightly stuck up at the front from where he had pushed some sweat away. He was smiling at me with an expression of knowing that I had never seen before, his look bordering on admiration. I liked it. It showed, finally, some respect. That's all I wanted. He might not have said the words after the day's work, but that smile and the look spoke more to me right then. What a lovely sight to wake up to. I rubbed my eyes to break the spell of the blue pools lapping at me and sprang out of bed, I was up now, "Your turn" was all I said, putting the safety catch back on the little Glock while I walked across to the other room to make another hot chocolate.

"OK, but I need a shower as well now," he answered and went straight into the bathroom as the kettle boiled.

I didn't know which way to turn, Danny had left the bathroom door half open as he undressed to jump in the shower. Just enough, I found, that from the glass of the picture on the wall behind the kettle his reflection was quite clear. Well, at least he didn't need to wash his pants, I was somewhat surprised to find.

Once the kettle had boiled I had no excuse to stay in the room and wandered back through as I stirred the powdered delight, moving only after being treated to a side shot of the flat torso and a muscular thigh as Danny stepped into the shower and disappeared behind the door. I could ill afford to let him see me looking, so retired to the other room to take the temptation, but not the image, away.

Dried and dressed, sans underwear again, Danny slipped into the bed that I had just got out of. He relaxed into the pillows and pulled up the blanket. I hoped he could smell me there and feel my warmth. He shuffled round to lie just as I had done. I thought about him taking my heat, almost feeling my skin underneath him. He preferred to have his gun between his knees while he slept on guard, as his hands rested there and he could get at it easily. I sat on the floor at the front of his bed with my shoes on, ready. I watched him as he drifted off slowly to a deep sleep.

Hours on stag later, I was thinking of giving Danny's blanket a tug from the bottom when a loud crash from outside the door jolted me away from thoughts of the interesting ways in which I could have woken him. Rolling over, my gun was drawn as I sped towards the door. I waited, knelt on one knee with the beds at my back. Weapon in front, staring intently at the door waiting for the intruder to burst in. I was panting at the sudden movement after sitting still for so long, my ears crashed with the sudden sound of my overstimulated heartbeat. Thump thump thump through my head as I waited at the door. The stillness of the following few seconds made my hair stand on end.

There were scuffles on the corridor outside. I looked briefly behind to check Danny was there. He knelt in a mirror position to me, guarding between his bed and Susie. I felt safe knowing he was at my back, Susie would know nothing as she continued to sleep through the drama acting out just for Danny and me. I edged towards the door and nodded to Danny, he turned off the light and I looked through the peephole. The night porter was bending over just outside. Quickly, I turned the door handle. As he rose up, I sprang through to pull him inside, splaying him on to the floor of the room. The door slammed shut behind him, guns out of view until we found what he was doing there.

"Oh, I so sorry, Miss," said the porter, staggering to his feet, looking at his shoes apologetically and wiping the runny egg from the front of his burgundy waistcoat.

"I so sorry, so sorry. I went knock on door, bring breakfast. The tray, it fall. I scared to tell, it all on floor, Miss," then he continued to rattle on in Hungarian. By the looks of things he was in dire trouble. Danny stayed to keep watch over Susie while I helped him pick up the tray and what was rescueable of our morning repose. He offered to come back with more, but I declined, thinking of the damage he could wreak with an armful of toast and butter.

It was time to leave. The risks increased the longer we stayed. We would go into the main town centre to recce the place where Casson would have been due to meet his contact. Townsend Street was a typical old part of Dublin with a long history in a city famed for revelry. The Long Stone pub was a family owned inn that went back centuries, but was ever popular now with the new breed of party goers, over on cheap flights to try real Guinness on Temple Bar and be convinced they knew Ireland well because of it.

Across the street was a café where we could see the pub clearly as well as finally get some breakfast. Susie was starving after the sleeping pills and none of us had eaten properly since the previous lunchtime. A slow feast of full Irish breakfast, toast, marmalade and coffee was laid out in front of us, to be ravenously devoured. We looked a small happy bunch, passing the time in each other's company. At any one time someone was looking out of the window at the activity in the street until we had a good feeling of the surroundings. I went for a little walk and came back soon after with the morning papers and a refill of coffee.

"The front door is secured from the inside. There is a service road around the back where the barrels are unloaded and a hatch into the cellar. There is also a yard at the back which is used as the smoking area. There is an umbrella outside for shelter just over from the back door. No vehicles can enter the yard and there is a high wall all the way round. We need to know next what the inside looks like. That should be easy – they have a website." I typed the URL from the poster in the window of the front door of the pub into my phone and waited for the website to materialise.

It didn't take long, the 360' virtual tour on the tiny screen showed all we needed to know of the bar areas and rooms.

"OK," I explained, "we will need to sit and wait for him. Danny, if you and Susie get in early and take a table at the far end of the main bar, here. I will come in closer to lunchtime and go into the other room. We can call each other and report then I will tackle him when we spot him." I had it all worked out, but Danny wasn't happy.

"Why don't you two sit together and I'll come in later, then *I'll* tackle him when we identify him?" he said gently, not meaning it to sound like a challenge. I took it as one anyway, so no matter what, we were going with my plan now.

"Oh, I thought about that, Danny, I figured it would look more likely to have a man and his girlfriend in there having a drink together than a man arriving on his own. Besides, two girls out on their own might attract some unwanted romantic advances and we need to keep clear of that." Danny appeared to be thinking it over for a few moments, then agreed it was the way forward. I was happy I had repelled the minor ripple of objection.

With an hour before the pub would open, we thought to take Susie's mind off things by taking her shopping. Dublin had some lovely places so we walked and talked and brought her back round in a big circle until it was time to get into the bar.

Inside, Danny bought their drinks as I walked round the back. I'd bought some cigarettes and pretended to smoke them while keeping an eye out for anyone entering through the back door. Danny could see the whole bar in front of him, but Susie's back was to the entrance. We couldn't risk the unknown agent recognising her and fleeing before we realised who it was.

The driver was on standby in the taxi rank less than quarter of a mile away. The phones were streaming live and now we just had to wait. Steadily, the patrons piled into the pub as the lunchtime rush came in. One group appeared to be out on a work's birthday bash from the local offices. They were loud and boisterous, but that wasn't what we were looking for. We needed a quiet man on his own, possibly with props such as a newspaper so he could look like he was just bumping into someone, or like he was going to be on his own. He would check his watch or phone when the contact became late. He would have a drink to blend in but then sit somewhere quiet, away from the crowds. He might order a meal, but he would choose a spot where more than two could dine. This is what we were lying in wait for.

I walked round the block and looked into the main road. It was time to call Danny, "Anything?"

"Not yet, we're just having a quiet drink."

"I'll give it until 12.30 then I'll come inside."

I walked back to the smoking shelter and noticed a man sitting at the picnic table underneath the umbrella. I nodded to him and got out my cigarettes. He was already smoking his so I asked him for a light. He offered me the lighter, a very expensive Zippo, suiting the smart man in the tailored suit and shiny Italian leather shoes.

"Thank you" I said, smiling a bright bubbly grin, but the man just sat and smoked, dropping his ash on the floor and flicking the butt across the table when he'd had enough.

My senses raced, the chase was on. The man was quite short, aged about mid-fifties, with dark steely grey hair and hollow blue eyes. He was wearing a long brown camel overcoat, open at the front to expose the neat suit, the belt flapping loose at the middle, slightly too high for his waist. His brown leather shoes were freshly polished. A stylish, designer led Frenchman.

He slowly made his way, panting and coughing, through the back door of the pub. I was on the phone again, "Did you get that one, with the camel coat and the dark grey hair?"

"Yes, I did. He went round the main bar to the other side of the lounge and is sat a table at the far end of the room. He ordered a single drink and opened his newspaper. Does it look good?"

"It certainly does. He was smoking French cigarettes with no filters, I have the butts bagged for forensics later on."

"We can see very well from here. It all matches and looks just lovely. Do you want to come over later and see it?"

"Yes, I'll come in five minutes and observe, then I'll tackle him."

I put down the phone and finished my pretend cigarette. I walked through the back door and moved to the other side of the bar to get away from the crowds. After ordering a bar snack I sat to observed my friend in the corner. Danny could see me clearly from where he was sitting and kept a watch over the rest of the area to make sure we weren't missing anything else. No other candidates came in. I was sure this was it.

At exactly half past twelve, the Frenchman looked at his watch. He looked around the room, over the top of his newspaper, and took a swig of his drink. He looked at his watch again. How long would he wait? I had already made sure he was waiting in vain, but he was only just about to figure that out.

He checked his watch again then finished his drink. As he folded his newspaper to leave, I sat down at his table. He looked at me with a neutral face as I smiled towards him sweetly.

"Thank you for the light, Monsieur," I said. He looked at me, this time with interest.

"And how, mademoiselle, did you know I was French?" he asked in a quiet voice, leaning a little closer to hear the response.

"Ah, Monsieur, you are smoking French cigarettes. I have just come back from there and know that smell and the brand you had in your hand outside, I smoked it myself while I was there."

He was no longer intrigued. He bid me a good day and went back to moving towards leaving.

"Has your friend not arrived?" He was getting annoyed with me now, he had to go, ignore the annoying girl and get out.

"But he's usually so punctual, isn't he?" I asked. He sat back in his chair and looked at the uninvited guest that was still smiling at him quite disarmingly. I toyed with the mobile phone in my hands, turning it over and over as he looked at me with half disgust, half concern.

"Monsieur Casson, he is usually so punctual, is he not?"

The look turned to murder in his eyes, I could feel him examining my body, pausing to ponder how he would get out through the quickest route once he had shot me in the chest as I sat opposite him. The smile fell from my lips as I caught the murderous intent on his face.

"Don't worry, Monsieur, he is quite safe. I have come here to show you where he is, but don't make any sudden moves, my dear friend, or you will not need to worry about cancer from the cigarettes." As I played with the phone I pressed three times on the keypad, calling the waiting taxi driver to speed towards us.

Danny and Susie picked up their things and walked outside to wait for him. I sat, my gaze locked on to the man who was right now plotting how to kill me where I sat. I moved my jacket to the side to show him the handle of my gun, not yet drawn but menacingly close. Closer than any weapon he might have concealed upon him. I then moved my other lapel to show him Casson's gun, taken from his warm corpse the previous day. He clearly recognised the weapon and the threat never left his eyes as he watched me intently for an opportunity to strike. Foolishly, he decided to try me out, but I was ready for the test. His hand rose towards his jacket. Mine was on it in a second, bracing his wrist with the knife from the table and setting it gently back down as the blade stroked against his veins. I smiled at him, reassuring him that he was about to do exactly as I said.

Three beeps back on the phone was the signal for me to ask our guest to join us outside. We linked arms, I pressed my tiny gun into his ribs as we walked towards the door, giggling and grinning at him, knowing he was searching his mind to find a way to get that bullet into me before I forced him to the waiting vehicle.

Outside, he might have mad a dash to throw me off but for Danny standing waiting, his own gun hovering over the man's intestines as we approached. He opened the car door and I showed him into it, waving a cheery goodbye as we stood on the footpath, admiring our prey as he was whisked away for questioning. I called Turtle from the street outside as we walked quickly away from the scene, "Done, the package is in the delivery van" was all I said, "Well done, talk to you later" and the episode was finished.

Our job was complete. It was time to get back to the airport for the flight to take Susie back home. We had bought her some new clothes and administered the doctor's medicine to take away the cravings, a little less each day, until she was clear. The doctor was to meet us at her house that evening for a check up as suggested. All we had to do now was to get her back safely. We got to the airport on the homeward journey, but could ill afford to relax. We were exposed as targets. If the man we had taken today was supposed to call in at some point this afternoon, the two snatches would start to add up. To top it all, Susie was a nervous wreck, we had to lead her on to the plane with one in front and one behind to keep her moving. Strange behaviour when we were, at last, taking her back to the safety of her home after weeks of ordeal.

Chapter 9

The next stage of our work was under-way, although Susie's nerves were of concern. We had brought her so far and were thinking that she would be glad to be going home, back to the bosom of her family and safety. Her body was recovering from the abuse of the last couple of weeks. She had regained her appetite and the sores on her arms were starting to heal. Her cravings were being administered to with the application of the buprenorphine the doctor had left us. All should have been well. The order of nerves now, however, was nothing like those that had gone before. She shivered whenever home was mentioned and glazed over so it was difficult to talk to her or snap her out of it. There was an unease at the situation, although we couldn't put our fingers on why, it made us especially careful.

Off the plane and the usual routine, a call in to Turtle using the mini scrambler at the airport phone. This was the established protocol just in case there had been an incident crossing a border. He would track us using our boarding cards as we arrived for the flight, then track the plane using air traffic control records. We had to call from the airport so he could see us on security cameras and tap into the phones to make sure it was definitely us calling and we were safe. If no call came in time, he would check customs and airport security to see if we had been detained for some reason or send up the alarm and get men out to find us. It was elements of the job like this which made him such an important part of the chain to make sure the officers in his charge were looked after constantly.

I was Turtle's full time responsibility. Now Danny was with me, it was important that Turtle kept him close as well. I called in, "Hey, we're down, where to?" I asked.

"Top of the morning to you, my dear, I hope you spent a pleasant night with your partner there – get much sleep did you?" He teased, playing on my distant dislike of the other officer, for once he was badly behind the times.

"I have an address for the senior Government official that you are about to meet." He was keen to impress on me the gravity of the situation.

"As yet he knows nothing of what his daughter has been through or that she is arriving home today. We have kept him out of the whole episode so that we can secure his work before we tell him. He will get a phone call once you are inside to tell him to go home. Its very important to keep this man happy. Make sure you don't upset him, take him his daughter back safe. Question him gently and try to see if he knows what the terrorists wanted from her. The driver is waiting for you outside, he will take you there. Good luck."

My unease increased and Danny read it on my face as I put away the electronics. Dr Fairfield's address was highly classified. You had more chance of getting into Camilla's bedroom than getting anywhere near the country's most productive weapons scientist of the last fifteen years. He had over three hundred patents in his name, his technical achievements had earned him a special personal award from the Queen, which was itself classified.

His work in the defence of his country was beyond reproach and he was guarded very closely. His route to and from work was monitored by special forces, he had a daily schedule that was registered, stating where he was going and with whom. The long arm of his employers could be felt wherever he went, all for his own good, he knew.

The driver made his way through the beautiful city of Malvern, nestled into the long low hills. We turned and headed out of the city, further into the countryside. About twenty minutes from the town centre the green lush farmland opened up. The famous hills could be seen in all their glory. As the clouds passed overhead the light played across them, throwing shadows and highlighting the myriad of colours on the side of the ever changing hills. We climbed a long incline that brought us high to view the landmarks and steeples of Great Malvern below. The road to Wyche was steep and few houses littered the route. Around a sharp bend at the dead end of Gordon Terrace stood a long high brick wall that carried along about five hundred yards until it came to a wrought iron gate with impenetrable steel plates behind it. No view could be seen to determine if we were in the right place.

The driver pulled in, his window slid down to reach the button on the intercom. I noticed that the cameras above the gate were already trained on the hot bonnet of the vehicle. Susie called to the driver just to push the coded entry keys as she told them to him. The gates clanged open, moving swiftly sideways to let the car through. The drive curved to the left as it rose up the hill from the gates through a large, well kept garden with a row of conifers and beech trees shading shrubberies and a rockery. The car passed the peak of the hill and we caught our first glimpse of the great house as it came into view. A large symmetrical house with a central pillared entrance portico, all built of local dark sandstone, set gloriously into the grounds. The house was fairly new, having been constructed in the 1920's as a grand statement of someone's new money status.

As we crawled up graciously to the entrance on the gravel drive, I looked through the tinted car window into the garden and carefully at the house. In between the flower beds and shrubs in the carefully tended landscaping, the occasional thin spike stood proud from the earth. The more I looked, I could see that they were laid out in a large grid pattern all across the garden and up to the house in each direction.

I had seen this before, the pegs gave out a frequency that monitored movement in the garden. If they detected movement or infra red signals, it would read back to the control centre in the house and give a grid reference for the cameras to home in on and use their detectors and thermal imaging to scan the area for intruders. This was as sophisticated a system as I had ever seen and rivalled any in the country. This sort of system was my worst nightmare in my professional pursuits, making it almost impossible to get to the house without being detected. The system would be capable of detecting personnel, raising an alarm and recording the intruder all automatically. Manual users would also be able to focus on the person approaching, take still photos and zoom in and out. The very best security available. I hated this place already.

The car pulled up at the front door which opened immediately to reveal a short, thin lady with neatly cropped grey hair wearing a mid length pleated skirt and crisp white blouse. She looked as though she had just finished playing golf or making the cricket tea, the very image of a genteel lady. Not as old as her clothes would imply, she stood in the doorway and waited to find out who her unknown visitors might be. Seeing us through the CCTV cameras as they alerted her to our presence, she would have been mystified to know who had the code the let themselves in.

Danny was first out of the car at the far side, he checked the outside of the house and the entrance, then looked both ways to see what was either side, through the garden. When he was happy, he knocked on the window of the car and I got out on the side closest to the waiting figure.

"Mrs Fairfield?" I asked, walking towards the front door and extending a hand to greet the lady now standing under the giant portico.

"Yes" she said sternly, "what can I do for you?" declining the hand and looking past me to the car as another figure was emerging. Danny was helping Susie out, looking either side for any signs that things were not right, ready to bundle her back in and tell the driver to take off. Susie's mother watched her, wondering who this stick and bone creature was, whispily floating out of the car with the help of the young man next to her. Susie was close to hysteria, her hands shook uncontrollably. She could barely turn to face her poor mother, still blissfully unaware of the earth shattering news that was about to be broken to her. Danny turned her around and held an arm under her elbow to hold her steady and guide her home.

Seconds passed as Susie's mother watched her walk closer, looking her up and down, still not registering. It was only when she stood in front of her, Susie could eventually bear to turn her face into her mother's and their eyes met properly that her mother saw the gaunt, haunted expression and recognised it as her own. Susie looked nearer forty than twenty, even with the two jumpers her frame was withered, not the healthy young teenager that went off to Ireland only ten months before. Her mother tried to believe that this wasn't her child, they had made a mistake, it couldn't be her, but as her eyes crossed the landmarks of her daughter's face, the pain of what she had been through was reflected in her eyes. She walked over to throw her arms around the girl and hug her for the first time.

I shepherded them, still entwined, into the house. Danny went ahead to check the rooms and the driver moved the car round the side of the house, out of view. We went into the main foyer of the house, down a wide corridor to the double doors at the end. They opened up to a lovely bright fresh yellow and white room with glass doors at the back leading straight to a terrace.

Susie sat down with her mother on one of the large settees and they both cried. Some tears of fear, some joy and relief and some just because they needed to come out. Her mother held her in her arms, Susie's head on her chest as she hugged her tightly, gently rocking as a mother does when cradling her babies to comfort them at bedtime. She patted Susie's back very softly, in time with the rhythmic side to side motion of the rocking, trying to calm her and stop the tears that never seemed to fade.

Susie sobbed and sobbed, soaking her mother's cotton blouse and silk scarf. In turn, her mother's tears streamed down her face and off the end of her nose into Susie's hair and onto her clothes. The turmoil of the last few weeks was over. The girl's emotions came flooding out, she had held up to everything that had been thrown at her and now she was home and safe at last. With each sob she shook herself free of the tension of what she had seen and done. Free from the drugs, the men who had kidnapped her and the danger she had been in until she walked back into the family home that had protected her for so long.

I looked on at the reunited couple. Susie apologised again and again, I felt she realised how foolish she had been. I also knew she would give up the safe arms of her mother right now if she could get a hit of heroin to calm her nerves. The regret poured over Susie like her mother's tears, down her neck, wetting her collar. Her body was trying to curl up on her mother's lap as she did when she was little and her father was away at work for the night, when she was allowed to stay up to keep her mother company.

Fear, shame, guilt, regret, love, all appeared in waves for the whole room to see. I thought about what I could say to her poor mother, who had no idea of what her daughter had endured. All Susie could say was "I'm sorry" to which her mother had no reply. She had no idea what her daughter had been through and no clue why she should apologise, she just hugged her tighter and brushed the tears from her hair with her hand.

Danny and I left them there for a while, waiting across the large reception room for the ladies to be composed enough that they could listen to the whole story. It was important that they knew the situation fully. We left them to run their course and did not get in the way.

A shrill ping from behind a pair of shuttered yellow doors in the far corner of the reception room made Danny and I turn with curiosity at the noise. The women were too absorbed to acknowledge our puzzled looks, so we opened the doors to find another small room, dimly lit with the far wall covered in CCTV monitors, all showing different views in and around the house.

The control desk commanded a view of each screen as well as the PC which controlled each item of high tech security. The ping was the camera at the front gate indicating that it was following a car coming slowly up the drive of the house with an on screen display telling us that access had been granted via a remote in car device. This was someone who could let themselves in and out as they pleased, someone with the keys to the castle. The master of the house had arrived.

"Are you expecting your husband home, Mrs Fairfield?" I asked, breaking them off as gently as I could from their bittersweet reunion.

"Oh, well," she said, glancing in to the control room, "that's his car but I wasn't expecting him so early. Come on" she raised Susie's chin in her hand "let's sort ourselves out for your father," wiping the tear streaks away with a tissue from both their faces. She held Susie's face and smiled into her eyes.

"I'm glad you're home," she said, very gently.

"I love you, Mum," Susie whispered along with another apology. Danny and I stood in defensive positions between the two ladies and the door of the room. Our guns were not drawn, but at the ready just in case this was another subterfuge and the car had a different unexpected visitor.

Dr Brian Fairfield was a very tall man, about six feet four at his full height, but all the years leaning over a laboratory bench had left him with a permanent stoop, his back caved and rounded at the top, leaving him looking like a man on stilts craning over to talk to a child. He bustled into the room as the owner of this domain. He had no interest in the two people closest to him, we were merely in the way on his route to his family. He strode past us both and focussed all of his attention on the figures standing beside the great hearth at the other side of the room.

Without a word he threw down his briefcase and overcoat and moved up to hug his little girl, pushing out his arm to combine his wife into the embrace and pulling them close to squeeze all three together back into one family unit. We turned away slightly so that they could have their moment privately.

"Are you OK" Brian asked his daughter, "I'm fine now I'm home," she replied, and buried her face into his lapels. Dr Fairfield turned to us and coldly asked, "She's clean now?" His demeanour was contrite and business like. We looked at one another, I answered, "She's on some medication to help her and the doctor will be here any minute to check how she's doing." The master of the house turned away again without a response for us interlopers. The little unit kissed and hugged some more. Susie was very much relieved, she composed herself enough to remember her manners.

"Oh, I'm sorry, I haven't introduced you . . ." she walked over to me and Danny, "these are the two that saved me and escorted me home, they got the doctors to help me and have kept me safe and well all week . . . I owe them everything." More tears welled up as she recalled what we had done for her.

The parents looked at us properly for the first time as a dawning realisation came upon them that we were not bringing her home from an illness but something rather bigger had happened to their daughter. I needed to explain.

"We are from your employers, Dr Fairfield. We have brought Susie home to keep her safe, but she has had quite a couple of weeks and will need some more rest." I slowly told them the story from the beginning; about the drug addiction, the arms agents, Tunisian terrorists, the kidnap and subsequent rescue and the Dublin squat, sparing them only the most shocking details. Now they knew everything. I could see the weight lifted from Susie in a vast release of pressure. She must have dreaded what her family would say and what they would think of her, but now it was all out there she looked strangely at peace and stronger than I had yet seen her.

I explained that our doctor would call on Susie regularly until she was fully rehabilitated. She was still at risk from the addiction and would need the support of her family to make it through, which they both duly pledged. The air hung heavy with the silence that followed while the parents looked at their daughter, marvelling about how lucky they were to have her standing in front of them right now.

Dr Fairfield had been in the secrets business for a long time, his cynical side would know that Turtle and his governors would have only acted to save their own secrets, but he seemed to warm to us. The duty of care we had shown his daughter and the lengths gone to for her protection must have counted for something and his distant manner appeared to come forward a step. The gate buzzer sounded to indicate a visitor. Dr Fairfield went into the Control Room and spoke to our doctor, waiting at the gate, who had come to see Susie. The cameras followed his car up the long drive and Danny met him at the front door. He briefed the doctor on everything that had happened since he had last seen Susie then introduced him to her parents. The doctor asked for a little privacy to examine her and the two ladies went upstairs into Susie's old bedroom to talk alone.

I took the opportunity to question the scientist about his work, "What can you tell us about the current product you have developed," I asked directly, "Nothing" was the response, "Its all classified, way above your grade. You will have to speak to your men in high places if you want any of that information," his jaw snapped shut as he finished his sentence. The distance between us pushing back into the conversation.

"All we need to know is the launch date, Dr Fairfield. That's what they wanted, the men who took Susie. They are planning something and we need to stop them. We can only keep her safe if we know their timescale. We know about the AnTTS with multiple capabilities, all we need is the launch date."

"That's all anyone wants," he muttered under his breath. His fingers drummed on his knees as he thought about the question long and hard, "You leave me with little choice," he seemed to have come to a decision, "We're launching to the Cabinet on Friday. There is a venue for the unveiling and we will have a demonstration of some of the capabilities." So that's what all the fuss was about, Friday.

"Where?" I asked, "No idea," he replied, "I just have to get on a bus when they tell me and it will take me where it needs to go. I get off and do my bit wherever I end up. I have already packed the demonstration AnTTS ready for the launch, along with spares if necessary. They are being kept at a secure site so they can't be interfered with. Top Security all round and I can tell you no more than that," his last word on the matter. We were a little further on, at least.

"Who else knows about the demonstration?" I pushed him for more details.

"Only the cabinet. Even their secretaries don't know, they each have a different appointment in their diaries but they will all meet in the same place. The various drivers won't be told what they are doing, just to deliver them to an address at a specific time. That's usually how its done." He looked down at the floor as he spoke, he was tired and distracted.

"I really would like to see to my daughter now, if you don't mind?" he asked, standing up to show us to the door. I felt as though we were being hastened away, without a word of thanks that a doting father would bestow on his daughter's liberators. An uneasy feeling alerted my suspicions. Something was nagging at me, "Of course, Dr Fairfield, we will leave you in peace. Here are my contact details and where we are staying, call if you need anything. Please ensure Susie gets some rest tonight and we'll come back to check on her tomorrow." I smiled at the scientist and turned away before he could object to our calling back. Danny looked at me as we left but said nothing – nobody had said anything to him about coming back the next day, I know, but I knew we needed to return.

As the car swept back down the hill and through the iron gates, Danny turned to say something but I was deep in thought and not listening. I hadn't enjoyed the unease in the house and was replaying events from the afternoon in my head to try and single out what had disturbed me. I wasn't sure. I needed to sound it out with Turtle. Danny recognised I didn't want to be disturbed and thankfully kept his silence so I could think.

At the hotel I made the usual checks and called in, putting the gadget on speaker-phone so that Danny could listen and interject.

"How was Dr Fairfield?" Turtle asked once we had reported all the details in order, "was he very upset at the news?"

"Yes, sort of, but he was more happy that she was home. They said they hadn't known anything until we told them," I added.

"We hadn't wanted to worry him until you had her home. Every parent worries more when they can't see for themselves that their offspring are safe. We wanted to wait then he could come straight home and see her immediately without being frantic for too long." My own cynicism knew that they wouldn't want to disturb him from his important work until the very last minute. They needed him working and not at home comforting his wife and worrying about Susie. The unveiling of their ten years work did not want to wait for one little girl. One little girl that would quickly have been sacrificed to save it. I tried not to think about that bit as I inadvertently shot an accusing glance at Danny. We all had jobs to do and everyone we killed was someone's family somewhere. I tried harder not to think about it.

"That's it" said Danny suddenly, I looked at him, puzzled, "That's what?" I asked.

"That's what has been bothering me about Dr Fairfield. Remember how he virtually ignored us when he walked in? Well, what was the first question he asked when he turned round? He had no idea who we were and he was not supposed to know about what had happened to Susie, but what did he say to us?" I sat and thought, then it came back to me, "Well, yes, I suppose it doesn't make sense. Turtle, when he came in he ignored us then he turned round and asked if she was 'clean now'. If he didn't know what had happened to her, how did he know to ask if she were clean?"

"You were right to say you would go back tomorrow, Blossom, well done dear girl for trusting your instincts." Turtle was deep in thought.

"Do just that and talk to the two women to see what they know about his work. Find out what Susie told them about her habit and who else could have told him," he instructed.

We confirmed we understood what he was asking us to do and signed off. There was nothing that could be done until the following day. Danny looked at me. It was still early in the evening, we had all night to kill.

"What do you want to do tonight?" he asked, not looking at me directly, maybe so I didn't think he was pushing me to spend time with him.

"Gym" was all I replied with a smile.

I was looking forward to a good workout. When I came back from getting changed Danny was already waiting with a rolled up towel round his neck.

"What's with the towel, are you usually a bit sweaty?" I teased. He smiled and unrolled it on to the bed to reveal a small gauge handgun in the centre, "Don't like to be caught out," he said, rolling the gun back into the towel.

"Neither do I," I replied and hoisted the three quarter leg pants to show him the leg holster with my little Glock Supercompact in it.

"Looks like we're all ready."

Danny was super fit and a little bit cocky about going to the gym. We warmed up in different areas but came together the start our routines in earnest. I joined Danny on the next treadmill as the power began to go up and the breathing get harder.

I turned up the pace and noticed Danny did the same after a short while. The pace was easy just yet so I turned up the speed on my machine to push a little harder. Within seconds Danny turned his up a speed higher. I had to stifle a giggle, he was trying to beat me. Well, if he wanted to do that, he was going to have to work a lot harder. I knew he would surpass me eventually but heaven forbid he thought it might be this easy.

I turned the machine up as far as I could manage; I could stand the pace at about the 20 mark so cranked it straight up and ran just about flat out. Danny took up the sport and pushed his machine up to the same level, the pounding of our feet in the empty gym resounding off the walls. The wump wump wump hitting the black matting of the machines grew heavier as we ran faster. The machines churned the never ending rubber belt round and our feet hammered along, individually at first but little by little our pace combined until we ran in time with one another. Our bodies were synchronised, beating the floor in time together.

We ran like this for minute after minute, neither wanting to be the first to need to stop. I was feeling the pain, after fifteen minutes or so at the frantic pace I knew I was done. My legs were turning to jelly, my lungs burned to burst. I was determined to take him to another five minutes, "Keep pushing, keep pushing, just one more minute", I kept myself going as I could hear his breath, rapid and blowing next to me in his effort to do the same.

I heaved myself on but at the twenty minute mark I could take no more, I stopped the machine and pretended to stretch again as I caught my breath. I couldn't admit I was tired, trying to control my breathing so I didn't seem to be gasping as much while I bent and stretched. It felt good to stop until I realised that Danny was still going. I thought he would have finished not long after me, but he was clearly fitter than I had imagined. He stayed on the treadmill while I cooled down my muscles then hopped off, smiling, "Well that's a good warm up," he moved straight on to the rowing machine. My heart sank.

Not to be beaten, I had to jump on too and tied my feet into the next rower in line.

"Fancy a race?" he asked, the dimple darting out as he teased me to accept the challenge. I couldn't resist, his smile egged me on, if only to spend more time with him.

"OK" I let my own smile slip out, "but you need to give me a head start." He was still up for the 2km race so conceded. His confidence gave me a little shot of excitement that reminded me of the massive crush that was only just buried beneath my stony surface. I tried not to imagine my lips pressing lightly against his face and neck, the sweat rolling down making me wonder what it would taste like as it disappeared into the tight vest. I licked my lips and looked away.

"Thirty seconds, that's all I'll give you."

I jolted back to the challenge ahead. Now was my chance to show the boyish upstart. I might not beat him but I would push him hard.

"When you're ready," he said, still smiling. I didn't care how pointless the race was, I would bust a gut to beat him.

I pulled back on the handle and the timer started to run. The distance clicked down as I pulled harder and harder on the handle that turned the heavy flywheel just past my feet. As the distance ran down, the timer moved on and when it got to thirty seconds Danny heaved on the machine and his timer started to move. His pace was so terrific I thought he would never be able to keep it up. I was calculating in my head how fast I needed to go as I pulled, increasing my pace as I felt more comfortable.

When I got to 1km left I looked over at Danny's display, he was moving up on me, fast. I was going to finish at eight and a half minutes, my calculations revealed he would finish at eight minutes. I had to go faster. I gasped one large breath and heaved hard on the handle, pulling it all the way up my body and stretching my aching legs to maximise each stroke. The excitement of the challenge made me want to giggle, I was trying so hard, wanting to win so badly. I looked across at Danny's display, I felt like screaming, but the race went on. He had almost caught me up.

My hands hurt form the rough wooden grip. My arms and legs ached from the exertion. The harder I pulled, my lungs burned more and I urged myself on to pull faster and faster. The seat underneath me hammered into the stop on the sliding rail and my hands came up to my chin as I tried to extend each stroke as far as I could. My stomach muscles contracted and brought my back upright to ease the tension on the handle and do it all again and again. The metres counted down. My body cried out for me to stop. I would not give in. I pushed harder to go faster still.

The sweat poured from us as we toiled at our machines. The displays clicked down, too slowly for both of us, we were both in agony now, puffing and grunting at our machines. Last few metres. Danny's face was contorted, his eyes screwed and a wild grimace on his lips, his teeth bared with the exertion. The race had turned into a battle of wills, My arms and legs screamed at me. I couldn't stop, not until I'd finished. I looked over at his display, he was ahead now and almost there, one hundred metres to go.

One last fling at the machines, trying to yank the handles out of their restraints as we laid horizontal in our efforts to maximise the strokes. Raw power won out and Danny finished, he let go of the grip and it flew back and hit the end of the flywheel with a loud clatter as soon as his machine beeped to tell him he'd done it. By the time his handle dropped my machine beeped as well and I was done. I was beaten. I sat with my legs still in the straps, my lungs fighting for air, sweat pouring from my head and back, streaming down my face.

"Well done," I said, "you win," and offered him my hand in congratulation. Yes, I was competitive but not a sore loser.

"I win?" he shook my offered hand, "You did it in less than eight minutes, that's fantastic, most men can't do that" he said, gasping, smiling, "Well done, I've never known a woman do less than eight minutes fifteen."

"Oh, so you know that you'd be OK with the thirty second lead then?" I accused, but pleased with the acknowledgement of my achievement.

"No, no," he defended himself, "I've never done faster than seven minutes forty before. You pushed me so hard, I thought you were going to beat me."

I didn't win, but he thought I might, that would do for me.

"What shall we do now?" he asked, still panting, looking intently at me, his eyes trained on my hot sweaty face with joy, a slight raise in the eyebrows, a flirtatious giggle in his eyes. I smiled back at him truly for the first time. We were alone in the gym, just the two heaving bodies smiling at one another. I slipped my feet out of my trainers, pulled at the tie chords on my jogging bottoms and let them fall to the floor. Danny watched me slowly removing my clothes. I rolled off my socks, looking at him as his eyes followed my movements, enraptured with the display as I intended. I put my leg holster into my trainers and removed my T-shirt, revealing the bikini underneath. I threw the last of my clothes on the floor then dived into the pool to cool off.

Chapter 10

We returned to the twin room we were sharing for the sake of a cover. With gentleman Danny in the room I didn't need to worry about unwanted attention in the night. Although the temptation was great, and I knew the thought had kindled in his mind when I was undressing after our workout, our professionalism was paramount here. Success could not be compromised and part of the competition between us was about who could be the best agent. That meant not succumbing to any distractions, no matter how interesting they may seem. It was getting late now, after everything we had been through over the last 24 hours we were both in need of an early night. I opted for the first shower. I wrapped my little gun in a small towel and left it to hand in the sink while the shower warmed up. Always a little insurance policy, just in case.

The heat of the water felt good against my skin after the cool swimming pool and hard labours in the gym. The water splashed down my body and hit the shower tray, the noise was like a waterfall as I plunged my head under the spray. I broke free of the jet as a bump in the next room put my body into alert. My heart rattled the inside of my chest with an extra large hit of adrenalin. Another bump and a slight crash. I felt the floor move as well this time. My dark animal pulsed inside me as I crept out of the shower.

I picked the gun out of the sink, unwrapping it from the towel quietly, drying my hands and face. I left the shower running to cover any noise as I moved forward to listen intently at the door.

There were voices in the room. Someone else was there apart from Danny. One more bump, I tried to gauge from the vibrations from the floor how many people were in there and where they were. There were two people talking and neither of them were Danny. I carefully cocked the weapon, muffled by the towel which I then wrapped around myself just in case I was mistaken and about to burst naked into the porter with room service.

I tensed against the door. It wasn't locked so there would be no click to give me away as I ran my hand over the handle, thinking about how it opened, which way to turn it, whether the door creaked or not. All this went through my head in fractions of a second, my nerves electrified, waiting for the right moment to attack. I grasped the handle with my left hand, allowing my right to grip the gun steadily at the opening as I turned the handle gently but firmly. The latch slipped back, the door opened towards me. My eyes were unblinking, waiting for the scene to unfold. I looked through the gap and saw two men, both with guns drawn, standing over a figure on the floor between the twin beds. It was Danny, blood pouring through his hair from a gash on his head.

They were asking him about me, where was I, which room number, but he was laid dumb on the floor, hence the bumping as they kicked and beat him to make him talk. Their accents were Dutch, that meant one thing, mercenaries. Guns for hire rather than officers or agents themselves, they would have no loyalties, working only for the highest bidder. They would have been told to pick up a pair of agents or dispose of them, whichever they could manage. The money to pick them up would be more due to the increased advantage in being able to interrogate them, but they would be paid for bodies as well if we proved too much trouble to bring in alive. I had been approached many times for this kind of service but had always declined the dirty business. I despised these classless, honourless ronin.

The mischievous part of me wanted to stand and listen to see how far Danny would go to protect me – just to see. Would he give me away or suffer in silence? He had been through interrogation training, just like I had, but the reality of the pain was always different to the exercise.

Through the tiny crack in the doorway I could see the two men clearly. The largest man was doing the beating while the smaller one in a slightly more expensive suit was asking the questions. They both had guns, which made things difficult for me. I would not be able to cover them both at the same time as they were too far apart. Danny was suffering, I couldn't afford to wait. I would have to shoot them both before they realised I was there.

I needed to know who they were working for. One of them would need to be left alive. Drop one, take one, bear that in mind, Blossom, don't kill them both. A feeling of giddy excitement came over me as I gripped my trusty little pistol, removed the safety and got ready to move. Focus, breathe, hand on the door, OK let's go.

In one movement the door opened fully. I dropped to the floor on a bended knee, firing one shot in the chest of the big man as I went down. He stood for a partial second before his knees buckled and he fell down directly on top of Danny. I was pleased, Danny was now covered from any danger if a proper fire-fight materialised. By the time the pleasing drop of the big man was making the passion of my aggression smile inside, I had aimed again. My next shot struck the smaller man in the shoulder, passing in through the shoulder blade and exiting via the collar bone, narrowly missing the main arteries of his neck. A spurt of claret passed in front of his shocked face. He dropped his gun and collapsed on the floor. I was on him in a second, gun at his temple so he could see it.

He gurned with the pain in his shoulder and neck. He was losing blood fast from the open wounds. I pulled off my towel and shoved it into the gaping holes to stem the blood on both sides of his body. I needed him alive. With the gun at his head I warned him to keep quiet. His eyes screwed shut at the agony but he nodded that he understood and his groans were stifled into the towel, he took a deep breath to control the pain and tried to settle down as the stabbing sensation ran down his arm and back. I pressed hard on both wounds to try and arrest the flow. The relief of dominating the contact made me buoyant with success, allowing my arrogance to flow freely. I felt powerful and alive, my senses inflamed. This would subside to feelings of guilt and shame later on, but the feeling right now made me forget that for a moment.

I reached for my phone, one push dialled Turtle, "Man down, man down" I rushed into the mouthpiece, "Danny is injured, we have one assailant dead, another with GSW to the shoulder. I need a medic, clean up squad and recovery." I turned to the man who I was still sitting on as he slowly bled, "Is there anyone outside?" I asked, he nodded.

"Is it a car and driver?" he nodded again.

"I also need a driver and team to be picked up outside our hotel. The GSW can't be left so you will have to send someone else in. Can you confirm."

"Instructions confirmed and a team is on their way. Are you injured?"

"Negative, I'm fine but Danny has had a beating. I have the injured man's mobile and am sending you a recognition text now. Can you trace the number and get some info back to me."

"Got it. It's coming up now." Turtle put the number into the computer to trace the owner. The data flashed up instantly on the screen, giving his home address and ID photo.

"He's Dutch, came into the country yesterday, he must be working hard to have been on to you already. I am sending you a copy of the messages he has had in the last twenty four hours to Danny's phone. Leave this line open and go see if he needs help." Turtle's steady voice was welcome to my ears and I began to calm down a little, the adrenalin surge subsiding.

I'd already got off of the wounded Dutchman and propped him up against the end of the bed so he didn't bleed out. The hotel's flowery curtain tie back that matched the bedspreads made an excellent sling and it held his arm where he could do no further damage until the medic arrived. I tied the other arm to the leg of the bed with the flex from the table lamp then checked him for any other weapons to make sure he wasn't going to be any further trouble.

I turned the dead man over and rolled him off Danny's back. Danny hadn't moved. I worriedly checked his breathing and tried to establish if he was conscious. There was a long cut to the back of his head where they had attacked him as they entered the room. I could find no other injuries but he still hadn't moved. Urgently now I pinched his earlobe and he flinched to get away. Relief flooded in to replace the adrenalin in my veins, he was conscious.

I spoke to him gently to rouse him, lifting him softly. His hands grabbed his ribs instinctively to support them as he tried to get up. They had kicked and beaten him with the table lamp, homing in on the ribs to punish him and cause maximum damage. I gave the commentary to Turtle on the phone as I picked him up and laid him on the bed. Turtle updated me on our backup, "We have a paramedic on the way and an ambulance for the one who won't be writing home to his mother. The clean up team is half an hour away, can you manage til then?" Turtle was calm under pressure and a steadying voice in the madness. He acted as if all this was perfectly normal and he would send in whatever aid we needed as it arose.

Danny's phone beeped several times as the messages from Turtle came in one by one. He searched for the handset but retracted his reach as the pain of his ribs shot through him.

"Leave it for now," I said, urging him to rest, "we'll deal with that later." I checked his pupils for signs of a concussion but they reacted normally to the light being thrown into them. He blinked and rubbed his eyes, coughing with the exertion and being stung by the pain in his chest. Now he was awake and as I brushed back his hair and wiped his face of the blood, the perma-grin appeared and he smiled a big fat smile for my attention. He looked so handsome, even with the injuries to his face. His eyes were slightly bloodshot, but they still looked soft and warm towards me as I gazed down into them, "What are you so happy about?" I questioned the grin and the dopey expression.

"It's you," he said, dreamily, "you're so lovely," he purred as if trying to lull me into his fuzziness. I ran a hand over his cheek, he was so sweet.

"Hmmm . . . am I unconscious and having a really great dream . . . . or are you actually on my bed with me . . . naked?" he dreamily asked.

Shocked, I looked down at myself, I had completely forgotten that I had pulled the towel off and used it elsewhere. Bastard, he was taking the piss again. His stupid smile confirmed it, I threw a pillow over his face and dashed for the bathroom to drag out my clothes. No time for underwear, I threw on what I had and slipped on some shoes.

Minutes passed until Turtle piped up again, "The medic is only two minutes away, can you get them access downstairs round the back, there's a fire door. The local police have picked up the driver of the car outside and have taken him away so there should be no problem. Passcode is Oysters." I gave Danny his weapon back then sat him up in bed so he could guard our captive while I took both my guns and went down the back stair case to the fire exit at the bottom. I listened carefully then eased the door open just as an unmarked car turned into the rear car park. A rotund black woman with a large paramedic bag stepped out into the light from the open doorway. A flash of an ID badge and the mention of Oysters, I ushered the lady up the two flights of stairs back to our room. I untied the Dutchman and helped him on to the bed so that the paramedic could see properly to his injuries.

He had lost a lot of blood so the cheerful Teresa set up a drip to get some fluids into him, stop the shock and allow him to stabilise before moving him too far. I bustled round the room packing our things and getting ready for the clean up team. Teresa chatted casually to her patient as she applied the dressings and bandages, with a proper sling to immobilise the shattered shoulder so she could get it fixed up nicely once they were in the military hospital. He moaned and groaned as she manipulated him into his support, but she seemed to be used to uncooperative guests, "Its OK, Princess, I've got a lovely carriage awaiting you downstairs, we'll soon have you fixed up. I've got some top class medicine in there for you as well, so no more moaning, Cup Cake, or you'll be getting more than one blast tonight." Her manner was disarming and her teeth flashed as her bright smile lit up the room. I had a little word with the injured man while he was waiting for his ride, making sure the spirit of generosity I had shown him was reciprocated and he behaved on his ride back with Teresa.

"Ambulance is outside," said Turtle, I went back down to guide them into the place. The room was busy now so Teresa asked if they could take the injured man out first while she checked Danny over.

"It's OK," I said as Teresa approached him on the bed, "he's staying with me, he just needs his ribs looking at."

"With this one, Honey, I'll look at whatever you like," and Teresa smiled her enormous grin at Danny, "Hello darlin', I know we've only just met but I'd like to run my hands all over your chest, if that's OK," she lifted his shirt and laughed.

"Funny," said Danny, "I was about to say the same to you." Teresa did her best to look shocked at the forwardness of this handsome young lad.

"Now then, Sweet'art, I might just take you up on that later," she giggled charmingly.

I tried to feign only moderate interest in the contents of Danny's shirt as I watched the examination as nonchalantly as I could from the other bed. Teresa progressed along his torso with her hands, appreciatively rubbing, pressing and patting each toned contour as she went. Once she had finished rubbing her hands all over the perfect physique she looked up at him and sighed, "Well that was nice but now I'd better get on with my medical examination." Danny was in agony, laughing more because he knew he wasn't supposed to. Teresa said he was badly bruised but not broken and although she did offer, while fluttering her eyelashes at him, to take him away for the night for close observations and a stamina test, I declined on his behalf and Teresa gave him some pain killers for the night, adding that he would be OK in a couple of days once the bruising had come out.

The ambulance men came back in to take the body of the dead man. They laid him out on the floor to bag him up. Teresa said her goodbyes, winking and waving with a tiny hand to Danny as she blew kisses through the doorway. The ambulance men gracelessly stuffed the large corpse into the body bag and I asked how they would get the trolley up the narrow stairwell.

"No chance," said one, "its too noisy to try and get the trolley up here, we have a much quieter method with dead men who have given our people a hard time." They hoisted the bag between them, carried it out of the room and down the corridor to the back stairs. I ran ahead and opened the door as they squeezed onto the tiny landing. I was marvelling at the prospect of them carrying it all the way down the stairs, but as soon as the landing door closed, they silently swung the bag between them and dropped it over the handrail after a 1, 2, 3. The body flopped to the ground and landed with a crump into the trolley mattress they had laid in the hallway, two flights below. The men slowly walked down the stairs, retrieved the body in the bag, popped it onto the waiting trolley and transported it into the ambulance. They waved up at me, standing awestruck on the landing, as they left the hotel and disappeared.

By the time all this excitement was over the other team had arrived. I helped Danny out of the room, taking our bags and leaving the clean up people already scrubbing the blood stains with a special solution that allowed it to be soaked into a pad for disposal, leaving no trace. They would scrub and clean, fix any broken ornaments, retrieve the bullet that had crashed through the man's shoulder then fill and paint any holes it made. In the morning, the room would look like any other. They would pack their suitcases with the material for disposal and make sure the room looked as it should.

We made our way down the stairs, out into the night where the car was waiting to take us to RAF Pershore, the nearest military base. The driver took the most circuitous route to ensure there were no further surprises.

I gave Danny his instructions for the night before allowing him to retire in the VIP suite in the officer's mess. He was to leave his door unlocked so that I could check on him regularly during the night due to his head injuries and he happily obeyed. My room was just down the corridor, I plonked my things down, got dressed and called my info in to Turtle. He gave me the OK to proceed, I picked up the local SF team and headed back out into the night.

As soon as I got back it was time to pad the few steps down the corridor in my bare feet to Danny's room. I put on a small light in the corner so that I could examine him properly. He was laid on one side of the double bed. He looked so calm and beautiful, his flat torso as well as other interesting lumps and bumps were outlined by the covers. I thought about the form underneath the covers and about slipping in at his side to feel the velvet skin next to mine, but checked out only what I had come in for. Pulse, breathing, eye dilation, all looked normal.

Like a hunter able to wake just before the dawn to track their prey, my body roused me three hours later. I had told myself that this was stag duty, my body would understand that and act accordingly, it didn't let me down. I made my way once more to the next room. I should have gone back to bed as I had promised myself, but I liked to look at his face, taking in every pleasing feature without the embarrassment of him knowing I was doing it. He hadn't managed a shower and I could smell his skin, bringing back memories of him reaching over me having just finished a workout in the Club. I licked my lips and caught myself thinking about how nice it would be to bend down and kiss his injured face better. I shook myself to stop it, admonishing myself for getting so excited at the mere smell of a man so close. It can't have been that long, surely. When I started to think of it, actually it had been a while, but this wasn't the time and I needed to concentrate on the work. Pull yourself together, girl.

I climbed on to the bed next to him and gently ran my fingers through his hair to locate the other wound. It was a swollen egg on his scalp with just a cut that had crusted over nicely to stop its bleeding. I would superglue it together in the morning once he had showered and washed the matted blood away. I laid quietly next to him, looking at his face and listening to him gently breathing. The long slow in, out, in made me relax and close my eyes.

It had been a long night, I opened my eyes to take in the scene, rousing myself from a very short but deep sleep. I blinked, the little light was still on in the corner of the room but something was different. I moved my head to the side and there was the vision of Danny laid in front of me. He had turned over to face me and was looking at me as I woke, realising where I was and that it was morning. I had stayed there all night.

I felt my face flare red. I'd had carnal thoughts about him last night and now I had woken up in his bed, him looking at me with that stupid grin on his face. It was a lovely sight to wake to but I couldn't be caught out. I virtually jumped off the bed, "Oh, I got fed up with walking up and down the corridor, so I thought I would stay here instead. That's alright isn't it?" my tone challenged him, but it was rhetorical and he didn't have chance to answer. His smile didn't last long as he remembered last night. He groaned, shaking his head as I was about to flounce out.

"Are you alright?" I came back a few steps, "Yes, I'm fine, I am just so sorry about last night," he confessed, "they burst straight in while my back was turned. By the time I turned round they had their guns on me and the big one crashed something into the back of my head."

"Occupational hazard," I offered, feeling where he was coming from.

"It could happen to any one of us. We're all at risk, it happens all the time. Don't worry." It could have been me standing there as they entered the room – would I have fared any better? I wasn't sure.

I came back towards the bed and looked intently into his eyes, "I would have been in the same predicament if I hadn't opted for a shower so early. Don't worry. As long as you're alright, that's what matters. We won last night, its fine."

Dan's competitive nature made him feel that he had failed. I would feel the same way, knowing I'd had to be rescued after a beating.

"Its not just that," he said, looking shame faced, his sheepish demeanour was of definite concern, "We should have been able to take the two Dutchmen and the people they were working for instead of having to nursemaid me out of there and back here to safety." His head hung low, he had just reminded me how stupid he was, but that was something I could help him with.

He seemed so shy and nervous, my proud heart went out to the sad figure on the bed. I knew just how to cure this particular problem.

"Well, you had better come with me and we'll see just how badly we did . . ." I trotted, pleased with myself, back towards the door, smiling, and beckoning for him to follow. Danny threw back the covers and got up a little stiffly with his bruised ribs. I instinctively took a step to help him as he stood up, then turned around swiftly as I realised he was naked. If only I'd known that last night. The regret of a missed opportunity grazed across my conscience.

"Would you like to put something on first" I offered, trying not to look or leave my mouth open for too long. Danny had a little giggle to himself and pulled on a pair of shorts and a T-shirt. Now we were even, we had both seen each other naked.

I led him out across the wide corridor, past my room to the door at the end. I punched in the key code to unlock the door then turned with my hand on the big brass door handle and smiled at him as I opened the door. Inside, the room had no luxurious furniture like ours, just three bare wooden chairs in the centre of the room. Two men wearing grey suits and hessian bags over their heads sat lashed to their chairs to inhibit their escape. White noise played loudly from the stereo in the corner. I was still smiling as the realisation dawned on Danny's face that these two men must be the ones who had ordered our demise the previous night.

He looked at me, mystified, I wore the smile that I very rarely exposed to him. We stood close together in the doorway, I looked at his lips, then into his eyes. For a second we connected, engaged completely with one another. Neither of us said anything but my heart seemed to bubble with excitement, for that extra long second I stood, thinking what I would do if he breached the small gap between us to plant a kiss on the impatient lips that waited and waited for him to move. Would I stop him this time? I wasn't sure now. The warmth he had created inside me made me feel unprofessional, but my lust for the beautiful man clouded over me again. He had waited too long, the moment passed, I blinked to disengage from him and he shuffled his bare feet on the corridor. I was only half glad he had decided not to make things awkward.

I closed the door again and padded back to his room to explain. Danny didn't know which question to ask first. I sat on the bed and he came over as I started to explain.

"We picked them up just after midnight. I went through the Dutchman's phone for the message telling him where he was supposed to meet his employers. It said they were at the Brubake Hotel in room 214. From there we knew exactly what the plan was. I sent the men in at the room next door, 216, where they were actually staying and picked them up while they waited for me and you to be delivered. They were bagged up and brought straight out into the car. I never even lifted a finger," I laughed.

"The team will soften them up for a while then start the questioning around lunchtime, so you see, we did do a good job and there was no detriment to having you here instead of there." I summed up, pleased to put him out of his misery. It had all worked out fine and I wanted him to know it. Danny looked at me, taking in the information and processing it.

"But how did you know they would be in the room next door instead of the room the Dutchman gave you?"

"That's the easy bit – we heard that agents selling black market weapons were using room 214 in that hotel so I bugged the room myself eighteen months ago. After a while they stopped checking for devices and that's when we started using it intermittently. We could listen in to their activities and it was clear that they weren't actually staying in the room but were close by. We had a breakthrough when we heard them actually on the phone telling the contact they were meeting where to come. It meant that as soon as they answered the phone they could gain access to the room. A little more digging and we found they had leased the room next door as well. When he said the name of the hotel, we knew which room to hit, rather than the dummy one. If we'd have gone into 214 they would have heard us and broken out while we licked our wounds and they wouldn't have used the room again." I sat back, very pleased with myself and the effect I'd had on Danny's face.

The list of captured terrorist agents was mounting up. We needed to be careful, we would be drawing a lot of attention within our secret community. We had identified and eliminated a series of links in the chain, with more to come. My childish delight at having beaten someone in the game seemed to amuse Danny. He said nothing but nodded his head in appreciation. I needed nothing else.

Chapter 11

Once we'd had breakfast and Danny had been examined by a somewhat less frisky doctor from the RAF Pershore military hospital, we were back in his room to talk through the day ahead. There was still business to attend to at the Fairfield house. I had a feeling that something was not quite right. How much did Dr Fairfield know about his daughter's drug problem?

We climbed into the waiting car to travel back to the beautiful Malvern house. Each of us travelled with our own thoughts. I thought that Danny looked like a chastened child, still smarting from the errors of the night before. I was hoping he wasn't feeling bad about me going out on my own and completing my own little mission. He had taken quite a beating to protect me instead of coughing up at the first opportunity. I tried not to think of how much I had enjoyed my role as nurse and the sight of him as he got out of bed that morning. The recollection made me blush, looking furtively in his direction.

We had no need to punch in the code today, as we drew up at the steel lined gap in the high wall the gates pulled back as the car slowed down outside. We were right on time and the inmates expected us. Mrs Fairfield stood once again in the doorway, smiling in greeting this time we approached, quite different from the unwelcome we'd received the day before.

"I'm glad you're here," she said, "the doctor is already upstairs so you can get his verdict as he comes back down." We stepped into the house at the lady's bidding, welcoming us in as old friends. We were her daughter's saviours, now here as guardian angels.

"Can I get tea for you," she asked, eager to mother us as most women do. I could see she paid particular attention to the boyish Danny.

"That would be lovely," said Danny. Ever the gentleman, I thought, knowing that the motherly old woman would love his innocent looking charms. If only she had seen him get out of bed this morning, there was nothing boyish about that. I smiled to myself at the memory.

Mrs Fairfield invited us to sit down in the large reception room while she busied herself with the tea things and home made biscuits on doilies. When she finally sat down, I asked how Susie had spent the night, "Fairly well, I think, your doctor gave her something. She went to bed early and slept until late this morning. Its probably what she needed, a good sleep. She always slept herself better when she was little and she was poorly." Mrs Fairfield poured the tea for each of us and an extra cup for the doctor, fussing over her guests as she talked, insisting on us having plenty of biscuits. I watched the poor woman who'd had a bomb dropped on her yesterday comparing the serious addiction of her daughter's to a cold she had as a child. I realised just how innocent this woman was at what had been occurring and a part of me wished I had the same innocence, but after the life I'd led, I would never be the innocent again.

"And how are you and Dr Fairfield coping with the situation?" I asked, feeling that it hadn't fully sunk in to them yet, "Well, we're fine" she answered, fretting about the teapot getting cold and where had she put the cosy.

"Have you and Dr Fairfield managed to talk about things?" I pressed her, trying to keep to the point. Mrs Fairfield eyed me defiantly. Too much so, betraying the insecurity I had detected, "He's very busy at the moment. He has some very tight deadlines approaching at work that he needs to make the final arrangements for. I couldn't possibly distract him at the moment," her manner was defensive at first, then softened slightly as she perhaps recalled a promise made, "but he says once the bulk of the work is finished we can all go away and have a bit of peace together, which should be lovely," she smiled at us, trying not to show that the façade was cracking.

"Where is Dr Fairfield now?" I asked, seeing she was trying to be supportive of her absent husband but maybe did not agree with his current list of priorities.

"He's at work, of course. He is coming home to see what the doctor has to say and should be back any minute. I'm sure he'll be delighted to see you both are here to check she's alright."

Susie and the doctor came down the stairs after a thorough examination to check on how she was feeling. She looked more relaxed than I had previously seen her, the colour was returning to her once ashen face. The medication was still required as the addiction was not yet beaten, but she had made a good start and with some more help she was expected to make a full recovery.

Susie was glad to see her rescuers again and greeted us warmly to smiles all round. Danny slipped outside with the doctor to get the low down on how she really was while I made conversation with the ladies about how Susie was feeling and how she had slept and eaten. Danny asked the doctor if she had given up any extra information and he said that she was recovering well physically but mentally she needed a stable, relaxed environment so that she could get over what had happened. She had said nothing more of her weeks in Africa but if anything came up he would let us know. At that the front door opened and in walked Dr Fairfield. His brow was wrinkled and he stomped into the house as if he had little time for this inconvenience, needing to be somewhere else.

He stopped as he saw the two men talking in the hallway. He shifted his feet uneasily then continued towards them, pretending he was glad to be home.

"Good day, sirs," he addressed them cordially enough, "and how do you find my daughter today?"

"If you would care to come into the lounge, sir, I can tell you and your wife together," the doctor ushered them into the reception room and took up his tea cup as he talked reassuringly about her progress to date and what the doting parents needed to do now. He neglected to mention how anything she said to him would be written into the secret report that went to the Ministry so they could assess the risks to their work.

The doctor said he would call again in two days and reiterated his contact details if they should need anything. Mrs Fairfield gratefully showed him to the door and her husband offered to do the same for us. I sat back in my chair, eager to let him know we were not as willing to be moved. I was more suspicious at the attempt to get rid of us, just as I had been the day before. I picked up my tea cup and made myself comfortable, settling in for further discussions. I politely asked Susie to go upstairs with her mother so we could talk to her father. This unwanted obstruction was not lost on the master of the house.

When his family left the room Dr Fairfield became annoyed at the intrusion, how dare we order his family about in their own home. I stood up and gently slid my cup and saucer across the coffee table. Danny closed the door to the corridor and the room seemed suddenly very still and quiet. The faint tick of a carriage clock on the huge mantelpiece came to me as I focussed my attention and cleared my thoughts so I could tune in to every nuance from Dr Fairfield's answers to my questions. Or lack of them, "What are you working on at the moment, Dr?" I asked, studying his response.

"Something way above even your boss's pay grades," he retorted. So, it was going to be a hard question and answer session then.

"Why did you send your daughter to Ireland?" I probed, knowing full well that Susie had been desperate to break out but wanting his reaction.

"Send her? No, she wanted to go," the scientist explained, frustrated.

"We only allowed it because it was close enough not to have to travel too much but far enough that she might be out of reach of anyone who might recognise her." He was acting defensively but at least he was opening up, I needed to push him again.

"Didn't you think that she would be at risk over there? Its been a hotbed or terrorism for the last thirty years."

"No, no, you don't understand. We tried to keep her here but she threatened to go anyway. We thought southern Ireland would be safe enough, nobody would know her there. She would have gone somewhere out of our control if we hadn't let her go to Dublin."

"Why was she so desperate to leave home?" I asked, deliberately provoking.

"She wasn't desperate," he answered, indignant at the accusation, "she just wanted to do what everyone else her age was doing, studying at university, making friends and going out. Gaining some life experience. We wanted her to be happy but we were always worried about her over here so her movements were very restricted – just as ours are, but its different when you're young," he tapered off. He sunk into the chair as he pondered what else he could have done to save his daughter from the fate she had endured on his behalf. He was sweating and took out a white cotton handkerchief to mop his brow and dry his eyes as he composed himself to carry on.

I allowed him a moment. I sat back on the sofa to keep myself at his level, wanting to force some eye contact. I stared at Dr Fairfield until he reluctantly returned my steady gaze. Now for the final thrust.

"You knew about Susie's drug problem" I said quietly, watching his reaction. He closed his eyes and the proud head dropped, exaggerating the heavy stoop as the bony fingers strummed through his thinning grey hair. He sighed. I knew we had him and sat patiently now until he was ready to respond, hoping he wouldn't keep up the pretence any longer. I could hear his breathing, stifling the sobs that had control of him, he cleared his throat but did not look up as he spoke, "One of her friends called me a couple of weeks ago and said Susie was in a bad way and she was worried about her. She couldn't be more specific and I tried to call Susie several times but could never reach her. Someone always took a message, saying she was fine and she would call me back, but she never did. I have been frantic with worry but I couldn't bear to tell her mother, she would have been out of her mind by now. I was planning to go over and see her after this thing at work calms down in a week or so, I already have the holidays booked." He looked up, searching for a sign of trust and belief from me. He couldn't bear to talk about it any longer.

"So who did you think we were when we brought her home yesterday?" I asked, understanding the pressures of the chief scientist's work, his service was his sacrifice. His life not his own.

"I thought you were finally the police bringing her home to tell us she had been arrested on drugs charges or whatever she had been up to while she was away. You looked like a pair of officials."

I looked at Danny for any sign that he had any more questions, but he shook his head. The eminent civil servant conducted himself well. It was perfectly plausible for him to have kept this to himself. It was logical that he thought she had been brought home from Ireland after some sinful behaviour had landed her in trouble with the law.

His movements were so closely guarded that he could not have rushed off to Ireland without having to explain why and would not want his employers knowing about his daughter's addictions as a possible risk to his work or status. He would have to plan the visit wisely and a quick check once we were away from the house would confirm if the holidays and travel plan had indeed been booked already.

Satisfied that all our questions were answered, Danny and I stood up, shook the scientist's hand and bade him farewell. He was sitting, distraught, in the armchair. He barely looked up as we saw ourselves out. We needed to get back to the base where all the agents we had caught were being held to see what information could be gleaned to lead us to the terrorists. Turtle was trying to gain clearance for more information about the AnTTs to be released but it had to come from the Home Secretary himself. His PA was preparing the paperwork. Civil Service never moved that quickly.

We closed the door behind us and were walking back down the wide corridor towards the front door of the house when a beep from Danny's mobile made him take it out of his pocket to see the text message. I could see him scrolling through the messages. There appeared to be more than one waiting for him. I wondered if a poor forgotten girlfriend was back home waiting for a phone call and in his excitement he had neglected his duties. Maybe that's why he hadn't kissed me that morning. I hoisted my jealous nose into the air to pretend I didn't care about the messages, walking quickly towards the front door to escape the unwanted girlfriend reminders.

Danny walked more slowly behind, looking puzzled at the screen in his hand. He pushed button after button to interrogate the device then stopped dead as I pulled open the large front door and walked through to summon the car. Two steps outside, Danny swept up behind and yanked my collar to drag me back in, crouching on the floor and drawing his gun as I tried to regain my poise. I looked at him and he nodded through the door, I instinctively knew the look of the hunter and obeyed without question. I saw that Dark Dan was in possession of my pretty friend, immediately recognising his animal within him as I did my own when it took over my persona. I drew my little pistol even though at that moment I had no idea why.

I had no understanding of what was happening, just the hammering of my heart inside my chest, I looked at Dark Dan to follow his lead. He was covering the front door and looking outside for the danger he sensed. When I looked at him for an answer, he showed me the message on the phone sent from Turtle last night, it was a photo message displayed on his screen.

The picture was of the pair of us together, the background a large garden with a row of conifers and some beech trees overhanging a rockery down a slope. The message read 'Capture/termination notice. Both subjects.' The picture was startling. I looked out of the front door where I now crouched with the other spooked officer close to my side. There was no mistake, the view from the front door was the picture on the screen. The text had been copied by Turtle from the Dutchman's phone last night. The order that had been sent to pick us up or terminate us had been given via this message. I scrolled through the other messages which gave our names and the hotel we were staying in. Every detail our killers needed were on Dan's phone.

I turned and covered the firing angles inside the house as Danny covered outside. At once, I realised the depth of Danny's instinctive response – the picture was a still from this house's high tech CCTV system. I pushed the button on my phone to send an SOS to Turtle, slipping the mobile into my jacket pocket for it to ring and confirm he had the signal. I was kicking myself. For the second time in two days I was sending up the alarm. I would hear about this at my next training course – the barrack room banter from the guys would imply an inadequacy to manage on my own, "Needing help *again*, there, Blossom" would be their taunts until I kicked their arses in the shooting range and unarmed combat. This was not good.

Turtle duly rang back immediately, the phone answered for me, "I need another team and vehicles to extract the three Fairfield family members to a secure location separately. We have been compromised but we don't know who by yet, it could be any one of them or all three. We are not injured but we are treating as a security risk and have drawn our weapons. Danny and I are about to go back inside and detain the three suspects. Please confirm."

" . . . . Er, confirmed. The backup team is on their way, ETA is fifteen minutes. Two further cars are being dispatched and should arrive just after, carry on with the rest of the manoeuvre. Out." Turtle had hesitated at the beginning of the sentence. The detention of one of their leading scientists was obviously of great concern and he was confused at the security breach, but this was not the time for questions. He trusted his field agents and got on with the organisation of the extractions. He would already be half composing his letter of apology in his head for when he was hauled up for a huge cock-up, but it didn't stop him serving his duty as his agents told it to him right now.

Our own car screeched round the corner and the driver got out in defensive stance, he had received the SOS and heard the report to Turtle. I motioned for him to stay where he was and keep the engine running. Danny covered the stairs and the rest of the house as we moved together cautiously back to the reception room where Dr Fairfield had been sat.

I reached the room first and listened in at the door. No movement came from inside. Checking that Danny was behind me, I pushed down on the handle then silently rolled into the centre of the room, landing on one knee with my gun held out in front, pointing at the chair where the Doctor had been. It was empty. The Control Room doors were ajar. I motioned to Danny, who made his way over to the open doors. He flung them aside and brought the tip of his gun down swiftly to the base of the doctor's neck so he could feel the cold steel pressing against him. The doctor froze in the big control chair, the monitors scanning the grounds as he was watching for us to leave.

"How dare you," he started to object. He did enough to develop the weapons but had no idea about dodging them.

"Hold nice and still, Doctor," said Danny as he wheeled the big chair away from the desk so he could see the big man wasn't armed. After a brisk check the doctor was made to stand up. A beep on one of the monitors and it automatically zoomed in to a car that had pulled up at the gates, Turtle came back on the phone, clear for us all to hear, "You have one team at the gate, are you able to let them in?"

"Confirmed. Letting them in now" Danny clicked the mouse over the option on the screen to open the gate.

Danny shepherded Dr Fairfield out of the room then through the front door into our car. The driver jumped into his seat, waiting for instructions and keeping an eye on his latest fare. He pressed the button to raise the bullet proof glass screen between him and his captive, it quickly scrolled upwards as the back doors locked. The doctor was sealed in, held securely in his luxurious leather and walnut trimmed prison. The driver could see him from the surveillance monitor behind his dashboard but could hear nothing through the sound proofing. The old man had apparently flipped. He was agitated, squirming around on the rear seat and chatting away to himself. The sweat poured from him as he stared intently out of the window. The driver moved the car forward to allow the other one room to pull up behind.

I met the second team as they stopped outside the door. They set up position in the hallway while I briefed them on what they were doing. One suspect was in the car, the other two females were upstairs and not aware they were coming for them. Caution was required so that they were not unduly injured, they were only suspects at this point. The team were to extract them as quickly as possible and load them gently into separate cars. They could draw their weapons but only fire if fired upon, they needed to see a weapon clearly before they were allowed to shoot and were only allowed to wound, not kill.

Danny led one team quietly to the stairs to retrieve the two women. Suddenly a scream from outside the front door of the house made my stomach turn with the horror it emitted. Both teams filed back to the doorway, I peered through to investigate the terrible noise. Under the large portico the second driver was on the floor, dragging himself towards me, his left foot pouring smoke from the side. A strange stench of burnt plastic and flesh accompanied the vision. I rushed out to drag him inside then searched the front of the house to find who had shot him but could see nothing in the serene garden.

The team medic took off the shoe that was still smoking to look at the injured foot of the man sprawled on the hallway floor. The driver had to be stopped from screaming, his mouth muffled to hide his pain from the rest of the house. With the shoe off it was plain to see the extent of the damage. The side of his foot was missing at an angle that also displaced his last two toes, but there was no blood from the wound, only charred, melted skin covering the hole where his toes had been. The medic looked at him, at first thinking he had shot his own foot.

"Check his gun," he ordered the next man to him.

"Its clear," said the man, confused that his gun had not been discharged and no ammo was missing. None of them could understand what had made such a strange injury that could cauterise itself as it passed through with such ease. I heard the curious commotion and moved from my defence of the front door to have a closer look.

The strange wound was like none I had ever seen, the smell of the charred skin and bone where the toes had been cleanly severed sent the team members retching and moving away. I was used to field injuries and could stomach the sickening stench, although it was particularly bad. The wound was certainly unusual. I turned the foot over to look at the rough underside, the cooking of the skin at the tender points had left a series of burnt blister bubbles that looked like the seam of a weld. At this, I recalled a trade journal with pictures of some metal that had been burnt in a similar way. I looked at the shoe, it had been sliced straight through, taking the owner's toes with the hunk of leather and plastic. There was no gunshot, this was a laser cut.

Danny saw the tension return to my face. My body stiffened, I ordered the area in front of the door to be cleared. The teams retreated into the house as I peered outside to try and see what only I knew was there. The trade journal had said that a special white laser with acutely accurate cutting powers had been developed and was being used in the diamond industry. Chillingly, I also remembered that the lethal white blade was invisible to the naked eye. I had no chance of seeing where it was. An invisible knife that could cut through steel and diamond was waiting for us outside.

I reached into my handbag, still sitting in the hallway, and took out my compact. The fine dust would be ideal. I blew it in front of me as I walked slowly towards the car. Step by step I made my way, inching along, blowing the loose powder out in front of me to try and detect the deadly weapon. I stopped and stared at the dust as it danced and rose in the air. One gust from my lips scattered the fine powder into a cloud that burst into a column of tiny sparkles as the laser caught it and exploded the particles, super heating them to destruction in an instant. There it was.

I asked for the fruit bowl that was sat on the hall table. The large turned wooden dish with a thick base was passed through as I stood staring at the broken particles for fear if I turned away they would disappear. I put the heavy bowl on the floor and slid it over to the base of the shaft of light with a kick. As it passed through the bottom of the laser a stream of smoke came up and the two halves of the bowl peeled apart with a quick plume of flame that immediately died out. As I looked up to try to see where the source of the laser came from it suddenly stopped. The signal had been cut and the sparks disappeared. Someone had turned it off. The weapon had been armed, used and stopped as it was discovered. Someone was controlling it, but who? Dr Fairfield was already secured in the car. One of the women? My thoughts turned to Susie. She had been in a delicate condition, she had spent time with the arms salesmen as well as the terrorists. Maybe she had been turned while she was lain captive. Her nerves at having to come home and have her secrets revealed to her parents might have been guilt at having forged links with the terrorists or having struck some kind of deal. We had to find her before more secret weapons were unleashed.

Dr Fairfield sat quietly now in the back of the car. Ever the perfectionist, had he known about a traitor in his house? We would have to take him away to find out. I signalled the driver to get him out of there, I didn't want him knowing that we were picking up his wife and daughter, we needed to see if this was a family affair. The car left the driveway and whisked the old scientist to a different kind of secure establishment.

I retreated into the house, Danny pulled me inside quickly, he had been studying the console inside the Control Room and had found screens for the security system.

"I have a menu for the front door arms system, but there is a separate method of turning it off from here that I can't find. There appears to be a remote controller. Perhaps there's a panic room?" We had to find it and secure the two women, quickly.

I renewed my contact with Turtle, we needed his help, "Was there another room in the house that could control an armed defence unit?" The house was maintained by the government for use by their leading scientist, any systems installed must be known to them.

"Yes, a white laser system," I was almost screaming into the telephone, Turtle had no record of any such system and was checking for the severalth time that he had heard me correctly. The information wasn't there, Turtle was locked out of the details of the family's home protection system. He couldn't help. We were on our own, the long arm of Turtle's information network had never failed before, but this time he was thwarted by his own team's defence mechanisms.

Danny disabled the arms systems from the main menu so there would be no further clash with our additional help. His impromptu team drew back to the bottom of the stairs and started again the gentle ascent. Danny was in the lead, gun drawn, stealthily making his way up the curved staircase. He reached the top of the stairs and listened to try and detect where the two women were. When he had seen the doctor coming down the stairs earlier, he had come from the left, so this was the way Danny slithered along, trying to gauge where the creaks would come in the old house's floorboards. He edged his way towards a door on the left of the top corridor. Muffled voices greeted his ears, faint and light, some laughter.

Movement in the room now focussed Danny's attention, the team at his back tensed and readied for a fight. Mrs Fairfield walked cheerily out of the room and was surprised to see Danny with several strange men waiting for her. She physically jumped. Her innocence looked to ask in a dazed way what was going on, not realising as a hunter would that she was their prey. No sense of danger came upon her and she stood still, obediently, as they checked her pockets then ushered her downstairs. Armed men in her house, but one of them was Danny. He had said there had been a security breach, so she must obey, of course. They were here to look after her. The men held her by the front door as instructed. We needed to check for the invisible laser again before setting foot outside.

Only the girl remained, alone in her room. I was wrestling with my emotions. I'd had a lump in my throat at their loving reunion yesterday when Susie had come back to the bosom of her family, what if now she was a terrorist collaborator waiting in there, ready to execute the next person to pass by. Danny listened outside her room, trying to imagine where the occupant was and the possible layout of furniture inside. He'd had a pleasant time with Susie during her interrogations and felt great satisfaction at her rescue. He of all people knew the risks and was determined she would come out safely. He had promised to keep her safe, what if now he needed to take her by force? I was ready to step in at any sign of hesitation.

He'd had no clues from the transcripts of her capture that they had any luck in securing her services, but what if he was wrong? We couldn't take the risk, she had to come with us. A few more moments in front of the door then Danny turned the handle and dashed in. Susie was alone on the bed, not scared but alarmed at his presence with the gun drawn. When two more men came in behind him she was visibly scared. She looked to Danny for an explanation, her expression imploring him to protect her. He tried his best not to alarm her further. He explained there had been a security breach, she was to come with them immediately.

"There's no time to explain," he insisted, "you must come with us, now Susie, please," his sense of urgency making her obey instinctively.

The two men bustled her down the stairs and held her at the opposite side of the door to her mother. Mrs Fairfield moved forward to hold on to her daughter, but the men restrained her, drawing her back to the side of the hallway.

"There is a car waiting for you outside, Mrs Fairfield," I used a reassuring tone so that she would not fear they were under suspicion. She was held next to the front door by two of the armed men, all standing in silence. I thought about their exit and where the laser could be placed. How could they get out without the invisible knife shearing through them?

I walked back into the hall and took a large picture off of the wall. It was a common landscape print in a gold leaf frame. Standing at the front door I launched the picture into the air like a frisbee. It spun and flew through the air until it landed on the gravel drive next to the car with the rear door open, waiting for its new passengers. The picture landed in one piece, undisturbed by any invisible menace.

"Go go go, get out there, now, her first" I shouted at the team, pushing the young girl forward. Two of them took Susie out through the door, along the same flight path that the picture had cleared for them and into the waiting car. They all jumped in, the car moved off towards the gate and stopped. The last car drove up and the back door opened as the first had done.

"Next, go, get going," I shoved the remaining team out and they ran, taking the bemused Mrs Fairfield with them and diving through the rear opening of the car. They set off immediately and waited behind the first. I was back on to Turtle, "We have all parties secure and ready to roll. They will be on their way to Pershore in just a second. Danny and I will stay behind and reconfigure the security system so it will only allow us access then try to disarm the weapons."

"Roger that, call in when complete."

We went back to the Control Room where we had picked up the scientist. Danny unlocked the front gate and allowed the two team cars to exit the garden and secure their guests. On the security control PC Danny created a profile of his own to allow him top access to all the features. When he had completed his details he was asked to place his finger on the printer scanner. It flashed and confirmed that his profile was now set up, he could log back in whenever he wanted.

There was still a lot of work to be done. He reconfigured the system to be on full alert and changed the alarm number to his mobile so he would know if there were any guests while the Fairfields were being detained. He also altered the keypad entry code for the front gate and left the cameras on automatic so they would start to record as soon as an alert was raised. He searched through the menus but could find no reference to the location of the other control panel for the arms systems, through his new access, he was able to turn them off but he knew it was only for now. The other panel would be able to override what he had just done. We were going to need help on getting the weapons out completely, that would have to be the next job, right now we had to search the house to find that missing control panel so the white lasers could be disarmed permanently.

We split up and covered every room in the house from top to bottom. The house was very large, it took some time to get through every room and check in each hiding place for a remote control for the security system. A small panel in the Fairfields' bedroom allowed only the facility to look at the monitors and cancel the alarms if they were disturbed in the night. We found no evidence of a panic room or another control system like the one downstairs. We would need help with this as well.

"Turtle, we can't find where this thing was switched on from. We have searched the whole house and there is no reference to where the panel is. We need help," I called in. Turtle had spent his time wisely while we were busy in the house, "I know more about the security system now. If you need some help you can see the man who developed it, guess where he works?"

"Would it be a certain laboratory facility in Malvern?" I asked.

"Well done, dear girl. I will set up the meeting for you tomorrow morning. Secure the house for now then come and entertain your guests this evening. They might have more information for you before you see the other scientist tomorrow."

"Got it. We'll lock up and come in. Talk to you later."

Chapter 12

At RAF Pershore we returned to our respective rooms of last night to change and get ready for the interrogations to come. I needed to think about my subjects, what made them tick, what would make them angry, what would cause them to clam up and say nothing. Should we be nice or nasty? The rules were clear, always start simply. Name, address, date of birth. Get them talking, keep them talking, press the right buttons and get the right responses. They would talk to me without realising they were being questioned. Well, I could hope.

Pershore was the perfect place for these interrogations, the site was used to train the RAF Police as well as other intelligence forces and the rooms that looked so luxurious and obliging were all wired for cameras and sound. Every part of the suite was bugged, including the bathroom. Cameras and two way mirrors were positioned to capture all movement in the rooms, with a small Technical Room disguised between the rooms as a cleaners store. All the data came back to this room for the monitors to show as well as the computers to analyse.

There was a light tap on my door, "Come in." Danny walked sheepishly in to the room, his swagger less pronounced as he made his way over to the end of my bed and sat down, facing the wall. I was laid on top of the covers and found myself arranging my hair and pushing my lips together, making them plump up with blood so they looked fuller and redder.

"You OK?" I asked as he was just about to say the same, "Yeah, fine," he answered, looking around the room as if searching for the words to say next. I didn't feel awkward at the silence this time and sat patiently for him to explain what he was doing there. He was wearing the Club uniform little vest and blue tracksuit bottoms, tied lightly and slung low across his hips. A stunning reminder of how good he looked in them, it pleased me to see him there, sitting on my bed, relaxed. He turned so we made eye contact, I raised my eyebrows quizzically – what did he want?

"I suppose we need to decide what we are going to do with the suspects" he said at last, "you know, who questions who."

"I guess you already have a plan, seeing as you're here to discuss it," I smiled sarcastically and tilted my head to force the question, "what were you thinking?" Danny smiled back, I liked that he wasn't offended by the sarcasm I whipped across him, he actually seemed to enjoy it at times. That could be telling.

"Well, I was thinking, I have already spent a lot of time with Susie, and her mother sees me as a rescuer rather than a spy, so I have their confidence already. If either of them are lying I should be able to tell as their attitude will change. I should be able to winkle most things out of them if I'm nice and polite with the mother. I can just carry on as before with the girl." He paused, I thought he seemed cautious about his next line of reasoning and wondered what he was about to ask.

"The Dr will be wary of any kind of questioning and will have been briefed just in case he was snatched, so it will be a little trickier. If you look after him I'm sure, with the experience you already have of questioning him, you will be able to get him to give up some useful information. He's an intelligent man and will have respect for your obvious talents," he paused again to see my fleeting reaction, I tried to remain icy but felt my face flush momentarily before he resumed, "you use your charms on the Dr and I'll use mine on the women."

"OK, it makes sense for you to continue your work with Susie while she's here. I will stay in the Tech Room and monitor her reactions. The room is fully wired so nothing should escape us." He seemed happy that I thought his plan was good enough to proceed with. He had been nervous when he first came in, I decided to throw him a bone and give him a little vote of confidence so agreed without changing anything. Besides, his thoughts echoed my own and I had formed the same plan myself, although mine was based on the fact that with him charming them, those women didn't stand a chance.

He was comfortable on the end of my bed, I wanted him to stay a bit longer and was trying to think of how I could keep him there.

"Right then, let's go over the ground-rules," I said, afraid that he was about to walk out. That was all Danny needed, he turned on the bed and laid down on his stomach, his upper body supported on his elbows and his legs bent so his feet could move around, crossing and uncrossing his ankles as we talked. We went through each person's roles and what we were trying to achieve. We set out the plan and made our preparations. More time in each other's company was helping us both to relax and I for one was glad of it. When Danny got up to go back to his room, the swagger had returned as he slowly made his way to the bedroom door. He smiled again as he walked through, I caught the grin and thought again how pleasant he was to have around, gazing after him long after he had left the room.

We were clear in our plan of attack, Danny went alone to question Susie as he had done the week before. They were closer now, had more of a rapport, he knew her a little better, there was a personal connection. He would need to capitalise on that so she would tell him what he needed. I watched through the monitors as they sat comfortably together in the beautiful VIP suite. They each had a small sofa which Danny had drawn together, one at a slight angle to the other so they could sit intimately but not directly opposite one another. Danny needed to keep an eye on her body language so he sat where he could see all of her. I recorded the interview from the Tech Room, so if he missed anything I would be able to pick it up. A tiny earpiece allowed me to communicate with him without Susie being aware. If she was obviously lying, the message could get through.

He needed to start simply with questions she would not suspect and could answer truthfully. He started with her surroundings, was she comfortable enough, did she want anything to eat, had she managed any sleep that afternoon. Then it went on to simple facts, date of birth for him to check, address of lodgings in Dublin, where she went to university. All of these were written on the clipboard that Danny had taken with him as a prop and excuse for talking to her, just to check a few details.

"Thanks for this, Susie, you're doing really well. So, there was a security breach at your house today, do you have any idea what that could have been about, where the threat could have come from?" he asked, trying not to scare her. Susie shook her head, looking towards the floor.

"I have no idea. When you came into my room I didn't know what was going on."

I wondered if Danny had caught that Susie only made eye contact when she talked about him coming into her room. His little girl had a crush on him. It changed nothing, he would have to press her harder, I reminded him in his earpiece.

"Did your parents know of your drug problem?" he asked after a short pause. The young girl looked down at her knees then out towards the window. She was ashamed of her problems but trusted Danny enough to talk to him about it, "No, they knew nothing. They are very simple people, they used to go out but as my father's work became more and more important, they went out less and less. The hassle of popping out anywhere and having to report in all the time became too much trouble so they hardly go anywhere that's not on the schedule any more. They know very little of modern society and how you get into the kind of circles where you do such things." She laughed, but in fact she wished she was still a part of that side of the family who couldn't understand how it all went on.

"They only found out yesterday when you brought me home. I was so scared I didn't know what to do. I wanted to tell them so badly but I was in too deep and the more I wanted to come home the more I just couldn't. I took more and more stuff to try and forget that they were waiting for me at home. They must be so ashamed." She looked again at the floor and towards the window, looking for a way out and an end to having to deal with the reality of what she had done.

"Do they have any friends or visitors?" he asked gently.

"My Mum has a couple of friends who come over to play bridge on a Saturday night if my Dad isn't working. Other than that she only has my Auntie Les, who she speaks to every day and goes over to see once a month. Its all on the schedule."

"What about your father?"

"He just works, really. That's his full on life, that laboratory. We have a holiday once a year for one week only then its back to the labs for him and back to the same old routine for me and Mum."

"So who do you knock about with when you're at home?" he wanted to keep her talking.

"I have a few school friends who live close to here, but I needed permission to go and see them and they all had to undergo basic security clearance for me to be allowed into their houses. It's a bit of a strain meeting new people under those conditions so I kept to myself most of the time." The tears were welling in her eyes. I had the feeling that she wanted to talk more but was unable to get the right words out. Danny must have had the same feeling, he nudged her on, "Did you make friends with any of the people in Tunisia?"

She looked at him, puzzled.

"Was there anyone there that you could talk to or make friends with? They sometimes have cleaners or housekeepers that are not connected with their work but are around the house and often get to know a person who has been kidnapped and maybe help them out or talk to them about what they are doing there. Did they have anyone like that?" he asked.

"No. It was just the three of them. They shouted at me in French and English. They threw me around the room like a doll. I had some basic meals but just noodles or rice that I could eat easily. I was sick a lot and in a lot of pain, the doctor said it was part of the withdrawal. I didn't have anyone to confide in or talk to."

"Nobody at all?" he had to be sure.

"No-one." She fell silent, the drips of her tears falling in spots on her lap.

He left it for a minute before he pressed her again.

"Susie, I'm here to help you, but you have to be honest with me. Can you do that, Susie?" She looked up at him nervously, her admiring glance wanting him to help her. He looked into her eyes as the strain started to break through, I spoke quietly in his earpiece, "There's something there, Danny, keep going," as I saw the girl's temperature increase on the monitors.

"Can you do that Susie, can you talk to me honestly, I need the truth from you Susie, do you understand?" She started to cry, the drips turned to blobs, falling free and fast.

"I'm sorry," she mumbled out as she wiped her wet nose and face, "it was my fault, I did it." Danny tried not to move, his body tensed expectantly. I watched intently from my hiding place next door.

"Did what?" he asked as casually as he could, fearing that he knew the answer but trying to be gentle in coaxing it out of her.

"It was my fault. I knew what I was doing and didn't stop myself," she was drained now and sobbed without checking herself.

"I knew it would be trouble. They said they would bring me drugs and that was all I wanted. I knew it was wrong but I didn't stop myself."

She broke down and buried her head in the cushion on the arm of the sofa. Danny gave her a minute, desperate as he was to know what she had just confessed to. I warned him from the next room to be patient but in the Tech Room I was on the edge of my chair, leaning into the monitors to get every nuance from the conversation. Just say it, for goodness' sake. Through the earpiece I told Danny to talk gently to her and get her to calm down, but he was there already. Susie collected herself and apologised once again after a few minutes sobbing into the cushion to hide her guilty face.

"Its OK Susie, I'm trying to help you, but you must be honest with me and tell me the truth. What did you do?"

"I couldn't help it, they said they would hurt my family if I refused but I just wanted the drugs. I . . . I told them the code for the gate to my parents house," she faded out towards the end of the sentence.

"Have you had any further contact since you came home yesterday? Have they been in touch again?"

"No, I have been in bed most of the time and haven't even told my Uni friends I'm back home, but don't you see, they said they would hurt my family and now there's this security problem and its all my fault. They must have used the code that I gave them to come to the house because I was too out of it to help them." She started to break down again, "Its all my fault, I shouldn't have told them the code." She looked up into Danny's face, her eyes pleading with him to forgive her foolish, drug induced mistake. She looked to the face of her saviour, the one who always came to her rescue, her own tense features softened as she leaned towards him, "Thank God you were there to help us or we could have all been killed," she insisted.

I could hardly hide my disappointment and I could see Danny struggling as well. Oh, dear, was that really it? Susie thought that the Tunisians had come for them and that's why they had to be evacuated. The poor girl.

"You're quite safe now. Its OK." Danny tried to appease her, "I've changed the code on your security gates and its just as secure as it always was. You did very well not giving them anything else when they asked you for it. I think you're very brave, actually," Danny offered, putting a reassuring hand on her shoulder. She looked up into his pretty face and saw him smiling at her. She was enthralled, I could see it. I wondered if that was how my own ridiculous face appeared when I looked at him. He'd won this one over as well, Susie's temperature started to reduce, I told Danny to come back to the Tech Room.

"I'll go get you some tea and toast," he offered and she nodded obligingly.

He swiped his ID card to be let out of the room and the door locked behind him as he walked down the corridor to the dark little chamber where the surveillance cameras and microphones were watching Susie in the room. She had walked over to the two way mirror that we were sat behind in the middle of the longest wall and started to clean up her face from the tears and the make-up. She licked a hankie and dabbed her eyes, cleaning the running streaks, trying to make herself presentable for Danny's return.

Susie wet her lips and smacked them together then fluffed up her hair. She pushed her hand into her bra and pulled up her breasts so they were more pronounced under her shirt.

"I think she likes you," I said from the corner of the darkened room, hiding the bitter jealousy from myself as much as him.

Danny ignored my teasing, "What does the voice analysis show?" He had asked Susie the factual questions so that the electronic lie detector could get a normal reading, he played back the recording and the oscilloscope pattern danced on the screen, the background was green for the factual questions, she was relaxed and in a non-stressful state. This was the base line for the rest of the analysis. The rest of the monitors looked at her pupil dilation size, comparing it with her normal response and her temperature and sweat levels as key indicators to tell if she was being deceitful. The analysis result was that she was not lying.

As he played back the rest of the conversation, her voice was becoming more and more stressed, but it was not lying, just traumatised. She had been telling the truth about the information she had given him. It wasn't her that set the lasers or given out our photo. Unbelievably, we were now focussed on the Mother.

"We need more information on the parents now," I told him, "try and find a gap in her knowledge of their schedule or some old friends that have just appeared in their lives, anything out of the ordinary." I instructed.

"Someone must have been contacted somehow last night for the photo to have been released, try and build up a picture of what they were doing and who with. OK?" He said nothing more, Dark Danny had taken over again, he was serious and intent in the dimmed room. His eyes looked black, he nodded and walked out. The tea and toast had been ordered and was ready while he had been in the Tech Room, he picked up the tray left outside and went back in to see Susie.

He tried not to notice the freshly plumped up breasts trying to peek out and look at him from under Susie's shirt. He poured out the tea as she buttered the toast and munched away contentedly, she still had a lot of weight to put back on and was happy to get her kicks from eating for a change. They sat in silence, looking comfortable together. She was happy now that she had got the burden of guilt out in the open. That's why she was so terrified at going home, but the lovely Danny had saved her again and no damage had been done. He started the questions gently again as she ate the hot toast. He asked her more about her parents movements and who the friends were who came to play bridge. They were the same since she was a small child and nobody ever replaced them when they were on holiday. Two spinsters that lived alone in Great Malvern stayed the night on Saturdays in the big house. They all went off to church together on Sunday mornings then they made their own way home afterwards. These were her mother's only friends and no other visitors had been recently as far as she knew.

"What about last night," he asked, "What happened after we left?"

"I wasn't up for long. The doc gave me a tablet to take after my evening meal and it more or less knocked me out. I'd had a nice time helping Mum prepare dinner, it was just like when I was little. I would peel potatoes and we would listen to the radio and sing and dance along. It was nice just to be home." Danny felt her tears starting to build back up, he had to keep the momentum and stop her from carrying on down this emotional route. He needed facts now, without appearing to rush her.

"What time was dinner?" he asked, trying to keep her on track to reveal the night's events.

"Dinner is always at 6.30pm," she replied, focussing as he required.

"We served dinner on time but had to wait to start as Dad was on the phone in the reception room." She looked away for a second, appearing hurt that her father could have ruined their family reunion.

"It was funny, though, Mum was totally nonplussed and she went and banged the big ornamental dinner gong in the dining room to tell him to hurry up." This made Susie laugh, she and her mother must have had a moment together as giggling schoolgirls doing something naughty, disturbing her father when he was busy.

"We really shouldn't have because it was probably work, it usually was. Anyway, it must have worked because he came through just after and we had our lovely dinner. I had the tablet and was pretty much knocked out after that. I went almost straight to bed and didn't wake up til about eleven this morning." So, Dr Fairfield had been on the phone at 6.30pm. That was one thing we could trace.

Danny thanked Susie for being so honest, he reassured her that the breach had not been her fault and that the house was secure now. He had a plan of the night's events and enough to tackle the Mother with. Susie would be back with her family very soon, he told her not to worry. He cleared the tray of tea things and swiped out of the room. Susie flopped out on the bed when he left, I could see her looking after him longingly.

She may have been dreaming of his image but I still had him in my sights. When he entered the next room, the charm offensive started again. He put Mrs Fairfield at her ease so that she could relax. He smiled a lot and reassured her that everything was fine. He just needed to check a few things with her, and he went through the sample questions for the voice analyser to gain its normal level readings. She was relaxed now, he needed to capitalise on that to get her to talk openly. They chatted together and he asked about her husband.

"How long have you been married, Mrs Fairfield?"

"Twenty three years this year," she told him, pleased with the rare achievement these days. Danny was working his magic, she was happy to keep talking.

"Where did you meet?" he sounded like a woman getting to know a new girlfriend. I was wary of him once more, the player that he was. His knowledge and cunning when it came to women was more than I had ever seen, how to get them to open up to him, his pretty face innocent and his manner charming. I needed to watch myself with this one. I didn't feel like being played no matter how nice it might be at the time.

"We met at University. He was in his second year and I was in my first. I thought he was very clever and he was quite handsome and funny as well. Carefree, he was, but very career focussed. He was always ambitious and I liked that about him at the time. We used to go out all the time back then and met at a mutual friend's house." She stopped, I imagined she was remembering a time when they were young and free, with little obligations and their careers all ahead of them. She looked at the table in front of her, maybe with their wedding pictures in her mind's eye, the simple service and afternoon tea. A quiet honeymoon in the country at his family's cottage in Devon. Her quiet reflection we didn't have time enough for, Danny needed to draw her more, "Do you still see many of your old friends?"

"No, we only see a couple now. As he has risen through the ranks at work we saw our friends less and less. He became more and more insular, but I have insisted on keeping our old bridge night on a Saturday."

"Do you play a regular crowd?"

"Oh, yes, it's the same two dears we have played since we moved to that house. They live in the village down the hill. They come over for supper then we play bridge until late, so they stay over," she explained.

"How do you know the ladies?"

"I met them when I used to work in the charity shop in town. We were all volunteers. When we started getting friendly, Brian had a security check done on them so they could come to the house. Because of all the complications like that we never bothered going to find any other friends. Its been quite difficult, really, but that's why I insisted we kept the bridge night going. Through everything else, we have always done that."

She looked sad, like she had wasted something and regretted it but was resigned to the fact after years of struggling.

"What are the two ladies called?" Danny asked, trying to break the spell of regret that had come over her and keep her talking, "Oh, its alright, they have their clearance, it gets checked every year to make sure they aren't carrying Semtex in their knitting bags" she snapped at him unexpectedly. I was taken aback by the strange outburst with a low "Wow" uttered into Danny's earpiece. He looked at her but she ashamedly refused to return his gaze.

"I'm sorry," she said, "Its sometimes difficult to serve your country when it imposes such strict rules on every aspect of our lives." Good, she was opening up now, if Danny carried on like this he would be able to get to the bottom of her frustrations.

"Empathise," I whispered into his ear.

"It must be very difficult for you, especially as a family, maintaining a normal lifestyle with a young daughter. It must have been very hard for you when your only child had to go all the way to Ireland to get away from the ridiculous regime imposed on you by Brian's work?" He tilted his head on one side and put his hand on his chin to show he was taking great interest in what she was saying and felt deeply about what she was telling him.

"Oh, you would not believe what we have gone through with poor Susie. When she first said she wanted to go to university Brian was terrified that something would happen to her. I had to argue the point with him that she had to have all the opportunities that we had to become independent and be able to do her own thing as an adult. She couldn't stay in our enclave forever, I told him. But of course he saw sense and his, I mean your, employers were more than generous in helping out, they planned and paid for all her trips, showed her how to keep herself safe, vetted her room-mates. They were really very good and helped enormously. I can't complain at all about their conduct."

We were going the wrong way, the feeling of dissent was fading fast. What else could he press her buttons about and get it back.

"Was it just because the house was such a prison that she felt the need to leave? I mean, I have seen some good security systems in my time, but that one takes the biscuit, how many cameras are there?" He smiled, still leaning forward to show that he was utterly absorbed in what she was saying.

"Well, Brian says it's the best system of its kind. There are cameras everywhere, I don't really know how many but I know you can see the whole grounds and the gate," she leaned in herself a little, talking in confidence.

"It must be a terrible nuisance, going off with every cat and hedgehog in the garden?" Danny laughed, determined to take her off guard.

"No, oh no, it's a bit more sophisticated than that. It will look at the image but if it doesn't recognise it as a human then it doesn't alarm. It was a bit wonky when they first put it in, but it works really well now and we very rarely get the alarm sounding," she told him.

"It all sounds very clever, so what would it do if it detected a person?"

"Well, the man who put it in comes to test it every so often and what it does is, the cameras all turn to the person and start to record wherever he is. The garden is all laid out in a grid and if he crosses two grid sections then the alert signal goes up and a message is sent to Brian's phone. We have a monitor in the bedroom and we can see what has set it off, even if it's the middle of the night. Its very clever you know. We can cancel it or send for help. If they go over a third grid then the security team are called automatically. Its all very well, but I have no idea how it works, if Brian wasn't there then I have no idea how to do anything on it."

"So you couldn't replay the recording and watch it again or anything like that?"

"Brian did show me a few things. He showed me what button to press to record and how to move the cameras around if I needed to, there's a little toggle thingy that you can select the camera then wiggle it around. I set it to record yesterday when you arrived unexpectedly with Susie because I didn't know who you were. Brian also showed me how to send an emergency alarm if I needed it and he wasn't there, and how to cancel an alert. That's all I need really, its too complicated for me with all kinds of gizmos on it. I don't even like using the remote for the video," she laughed and Danny laughed too. Was she really such a technical dunce? She had already admitted she recorded the images of us arriving.

"What other gizmos does it have? I've seen some of these systems with remote controls and all sorts of things. The weapons systems on them are fabulous aren't they, all built in," he elaborated to encourage her to join in and fill in the details.

"Oh, Brian would never let any weapons near the house. When the special forces boys came over they wanted him to have something but he refused, saying his house was not an armoury."

"What about a remote panel. Can you work the controls from elsewhere in the house, like a panic room, don't you have one of those, I thought they were standard for people of your stature within the protected community?" he was making the statements more challenging, forcing her to defend her defence systems.

"We never had it done. They were supposed to come and put one in during last summer but we were just sorting out Susie's university place and we never gave them a date to install it. We never got a panic room so the only control panel is in the main room downstairs."

She must be lying now, the laser was turned off when there was nobody in that room and it definitely showed on the screen that it was under remote operation.

"So if I came to your house and you were alone, what would you do to stop me from getting in?" Danny asked innocently enough, "Well, Brian says that the system would stop anyone from getting close without telling me, and then you would have to get through the gate, the garden and the front door or a window and everything is alarmed. You wouldn't be able to do it," she assured him.

"Yes but all that does is send up an alarm, you haven't stopped me from getting in," he pressed on.

"We have a hotline to the local police as first response then the security team are less than half an hour away, you wouldn't be able to get inside in that time," she was polite but insistent.

"What if I said that I could turn up your house and get in whenever I wanted, what would you do then?"

"No, its impossible, we have one of the most secure houses in the country. Brian says it's the most sophisticated system ever made. You would never get in." She was becoming slightly upset that he imagined her husband had such a lax system. Exactly what he wanted, he pushed some more.

"I'm quite sophisticated myself, what would the system do apart from sending a text message? That wouldn't stop me, would it?" He insisted.

Mrs Fairfield was shocked to be challenged this way, they had tested the defences with armed servicemen and they had never broken in, not once. Her image flushed on the screen, her temperature rose with every challenge. I felt he was close.

"Well, how on earth do you think you would get in when so many have failed before you?" she demanded.

"I'm ingenious" he answered, allowing a second to collect her thoughts at the young challenger.

The questions had made her flustered but not offering an answer. He wasn't getting the reaction we needed about the weapons systems installed. I screwed my eyes up at the monitors in front of me – this line of questioning wasn't getting us anywhere. She wasn't going to tell him, if she knew at all. I was starting to wonder if she knew anything about what had happened that afternoon with the driver and the laser. I nudged Danny to move on.

"It would be easy to get into your house," he was smiling at her again now, "I would just ring the bell and say 'Hello, can I come in?'"

The old woman mellowed to him again, "You were teasing me all along. You are such a charming young man, aren't you. Of course I would let you in, you are always welcome in my home after what you did for my poor little Susie," she giggled, like a flirtatious girl and put her hand momentarily on his arm in affection without being unseemly.

"Can I get you some tea, Mrs Fairfield?" he swiped out of the room to see what I thought of the encounter and what to do next.

The Tech' Room was darker than before, Susie had turned off her light to get some sleep after finishing her tea and we had to keep the light low so she would not see us behind the mirror, even with the blind down. I was waiting for him. The voice analysis showed that Mrs Fairfield was telling the truth. She was not anxious and her temperature never rose throughout the interview. She maintained a level reading and only rose slightly when he challenged her, but even then she believed what she was saying to him and thought for sure that he could not break into her fortress of a house. She had been completely unguarded in her responses and the computer had given good information.

"She's not showing any signs of lying, she genuinely thinks you're a 'charming young man'" I teased. I also believed her account of things and was struggling to explain what we had witnessed at the house. We were out of suspects, it all hinged on who was in control of the remote panel that showed on the main screen – they were the only ones who could have set them and turned them off as they watched on the monitors. Danny and I thought about the implications for a while in silence when a light went on in my perception.

"We have been thinking this the wrong way," I said, "think about it, the weapons system and the security facility were both developed at the Dr's research laboratory. Maybe the man who set up the defences still has a panel back at the workshop in Malvern? Maybe that's where the laser was switched on and off from? What if it was a misunderstanding and he thought the agents coming into the house were there to attack the family and he was defending them?"

A whole host of possibilities opened up to us both. The location of the panel was still important but didn't answer how the photos of the two of us got to the hands of assassins sent to hunt us down. We still had suspects within the house. We had questioned two out of the three and it was time to move on to the main man.

"Get a bit more background on the husband, friends, hobbies, family, etc. then I'll go see the old man. While you're in there I'll tell Turtle that there could be another possibility and get him doing some more research" I advised. Danny nodded, turned and left, picking up the tea tray from outside the room once again.

"Here we are, sorry it took a while, I couldn't find any biscuits for you. Would you like to be Mother?" which of course she did, fulfilling the function of her existence as she felt it to be. She poured the tea and they both sipped at their cups, maintaining a comfortable silence.

"You say you have the two ladies who come over for bridge, does your husband not have any family that comes to call at all?" he asked, halfway down his tea.

"His mother died in the spring," Mrs Fairfield looked sad and relieved at the same time, "She was very infirm but he was utterly dedicated to her. Its because of her he got into this line of work in the first place. She had been a Bletchley girl during the war, decoding German transmissions, and she pushed him into doing something for his country as well. We didn't know about the work at Bletchley for years, it was only after her first stroke that she told us. The work had been so secret that nobody knew, not even her own family. Brian loved his mother and was devastated when she died, but he's getting over it now with the fishing."

"Fishing?" Danny asked.

"Yes, he used to go and see his mother on a Saturday morning, quite early, and stay until lunchtime. He found the gap too awful and just moped around the house in a bad mood until a friend at work told him that he went fishing at that time and invited him to go too. He was reluctant at first, but went once and was hooked," she laughed softly, "pardon the pun."

"I thought he didn't have any friends, from what you had said before," Danny was annoyed that she had not mentioned this until now.

"Well, I thought you meant outside work, I mean a work colleague can't do any harm, can he?" She was surprised at the interest in a simple work relationship spilling out of hours.

"And what is the name of this work colleague?" asked Danny in what I had to highlight to him was a curt tone.

"Peter Bowson" she replied, not thinking him important, it was only fishing. Danny asked if there were any other friends or family that she had not told him about, or any other visitors to the house, but she was adamant that there were no others. Peter didn't call at the house and she had never met him. Brian met him at the gate and they went straight to their fishing spot on the river. If they caught a really big fish they would text her a picture before throwing it back and sometimes he was holding it, but other than that she had not seen him.

"So he couldn't be having an affair or anything, its definitely a man he's seeing," Danny asked, deliberately provocative to shake her up a bit once more. His prey looked at him, surprised. She had obviously never thought that he was capable of having an affair. The thought had not entered her mind, I could tell. She said nothing, just looked at him as if he had hurt her inadvertently and shook her head slowly from side to side.

"No, he's not having an affair, I'm quite sure. In fact, he has talked recently for the first time about the possibility of retiring so we can spend more time together, he has never said anything like that before. I think it's the first time he has actually thought he could manage with not going to work. He knows now he could spend some time down by the river and be quite happy not doing anything but catch fish." I could tell the question had made her think, though, he had obviously changed since starting the fishing. That was interesting.

Danny didn't need any more. He had plenty to think about and plenty of lines for me to chase with the man himself. He tidied up the tea tray and the gentle lady helped him stack the cups and saucers neatly so he could balance the tray easily.

"Do have a pleasant night's sleep, Mrs Fairfield. I will be in to see you in the morning. Don't worry about the house, its quite safe now and Susie isn't far away, she's sleeping at the moment so you will see her in the morning as well. Goodnight, Mrs Fairfield, if you need anything just dial '0'."

In the Tech' Room I showed him the analysis again. She was still very convincing at telling the truth. Danny stood behind the high stool that I was sitting on to control the computer and replay some of the audio captured. I had marked the points where Danny had been a little sharp to show him her reaction.

I stood up and moved towards the door. It was Danny's turn to stay in the box now. He was to do some research on the name of the fellow fisherman while I was questioning the good Dr. and I would be back in to see him soon. He settled onto the stool to take control of the lie detecting machinery.

I checked my appearance in the mirror, I wanted to make sure my hair was all in the right place and I was dressed properly before going in to challenge the senior scientist. He wouldn't be noticing my hair, I knew, but my confidence needed tricking into making sure I was as well turned out as I could be. Slightly nervous and wary of Danny watching, I knocked on the door but received no response. After a second knock I swiped myself into the room anyway. Dr Fairfield sat on the sofa in the middle of the large suite. The surroundings were rich and luxurious, the furniture more at home in a plush hotel than a military hostel. He did not raise his eyes as I made my way slowly towards him, "Dr Fairfield, I need to ask you a few questions, if you don't mind" but he gazed, open eyed at the floor. I felt a sinister presence in the room and instinctively rested my hand on the gun tucked into the back of my trousers. I sat down opposite the old man and waited for him to acknowledge my presence. After what seemed like minutes, he raised his head and our eyes locked. He maintained the gaze for a long time, almost trying to see through me as if my eyes were the windows to my intent, but when I gave nothing away he dropped his head once again, "I will answer nothing. Do as you will. You have no right to question me. I answer only to the Minister, get him here to ask your questions."

I waited to see if there were to be any further outbursts but he sat, rested, staring at the floor. He did not appear to be disturbed but was still sweating. His only other movement was to mop his brow with the little cotton hankie then return it to his pocket and sit motionless once more.

Danny was talking in my earpiece, there was no personnel record of a Peter Bowson at the DRA, I needed to get some more information about the fishing trips from him, just in case his wife had the name wrong.

"Tell me about your hobbies, Dr," I said, trying to encourage him out of his cage, but he said nothing. Not your typical angler, I thought, most of them can't wait to bore you into submission about bait and how intelligent trout are, actually.

"Isn't your fishing interesting enough to talk to me about?" I asked but his glazed over eyes gave me nothing at all.

"Do you know why we had to evacuate you?" I tried again with the same response. One last attempt, "Dr Fairfield, if you are here, where do you imagine your family are?" At last, he twitched his eyes, looking into the fireplace in the comfortable room. He had not thought about that, surely they were still at home? He looked at me, wanting desperately to ask where they were, searching my face for clues that would tell me they were safe. He found none. The sweat poured from him.

"What do you mean?" he said at last. My move.

"I just wanted to ask a few questions" I continued as if nothing else had been said. I checked the factual data that we needed, name , address, date of birth, then moved on to the fishing, but he clammed up at that point, demanding I told him where his family were.

"They are quite safe, Dr. We will be holding them here until we have finished our little question and answer session with you, so its all down to how far you are prepared to co-operate, the sooner we get the information we need, they can go home. So, just talk to me about the fishing, Dr." The flames were reflected in his eyes as he sat, staring into the hearth. He was giving me nothing, refusing to chat about his hobbies or his work.

"Get the Minister if you want those questions answered, I've told you what you have a right to know." He sat back on the sofa and closed his mouth. No matter what I tried, he would not acknowledge my presence again. I would have to try again the following day when he had time to think it over. A night away from his important work and worrying about his family would make him more receptive.

When I returned to Danny we shrugged at one another and acquiesced to trying again in the morning after our visit to his workplace. More information would be there that we could use to make him more open for questioning. Once he knew we had been allowed in to his inner sanctum by his superiors he might see us in a better light. We could also get to see this fishing buddy of his and see what information he could give us.

"What shall we do now?" Danny asked, "Gym" I said, smiling as I knew that even with his ribs in a mess he would still not be able to resist the challenge, and this would be one of the only chances I would have to beat him. I would spare him the rowing machine, though, as I was feeling generous.

Chapter 13

We pulled up outside the laboratory location nestled between the beautiful, long green Malvern hills. The cream prefabs with the peeling paint and leaf encrusted gutters did nothing to betray the importance of the work being conducted inside. The world's most highly advanced technology was being developed in what looked like a series of small cabins and 1940s brick buildings. The fence was unassuming and the simple faded sign at the gate, reading just 'DRA', was the only clue that we were in the right place. A blank space appeared on the Satnav screen, this place did not exist.

The Defence Research Agency was started during the Second World War, initially to develop ideas such as RADAR. They moved to the quiet Malvern site from the south coast of England following a successful British Commando raid on the equivalent German establishment. When they looked at the location, they found that they could come under a similar attack from German forces and moved the whole operation inland. The Malvern Hills gave excellent cover from enemy viewpoint and any planes in the area could be quickly spotted and targeted. The site was then used to develop all technical weaponry as well as defensive initiatives, right up to the present day. Their successes included infra-red signalling, thermal imaging, voice recording and recognition, biometrics and of course they perfected the indispensable RADAR. Any technological advancement to hit the modern market place was at least ten years behind what they were already doing in the Malvern facility, right here in these little huts. Dr

Fairfield himself had over 5,000 UK patents in his name after his stint in the laboratory since starting here straight from University, all in the name of the defence of his country, not gaining any fiscal reward for any of them. He was making his way through the ranks aided by the height of the Cold War and the prospect of nuclear war in Europe. A time of massive technological achievements and change; a time where he could capitalise well on his success, catapulting himself through the innovative ranks. He had burned brightest among the many scientific minds, now Head of Development. A worthy status and a five digit salary, but if he fell into enemy hands the whole of the UK's defences would be at risk. He was protected day and night.

Security allowed Danny and I entry through the front gate, we were told to follow the road to the right and park at the visitors car park round the back. We had no driver today, only us two were permitted entry to the inner sanctum and we would have to be on our best behaviour, Turtle had warned. Danny drove round to the right, the road was enclosed by a large brick building on the left and a steep embankment with trees and shrubs on top with the fence surrounding it on the right. The road was dark and wound round to our left as it passed the back of the building. The vista opened up to us as we rounded the next corner, a glorious sight of a wide metropolis greeted us. A vast sprawling network of hangars and specialist buildings, each with its own compound and security system surrounding it. All of this had been invisible from the outside road and every building was painted a dark green to blend in with the background so they were very hard to see from aerial pictures. The roads themselves seemed to sparkle with a strange blue tint which looked sort of blurred as the light hit it directly, the special tarmac mixture could not be captured in photography, it acted like a light source when you tried to take a picture of it and each image would be refracted, giving an inaccurate recording of what was actually there. The tarmac covered the flat tops of the buildings as well, to further blur the lines of the buildings against the roads from the air.

This place fascinated me, I couldn't wait to be inside, my inner nerd was pining to know what technological advancements I was going to be using in a few years time. We were both nervous with geek-like anticipation.

Danny parked in the single Visitors bay and walked to the nearest door. For security reasons, none of the buildings were identified and the only marking was a small brass plaque which read in etched letters, 'Reception'. I checked we had the ID of the person Turtle had arranged for us to meet and pushed open the old green wooden door. We stepped through into a long narrow corridor. In stark contrast to the dark green outside, the corridor was bright white, there was a steel door at the other end and I immediately wished we had not come in together.

When we reached the end with the door and there was no handle on our side, I realised we were in a monitored area. Cameras would be on us and, depending how long it took to open this door, we could be being X rayed as well. Just as I thought, Danny was close behind me yet it took several seconds for the magnetic lock to snap open and the door to swing back on its hinges, we had been X rayed and photographed on the way in. The doorway opened up to a very modern, neat Reception area with a glass desk and a set of plush chairs and low tables. The desk glowed with a reddy tinge that slowly swirled and moved within itself. The middle aged lady behind the desk already had our IDs confirmed from our photos and smiled warmly as we approached.

Like a child in a sweet factory, I was trying to take in every detail so I could relive the moments later on, the lady's badge just said 'Nancy', "Welcome to the DRA," she greeted us, gesturing to the far wall opposite, "If you could stand over by the wall, Mr Falkes, a tray will open in just a second." Danny stood where he had been instructed, part of the wall popped open and a lined tray stood out.

"If you could just place your weapon in there for me, Mr Falkes, then we can proceed to signing you in." Nancy was still smiling but I was not. What the hell was he thinking, bringing a weapon with him? He should have known they wouldn't let him in here with it. Danny placed the gun on the tray with his spare magazine of ammo.

"If you could push the tray closed with your right index finger, please, Mr Falkes. Thank you." He pressed the front of the tray and it scanned his fingerprint. As the tray closed into the wall again a puff of air came past him and the tray clicked snugly into its resting place. The system had taken his fingerprint and also a sample of his personal odour. Even if someone else replicated his fingerprint, they would not be able to open the tray, the system would electronically 'sniff' the person trying to gain access and if the smell didn't match Danny's, it would remain firmly shut. I had read the piece written by Dr Fairfield himself on the technology and its many uses.

"And now, Miss May, if I might take your coat?" Nancy was still smiling, but her demeanour suggested it was not a question. I was not for giving it up, "Thank you, but I'm fine. I will leave it on."

"I'm sorry, Miss May, but I cannot allow you into the facility with that coat on." Nancy was most insistent but not for the first time,

I felt threatened by the intrusion. I also never enjoyed being told what to do. I turned to square up to the lady behind the desk, who had sensed my defensive qualities, "Miss May, I'm sorry, no explosives are allowed to be taken inside – the third button down on your coat, its one of ours," Nancy explained.

Of course, in my excitement I had forgotten the emergency charge built into the button. I handed it over, a little sheepishly at having challenged my gentle host about it. Danny looked at me, evidently suppressing a snigger after the daggered look I had thrown at him for bringing in the gun. Once the coat had been secured away behind the Reception area, a whiff of air came past as though someone had opened a door nearby. The glass desk now glowed green, the checking system had not detected any further sources of explosives on such risqué visitors and we were cleared to enter the facility.

We signed in, our mobile phones, pens and watches were taken and we finally received our photo ID badges in exchange, printed directly on to the cards which had to be displayed at all times. We were taken into an ante room to watch the Health and Safety video before entering the facility. This brought it home to us both what we were dealing with in this place, the video warned of the different types of audible alarm we could hear while in the buildings, one for fire, one for chemical hazards, one to evacuate another to stay inside. All different, each with a set of instructions. We would be escorted so we should remain with our host at all times. I hadn't thought about nuclear activity in the area, we both grew visibly more excited still. I walked out of the room with the sounders still ringing in my ears, hoping I would not be hearing them again that day.

The man we had come to meet was waiting for us as we came out of the ante room. The name we had been told to ask for was Mr Johnson but there was no way of knowing if this was his real name or not. He greeted us warmly, if a little seriously, then ushered us into the main building behind the Reception. We walked through various corridors while he talked about some of the achievements of the laboratory. He seemed very proud of their work and was happy to answer questions, leading us through to the workshop. His briefing seemed to be concentrated in my direction, almost ignoring Danny altogether. He manner was overly genteel, bordering on smarmy, and I began to think he fancied himself as rather the ladies man. I could use this later on. For now I just wanted to keep him talking and he was more than happy to oblige, smiling and flattering me as we passed each new section.

The undulating corridors that linked what once were individual buildings together to form a warren-like network of paths and tracks between the structures took us through the different departments. Each stark white corridor was the same as the next, labs on the left, offices on the right. A code next to each door so that it could be quickly identified in an emergency was the only marker in halls full of nothingness. The lab windows were mostly blanked out so it was difficult to see as Mr Johnson spoke about what was happening in each one. As we walked by he would drop in that this section had developed the thermal imaging camera, another was working on the latest in solar harvesting. It was all a blur to us, with no features or landmarks to point out the difference. The corridors were a labyrinth, my excitement turned to unease as I struggled to remember the route back. I didn't like the feeling that I didn't know my way out – always have an exit plan was the number one strategy to keeping myself safe and here I felt exposed.

I turned, noticing Danny tagging along behind. He was an expert flirt and must have recognised that this man had taken a liking to the girl of the party. He didn't look pleased, more so because he was persistently ignored as Mr Johnson concentrated on me alone. I was very much amused and determined to capture all of the attention just to tick him off. The man kept on talking and looking at me, so I pretended to be utterly enthralled by him, until we reached an office opposite some labs marked 'Security Lenses' with a piece of masking tape stuck to the door. Very high tech', I thought, unimpressed.

Mr Johnson settled us into his office and offered drinks which we refused. All we wanted was the information on the Fairfield's system, "Yes, I oversaw the installation of the security suite at their house personally and was responsible for the updates," he looked at me to see if I was impressed by his personal seniority, but I was all business for now, making him try harder to impress me.

"What sort of updates?" I asked.

"Well, we've had some software upgrades and the digital mapping system has been improved since we first put it in. The thermal imaging is the same but the recognition system and alarms have been updated significantly as we have refined the system."

"Do you use these systems as test beds for your own research?" Danny felt the need to interject and remind us both he was still present. Mr Johnson was annoyed at the intrusion to his building of our rapport, he answered curtly, "Yes, its important to have real usage of the systems to iron out any potential problems. That system has been in for five years but this stuff isn't even on the market yet. Only a few places are deemed important enough to spend the money on, but Brian's was a development excuse so it was OK." I crossed my legs in front of him. As the newest female on the block he felt the need to make his move, despite probably being married with several children. It was many a man's game. His pride came from his conquests even if they were only ever in his head. If I was nice he would go home telling himself that I was desperate for him. I would encourage him for as long as I needed his help. The long crossing of my legs in the pencil skirt didn't escape Danny's attention either and his face spoke thunder in the small room.

"Brian gives us a weekly report on everything that has happened within the system. If there's a problem we write a patch and download it online. We do a full security test once a year to check everything works, and of course, it always does," he was smiling at me again to emphasise how clever he was. I looked at Danny and it was clear he'd had the same thought. What if the remote panel we had been searching for was a simple PC or laptop connected to the internet? I got a sinking feeling, a knot wrenched at my stomach.

"The system is connected via the internet?" I asked, dreading the answer but he shook his head, "Sort of, but not really," I looked quizzically at him, "Sorry, I'll explain, part of the development of this system is to use the next communication tool that is coming out. It uses phone lines the same way as the internet, but is so much faster than broadband we have had to develop new technology to make it work. Its actually two steps ahead of broadband, not due to the manufacturers for three years yet. We will finalise the development then drop it into the market for the manufacturers to start making the merchandise. The Glowband connection is just between the PC in the lab here and Brian's system, so this is the only place that can talk to it just now. We're using the technology for military communications exclusively at the moment because its so much faster than anyone believes is possible. Its all part of the element of surprise. By the time Glowband is out in maybe seven or eight years, we will be on to the next thing and change it. That's the beauty of being ahead of the market," he was so proud, if he were chocolate he'd eat himself.

We both sat and thought for a second, "So from the PC here in the lab you can control the cameras, the recording and the arms systems?" I slipped it in subtly with the mundane items, but he didn't miss it, "No, no. It doesn't exist, the arms system. We included it as a possible bolt on for later, but there is no arms system included in the security programme. Brian wouldn't have it. Even if there was, we can't control anything from here. The connection allows access to the processor only, the operation is only available from the Control room at the house." If he was lying he was damn good at it.

"What about the remote control panel, where is that located? Is it within the house?" I pursued him further.

"Again, this is a development prototype. The remote facility was never used. We put it into the software but didn't give them an extra panel, its still sitting here in the workshop. Actually I don't think it would even work any more, Brian has robbed a few of the bits for other projects so there is no working remote panel."

I needed to figure him out quickly, we needed the truth. I leaned forward on my chair and looked directly at the man sitting behind his desk until I knew he was listening intently to what I was about to say, "Mr Johnson, you say that these systems are not available, but we both saw them working at Dr Fairfield's house yesterday. How do you explain that?" My gaze never flinched, he knew I was asking him to tell me how it might be possible, but it seemed he had no idea.

He wrestled with the facts for a while, looking confused at first and a little offended. It was his system and he should know about any updates, but the basis for the facilities were there so Dr Fairfield could have the other parts added whenever he wanted. On the annual test, Mr Johnson ignored the remote and arms menus because he thought they didn't really exist. He had to come to terms with the fact that his superior could well have altered his prototype and not told him. He clearly felt ashamed in front of me, his pride had been dented. He had to admit it, talking more quietly now, "Well, the programme is all set up, if he wanted to, he could have the add-ons installed and not need me to set them up. He could get someone else to do it for him." After building himself up so well it pained him to admit he was not indispensable.

"So, if he wanted to have a remote panel built and set up, he could do it without your team?"

He knew I was being kind and mentioning the team and he seemed to warm to me further for giving him a way out and sparing his blushes, "Yes, as long as he had the technical frequencies that each command worked on, he could have it emulate the commands he set up. Of course, he had all of the frequencies in the control manual that was written for it when we installed it, so I guess he can do whatever he wants."

"And what type of arms systems would it support, do you have those developed as well?" I gave him a stony look that told him he wasn't off the hook just yet.

"We don't develop weapons systems in this department, but if they were to be used, it would only need a simple digital controller with basic commands, for example a location to tell them where to work, arm, disarm, fire, aim commands possibly, that would be all, the processors, etc. are already built in."

At last I was satisfied he was telling the truth. That meant we were still trying to locate the remote panel and that it could take the shape of any type of controller. This was getting harder, not easier the more information we got. We were now looking for a needle in a haystack unless the old man was willing to talk. We would have to go back to the base to find out, but we had other business before leaving the DRA.

"Thank you, you have been most helpful Mr Johnson," the sweetness was back in my voice and I smiled at him to let him know he had done well, "if we could just impose on you for one further thing, could you locate a Mr Peter Bowson for us? He works at this facility and is known to Dr Fairfield, we just need a quick word with him. Thank you ever so much," I sat back in my chair and swept my hair back off one shoulder to expose my neck for him to see. He immediately started to look the name up on the Staff Search with the directory of each employee's extension number.

"I'm sorry, I can't find the name, do you know the department?" but we did not.

"Its alright, I will take you back to the Reception, Nancy has a photographic memory and will be able to find whoever you need, she knows everyone who has started here for the past fifteen years at least. We call her the Oracle," he laughed, light heartedly, attempting humour now to win me over and I faked minor amusement.

Back down the labyrinth of corridors, we passed a place that I did not recognise. The hackles on my neck rose up and I became very wary of our position, he was taking us a different route back. This I did not like at all. The man was still chatting away, but I made only moderate responses now as I tried in vain to get my bearings in the bleak white landscape.

"That's it over there," he pointed to a shabby looking cabin set slightly back from the corridor and Danny, who had obviously been concentrating harder than I had, asked if we could go in.

"Its probably locked," Mr Johnson said. Smiling admiringly at him, I asked if we could just try it, if it was locked then we could carry straight on to the Reception, no harm done. He relented, eager to please and probably convinced that the office would be locked anyway. He took us through the outer door that led to Dr Fairfield's private office. He held the door open for me, I in turn held it for Danny, placing an object into his other palm as we walked through and pressing it home so he could feel it. Mr Johnson gripped the door handle and gave it a tug, "Just as I thought, locked. I'm sorry, my dear, well never mind," he ushered me away with an open gesture and a gentle arm on my shoulders as an excuse to touch me and have me walk closer to him. I smiled at him, positioning myself between him and Danny, whose hand was on the office door, "Oh, its quite alright, Mr Johnson, thank you for bringing us over and trying, we know how busy you must be, someone of your position within the organisation. I'd hate to take up any more of your precious time, sir." He was blushing with pride until Danny called us back moments later. He stood with the door ajar, gesturing the civil servant back to accompany us inside,

"It was just a bit stiff," he said, passing the lock picking kit back into my waiting hand as he held the door open for me. We were getting to be quite a team.

A quick search of the office revealed nothing of any potential control panel or any evidence of an arms installation. One of the photos on the bookshelf I recognised, it was of the mysterious fishing partner and himself with a particularly large fish, looking very proud. They were wearing summer clothes on a bright sunny day in the country with children playing and a pub in the background. I took the photo out of the frame and put it into my pocket. Mr Johnson did not look pleased at this and began to get nervous.

"Just borrowing it," I said, "I'll give him it back when I see him later this morning, its OK" With no other evidence of a remote panel we would have to go back and try him again, unless Turtle had managed to have the access unblocked. We needed our mobile phones, it was time to head back to the Reception.

Mr Johnson reluctantly gave me a long goodbye then curtly shook Danny's hand in rough acknowledgement of his presence. Nancy was waiting for us and I asked for our phones.

"Do you recognise this man?" I asked Nancy, showing her the picture from Dr Fairfield's office. "Not the man with Dr Fairfield," said Nancy, "but I know the place. That's the White Lion at Holly Green. I used to court a young man round there and he took me for picnics along that stretch next to the river. There's a lovely bridge over the Severn there. Sometime around 1963 that was," she added.

"And do you know which department Peter Bowson works in?" I asked but already knew the answer.

"I'm sorry, there's nobody of that name working here. I know every name and face personally," The urgency to trace this man became apparent. We took our possessions back, Danny was 'sniffed' then told to press his finger on the wall to retrieve his gun from the little tray.

"Where to now?" he asked as we passed back through the security gate and out into the normal world once again, "We'll find out if they have a pint with their fishing then back to talk to the good Doctor. He seems to have some explaining to do." Danny accelerated away. I collected my impressions of the morning's developments and thought in anticipation of what the rest of the day might bring.

The White Lion Inn was a picturesque little pub on the village green. The river ran through the edge of the village, the bridge and embankment being popular spots for fishermen. It was a quiet location with just a few shops and a small rural school nearby. If they were out here fishing all Saturday morning, what would they need from the local neighbourhood? Perhaps a pub lunch, a sandwich from the local shop? That was all there was available here so we decided to try the pub first, the most likely candidate for two men out on their own since the early morning.

We trudged up the gravel drive to the double doorway under the porch which led to the main bar. The pub was hundreds of years old, a former coaching inn, still with the stables at the back, converted to rooms for paying guests now. Danny ordered our drinks and we stood at the bar, the only people there, to try and engage some conversation with the landlord.

I held out the picture from Dr Fairfield's office. Danny and I chatted about it, pointing out the landmark of the hotel we were now in, the white lion statue on the top of the porch clearly visible in the background. The landlord was interested in our visit and it was easy to engage him. I showed him the picture we brought, telling him our friend had recommended the area. As Danny was a keen fisherman, we were checking it out for a potential fishing trip. Danny's skills of manipulation being used on a man for a change, the talk turned round to the man in the photo. He casually asked if the landlord knew his friend Peter. When Danny said he came over on a Saturday morning, he knew exactly who he was. He ordered a lunch every time they fished there, him and his tall friend.

"Ha, he's so funny." Danny scoffed, "I don't know any other man in this day and age that still pays for everything by cash. When we go for a meal or anything, there's never a card to be seen. We laugh about it all the time, its so unusual these days, isn't it" Danny threw the conversation back to the landlord for comment, but he had to disagree, "I have to pull you up there, sorry young man. Your nice friend always paid by credit card for both meals, he would keep a tab open for them both to have a couple of drinks as well, so I'm afraid you're quite wrong there," he advised.

"Are you sure?" he asked, amazed at the revelation, "maybe its something he had years ago and doesn't use now. When was he last here using the credit card, it must have been ages ago,"

"No, no, definitely not. He was here the week of the gala, only two weeks ago and I tell you now, boy, he used it then."

"Wow, it was the first time I've known it," Danny admitted, "wait til I tell the guys back home," he exclaimed, "Old Pete does belong in the 21st century after all." We all laughed, carrying on the joke at 'poor old Pete's' expense. Danny said it was a lovely spot and we would definitely be stopping here for lunch ourselves when we came on our fishing trip. We finished our drinks and went outside to the car.

Turtle traced the records, the little inn was so far from anywhere that there was only one card used over the weekend to set up a tab, according to the credit card records, and that belonged to a Peter Bushell. He was able to quickly get an address. This man had a family and a national insurance number. It was only a matter of time before we picked him up. Turtle found his passport ID and sent the picture to my phone. It was the same man as the fishing photo. After sending the data through, Turtle did another search on the picture to find that this man had been to Tunisia at the same time as Susie had been there. His photo also matched the description of a man they had been interested in a couple of years ago for suspected illegal arms deals in the Gulf, but they had lost visibility of him after one of our officers had a car accident while following him. Turtle would get the local boys to pick him up at home while we went back to talk to the doctor. Peter Bowson, or Bushell had become suddenly very important by his absence, but we were on a hot trail and shortly would see exactly what his involvement was.

Chapter 14

The plan of attack had been revised and rethought. Turtle was on to the DRA personnel records and Dr Fairfield's security system, hoping for a decision within the hour as to whether he would be able to gain all the details we required. The Tech' Room was up and running again, the subject this time was the eminent scientist. He had spent the night in the comfortable surroundings, but recordings of the night showed he had slept badly. I hoped he was worried enough to tell us what we needed to know. We needed to find the mole who had betrayed us to the Tunisians.

I observed him in the room for a short while to gauge his body language and see what kind of mood he might be in. At the forefront of my mind was that he would be trained against interrogation techniques and would not fall so easily for my usual little tricks and capers. I would have to convince him it was in his best interests to talk to me. I thought back to the previous day's confrontation at the house, he was tight lipped until he was convinced we could gain nothing from the information he was giving us. It gave me a starting strategy at least, I should make him think that we knew it all already. Even if I made up something ridiculous, the man of facts and science would be tempted to dispel my myth rather than allow it to carry on. It was a start to get him talking, something that had proved the most difficult thing last night. Ready to go in, I nodded to Danny to start his observations.

"Good afternoon, Dr Fairfield," I was cordial towards him without being warm, "Well, we've had a very interesting morning at your workplace, Doctor. How on earth do you find your way around with all those white corridors all looking the same?" He made no move to look interested in anything I had to say.

"The man that developed you house security system was very helpful. 'Mr Johnson', as we will call him," I looked for a reaction but received no reward, "he told us all about the weapons system and how it could be controlled. He explained about the Glowband connection and how very few people knew about the controls other than him. Good system isn't it?" I looked at the doctor as he started to fidget in his chair. His discomfort needed to be increased before I would get the reaction I required.

"So it is obvious really that Mr Johnson must have fired the laser that injured one of our men. Did you see that yesterday? He shot one of the agents that came to your house. Took the side of his foot right off." I circled around the room, he remained glued to the sofa, his eyes never lifting from the fire in the hearth.

"Shame really, after so much hard work for us that someone as valuable as him should have to go to prison. Don't you agree Doctor?" He sat, shaking his head.

"Of course, your testimony as the prosecution's star witness should help put him away. As soon as you vouch for the fact that only Mr Johnson could have fired the weapon, he'll find himself going down for a fair old stretch." The doctor sat in silence but switched and moved position slightly as if trying to gain some comfort in the old chair. I continued to stroll around the large room, watching his pain.

"We had no choice but to arrest Mr Johnson, I'm sorry he's a friend of yours, Doctor, were you close? Oh dear, you have clearly been betrayed," I let the word hang there for a second, "we're looking at other potential crimes from his office now. His work has been suspended and his team disbanded this afternoon. You know how fast these things work when some breach is discovered. All his achievements will be written off. His private life is already coming under scrutiny. I took a phone call just before I came in to tell me about his name as a ladies man apparently coming to light and looking slightly distasteful. His poor wife, eh? Do you know her?" I persisted. My dark demons were good at mental torture as well as physical. I always thought women were better at interrogation than men, not threatening and abusive, but ruthless and unmerciful when the subject matter required.

I had reached the point I had been aiming for, the Doctor stood up; the veins in his temples throbbed with rage, his teeth gritted and his face contorted in anger. I looked smugly at him, waiting for the tirade of abuse that I knew was brewing within him. The charges were ridiculous, but he could say nothing without incriminating his own family or friend. He either gave up an innocent colleague or his own family. He mopped his head and face with the little hankie once again and slumped back onto the sofa, pressing a cushion into his knees, kneading it like dough and shaking his head, "You're wrong," he blurted, "he knows nothing, he's such an arrogant ass, he'll tell you he can do anything. Especially you . . ." he started, darting a glance at me but refusing to finish the sentence. I tried to draw him further, "Really? The evidence is all there and his own testimony points directly to his office . . ."

"You're wrong" was all he would say, over and over as I expanded the lies to torment him further. At last, he pushed his hands into the cushion, rocking back and forth, refusing to say anything else.

I scoffed at his pitiful state and said I would return shortly for him to sign the statement for the secret service to use as part of their evidence.

Danny waited for me in the Tech' Room. I looked at the monitors to see how the doctor had reacted to my torments, he was still simpering into the cushion. Then I looked at Danny, he had a strange expression fixed to his face, "What?" I asked, wanting to know what it meant.

"I think I've got it," he said, rewinding the recording of the Doctor's outburst when he stood up to confront me but was unable to carry on.

"Have you wondered why he keeps his jacket on when he is obviously so hot that he needs to mop his brow every two minutes when you are talking to him?" I thought it was a nervous reaction.

"Look closely," he added, too eager to wait for my answer, and zoomed in to the picture on the monitor so that just the Doctor was in the frame.

"See anything unusual?" he asked, enjoying my confusion once again, "No? Look again, this time in colour," he switched to the thermal imaging camera. The whole of the doctor's jacket was red with heat when the rest of his clothes were cooler blue or warmer green in the hot areas like the crotch and joints. I watched the image closely as he got out the hankie and mopped his face, "What's that?" I asked as a tiny white hot spot was revealed when the hankie was taken out of the pocket. The jacket was producing its own heat signal and it pinpointed to a single spot within the breast pocket as a very hot source. I looked at Danny with a light dawning on me. Danny's giddiness infected me as the possibilities presented themselves. I felt a sudden rush of excitement, "Let's see how attached he is to that fancy jacket. Turn up the heat to 30'C in that room and see how hot he has to get to take it off."

The heat rose quickly in the mild autumn coolness. The subject alone in the room was stifled and sat up as it reached 25'C. The sweat poured from him but the jacket remained in place. The heat increased, becoming unbearable, then he did the thing that made us almost shout for joy in our little enclave, he checked the inside of the jacket, behind the breast pocket, to see if the heat was coming from there. We were right. Once he knew it was the room getting hotter, not his jacket, he took it off and laid it over the back of the chair. That was the moment to strike, I ran out of the Tech' Room straight into the hot suite.

"I'm sorry, Dr Fairfield, there seems to be a fault on the central heating," I apologised, moving the radiator valve pretending to turn it down as Danny reduced the set-point to normal levels and engaged the air conditioning to cool the room quickly. I stood with my hands on the back of the chair where he had thrown the jacket, "The building is quite old and the heating system goes a bit wonky every so often," I laughed, best friends now, and offered to take his jacket and shirt for dry cleaning, picking it up and folding it over my arm, "I can bring you some clean clothes while I get these laundered for you, if you like," but he did not like, apparently.

"Could you please just put my things down and leave now," he raged at me. I fumbled with the jacket for a little while longer, insisting that I provided some service as recompense for the faulty heating, but he fervently declined all attempts so I left him to stew.

"Did you get it?" asked Danny, excitedly. I produced a tiny piece of cloth, the lining from the Doctor's precious jacket. I had snipped it out from inside the sleeve while we talked. The material was the power source for the tiny processor hidden behind the breast pocket of the tweed jacket. When I picked it up, I had felt the controller and the slight bump of something in the collar of the coat. The material acted like a battery, using the Doctor's movements to store tiny amounts of electrical charge. The miniature processor used very little energy and as long as he kept moving, the controls would work indefinitely. Mr Johnson had told us a few commands would be required to arm and fire the laser system. Once we isolated these, we could figure out how he had activated and fired the weapon. Danny rewound the recordings, maybe the buttons were the keys or something in the inside pocket.

Danny checked the recordings of the thermal images to see what showed up while I rang the driver that had brought him back to the base the previous day. When I quizzed him about his passenger's behaviour, he had remarked that Dr Fairfield had not been touching or playing with any buttons, pockets or items of clothing, but the poor fellow appeared to have been greatly stressed because of his habit of talking to himself in the back of the car while I was blowing the dust about outside. He had been even cleverer than we thought, a true leader in his deadly profession.

He was certainly one for using all of the innovations at his fingertips, the voice recognition software within the jacket would take direct commands and transmit them to the security system to arm it and fire the laser as well as turn it off when it was discovered. The X-rays from the camera in the room that Danny had been checking confirmed that the jacket had a series of wires running through it, with a couple of buttons hooked into the system as well. We could only speculate what they did, but explosives could not be ruled out and a guard was placed at the door of his room at a safe distance just in case he decided it was time to leave. Dr Fairfield had fired on the driver, talking like a madman to his coat to arm and fire his deadly rays; it wasn't a giant leap from that to sending the pictures to have us terminated.

Turtle was silent at the news. The consequences would be dire if this information got out, but it gave him the leverage to gain access to some of the data denied to him before. First the doctor's phone records were released. The call the doctor made that had disturbed his evening meal that night Susie came home was to a mobile triangulated to the Brubake Hotel. He had sent the assassins after us, using the details we had given him to lead the Dutchmen to our hotel. We had him in our grasp, but the consequences of Britain's top defence scientist being in the control of terrorists sent a shiver right through me. The shock of our discovery was unwelcome in every respect. As it dawned on us all at once, Danny and I sat looking at one another as if to check if this were all real and not imagined. We had to know what they were planning to do with the AnTTs.

The launch was to be made the following day, we didn't have much time. First we had to get the jacket away for fear of the other unknown powers he had in its command, "Set everything to record and come with me," I ordered, exploding into action as the confusion of fog lifted from me. Danny pushed all the necessary buttons then followed me out of the room. I burst in upon the Doctor, walking quickly to where he sat, standing over him so that he couldn't get up.

"Take it away," I instructed, Danny swept up the jacket, still over the back of the chair as its owner was relieved to be rid of it for a while until he cooled down. Danny turned and swiped out of the room. Dr Fairfield shuffled in his seat but was unable to make any move to stop him. He hung his head once again as I stood still above him. He was an intelligent man, we both knew the game was up.

"Very clever," was all I said, making my way across the room to settle in for the long haul of trying to get him to give up his involvement. I softly placed myself into the armchair, sitting up straight and looking directly at him, "Well, at least your friend Mr Johnson is off the hook, isn't he?" The powerful executive seemed feeble now. He appeared to have aged ten years in two days, but also looked resigned to what had happened – almost relieved. He sat back in the chair for the first time.

"Was it the thermal imaging that gave it away?" he asked after a short snort and a long sigh, looking up at me, his captor, to admit defeat. The perfectionist in him still wanted to know how well his experiment worked and what had betrayed him. At the end of his carer he still needed the closure of knowing how well his work had fared.

"Why?" was all I answered and his eyes began to pool with tears that he couldn't fight back. He shrugged his shoulders and looked down, "It doesn't matter now. The damage is done. We'll all be killed tomorrow if we try to stop it. They had it all sewn up, I was just the last piece of the jigsaw, the date, that's all they needed from me. They had everything else already." He paused in his recollection of the damning evidence, "I could have retired . . ." he drifted off into his own little world but I needed him back. I sat next to him on the sofa, dropping down lightly but banging a hand on the coffee table to focus his attention back into the room.

"What are they going to do at the launch?" I was urgent in my enquiries now, my voice raised, my tone demanding. The scientist had flipped, the pressure was too much, "Its no use, they'll kill us all if you try to stop them." I needed more information but in his delicate state of mind I couldn't get through to him to give it up.

The clock was running down. The terrorists had a plan for the following day. I needed it now, "How will they kill us all if we try to stop them tomorrow? Doctor . . . I need you to concentrate, what makes you think they will kill us tomorrow?" The old man was getting older by the second, gradually fading away in front of me, his eyes full of tears, shaking his head in despair.

"The AnTTs," he said, looking at me for the first time, "they will use the AnTTs. If anyone who is supposed to be there doesn't come to the demonstration, including me, they will use the AnTTs and detonate them somewhere else, it could be a public place, or my house, or anywhere they choose. They have some of the demonstration AnTTs sent out last week and a controller. They could use them anywhere. You can't stop them," he faded out again, the terror of the situation gaining on him. My breathing came quickly as I tried to piece together the threat he was too scared to admit.

I could see he was struggling so softened my approach to the poor tortured soul.

"Doctor, I'm sorry. Can you please tell me everything you know, so I can help you. We have to stop them." With all the cameras in operation, Dr Fairfield unfolded the story before us.

"I don't know what they're planning, I only know what they'll do if anyone interferes with it," he spoke quite reasonably now, the insanity subsiding as he calmly revealed the hell to come the following day.

"They said they had the AnTTs and would use them if I didn't keep quiet. Me, and all the other guests, had to turn up for the launch otherwise they would unleash terror on the streets. They said they would be watching, and if there was any attempt to interfere, the AnTTs would be detonated at a place of their choosing," he said.

"Tell me from the beginning," I gently prompted him, "when did you first get involved? I need to know every detail." He took a moment to rub his eyes and compose his thoughts. His manner was simple now, almost child-like. I was desperate for the words but would need to be patient for him to be steady enough to give me everything I needed.

"They first contacted me at work. After my Mother died in the spring someone suggested trying fishing. I'd never really had a hobby – at least not as an adult. My father had died when I was young and I had only a small recollection of fishing as a child. I had a gap in my life and decided to give it a go. I was given the number of a man called Peter Bowson who said he was a retired agent, working for MI6 as well as the DRA on certain research projects. He wasn't in any of my teams, which I saw as a relief as we were less likely to stray into work talk."

I shifted in my chair and gave the Doctor a moment while he thought about how events had turned on him within so few months.

"Peter showed me how to fish and we talked while we fished. We got on well, he was a really nice guy. He had shared a lot of stories about his work and travels, people we both knew, never enquiring about anything I was up to and appearing not to care. Then one day he looked upset. I asked him what was wrong and he told me that through his old Police contacts, he had heard Susie was in trouble with drugs in Dublin. I was shocked, of course. I wanted to go to see her, but he said not to worry, he knew some people who could help me out. He said that if I went I would have to book the journey on my schedule and then it would be public knowledge about my daughter being in trouble. I knew what he meant – our employers don't take kindly to any sort of risk with their people or their work. I had seen a man lose his entire career after a suspicion that his wife had a gambling problem came to light. We never saw him again and his work was split up and given to other staff for safety."

"Peter said it was best to keep quiet, his fiends would look after things and get her on the right track. I thanked him for his help. Ha!" he snorted, clearly unimpressed as an afterthought of his new best friend. I would not need to point out the error of his ways in trusting the man that had manipulated him so easily.

"My work on the AnTTs was just coming to a head, ten years of the most innovative and striking technology I had ever produced. It was the absolute pinnacle of my achievements and to be the crowning glory of my career – we're talking potential knighthoods here," he glared at me so I understood his commitment to the project and of course to his own glorification. "I couldn't risk it being stopped, I had no choice but to let him make what arrangements he could to get Susie back under control. I was still in contact with her at that time, although neither of us mentioned anything about it when we talked. Susie assured me she was fine and I thought it had all been worked out when she told me she had met some new friends and was getting on well at school. I thought Peter had kept his word." He looked sad at being fooled so badly by someone he trusted.

I hoped the recounting of the story would unburden him of the stupid guilt that would have plagued such a clever man since the sorry episode began.

"After that, Peter started asking about my work, casually at first, then more frequent. I knew he had a high clearance so would give out a few little details that he could have come across anywhere within the labs, but I avoided anything else. That's when he started to get more demanding. He kept saying that he had done me a favour in helping out with Susie, but if I didn't give him the information he wanted, she would end up on the streets. I refused. I told him I wouldn't see him any more and he wasn't to contact me again. That was when Peter told me that Susie was in real trouble. He said they would take her out of it and clean her up for me if I gave them the date they wanted. He threatened to tell my superiors about Susie and how I had covered it up. He wasn't specific about the AnTTs, he just wanted the big project I was working on."

"The whole project had been more secret than any other I had worked on. Even the departments involved didn't know the full extent of what the devices could do, each one only had a small part of the brief to achieve. Only myself and two others knew the full story so I took a gamble that they knew nothing real about it and it would be safe to give them just a date. I said if they brought her home safe, I would give them the launch date. In return they promised to pay me for my services, giving me enough money to retire a wealthy man. I wasn't interested in the money, but the thought of retirement was very appealing. Whenever I'd broached the subject with my managers they said we could discuss it after the next project was finished, then the next, then the next." I gave him a moment to think as we both considered our employers and I wondered when I would be dreaming of retirement.

"Then I lost contact with Susie. Her friends were telling me she was fine and she would call me back, but she never did. I hoped that Peter was being true to his word but I knew I couldn't trust him now. I didn't know what to do. I was hoping I'd been unable to talk to her because they had taken her to a local rehab centre, I hadn't realised they had actually kidnapped her to get the information I had promised them. They must have thought there was a chance I wouldn't part with it once she was clean, so took matters under their own control. After you two brought her home and I found out about the kidnapping, I called Peter that night to tell him I would tell the Police, but he laughed and said that our conversations had been taped. If I refused to co-operate I would be branded a spy and a traitor," he scoffed at the irony after all his years of devoted service, literally handing over his whole life to the betterment of his country.

"Peter said he would send the tapes to the Minister if I tried to interfere. He said he would deal with you himself and made me tell him where you were staying then give him the photos for ID."

The more he tried to cover things up, the worse he made them. He was a broken man, trying everything to save his family and his career. After a life of solitude, starved of social attention, his only mistake had been to trust someone who he thought was in the same position and been careless. He so desperately wanted his little girl to be safe and the pressures of his work had clearly affected him for some time.

He looked weary, I felt sorry for the wretched figure until I remembered the white laser and the severed toes still smoking in the burnt out shoe, the man who may never walk properly again all due to this egotist trying to save his own skin.

"At the house, we put you in the car, what did you think was happening?" I asked him, trying to get to the bottom of why he would attack his own colleagues.

"I'm sorry," he apologised.

"I regretted that deeply, I didn't mean for anyone to get hurt. I just wanted to see if you could detect it. I'd wanted to try it for a long time and it seemed like the ideal opportunity with several of the type of professionals that it was constructed to evade. The voice activation was slightly off and the laser swiped across the path in the wrong direction. I couldn't turn it off fast enough to stop it. It was pleasing to see it work, though, if in need of some refinement." A hint of pride broke over his features, stopping short of a smile that I wasn't sure he remembered he owned.

"In other words, you were testing it on us. We were part of your experiment—your research? Would we have been included in your report on how well it worked?" I raised my voice again now, "a man walked through that beam and has lost his toes because of your little system test, do you realise that?"

He stood up and strode around the room, a different man now, once more he was the scientist, Head of Development, leading voice in all technical developments. He was used to being challenged about the ethics of what he did and his simple response was, "Well, if its going to work at all, it needs to be right, don't you think?" The perfectionist in him had got him this far in his career and this system was no different. I used the weapons he developed, so which one of us was truly morally superior? I had no high ground on this topic.

Turtle was watching the live stream of the feed from the cameras in the room. He and Danny watched in horror as the plot was revealed, but we still had no idea what the terrorists were planning. We needed more – how many AnTTs had they taken, who had given them the information, who was behind it and what did they want. We simply weren't going to get it from the doctor; he had told us what he knew, I was sure. I thanked him and left him alone.

Right down the corridor was one further possibility for information. I had not managed to get to the captured men in the other room that had been picked up at the Hotel. They had been softened up for a couple of days, maybe it was time to pay them a visit. The arms dealers were my next call. They had been separated by their interrogators, I could isolate each one to get out of them what I could and make out that the other had told me.

There was no time for introductions, I ran in through the door and jumped at the chair in the room, knocking it over backwards. The impact of the chair crashing to the floor smashed into the man's hands, tied to the back. A yell came out from under the hessian bag as I came back to the strewn figure and sat on the front, with the man's knees underneath me, crushing his arms at the wrists and straining the shoulder joints. He tried to squirm free but my feet hemmed him in so any wriggling proved futile. My position of power over the stricken agent tempted my dark inner animal into the violence it so enjoyed. The darkness of its presence came over me but I had to resist the urges it was forcing upon me.

I sat and waited for him to stop, as an intelligent man would, learning that he was wasting his energy. As he eventually calmed down, I bent my face down to the bag, where the ear would be underneath, and gently coaxed him that he would do better to stop squirming and listen.

"I know about the plan for the launch, I know about the fishing trips, I just need to know how many men were going to be waiting for us tomorrow?" I murmured in a soft voice. The man grew very still and quiet. I repeated the statement, waiting for him to react, but he remained defiantly quiet.

Again I pushed the invasion of violence to the back of my mind, although I had no time for simple silence, beating him randomly would probably not help. I had other forms of pain that I could control more effectively. I wrestled the chair into position so that the bars on the back were directly over the ends of his fingers, trapping them at the nail, the full weight of his body pressing against them excruciatingly. He yelped under the hessian mask, grumbling that he knew nothing.

"You were the one who waited to hear about whether I had been picked up or disposed of by the Dutchmen – would you have been any kinder in my treatment after you planned to kill me when you were finished?"

I slammed myself down onto his knees, the feeling of red hot nails being pushed through the ends of his fingers would be ripping through his hands all the way to the shoulders as the nerve endings were trapped and torn. He tried to stop himself screaming, a muffled grunt came out as I pulled off the hessian bag. I pulled back in disbelief, rising from the chair. Right here in front of me was the face from the photograph, the fishing partner, Peter Bowson. The search was over, I had the main culprit held by his fingernails under my feet. I wanted to shout for Danny to come and look, but the business was still at hand, if not intensified now this leading agent was here and subdued.

I heaved the man and his chair back to their feet so that the blood would rush back into the ends of his fingers and the pain come with it. The skin would burn with the agony, his white nails slowly turning pink and glowing with the sensation. He looked at me, his eyes cold, refusing to acknowledge my advantage. He looked bedraggled from his days of softening up, but he was apparently not beaten yet. I needed some leverage to get him to talk. I only knew a couple of things about him but they were incredibly useful ones.

"Mr Bowson, very nice to meet you. Tell me, does your wife always think you're on a business trip when you are actually out helping terrorists and blackmailing innocent people?" A flutter of a reaction was fleeting but I'd caught it. At the mention of his family, he looked at me, then regained his steely composure. The Police had been to pick up our dear prize at his home, making the pretence to ask him about an accident he had supposedly witnessed so as not to raise the alarm, but his wife had insisted he was on a trip and not available for contact until the weekend.

This was not going to be easy. We both knew he only had to hold on until the morning. I needed to exert more pressure, quickly, there was no time to build a rapport or wear him down, it had to be all out attack.

"Maybe we should bring her in and ask her exactly where she thinks you are. We were trying not to alarm her before, but now that we know where your loyalties lie, I don't see why the wife of an arms dealer working with terrorists should be spared any disgrace."

He sniffed at me and looked up at the ceiling, pretending to take no notice of my threats. He wasn't biting, I needed to continue, "Of course, if the wife is in custody, what will happen to the children? They're only little and you have no family to take care of them. I suppose they will have to go into care until all this mess is sorted out." His expression didn't alter but he started to sweat, a solitary bead making its way slowly down his temple, turning into a trickle as it joined other tiny drops on their way down to his chin. I knew the pressure was working when he turned that side of his face aside, but would he yield in time?

"It can be so difficult to get your children back once they have gone to social services, though, can't it?" I went on, as if we were having a conversation over the garden fence.

"It's a shame, the stories you hear about what goes on in these isolated places. I'm sure that won't happen to your children though. I'm sure they will find a nice uncle that will look after them really well. Very cosy, take them to bed at night, tuck them up tight . . ."

I left it there, the images would be spinning around in his head, too much for any parent to bear. He screwed up his eyes as if to block it out. The pressure was building, I could see it.

"How many men will be waiting for us tomorrow?" I asked again. He sat in silence, back to business, refusing to hear my questions. One more violent outburst was required, I would need to keep myself in check as my heart pumped with the force welling to be let out.

I growled at the traitor in my grasp, with a crash I threw the chair on to its side on the floor. It slid over the floorboards and came to rest closer to the hearth. The man attached was now on his side, suspended by the chords that held him. I had a run up then punted the chair so it rocked and spun on the floor. When it came to rest I sat on top of the chair so he was unable to move, his eyes were clenched tight, waiting for the next strike.

"How many men?" I asked again, kicking the man's shins with the backs of my heels.

"Very well," I said and pulled out my mobile phone. I dialled my other mobile, safely tucked away at home and had a fake conversation with my answer phone, "Yes, its me, can you pick up the Bowson woman in Canterbury and send her for questioning . . . no, to a secure location, yeah somewhere nice and quiet. No, not the Police this time, use our own men and they don't need to be too polite, yeah? And don't forget the children, they are both at local schools . . . yes, that's right. If you get Social Services they can take them straight away. Thanks, yes, OK."

I snapped shut the phone and looked down at the captive. He was resting his head against the floor, staring into space.

"I just need to know how many men. I can help you get your kids back if you help me, but you have to do it right now."

"OK" came a little whimper "four," was all he said. He closed his eyes again and dropped his head back on to the floor. I acknowledged that he had made a first step and hauled him back upright. I congratulated him on being sensible and had another fake conversation with my phone about making sure the children went somewhere safe and that it was only temporary, no need to get Social Services involved as the parents would be returning for them soon.

Bowson took a deep breath. Now was a dangerous time, I had no reason to take him at his word but not many choices either. He had to expand on what he'd said in order to convince me he was telling the truth. I searched his face for a clue to what he was thinking. Something had changed in his expression, something that made me trust him less rather than more. I could not believe what he was saying but had to continue anyway in the pretence that I believed him. Maybe something he said I would be able to use.

I stood by the large hearth and leaned against the oversized mantle. He drooped on the chair, his head falling forward from the days of effort he had already undergone. I would allow him a few moments of silence before I started with him again.

"Where are the stolen products being held?" I asked. He raised his face to look at me. Murder was written in his eyes, I felt the cold stare of a predator plotting my downfall. I held his gaze, unafraid of whatever he had in mind. I could almost taste the desire to lash out at me, all there for me to see, he hid nothing of his intent.

"We took the controller to a safe place but the AnTTs are already released, ready for the target setting tomorrow," he said the words clearly and slightly too loud for the distance between us. "You best option is to tell me all you know. Now that you've started you might as well give up the rest. How many AnTTs do you have and where were they released?" I persisted, despite the threat he was emitting.

He was trying to look as beaten and lost as he could, but the effort seemed too much, something didn't ring true about his manner. My senses were on the alert, unable to pinpoint exactly what wasn't quite right here, was it just him trying to fool me into believing him, or was I just disappointed that he had decided to co-operate just as I had started to unleash my inner demons?

"We took the AnTTs and controller from the batch sent for the launch, mid transit," he continued.

"A foreign agent has the controller. I'm just a go between for the Tunisians, getting the information they needed in return for a commission on the arms deal once they've done it." He was talking but my suspicion at what he was telling me was overridden by the fidgeting of his position on the wooden chair. So far he had told me nothing we hadn't figured out already and my suspicions at his sudden forthcoming nature, so quickly after such a slow start, were rising. He wasn't just simply lying, there was something else wrong with this picture that I couldn't ignore.

I looked at him, sitting quietly in front of the hearth as I rested on the great mantelpiece. I paused for a moment to think. My eyes must have drifted from him for a second and within a breath he was on me. The ropes that had held him dangled hopelessly around one wrist as his other hand hoisted the wooden chair towards me. The sudden nature of the attack took me momentarily by surprise, I gasped as the chair legs sped past my face and the cross piece struck against my neck. He held it there, squeezing tighter as he pushed it far enough to make the legs jam into the wall behind me, pinning me against it.

As his body caught up with the sturdy arms that held the wooden noose against my neck, the pressure of the blood trying to spurt through my veins made my head throb with the effort. I gagged and tried to cough, the pressure forcing me to try and move. My arms and legs felt like lead as the last bit of air was used up flailing and thrashing to reach the treacherous agent. He was too far, my legs missed their target, my arms pinned with the other cross piece to prevent me breaking free. I felt dizzy, the pressure in my veins made them want to burst. I couldn't stand up, my body became heavy. A cloud of blackness started to form on the outside of my vision, I was losing it, I was going down. I looked at my assassin's face, my own redness reflected in his rage as he pushed harder and harder. I looked into his eyes to find a sign that he did not intend to kill me, but I was looking for a scrap of humanity that did not exist. All I saw was murder, his face contorted with the effort of taking my life away, but in the bottom of the expression was a distant joy, he was having fun at the prospect. He wasn't protecting himself, he was teaching me a lesson. A lesson he had given before, I could tell.

My shirt sleeves were trapped under the feet of the chair as I tried in vain to haul back my attacker. He squeezed the chair tighter against my neck, pushing with his full body weight, the wood digging in as my arms flopped hopelessly by my side, unable to break free. I was quickly running out of breath.

I realised I had been careless and over emotional in my desperation to get the answers I needed. He had seen the errors and was now capitalising on them, at my expense. I looked at him as I felt my breath slowly ebbing away. A sudden determination not to let this be the last image I cast on the world, him laughing as I helplessly tried in vain to stop him from taking my life. A sudden calm and resolve came over me, one that had saved me on more than one occasion. My life's experiences flashed in front of me as my brain searched for a solution. The black cloud continued to close in while I imagined how I should escape. If I left it seconds more, I would be too late, his dirty work would be done, I had to act now. Wake up Blossom.

As a last effort I shook my head to clear the black cloud then put my arms by my side, standing perfectly still to conserve the air I still had left. The panic of dying had gone from me, the chair was robbing me of my breath but my thoughts were clear. I relaxed and turned my head to the left as far as it would go. The muscles surrounding my windpipe turned with it and formed a barrier between the wooden rail at my throat and the quick death he was dealing to me. I had gained a small gap through which I could just breathe.

Still relaxed, I took in one long steady breath as he pushed harder on the chair but the legs were solid against the wall and he could go no further. With a shout and an explosion of power that came from my stomach, I threw back the killer, freeing my arms and grabbing the chair in one fluid movement. With him still attached, I made a rapid twist of the chair and my assailant spun with it, having to let go or both arms would be ripped from the sockets. He had his back to me now, I took a great breath and heaved the solid wooden seat across his rounded back. The crash of the chair into his soft flesh and stiff bones made a crunching sound that I wondered if it was wood or torso splitting. Two legs splintered off, the sound of cracking wood resounded through the empty room. His semi broken body slumped to the floor. I took hold of one of the splintered legs and forced it into his neck, jabbing at him until he stopped trying to get up. One sharp blow to the head with the wooden baton and he lay unconscious before me as Danny ran in.

"I think we might need another chair" I said, walking out to fetch one.

Chapter 15

We had a couple of hours drive to get to the air force base where the AnTTs were being kept. Finally, we had time to chat. Danny and I whiled away the time in surprising comfort. We could have further dissected the day's revelations, but we both chose to leave our dutiful world for a little respite as normal human beings, getting to know each other as the strangers we really were. Our team was beginning to gel now, fellow soldiers in hostile work, but our private lives were still undivulged. It was usually safer to operate that way in our world. I had been determined to keep my distance but the feeling of trust we had established made me weak. When my phone rang with The Muppets theme tune, I decided to answer it, despite already knowing it was my Mother.

After the usual apologies for not calling more often to update her on how busy I had been, Mum started asking about my cousin's wedding the following day. Was I coming? Who with? Why not? How did I think Edward will feel, knowing I'm his favourite cousin? With the day that I had planned, there was no way I would be able to get back and head off to a wedding.

"Mum, I'm busy at work. We've got a big launch tomorrow and I can't miss it, its all my project and it will fall over if I'm not there," I implored her to forgive me. For a second I must have forgotten I was talking to my Mother, "I never even said I was going to come to Eddie's wedding anyway . . ." I tailed off, knowing that this particular piece of defence work was, in Mum's world, quite irrelevant. A tirade of abuse stung me through the airwaves. Mum expressed, at great length, her disappointment, wanting to make me feel guilty and succeeding very well. I soon wished I'd let the bloody thing ring.

While I was deftly reprimanded by my nagging Mother, Danny sat back, listening for the first time to my domestic strife. It was his first insight into my other life and he laughed as I was made to look shamefully guilty about my prospective non attendance. I saw him laughing at me being told off and started to frown at him, growling disapprovingly as I pointed to the phone and told him to be quiet. It seemed the more I told him to stop, the more hilarious he found it, until I was trying to suppress a riot in the driver's seat. He laughed, making faces and wagging his finger at me. I could hold my sniggers no longer, Mum must have heard them and thought I was laughing at what she was saying, unleashing another bout of woe in my direction.

At that, I smacked Danny on the arm and told him to be quiet as I explained to my Mother that there was someone with me in the car and he was making me laugh to annoy her. I apologised and calmed down. Mum seemed to be so pleased that I had a man in the car she forgot about her nagging duties, for the rest of the call she tried to winkle out of me who it was. That was as difficult as the rest of the conversation. When I would offer no more than him being a work colleague, Mum passed me on to my Father. He wanted to know if I was still working on the same job as before and when the deadline was. I hadn't been able to update him since the Datameet so he was behind in our week's activities. It wasn't possible to speak candidly to Dad in front of Danny. Our work was not supposed to be talked about with anyone else outside the community, so I answered him cordially, explaining that the following day was the big finale, one way or another. He seemed to understand, asking no more questions while the obvious third parties were around.

When I said I had to go, Dad sounded fed up, "Nobody wants to talk to me any more," he complained, "your Mother has been on the phone with her Samaritans work a lot recently. You haven't called in days. There's only one thing anyone wants to discuss and its this bloody wedding tomorrow – and you're not even coming!" I took the hint.

"I'll be there if I can, Dad, I just don't know how long this thing is going to take tomorrow. I promise I'll be in touch as soon as I can. I'll send a car for you anyway; if I'm in it, all well and good, if I'm not then I'll join you when I can. OK?" it was the best I could do.

I put the phone down and looked at Danny angrily for getting me into more trouble with my Mother. He looked back at me and we broke down into fits of laughter. Real laughter that makes the tears run down your face and your stomach hurt with the joy of it. For so long I had thought he was always laughing at me, but now his sense of humour had been uncovered I reacted to it well, having finally learned where it was. Our trials had brought us closer on a personal level, he wasn't a mere distraction any more, he had proved his worth, the bruising on his sore ribs being testament to it.

The journey was pleasantly spent, soon we were following the red signposts indicating the directions we needed to get to the base. Our work persona's were back in place, no time for frivolous banter now, we had a job to do or the carnage the following morning would be a national disaster. Danny turned off the main road in the small Nottinghamshire village, the mile long access road showed the base's mission statement and resident squadrons. Armed Guards from the RAF Police stood by the gate. The lateness of the hour didn't matter to them, they would be on duty throughout the night.

Their breath steamed in the cold night air, hitting Danny as he wound down his window to show our military ID cards. The young private pushing his face through the opening in the hope of getting a little warmth did not recognise the highly specialised and rare ID cards that covert agents were issued with. These were the equivalent of 'Access All Areas' passes to any base home or abroad that we might care to make use of. He hummed and looked to his sergeant, comfortably sat in the heated guard-hut, to come over and help him out. The sergeant saw the two cards, jumped back, pushing the confused private aside, and saluted us.

"I'm sorry Sirs for keeping you waiting," he apologised, "but the security level has just gone up a notch to 'Specific Threat' and we aren't allowing anyone in who isn't cleared for access before they arrive".

Danny and I understood only too well. Word of a threat had got round and the military were getting ready for a strike, but they didn't know where. Neither of us had thought to call ahead to book our place. We sat numbly looking at each other, kicking ourselves for the lack of forethought. The sergeant walked back to the hut and pushed the button to raise the barrier, "But you were booked in about an hour ago, Sir, Ma'am. Have a pleasant evening" he said, the barrier lifted and Danny nodded approval as we drove through.

"Turtle" we both said in unison, he must have done our thinking for us, not for the first time.

Waiting for us at the Bomb Dump was a small, round gentleman with a black King Charles spaniel running round his short legs. He seemed pleasant enough as he walked out to greet us, "Hello, I'm Mark, and this is Maddie". The dog did a few laps then excitedly jumped at Danny, wagging her tail then rolling over for her tummy to be tickled when he responded with some attention. While Danny obliged, I booked us in at the control desk, using ID numbers instead of names, as we were entitled.

"I've been instructed to escort you to bunker 407. Your car will have to wait outside. If you have any contraband it needs to be left here in the cabin. I'm afraid all car keys, mobile phones, lighters, calculators, watches, anything electronic that could cause a spark will need to be left behind." The risk was too high in the explosive dust filled environment.

Mark chatted happily on the walk down to the bunker, not at all bothered at being called back to site after his day's work was complete to let in two strangers, "I already had a recall for a bit later on, so I knew I had to come out anyway. I just came in earlier and walked Maddie for a bit." At the mention of her name, the well trained spaniel came running to her master. He patted her head then shooed her away so she could run back to the rabbit's trail she had been previously following.

Then the fishing started as he gently nudged for more information to try and find out who we were and what we were doing there. I find it half amusing when someone with no concept fires their imagination to put us into a story of their choosing, half guessing what we're there for and filling in the gaps themselves. I'm always tempted to make something outrageous up, but you never know where it might lead, so my experience kept me enigmatic, answering the gentle enquiries with vague and cryptic replies.

The walk down to the last but one bunker, with the dog running up and down in excitement, was a long one but gave me a chance to see the layout of the Bomb Dump and assess whether it would be possible to break in here and take the AnTTs. Under equally gentle questioning about his lovely tree bordered domain, seemingly to pass the time during the walk, Mark said that the surrounding security fence was alarmed, the area covered by CCTV cameras back to the Guardroom and the outskirts patrolled every hour. They did have the occasional false alarm on the fence but it was usually nothing once it was investigated. I knew that these blips could easily be used to break into the area, but the CCTV would be a bit harder to fool in this open expanse of short grass and no cover.

All weapons and explosives had to be registered and stored correctly and the specialist ones we were after were no exception. The log sheets from Malvern said that four crates of AnTTs and two controller boxes had left their facility the previous week, delivered to RAF Cottesmore's bomb dump, where all ammunition was kept in secure bunkers, in case of explosion. The bunkers were constructed from four feet thick reinforced concrete, layered over with turf on the outside and angled walls to deflect a possible blast. The electrics inside were all spark free and a lightning protection system meshed the outside so that nothing could penetrate to the explosives within.

The bunker itself had two large metal blast doors, connected via an earth cable to the outside wall and the lightning protection system so that no sparks could pass between them as it was opened. Mark took out the key, unlocked the first latch, then the padlock on the hasp and unbolted the front of the doors to release them from one another. He turned the great steel wheel, like a lock on a submarine door, until the whole sturdy metal chunk creaked towards us. This was a slow business, the handle winding and shifting the foot thick metal block surely out of the doorway. I looked round, to see the CCTV cameras were now trained upon the doors, watching our every move. As the door passed by, the sulphurous smell of explosives dust hit my nose with a chemical tinge that set my teeth on edge. It was the same smell as the firing range, only stronger. I watched the switch on the door operate to alarm the Guardhouse and log when someone opened the heavy doors. If you were gong to break in here, there were several rings of security you would need to have control of before you started. Every aspect of this area had a separate alarm system. You could get easily into the grounds but not into the bunker without being seen, and no chance of burying through the concrete. Mark reached across the control panel on the outside of the building and switched on the interior lights. High on the ceiling they flickered and jumped into life.

Inside was an almost bare concrete enclosure. The lights were so high that by floor level it was quite dingy, adding to the air of decay in the fusty old building. Across one wall was a set of racking with crates and boxes on it, "These are the ones I've been told to show you," Mark handed Danny the paperwork that came with their arrival. No fool, he subtly hung around, offering his help with the heavy boxes, interested to see what was inside and what was so important that we needed to see it at this time of night. Danny looked at me. As kindly as I could, I obligingly ushered Mark gently out of the room to stand outside and wait for us to come back out.

"Thank you so much for your help, Mark, you've been brilliant, this is just what we needed. You can wait outside now, we can manage everything from here . . ." he knew he had been rumbled and stopped his pursuit of information on the contents of the boxes. Back inside, Danny was examining the paperwork, "The delivery note is the same as the one from Malvern, four crates plus two controllers. Danny wandered over and looked at the first box, 'Danger Explosives' was stamped on the outside in red letters. They were all identical apart from the two slightly smaller controller boxes.

A crowbar opened the first crate, revealing inside a set of ammo boxes. These ones differed to the standard box, being heavily secured with cipher locks and marked 'Top Secret' on the lid. This is what we had come to see. The tension rose within the room, I could feel goose pimples forming on my arms and a nervous feeling fluttered around in my stomach. Danny fumbled the box and it came out of his grasp. We both gasped as it hit the floor, reinforcing the sense of awe at the revelation that was waiting for us behind the locked case. He looked at me and gulped. I gave him a little smile as encouragement to carry on.

Turtle had sent us the numbers for the locks, I'd quickly jotted them down as we pulled up outside in the car, remembering I would not have my mobile phone inside. The small piece of paper shook a little as I uncrumpled it from my pocket. Now we had to be meticulous. Every box's serial number needed to be checked and the appropriate cipher code found to open the locks. My nerves jumped as Danny put in the code, releasing the catch on the top of the box and allowing the lid to open. We both paused, neither one daring to be the first to disturb the billion pound development that had taken ten years to be manufactured and rolled into the anti-static film pockets that sat in the box at our feet. I nodded at Danny to open them, trying not to let him know that I thought my hands might be shaking too much to handle the tiny weapons.

Inside the rolls of plastic film were thousands of tiny black dots. Each little compartment contained a hundred of the devices, no bigger than the head of a drawing pin. We looked at each other in amazement, barely believing that this was the super weapon we had come to protect. The little dots looked more like cake decorations than a threat to our civilisation.

Danny held one up to the light, the glinting of the tiny legs, finer than a human hair, was the only clue that they were there. The miniaturisation was so complete that these AnTTs could be anywhere at any time and remain totally undetected. I had seen many deadly technological developments in my career, but with this I was both amazed and horrified. My inner nerd came to the fore, amazed to see the highest level of technology right here in front of me, then the realisation struck about trying to find the ones that were supposed to have been taken. The possibility of finding a number of these tiny devices, which could come together to form a single giant bomb filled me with dread. The task we were trying to achieve now looked enormous. These tiny death bringers had already been released. How were we to find such a needle in the haystack of the UK?

The sudden sense of urgency overtook the pair of us. A swift glance was all that passed between us and we knew what we had to do. Turtle would need to know how many we were looking for, and fast. There was no time to count them all, at 50,000 to a box, a rough estimate would have to do. We needed to report back as soon as possible, but with no phones in the remote bunker, we had to work fast then escape to the outside.

We took a little time with the first crate, checking and rechecking then logging all the numbers. Speed was paramount now. We worked as a team to pull out, count and log the contents. Pack after delicate pack was laid out on the dusty concrete floor. The first and second crates tallied, both had the correct contents. The tension mounted as the third was unsealed and prised apart, I desperately wanted it to be full as the others had been. The side popped off with the crowbar to reveal a row of metal boxes that were not the same as as the ones in the other crates. They were thicker, of a similar weight to the full ammo boxes, but all were empty. My heart sank. We really were on the hunt for the tiny devices, a prospect that left me drained at the thought.

The third and fourth crates were both full of the dummy boxes, carefully weighted to feel and sound like the full ones. Two crates of AnTTs were on the loose. They could be anywhere, waiting to be activated, ganging together to strike where they could not be detected, lurking in the streets, hiding from passers by in the cracks in the pavements. They were useless without the controllers, these were next for the stock check and the final hope for me that a disaster could be saved.

My heart pounded with anticipation as the fasteners were pulled away from the final box. Everything was riding on there being a controller here. Danny's hand was hesitant at dispatching the last of the crates, the room was silent apart from the creaking of the staples holding the side in place as Danny strained to bust it open. The wooden panel crashed to the floor, sending up a cloud of dust that made me turn away. When I turned back round, I knew that the little box nestled into the packaging paper was not the same as the first one we opened next to it. I looked at Danny, both of us realising the situation now upon us. Everything the doctor and Bowson had told us was true. The crates must have been swapped mid-transit, but how? The only thing we did know was a terrorist attack was planned on the Cabinet the following day, and if we tried to stop it, the AnTTs would blow up somewhere else at a random day and time. We had less than twelve hours to find 500,000 minuscule weapons, ready to destruct.

The mission was urgent but the project still classified, we put the boxes back together and relocked each one carefully. The crates were secured back together and returned to the shelves. Once we checked the area, I went outside to find Mark sitting on the edge of the far wall, whistling to himself as the spaniel ran back and forth between bunkers. At the sight of me emerging from the dusty tomb, Maddie ran up to greet me, wagging herself almost in two, but at the sight of Danny, she jumped and dashed over to get a tummy tickling, the tail bouncing on the floor as she enjoyed the attention. Lucky bitch. The affection poured on her as she lay there, sublime, made me wrinkle a little as a shot of jealousy rushed through me. I reminded myself this was not the time as Mark had joined us, searching our faces to see whether we had found what we wanted, "Everything OK?" he asked, on another fishing trip no doubt.

"We need to get back," I answered, the enigma returning.

The walk back was considerably faster than the walk in. I thanked Mark and his loving companion for their help and retrieved our possessions from the cabin. Danny had gone to start the car when a hired roll-back van arrived and pulled up in the car park next to the gate. Mark came back out as I suspiciously waited to see who the late visitor was. The plain clothed driver produced his military ID and paper orders for the movement of three crates stored in one of the bunkers. The number was the one we had just returned from. My suspicions grew as I inspected each paper in turn for a clue as to where the boxes were being taken, but the delivery address was shown only as a grid reference, "Where are you taking them to?" I asked, tapping the co-ordinates on the paper, "We just take them to this grid point and wait until later. We get a couple of hours kip then the Satnav wakes us up and tells us where to go and what time to arrive. Pain in the arse it is, they never give us enough time and we're always last minute.com," he sniggered at his little pun, "til then we don't have a clue." said a slightly sleepy looking driver who appeared about as uninterested in his orders or his cargo as he could be.

"This is the pick-up I was expecting," Mark interjected, seeing my unease grow. "I had my own set of orders to take them to the bunker and allow them to take the crates."

So this is what he had been waiting for. We had been mere interlopers in the night's work of getting the crates to their destination. The paperwork showed the serial numbers of the crates to be taken, the ones with the AnTTs and the controller in were to be put on the truck, the empty ones would stay. Someone knew which crates were empty. This driver was to pick up the ones for the demo the following day, the empties would not be discovered until after the launch was complete, by which time the damage would be done.

I thanked Mark again and we said our goodbyes with a final petting for Maddie. As Danny sped away from the base I finally had chance to call Turtle. He had good news, "I've been given the destination for the meeting tomorrow," the edge in his voice sounded pained, I could tell he had gone through a lot to get the super classified information. Most of the people attending would not know where they were being taken until they arrived.

"I've sent the information to your phones and there will be some drawings of the layout in your room by the time you get back to Pershore. If the AnTTS have already been released, and after everything you've found we have to believe that they have, then we are looking for the controller. The extent to which we are exposed means that we can't put out an all points alert that the AnTTs are on the loose and the Cabinet in danger. Whoever planned this has gone into meticulous detail, down to substituting the correct crates to ensure the empty ones are not discovered. Someone knows everything about this project and are using it for a terror attack," he sounded grave. Turtle had no time for mole-hunts. Whenever the subject came up a bitter outlook came across him. He had been around in the fifties and sixties when mole hunting was all the rage and nobody felt safe from prying eyes. Suffice it to say he trusted very few people. I was in an honoured position.

"You must exercise extreme caution," he continued, business-like but reserved. "I am in touch with Special Forces, who are making their way to the venue to search as well as they can without arousing suspicion. The security arrangements will not be changed, the on site team have just started scanning the area for explosives, which is nothing out of the ordinary in the circumstances. They have been told to expect some extra men being made available, nothing else. We have to do everything as it would be expected otherwise the mole could raise the alarm and the AnTTs blown up elsewhere."

"You now have until 0300 to have a plan and a list of equipment you will need to save the Cabinet. The relevant ID will be waiting for you to enter the venue tomorrow, you will be there as government secretaries, come to make sure all the arrangements had been made before the start of the meeting. Suitable clothing is on its way." I looked at Danny as it all became very real. He stared at the road ahead, concentrating hard on making his way back quickly while listening to Turtle's instructions.

"You may arrive at the venue no earlier than 0700, so you can't bump into another team and give the whole rescue mission away. Do you have that?" Turtle was clear in his instructions, let the other special forces try to scout the scene and pass back any information they could, then we would meet the team in the morning on site and give the instructions for the plan, "Yes, got it," we both agreed in chorus, sounding like naughty children promising to behave, "Sleep well," advised Turtle as he signed off, knowing full well we would barely snatch two hours before getting ready for our longest day yet.

Chapter 16

Just as Turtle had promised, the drawings and photographs met us at the base. I unrolled them hungrily to find the location was a stately home in the heart of Oxfordshire. The house was in private hands but open to the public, although it would be closed for 'cleaning' that Friday. I studied the pictures of the glorious structure, a 16th Century classic building of red brick and Ionic pilasters, their fluted shafts embedded into the walls with ornate spiral tops and bottoms. The front was symmetrical with a grand staircase leading up to the door in the centre of the house. The five front bays went up for three storeys plus a basement below. The wings at either side, constructed to match the central body of the house were added some time later along with the chapel and outbuildings that made up the rest of the property. Across the ornamental lake at the front of the house were stables and farm buildings in a yard, hidden behind the trees. Photos from inside the house showed high ceilings, plasterwork to mimic the Italian style and a carved wooden chimney in the original drawing room.

A bird garden and an orchard made the view over the formal layout at the back of the house ideal. I would normally enjoy visiting such a place, but tomorrow would be different. A feeling of dread swept over me, how were we ever to find a threat that we couldn't see from the world's most ingenious weapons developer. I was drained, not knowing where to start. My stomach growled as if in sympathy with the rest of my feelings, we had missed our evening meal so

Danny sent out for Chinese and the Guardroom obliged by bringing it up to his VIP suite where we poured over the data in front of us.

On the floor of Danny's room, we sat with the drawings rolled out in front of us and cartons of Chinese dishes scattered between. I helped myself to the noodles with the chopsticks, trying not to spill them down my top and make awful sucking noises as I slurped them up ravenously from the box. Danny sat opposite, his tidy manners allowing him to eat sensibly. I watched him, fighting the urge to go over and feed the sloppy noodles to him one by one, dangling them into his mouth from mine and having his tongue tangle round them and draw them in while the gravy dropped on to his chin and pristine white shirt. The image in my head was tantalising, the raw sexuality of the simple act took me by surprise. I pushed myself to avert my eyes from his expertly pressed white shirt and concentrate on the 0300 deadline, but as long as we sat and ate the underlying desire that still hankered to be released despite our new comfort together made me feel contaminated with its presence.

Once the dinner debris was cleared away it was time to finalise the plan. Sniper positions, firing angles and evacuation procedures all had to be discussed. We needed little equipment apart from weapons, a communication system and one special box of goodies that I would have picked up from home during the night. Every detail was covered as well as we could, although the time flew past all too quickly for either of us to feel comfortable. Turtle was on the phone, it was 0259. I relayed our immediate action plan to my keenest friend and greatest critic. I felt that my sales role was being tested, having to present a complete plan while leaving out the doubts I felt about how many men the terrorists would have and that we would have no idea who was working for them. I tried to portray some confidence but the fact remained that it was a mammoth task and the location of the AnTTs made it even harder. They would not appear until the last minute, the point when you might see them was the point when they were due to explode. In enemy hands it was a true matter of terror.

Turtle gave us the contact details of the SAS Commanding Officer, Major Jim Williams, that we were to meet in the morning. He was already on site with his men, clearing where they could of the grounds, normal procedures for a Government visit. He would update us on the site and take the orders when we arrived. The plans were made. There was nothing else we could do except wait. I climbed on to the bed. I knew I needed to sleep, but wanted to stay with Danny in case we needed to move quickly, or so I allowed myself to believe. I laid down on his bed and closed my eyes, enjoying smelling him on his pillows. Danny cleared the sofa so he could snatch some sleep there without disturbing me, he wouldn't creep into bed with me uninvited. He took a spare blanket and laid himself down, but moved and shuffled as he lay awake, unsettled. I lay there, wondering if he would think me too forward if I offered him the other side of the large bed but feeling guilty he was on the sofa. The quandary overtook my plans for sleep and the difficulties of the coming day. I opened my eyes and turned over to see his back confronting me, the physical barrier between us spending the night together. Pangs of guilt and lust gnawed at me but I couldn't bring myself to invite him in. I needed to stay focussed, the thought of him so close distracted me too much, something I had only just learned to conquer, I couldn't afford to regress. I turned over and smelled the pillows again but only managed to fall asleep when I drew one close to me and wrapped my arms around it for the short time I would be allowed.

My body woke me at 0545, it was time to move out. I turned over to find Danny already sat up waiting for me. A brief grin and his dimple flashed at me. I liked it and flicked a smile back as I got out of his bed and returned to my own room to dress in the civil servant's clothes left for me. By 0600 we were both washed and dressed, meeting in the corridor between the rooms as we each came to call for one another. The subconscious link made us both give each other a nervous smile of recognition at what we were about to attempt.

Our new ID badges and names were ready for the secret service driver assigned to pick us up. Each driver had his own assignment and would pick up members of the party to go to the Oxfordshire address. As each one arrived they would book in and the visitors ID would be checked. Once they were cleared to enter, the driver would take up a surveillance position to guard the location and others would be freed up to patrol subtly in the grounds. The SAS would be on hand as covert backup should anyone attempt to enter the grounds. They would be dug in from the early hours of the morning. All parties were to be on site for the coffee reception at 0900 then the briefing and demonstration to start at 0930. Our time-line was set.

We travelled in silence through the green countryside, watching the fields and trees pass by. The plan was made alive for me as I acted it out in my head time and time again. I thought about the people in the houses and streets as we drove past, blissfully unaware of the plot being seen out to destroy their Government and leave the country in chaos. I hoped our plan was good enough to save them.

The large gates were open when we arrived, the winding road lead up a long drive through the deer park and constructed avenue. The first sight of the house laid it out spectacularly within the landscape, the symmetrical façade was complimented by a grand stone staircase leading to the front terrace, the bays of the windows on the ground floor opened up to take you directly into the various rooms. The drive led around to the side of the house, where an archway led to the inner courtyard. The car pulled up. A suited man wearing dark glasses, a curly wire hanging from his left ear, opened the car door and we both stepped out. The standard uniform of the security agent, dark suit, white shirt, neutral tie, always made them stand out when they were supposed to remain in the background. I put on my own special glasses as I rounded the corner to face the entrance. We were ushered gently but quickly inside the building, up the stone steps to a large rear door. As we crossed the courtyard I tapped the side of the glasses frame, one lens remained clear, the other displayed a thermal image of everything I saw, superimposed on to the inside of the lens. I scanned the scene outside. The cool spots stood out in the security men's suits where their guns were holstered and the heat signature from the car's bonnet as it drove off to park in another part of the courtyard glowed red with the engine's efforts. I just had time to look up and see a figure carefully concealed on the roof. Without the thermal image he was invisible, a man in black with a hood and a gun in the shadows of one of the chimneys, watching us as we entered. Special forces would be all over here today, but did they know what they were up against?

We showed our ID badges and fingerprint scans confirmed we were allowed to enter the main building. A woman in her late thirties wearing a smart suit not unlike our own props came sashaying towards us with a large tired smile that never made it to her eyes. She introduced herself as Melanie and explained she was one of the DRA secretaries working in Whitehall and had helped to set up the demonstration. Her manner was defensive, this low worker gave the impression she had managed everything so far on her own and could do without us snooping on her progress and checking up on the arrangements. Danny felt it too, we needed her guidance to all that was happening, so took the charm offensive forward to get the information quickly.

She showed us the meeting and reception rooms and a copy of the itinerary. Danny chatted and smiled, complimenting her all the time about the professionalism of the planning. It was my turn to feel left out as the two walked and talked and I trailed behind. Melanie looked directly at Danny, her eyes soft with the longing for his smile, as she asked if there was anything else she could do for us. She had said the word 'you' as a plural but she was looking at only one of us. It was my turn to exert my presence, not just for my own pride. I thanked her for her help, assuring her all was well prepared. Danny and I went through the motions of checking the catering and seating arrangements for the VIP guests while we refined the timing of our plan to include what we had learned about the itinerary. The army catering corps welcomed us into the kitchen, their enormous chef barely seemed to fit behind the range. His cauliflower ears the trademark of either a boxing or rugby pedigree. I made a mental note not to complain about the soup.

The kitchen checked, our path was blocked suddenly by a man in a dark suit. I touched my thermal glasses again to see his heat trail and found the SAS logo in a warm patch on his shoulder. I shook his hand and introduced us both, this was Major Williams. The top floor of the building, right under the painted white eaves, was empty, an excellent place to chat. He took us there where we had no chance of being overheard. The family who owned the house were on holiday in France, they had made the house available through a friend in the Cabinet office, if it was required. They used this part of the large house as storage for all the artefacts they did not have room to display. Hundreds of old tea chests and dust covered furniture filled every room. I liked Jim's thinking in bringing us here, we would be able to see immediately if there was anyone in a room by the fresh footprints. If the dust was undisturbed when we entered, we were sure to be alone.

A good thick layer of dust covered the floor. Happy his message would not be wandering off, Jim closed the door. He briefed us on the layout of the rooms, the positions to be taken up by the secret service and the dug in sites of his men around the grounds, all drawn in the dust on the floor. I went through the plan and how we wanted him to help. Afterwards he scratched his head, unsure.

"Well, if you say so," he said, you're stuff is over here. He led us across the corridor to a room that had obviously been recently disturbed. We found the cases full of weapons and communication equipment delivered during the night. Everything was present apart from the items coming from my own house. I wasn't sure they would actually work but without them there was an extra risk we could not afford.

We had been checked for weapons as we arrived, so the little guns we secreted about our bodies should remain undetected. My comms were contained in a pair of clip on earrings and Danny's took the form of a tie pin. A small earpiece was carefully gummed into his ear with a tear off strip so it could not be seen from the outside. A mic check hooked us up with each other and Major Williams so he could hear our conversations and act on any instructions when the time came. There was no hiding place, every word would be transmitted.

By the time all the plans were in place, I could see from the window that other cars were starting to arrive, various men in suits were being ushered up the steps to sign in and go for a coffee in the

Grand Drawing Room. Each drop off was timed exactly so they knew who each arrival was before they booked in. The nerves hit me in the stomach for the complexity and scale of what we were about to attempt. There was no room for error. I had logged every member of the Cabinet as they had arrived, as well as heads of the armed forces. They congregated downstairs, not understanding the potential devastation that was about to be unleashed. Only one or two of the people waiting for the demonstration had any idea of exactly what they had come to witness.

The inky darkness that shrouded my inner self started to filter out like a cloud rising from the desert. The need I had to endure the excitement of my filthy trade pushed me fatally on, despite the potential consequences. I wanted it to all happen now, hungry for the rush, but I would have to wait. This mission was all about patience now, the growling of the dark animal would have to be suppressed until it was time to be released. I looked across to Danny, his eyes flamed intensely, his own darkness was upon him and I was excited to see it flourish.

I would not have to hinder it for long, it was almost 0930. Two vehicles arrived in the courtyard. The hired van and army driver from the Bomb Dump the previous night pulled up next to the kitchen entrance. He got out and rolled up the back door, revealing the crates retrieved from the bunker. The other vehicle was the minibus from the DRA, with all the necessary staff on board to make sure the demonstration went smoothly. This included Dr Fairfield, released under escort so the terrorists watching would not suspect there was anything amiss. Dr Fairfield went over to the van and gave the weary driver instructions what to do with the precious cargo. The other DRA staff then proceeded to fuss around the crates to get them inside and ready for the demo as the man of the moment went to enjoy the due praise of his superiors and a coffee, his escort ever present.

It was time for me to go. I left Danny watching the arrivals to make sure they all turned up on time while I walked back downstairs with the SAS commander to check everything was in place. Each one of his men reported back that all was clear and there was no suspicious movement in the grounds. The main gates were locked with the sign fixed to say the house was closed today for cleaning. He checked with the security team. All guests had arrived safely as planned. They were proceeding with their patrols and shutting down the reception desk. All was normal and as it should be, yet my heart beat harder with every step we took closer to the main room. The Prime Minister, his Cabinet and Chiefs of Staff were all having coffee two doors away, any minute they would be moving into the Dining Room for the main presentation. I looked in for a final check, finding Dr Fairfield there with his presentation notes and a handful of the AnTTs for the guests to handle. I hoped Turtle had provided the smart suit he was wearing, just in case there were any more surprises in his other jackets, ready to be revealed.

The large glass double doors from the Dining Room led to one of the front terraces on the east side entrance. The fresh autumn air breezed in, filling the room. The terrace was empty apart from a tripod with a controller attached, pointing out to the greenery of the garden. I wandered over to see how well guarded we were at the front. Security was posted at each corner of the building but no closer. Nobody was present at the large front staircase, as if the area had been deliberately cleared. The only blot on the landscape was a car that had been parked on the driveway a short distance from the house, just past the lake. I was surprised to see it there, completely out of place in the carefully cleared area. The rest of the scene was blank all the way to the stable buildings.

From the edge of the room I watched the Doctor making himself busy with his preparations for the crowning glory of his career. I didn't know whether he hadn't seen me or he was choosing to ignore my presence, but he showed me no acknowledgement and continued in his tasks. I left him to it, the victim of his own hunger for recognition and power.

Jim rushed in to meet me, slightly out of breath, "The last delivery has just arrived," he took me to the courtyard. My sales case was there, we might yet be able to make this plan work. Time was short. I opened the case and took out as many of the little black modules as I had. Jim and I passed back to the Dining Room but they were about to move the VIPs in. We had to act quickly without arousing any suspicion. I stole back into the room while Major Williams used his rank to delay the entrance of the party until I was finished. It was tricky, but each module was installed in a different section of the room. We could delay no longer without someone trying to find out what I was doing. As I walked out, Jim gave the nod to the MC and the important guests were asked to move into the Dining Room.

The meeting started. Jim and I waited outside for any sign that something was wrong with the presentation. Muffled by the large oak door, I could hear the Doctor's speech, talking about the background to the developments, how long it had taken him to achieve and the capabilities he had endowed his ultimate weapon with. He handed out the de-activated AnTTs for his audience's amazement, just to secure the impact he desired. He had a sense of the dramatic and wanted to impress them before he left their service. I had to hand it to him, the whole event was an advert for him and him alone. He never once mentioned any other name and the brief acknowledgement of the team was quickly passed over. The self-glorification was sickening to hear, if the circumstances had been different, this would have been a definite tilt at a knighthood. As it was, all I heard was a simpering attempt to curry favour with the men who would soon be signing the papers to incarcerate him.

Danny was talking in my earpiece, he had moved position so he could see the front of the house, "The security team are keeping a safe distance from the terrace and patrolling around the courtyard and cars constantly," he was telling me. A rush of nerves flew over me, "Keep watching, something's going to happen in the grounds," I instructed, a feeling that what we had come for was about to materialise. I heard the Doctor saying that he had arranged for a demonstration of the AnTTs capability and asked the assembled audience to keep an eye on the car parked just outside. I ran into the next room where I could see the car clearly, "Danny, the AnTTs are on the move," the hush of anticipation made me almost whisper, "tell me what you can see."

"I've got the binoculars, I can see the car clearly. Nothing is happening yet," he commentated. The Doctor was still talking in the other room, my eyes were glued to the car and the surrounding area. I was torn not to be able to hear the Doctor's words more clearly, but my intrigue at the AnTTs capability needed to be satisfied. Just how powerful were they really? I had to know what we were up against.

"The car is turning a strange colour, it seems to be getting darker," Danny was as excited as I was to witness the deadly demonstration. I strained at the vision, pressed against the glass. Slowly I could see what Danny had meant, the red car looked to be turning a darker shade, a black curtain was rising up from the ground to swallow the sills and the bottom of the doors. I could hear a ripple of voices from the other room. The Doctor's tone was raised, he would be enjoying the amazement of his audience. He was explaining the AnTTs could be summoned to a particular spot, how they would be undetectable individually and only appear as they infested their target. The car got darker still, turning black before our eyes, even the windscreen clouded over.

"Blossom, its weird," said Danny, "there's a strange movement on the surface, like a wasp nest, appearing solid but made up of thousands of tiny bodies all churning and shifting. The AnTTs are all over the car. My God, it's amazing."

Next door, I could hear movement from the guests. Chairs shifted and voices were hushed as Doctor Fairfield proudly explained the homing system and the wide range of miniature electronics packed into the pin head of space to allow their target to be identified. I looked out of the window on to the terrace, he was pointing the controller at the car to make the AnTTs swarm over it.

A readout on the controller totalled the percentage of the AnTTs in the area that had been activated and were present at the target. When it reached 96% he announced, "but the AnTTs can do more than find their target, they have the ability to position themselves to form a line to cut through a cable or communication line, or they could be combined as a bigger charge to take down a bridge or bunker, and with enough AnTTs one could do this . . ." he hit the button on the controller, the black mass shimmering on the car erupted in an explosion that rocked the ground and rattled the windows.

"Go go go . . ." it was the cue to start putting our plan into action. Jim radioed his troops to move in a decreasing circle, making their way covertly to a distance of a hundred metres from the house. I burst out of the door and ran to the nearest Security patrol,

"There's been an explosion," I yelled, "the Cabinet have been hit. You've got to get them out of here!" His face was anxious but he didn't panic as I wanted him to, "Come on, come on!" I shouted at him, grabbing his jacket and dragging him towards the Dining Room. I had already cut his communications wire when he tried in vain to get some proper orders from his Commanding Officer. As we got closer, Jim ran up from the corridor, shouting, "Where the hell have you been?" he rounded on the poor exasperated guard, "The meeting is to be evacuated, there is a specific threat in the building. The SAS are closing in, we need to get the Cabinet out covertly. Where are the rest of your men?"

"They're mainly outside, Sir, but my comms are down . . ."

"Oh my God, they've got to the comms links already. OK, start moving them through there," Jim guided him to the basement door where they could escape without being seen. I ran around the house finding more and more men to help with the evacuation.

As I came across them one by one, each had their comms cut and were sent on the mission to get the VIPs out of the house. It had to be done quietly, we didn't know where the mole was hiding and the risk of being blown up wouldn't leave us until he was found. Jim tried to keep them all moving, telling the security team there could be snipers present and they were to stay under cover until the cars came to pick them up. Other Security men arrived and started to help, instinctively obeying orders just as we had planned. The Ministers and Chiefs were still reeling after the demonstration. The windows had rattled and the chandeliers tinkled as the wave of air passed over them following the explosion. These people were not used to being in areas where bombs were let off and as the Doctor was basking in his own glory at the effect he had on the distinguished company, the Security men and SAS Commander burst through the doors to remove them from the area. They were quickly shepherded down the corridor to the basement door. More men ushered them down the steep steps and into the cellar. Some had been sent outside to bring the cars round to pick up the guests away from the courtyard so they could escape unseen.

"Major, how many men do you have in the grounds?" I asked when I had found as many Security men as I thought we needed, "Only four patrols, sixteen men." That was enough, "And how many on the roof?" I asked, "None." The answer hit me like a rock. I felt myself frown as I thought back to when we arrived that morning.

"None?" I asked, the light dawning on me as to whom I had seen. Jim didn't like the look I was giving him, he stood squarely to me to reinforce what he was saying. Its not that I didn't believe him, I just couldn't see how a man on the roof could have been missed.

"The drawings we were given showed no access to the roof from the inside of the house and there was a note on saying it wasn't safe to cross," he explained, "I had to position my men in the grounds only was the instruction I was given."

I racked my memory to find the image of the drawings I had spent the long night studying while not making love to Danny. The third floor clearly had an access point to the roof shown at the top of the stairs coming from the servants quarters. I thought twice but could clearly recall the hatch. I told Jim of the man I had seen up there that morning, with the black suit and hood as his men would wear. A knowing look passed between us, the terrorists had been watching to see that the right people had arrived.

"You check the VIP's exit," I told him. The threat was now very real.

"Danny, the roof," I called, "I heard," he said, "I'm already on my way over to the steps."

I went back in to the Dining Room to make sure everyone had been taken out and found the Doctor in there with his escort, refusing to move from the head of the table.

"You! I might have known," he said as he realised his tormentor had returned, "you have ruined my demonstration as well as my career," as if I had poured water on his fireworks on bonfire night.

"Doctor, I'm sorry but you have to leave, the others are being taken away from here, the AnTTs are about to be detonated," I pleaded with him to go.

"Its no use," he said, resignedly, "if you take me away from here they will kill me to be sure, just as they said they would. I was only trying to save my family, you know. They were going to hurt my little girl. I had to tell them. I couldn't have won, they would have hurt Susie . . ." he drifted off into his madness, the pressure of the past few months finally breaking him into a shell of a man. Part of me felt sorry for him at last, the pawn of our masters desire, all he wanted to do was retire and lead a quiet life with his family.

I shook his hand and told the escort to get him back to the base as quickly as possible, enlisting one of the Security men to help. I looked over the terrace for any sign that the rogue AnTTs were on their way but nothing was visible. The controller was still on the tripod, the screen displaying the number of AnTTs in the area, 66%, 69%, 72%, the number was increasing, they were on their way, but to where? I looked outside, the two guards were still at the corners of the building. Everything looked as it should, whoever was watching would not be suspicious of anything they had seen so far. I looked across the lake to the buildings at the other side of the trees.

The old stables stood on the far left, with the farm and barns further back.

I put my glasses back on to look over at the buildings, seeing them more clearly through the trees. There in the shadows, hidden to the naked eye, was a red glowing figure. He must be all in black to be concealed against the wall under the pillars holding up the Roman façade at the front of the stable block. I tried not to focus on the figure and moved my gaze sideways slightly. As I moved my head sideways, a flash of colour in the air caught my attention. I could see a vague straight line pointing at me from the direction of the stables roof. It was the laser signature of the controller, pointing at the terrace as the target for the AnTTs to assemble. The controller next to me read 79%. Down the stairs a series of black specks was appearing. The AnTTs were almost in a group, not leaving me much time.

I grabbed Jim and told him where he needed to send his men, straight to the man hidden in the shadows. He radioed for two patrols to head to the stables and apprehend anyone in there. I needed to check on Danny.

I ran up the two storeys of stairs to the point where the roof stairs were positioned. The door at the top was already open.

"Danny, I'm on my way up the stairs to meet you."

"Confirmed," he responded, "There was definitely a man in a hood but he ran and I lost sight of him on the other side of the roof.

He might be trying to get down, so be very careful," he warned. *I climbed the stairs to the top and hauled myself out on to the flat section. The ledge to one side was waist height and a narrow walkway ran between the slanted peaks of the different levels of roof and the ledge. I left the access door open and made my way to the position I had seen the hooded man earlier. The main house was the central block, with two wings added to match. Where the south wing had been attached to the main building, the bottom of two apexes came together to form a valley between them. I looked across and saw the man there, walking along the other ledge to get back down to the stairs.

For a split second we looked at one another. The wind blew against me, tangling my hair and whipping it across my face. I held my breath, both of us standing, waiting, wondering who was the quickest as time stopped before the battle began. He reached for his trigger, pointing the assault rifle towards me. My dark cloud burst inside me as the animal was let free. A fire-fight was coming and only one of us would walk back down the steps. A rush of adrenalin roused me as the burst of suppressed fire came from the weapon. I rolled as I dived behind the roof, bullets spinning and ricocheting off the copper sheets.

With my head still below the danger line I heard another weapon fire, pop pop, a handgun this time. I peeked out from behind the parapet in time to see the hooded man fall on to the flat section of roof. Danny stepped out from the other side with his gun drawn, still smoking. He checked I was alright then cleared the hooded man of his weapons. No pulse showed that he had hit his target accurately, the left side of the hood oozing with red life as it flowed out of the terrorist's body.

It was the first time I had witnessed Danny's proficiency at this side of the job. I looked at him differently, as if he had just completed a jigsaw for me. He took hold of me, helping me up. I let him, even though I didn't need him to. A quick flash of a smile from me was all that gave me away, we headed straight back downstairs. Only one out of four tasks was complete.

On the Dining Room terrace, the controller had reached 86% in the few minutes it had taken to rid us of the man on the roof. The AnTTs swarmed and writhed en masse, spilling in to the main room, with others still crawling along the carpet from their hiding places within the house itself, checked and checked again to make sure no explosives were present, all the time lurking in the darkness, waiting for the call to serve. The amount of explosives in each device was not enough to trigger the sniffer machines, but when they were all together, the result would be combined, leading to a massive blast. I saw the mass outside the window and hoped the measures I had put in place would protect us.

Major Williams had detained two of the Security men, found trying to get out through the kitchen and, rather surprisingly, caught by the Catering Corps. The Major could barely suppress his amusement at the mammoth of a chef that had tackled the men single handedly. Unhappy at just having finished chopping up the dozens of chickens for lunch and finding the party had evacuated, he put his enormous cleaver, still in his hand, to good use when the terrorists entered the kitchen looking for a way to escape. They brandished their guns in front of the terrified kitchen staff, not so used to the rough and tumble of actual soldiering. It should have been an easy way out, but the irate chef was in no mood for giving up his carefully planned menu for nothing. He roared, flashing his cleaver. The terrified terrorists, amazed at the revelation, panic fired into the pans hanging from the rack above the cooker. The crashes as they clanged and fell scaring them even more. The rest of the staff ducked for cover. The chef dived for the two men and hit them round the head with a large copper fish kettle, sending them reeling to the floor, dropping their guns. As they struggled to get back up, the army staff stood over them, their own guns trained upon them. They were tied up and left in the hallway, to collect later. The catering staff evacuated. The SAS Commander congratulated the Chef, giving him marks for presentation and sent him on his way. The DRA secretaries were taken to the out buildings to make sure they were safe.

The SAS patrols were closing in on the last man standing. They surrounded the stable block as Danny and I walked slowly from the house as if just taking a stroll in the gardens. There was no sign of the man in the hood or the patrol we knew were present, each one was cleverly concealed. My glasses were reactivated, scanning the area to see what was hiding. I found two SAS men in the shrubs at the foot of the stable block, one either side, but no terrorist in the shadows above.

The controller was on the roof of the building, I could still see the faint trace of the signal line focussing on the terrace. He could not be far away. We entered the building, loudly laughing and talking as if passing the time. No livestock was in here now, but the dank earthy smell remained. The wet cobbled floor echoed as we stepped towards the wooden stairs that led to the byre above. I saw the trace of a heat signal, the air warm in the corner of the room as we climbed the stairs. I stormed the area, but the trace was false, our prey had moved on. The air still hung with his body heat, he couldn't be far. The last stair creaked as Danny took it, I heard the click of a weapon being cocked from the other side of the wall. The window was open, the controller on the other side. There was nowhere else for our friend to be.

We stood either side of the opening, Danny poised to climb out. Suddenly the old wooden boards groaned and shook under our feet, the sound of explosions reached us from the grounds. The controller had been activated. I felt the pressure of excitement as the inner darkness flooded through me. After a quick glance at me Danny jumped in one movement through the window on to the ledge beyond. The house was masked with smoke from the explosions, I could see nothing of the grand venue. My concerns for what had happened up there would have to wait. I was on the hunt again, my instincts feeling where my prey would try and flee to stirred me into action. I ran back down the stairs, into the byre. Above my head I heard a shot. For a second I thought about Danny, he was certainly hunting too, I had seen the darkness in his eyes as he jumped through the window but the shot was not aimed at him, "Bastard, missed him," came over the earpiece, his pot shot had gone astray. While I breathed a sigh of relief, I collected the two SAS men from the entrance to the stables and we ran around the building to catch the man in black as he tried to find a way out of the net that was drawing slowly tighter.

"He's away over the rooftops," Danny's breathless voice commentated as he pursued his man over the slippery slates of the stable and jumped down to the barn below.

I lost sight of the pair as we skirted the barn to head them off at the other side. Danny jumped from the barn roof, rolling over as a parachute landing, his gun out and ready as he came to a halt, scrutinising the vicinity to see where his target had disappeared.

Danny and I looked at one another. Our mark was gone. I fumed at having lost him. I burned with the determination to bring him down. The only other path was into the barn, like a fury I ran in.

At the far side I could see two of our own masked men, guarding the exit. He was trapped.

"Stay here and guard this door," I ordered, "and get some more men over here," the SAS men radioed for two patrols to make their way to the outbuildings.

Compared with the bright sunshine outside, the barn was dark, my eyes not adjusting quickly enough for me to run straight in. I activated my glasses, but the latent heat inside the rough structure made too many patterns for me to be sure which way he had gone. In the darkness, Danny and I moved furtively along each wall, past the hay bales and sacks of feed. My body hardened as my senses detected a movement up ahead, Danny walked further in, his gun ready. There was no time to duck as a pitchfork handle swung from behind the bales and clattered into his chest, knocking him flat on his back and pouring out his breath. His damaged ribs were not yet recovered from their recent beating and it was the worst attack he could have feared. I fired into the mass of hay where I imagined the strike came from, then dived over the bags of feed to get to Danny, my heart racing. He waved me on, just winded. My determination to catch the terrorist heightened, as did my wariness at pursuing him further into the dark shadows. My face flushed as my heart ran faster, the blood pumping through me making me rage on to hunt him down.

Alone now, I had to maintain my search for the masked man, carrying on carefully so I didn't suffer a similar fate. I flushed through the path laid out through the barn without finding a single clue as to where he had gone. I emerged in the daylight on the other side to find the SAS guards having seen nothing of what we were chasing. Nobody had come out of the barn. He must be hiding somewhere inside. I grew more anxious to have my hands on him. I would burn the barn down to make him run to me if necessary. I turned to storm back in, I would find this man and kill him where he stood. Suddenly I was yanked backwards and pushed up against the wall. The shadows surrounded me, the masked man in front of me was pulling off his hood so I could see his face. My lovely Macca was presented to me.

My elation at seeing him leaped through me, my eyes grew wide with delight and I smiled, excited that he was there. He smiled back and gave me a quick kiss, "There's more where that came from my wild Blossom," he said, and I wanted more, lots more.

"Later," I said, still smiling at him. Seeing him in front of me, his rugged frame pressing against me in the darkness, I was more determined than ever to get this job over with as soon as possible so we could re-make our delightful acquaintance.

"If he didn't come out he must still be in there, go round the other side and wait for me," I ordered. Work first, I knew Mac, he would do as he was told. He took three men and surrounded the barn as I went back inside to try and flush out the terrorist.

I crept through the still air, making my way back towards where I had first come in. I waited patiently this time for my eyes to adjust to the low light. The shroud of darkness lifted slowly as my eyes compensated and I could see above me that the hay bales were piled to the roof with a series of different levels running across them. It would be possible to hide or climb up there to see the whole area. That's where I would be if I were being pursued. I wondered if my quarry was in there somewhere, waiting for me to stumble unwittingly into his firing range. The animal pounded inside me, every footstep I made was gentle and considered in the rustling of the hay beneath my feet. I could not be shaken now, my focus entirely on the dangerous beast I was hunting. A movement came into my peripheral view, up above to my right. My gun pointed to where I thought the something had moved, my finger ready on the trigger. I kept low as I stalked through the bales, climbing up on to the first one to gain a little vantage. I saw Mac pass through the large door at the far end of the barn, two others shot across the end of the building and hid within the darkness, their hoods still in place. They were closing in, if he was here he would have to make his move.

Their eyes not yet accustomed to the dim light, the SAS patrol held back for me to flush our mark towards them. I moved less stealthily now, the confidence I drew from Macca's presence made me bold in the hazy half light. I knew my back was covered so went directly on the attack, hoisting myself up to the next level of hay. I looked around to see a man diving from the top bales down to the next level and running across them, heading for the hatch where he could get back on to the roof. I fired a shot as he darted behind the hay, the SAS men had no sight of the dark figure but laid down fire in the general direction that I had aimed.

I jumped across to follow the terrorist to the roof, I didn't need to take care, I trusted the SAS completely having trained in their own killing houses. The firing stopped just as I ran across the pile of bales. The terrorist jumped up and hauled himself through the hatch. Suddenly Danny was behind me, he had his breath back and had been lying in wait for the opportunity to strike, thwarted when our mark had doubled back. We ran together along the tops of the bales. The uneven surface of the teetering hay made me watch my step so I didn't fall down the gaps. I didn't see the arm come back down through the hatch with a gun in the hand until it was too late. Danny fired a shot, missing the target but ricocheting off the side of the building. The gunman fired, Danny dived over and rugby tackled me, slamming me on to my back and covering me with his body to protect me from the bullets heading our way as they cracked over our heads. The arm retreated. Danny leapt back up and dragged himself on to the roof through the hatch. Our foe was making his way down the tin shelter to jump back over to the stables.

He had no place to go, the SAS men cornered him behind the ledge of the façade where he could no longer be seen, but his arm could reach out and take random shots at anyone who ventured to get him down. Macca moved to the stable building and started to climb up the near elevation to get to the façade, the only way of getting him down would be to knock him from the ledge. Macca clipped on a rope and swung from his side round to where the cornered beast was hiding. As the terrorist moved across to fire at him, he exposed the right side of his chest. Taking aim and firing in an instant, Danny's bullet finally hit the target, slamming into the chest with a spurt of claret that shot into the air for all to see. His weapon dropped as Mac put out his two feet and rammed the terrorist from the outcrop of stone. I had just reached the edge of the roof to see the cloud of dust fly as the body crashed to the floor outside the stables and six SAS patrol men made sure the job was complete.

Macca slid to the floor on his rope and shook Danny by the hand, thanking him for the excellent shot that had saved his life. Danny was quiet, merely nodding in acknowledgement. No drama between the warriors, just a manly clasp of hands. I ran up to take a look at our man, slightly bitter that I had not fired the fatal shot but glad the threat was over.

Macca moved away, but I'd had another flash of inspiration, "Wait! Macca! What are you doing this afternoon?" I asked, my grin still spoke more words to him than I could say out loud, "Nothing, why, do you have plans for me, Miss?" He tried to appear aloof, but he turned to face me displaying his broad shoulders, dropping the tip of his rifle to hold it casually in one hand, a picture of masculinity.

"Mac, I need a date for this afternoon, a family wedding with an overnight stay in the hotel. What do you say?" I knew exactly what he would say.

"I'll see you later, then Blossom," he shouted back as I waved him off to go and report back to his Commander after making the arrangements.

Danny stood at the far corner of the building. As the other troops made their ways back he turned and looked at me. I felt uncommonly self conscious with the hay and dirt still on my face from leaping across the bales. His face was enchanting. The way he looked at me was mesmerising. His swagger seemed enhanced as he walked towards me. His eyes were bright, the sun looked to be shining from his face. I stood, limp, not knowing what was going to happen next. His arms enveloped me, swallowing me up as he hugged me tightly. The pleasure of the sensation felt somehow strange, the comfort derived from being in his possession brought out a warmth I had rarely encountered. I hugged him back, he wasn't the same to me now, he wasn't Danny the hunk, Danny the fit body, Gorgeous Danny. He was my colleague, my team-mate, maybe even my friend. I didn't wince when he looked at me any more, the dimple didn't scare me into thinking he was trying to undermine me. I was comfortable with him now, as he evidently was with me.

I looked up into his face, his blue eyes sparkled, seeming more radiant and gentle than I could remember.

"Your heart is racing, its nearly thumping me away!" I said as he still held me close.

"Blossom," he said quietly, "the only reason my heart beats is to remind me to think of you," and he touched his lips to mine gently, our solemn kiss lasting long tender moments in the warmth of the sunshine.

I felt vindicated by the emotion he was emanating, he did have some respect for me after all. That was all I had needed from him. I kissed him back, briefly, then pulled myself away, mindful of the appointment I had just made for later in the afternoon. I was torn. This was something I had not anticipated and the surprise made me dismissive, "Yeah, right," I laughed, "Its only an assignment, you know, we're not engaged." It was all I could do to give myself time to think as I pushed him away, giving him a punch on the arm and rustling his hair.

"Nice try," I said and walked over to the other SAS team to jog back up to the house.

Chapter 17

The troops gathered at the stables to inspect the body then made their ways separately back to the house. I walked up with my old SAS friends, Danny lagged behind, the spring wanting from his step. I felt terrible at the dismissal but I had a date already for the afternoon that I could hardly break now. The troops were all shouting and laughing, celebrating the win. Danny didn't join in. He was probably more bruised by his ego than any genuine feeling of rejection.

At the house I went to inspect the damage caused by the blast. How much of the beautiful old monument would still be standing? I wondered how the family would react when they came home from their lovely holiday to find a substantial insurance claim wanted. I greeted Jim, congratulating him on a successful operation. We walked through the building, Macca's unsubtle wink as I threaded my way down the corridor did not go un-noticed. My face burned as I remembered my microphone would have transmitted my half of our conversation to the Major and to poor rejected Danny.

The door to the Dining Room was a little stiff. I entered slowly, expecting to see the 16th Century plasterwork and the carved wooden chimney breast lying mortal on the floor. The room unveiled as the door opened, surprise and relief passed over me, all was as I had left it that morning. The grand room was intact. On the terrace, the once writhing mass of AnTTs were now still, their threat neutralised at last. It looked like a pile of tiny black plastic beads. I walked over to where the majority were piled up on the spot that had been pinpointed by the controller. The signal scramblers from my sales case I had only just managed to plug in before the meeting had saved the beautiful building.

If, as I suspected, the AnTTs were able to home in on the controller positioning but unable to receive the signal to fire, only the ones out of range of the blockers had exploded. With this controller active the AnTTs could still be detonated. I needed to secure the other controller and remove the signal scramblers to make the area safe once again. Major Williams came in behind me with the controller his men had retrieved from the stable roof. The lovely Melanie had been evacuated to the safety of the outbuildings, now she entered behind Jim to see what all the fuss had been about. I saw her come in but wasn't interested enough in her to chat. She was probably looking for Danny anyway.

I waded through the plastic beads trying to tread on as few of the multi-million pound developments as possible to get carefully to remove the last controller from the tripod. I turned round to Jim triumphant but my smile was soon wiped out as I saw him kneeling on the floor with a small gun thrust into his neck. The young woman in the smart civil service suit and sensible shoes had gone unnoticed by all the VIPs for most of the day. That was her greatest strength, nobody looked at the secretaries or noticed the support services in an operation like this. A select few unseen personnel had combined to plan and execute this operation. The mole needed to be someone who had access to all the relevant information. Melanie had been key to the event and had organised most of the personnel and departments involved. I admired the obvious intelligence of the resourceful young woman.

"You're working for the terrorists?" I asked.

"Why would I work for anyone else?" Melanie sneered back. She ragged the Major by the hair, "These people disgust me, they deserve to die. They are happy to send so many others to their deaths in the name of freedom. They murdered my husband in Afghanistan. Serving his country, doing their dirty work for them. These wrecks that call themselves men, they are nothing compared to my husband and now he'll never come home. These uniformed pigs will all die eventually, but I will make more money than you could dream of by selling these controllers to the highest dirty bidder to allow them to do my killing for me. I won't have to lift a finger," she was smug now, trying to impress me and the Major with how well she had done to get this far and show how clever she ultimately was.

I saw through the smug bluster, intended to intimidate. Unlike Melanie, I had been in these situations before, the amateur had made a simple rookie error, maybe seen a couple of movies and thought that the one holding the gun had all the power. I knew better, but would play along until I could regain the advantage, "So you gave them the information on the AnTTs they needed to plan all this?" I just needed to keep her talking for a little while longer.

"I work in the DRA office in Whitehall, all Top Secret plans are copied and written up by puny insignificant secretaries just like me. Nobody even knows I'm there, but I see and hear everything. I made all the plans, booking venues and arranging transport," she said, wrenching the Commander's head back and shoving the gun further into his throat, "and giving false layout drawings to the foolish troops so they couldn't interfere," she laughed in his face as I edged myself slightly forward.

I took tiny steps, circling slowly at a safe distance towards the large dining table. I kept well away from the deranged woman so she felt no pressure. I dropped my shoulders and looked down at the floor, my image depressed, defeated.

"How did the terrorists turn you? You could have been investigated if you were seen fraternising with them in public," I asked, I needed to be a little closer still.

"The terrorists didn't find me, I found them. It was easy to get them interested and we stayed well away from the areas I knew were under surveillance. I will be rich for life once they see what I've brought them. Now hand it over, my hand grows tired and I need to be moving on, thank you very much."

I had walked slightly closer as the arrogant woman enjoyed her moment of recognition. Melanie had clearly rehearsed her lines just in case she had the opportunity of letting everyone know she was the mastermind behind the whole plan. No other organisation was getting the credit for her work any longer, she was the one in charge now and it felt good. She looked nervous but elated, it must have been easier than she thought to bring the big man to the floor, once he saw she was the one with the gun. I wondered which exit she thought she was going to escape through.

Melanie pushed the gun more forcefully into Jim's throat. A little closer still, I made to hand her the controller. Melanie was not trained for the red mist of confrontation. It would cloud her ability to see me moving stealthily closer to the huge dining table. Melanie hissed at me to hand over the controller, "Alright, you win," I raised my hand to throw the controller.

Melanie shifted slightly to take hold of he device, in an instant I turned, my other hand spinning about my body and colliding with the giant tea urn, left there when the room was evacuated, smacking it from the dining table and launching it straight at her. The secretary did what any civil servant in a smart suit with hot tea heading towards them would do, just what I was banking on, she instinctively leapt out of the way, drawing back so the brown liquid would not stain her best clothes. I quickly pounced, wrenching the gun out of her soft hand and knocking her flat on to the floor. She might be clever enough to have plotted with the terrorists, but I knew a fellow warrior when I saw one, and this limp skirt was a mere wannabe, thinking that a gun would make us take fright.

Jim spun on the floor and landed a skilful kick, standing up without removing his boot from her neck. He was clearly embarrassed at being caught out by the non-combatant and looked at me pleadingly as his team came running in.

"Its OK," I chirped in, "this little witch is the one that gave us away, she just attacked me and the Major here saved me, thanks mate," I shook his hand gratefully. Danny pushed his way through after running all the way from the stables, "I heard the whole thing over the radio mic," he made his way past the astonished men, "Well done, Sir, good work." He shook Jim's hand and looked sorrowfully at me.

"I'm glad you're OK," he said quietly, his head drooping. I watched him as he dropped his radio kit on the table and walked slowly back out of the room. He would have heard the real tale over his earpiece.

As he sidled past, Macca slapped him on the back heartily, "Now then, pal, you did me a good turn back there, nice shooting, Tex. If there's ever anything I can do for you, you just have to ask." Danny acknowledged his words, nodding in thanks, but offering no response, just walking away down the long corridor, alone. Jim saw the melancholy stroll and took Macca to one side for a quiet chat after giving up his tender captive for his troops to secure.

I called in to Turtle to tell him the good news. He listened intently to the full report but not enough questions were forthcoming for me to believe he was truly listening. I asked what was wrong. Turtle hesitated, whatever this was, it was not good news. I composed myself for the words that I was about to endure. After a tangible sigh, he told me that Dr Fairfield died on the way back to the base for further questioning. My world stood still. That was the last word I was expecting.

"What happened?"

"The escort was a mile or so out of the gate when he heard the noise from the house over the radio as the explosions passed through the grounds. At the same moment he thought a shot had been fired through the car as the Doctor's chest burst out in front of him." Turtle explained. "On first examination, we think that the terrorists had got him to swallow one if his deadly creations, whether he knew it or not we couldn't say."

I felt the guilt that haunted Turtle at the news. He had warned us of his impending death and we had used him despite it. The act of evacuating him was supposed to save him, but taking him away from the signal blockers had actually been his demise. Did he know about the device within him? We would never know now. The terrorists could command him to do as they wished, ever with the threat that they could detonate the tiny bomb inside him. How many others had they planted? Maybe they told him his family were sabotaged as well? A life of service taken violently by his own creation.

"His family . . ." I started, but Turtle already had an answer ready, "It's OK, we have the area around them jammed so no signals get through while we find out if they have the AnTTs inside them. We're trying to find out now if they can be scanned without setting anything off, just in case." Dr Fairfield would be celebrated as a great British hero, the record of this incident would have his name wiped out so that no harm could come to the great man's history. His family would be looked after and finally get their peace and freedom.

Now he had given me the news, he had a thousand more questions, as usual, but I heard my Mother's voice ringing in my head. I had an appointment for that afternoon. If I left now I could just make it, "I'm sorry, I have to leave. Its my cousin's wedding this aft and if I don't get there my Mum will kill me, its very important to her. I'll call in tomorrow and report fully, you can get the rest from Danny. Put him on? Well, I would but he's talking to someone." My eyes smiled as I caught site of Macca standing next to him, "Call him later. Go to go, bye" I cut him off, snapping shut the phone and dashing to the car. The driver pulled away as Danny watched. I left with him in view, his swagger evident as he walked steadily up to the other car and got in.

Not many hours later, I was finally dressed in a softly tailored peach Chanel suit with cream silk vest and pearl accessories. I'd had the corsage and buttonhole sent over and was pinning mine to the beautifully tailored lapel as the stretched limo arrived, dead on time. The chauffeur got out to take my overnight bag and placed it gently in the large boot. The rear door opened and my date got out to welcome me in.

I stood and stared at him, he looked delicious. It was the first time I had seen him ready to go out. His light brown suit was beautifully tailored, the cut showed off the broad shoulders and slim waist. His shoes were shiny, as a military man's should be and he was, finally, freshly shaven. I gulped back the temptation to forget about the wedding and send the car on empty when our bodies touched gently as I pinned on his buttonhole. I looked at my handiwork and admired the rest of the view, "Good," was all I said, "Make sure you're polite to my Mother." He held open the car door for me to get inside. We sat reservedly in opposite seats on the way to collect my parents. The tension was evident, making it all the more exciting. When he glanced over at me I looked away. I barely dared look at him, let alone speak. The toughest test was yet to come. We would be with my Mother within a few minutes. We sat in silence, the quiet engine purring up ahead, this was no time for questions.

I knocked on the front door impatiently. I was the one that was a little late, they should have been out there waiting for me. My Father came running out, his tall, lanky frame covering yards with each stride, he ran to the end of the garden path, then ran back and kissed me on the cheek, "Sorry," he said, "its your Mother, she takes an age to get ready," and dashed back to the car, cursing his wife under his breath.

Mum came hopping towards me, one shoe not tied properly yet and equally blaming her husband for them being late out.

"Hang on" I said, making her stand still while I bent down to fasten her shoe. I stood up, looking nervously at her. Mum stopped pushing her corsage into her pin and asked me what was wrong.

"Mum, I've brought someone with me," I said, waiting for the eruption of undisguised relief.

"That's nice dear," was all my Mother said aloofly, and she walked gracefully to the car, leaving me with an open mouth. Normally she wanted a million details, where does he work, where do his family come from, how did we meet, where did he go to school. I knew nothing about him, really, and was so relieved not to have to face the barrage I just stood there. Maybe this wouldn't be so bad after all.

"Come on, hurry up, dear," shouted Mum over her shoulder as she reached the car door that was being held open by the smart young man. She turned to me and nodded approvingly. Elated, I ran down the garden path and jumped into the car, calling to the driver to get going. I was excited to be with him, my heart raced, I couldn't help but smile. Nothing else mattered in the world, I was divinely happy. I took a deep breath as we all settled into our journey, "Mum, Dad, this is Danny . . ."